Diversion Books
A Division of Diversion Publishing Corp.
443 Park Avenue South, Suite 1008
New York, New York 10016
www.DiversionBooks.com

For more information, email info@diversionbooks.com

First Diversion Books edition June 2015.
Print ISBN: 978-1-62681-549-0
eBook ISBN: 978-1-62681-548-3

THE
EUTHANIST

ALEX DOLAN

DIVERSIONBOOKS

This book is dedicated to my parents and to Sabrina, for cheering me on. Also, thank you for loving me despite my faults, such as ending sentences in prepositions.

CHAPTER 1

Every autumn is tarantula mating season around Mount Diablo. Horny male spiders roam through the twiggy grass to find their soul mates in a sort of spider Burning Man. They say spiders are more afraid of us, but that's bullshit. They don't even see us. They incite terror with their furry little legs and never know the havoc they wreak in our lives. If you were like me and grew up having nightmares about tarantulas, you would probably avoid the area like a nuclear testing zone.

Normally I'd have steered clear, but on this day I was driving through spider country to see a client. Bugs shouldn't scare a grown woman, but driving here made me nervous. A shrink once told me being afraid of spiders meant I wasn't aggressive enough. Then we talked about my stepdad.

He asked, "What is your stepfather like?"

"He's the sort of man who places a dead spider on your alarm clock to see how you react."

"I don't understand the metaphor," he said.

"It's not a metaphor. My stepfather put a dead tarantula on my alarm clock when I was nine. So when it went off, I hit the spider instead of the clock."

My doc dropped his notes. "Why the hell would he do that?"

"Because he's a fucking sociopath. He sat by my bed when it happened, I think just so he could see the look on my face."

"How did you react?"

"How do you think? I screamed my head off."

The shrink had eyeballed me the way that psychic magician

looked at a spoon he wanted to bend. I think he was wondering if I was lying, and if not, what he should do with me. "Do you speak to him?"

"Not since he went to prison."

After Gordon's spider stunt, big hairy bugs petrified me. The alarm clock wasn't the only time he pulled that crap either. He hid another one in my underwear drawer, and another at the bottom of a Balinese tin box where my mom held her "guilt" chocolate. The fear wasn't irrational, not if you half expected them to pop up like Easter eggs. I still shake out my shoes in the mornings, in case there's one curled up in the toe. Once I was old enough to have my own apartment, a Zen chime dinged across the bedroom in the morning, so I had nothing to slap on the nightstand.

Because of my fear of spiders, I cautiously rounded the hairpin turns through the foothills of Clayton. Hands at five and seven o'clock. One of those fuckers came out of nowhere—a brown spider the size of my fist boogied across the road. If I'd seen it coming, maybe I would have sped up and smushed it under a tire. But it flew into the road like it was in the Olympic trials, and, for whatever reason, I jammed on the brakes. On this vacant road with the paper clip bends, the car *erked* to a standstill. The spider paused. Tarantulas are predators themselves, so they know what hunting behavior looks like. It sensed the enormity of the vehicle, its hot breath and growling motor hovering over it. For a moment, it might have actually been afraid. But then it skittered across the asphalt and into the wild brush off the shoulder. Maybe later when it wooed its amour, it would recount this story so it could get some spider cooch.

My hands strangled the wheel, forearms buzzing with the motor's vibration. I hated myself for being spooked.

Behind me, the driver of a matte brick truck blasted the horn. I found the honk comforting, human. I wasn't afraid of people who weren't my stepdad, not even a big ugly guy like this one with the Civil War sideburns. The horn ripped a second time. Stopped in the road like a moron, I might have felt bad, but he mouthed swears at me in the rearview. His grill kissed my bumper, and I could feel the tremor of his engine. Maybe I didn't step on the gas because I wanted to provoke a reaction. My shrink liked to tell me I was combative. Whatever. If he stepped out of his rust monster, I'd make quick work of his knees with the tire iron I kept on the passenger floor. I made him go around me, smirking at his tobacco-spit frown as he passed. If I were dressed down he might have called me a bitch, but one look at me and he diverted eyes back to the road. If you stare at someone just the right way, they'll know they're in danger. Or maybe the wig just threw him off.

I remembered my client, Leland Mumm, was waiting for me. He didn't deserve someone to come late with shaky hands, whether those shakes came from arachnophobia or road rage. Not today.

IPF, or idiopathic pulmonary fibrosis, was killing Leland Mumm. Since his diagnosis three years ago, my client's lungs had stiffened with scar tissue. He described his breathing with two words: shredding lungs. Talking hurt, so he chose his words parsimoniously. For example, he would never have used the word "parsimoniously." Leland's lungs no longer transferred oxygen to his bloodstream, so the rest of his organs didn't get the oxygen they needed. Piece by piece, his insides were slowly suffocating.

Brutal way to go. Not Desdemona's gracious death in bush-league productions of Othello. From what Leland described, it was more like a pincushion bursting in the chest. Doctors weren't much help, because medicine didn't really understand the disease. With IPF, the agony is constant, and it can take five years to die.

In Leland's video interviews, he had trouble sitting up straight. He tipped to the side after a few minutes. Eventually we had to tape him in bed. Not the most flattering angle, but I adjusted the lighting to minimize the eye rings.

The video conveyed personal messages to friends and family. Last wishes. I burned DVDs to be mailed out when he passed, so he could explain why he was doing something most people would think was nuts, even selfish. Ten years ago, before I got started, clients might have sent their last messages by post. Some still wrote letters. I preferred video because it felt more intimate. In case cops in black riot gear rammed my door, the video also proved I was working with my client's consent.

When we first met, Leland could manage more words before his lungs pinched. He insisted we record a message to his wife, who had passed away a few years ago. In short bursts, he pieced a story together about when they first dated. The moment he realized he loved her. They were walking along the endless Berkeley Pier when a fisherman yanked a crab out of the Bay and it flew into her. Leland had known then he wanted to protect her. I'll admit, I admired the chivalry. When he got to the word "crab," he twisted in the sheets with a shock of pain.

I spoke to his pulmonologist by phone, but, paranoid about the legal fallout, she refused to meet me in person. Dr. Jocelyn Thibeault. She sounded austere, over-enunciating her English. I imagined her thin with telephone pole posture, probably in her fifties. She mailed Leland's medical records to a P.O. Box so I could peek at the X-Rays. I'm no pulmonary specialist, but the doctor talked me through the radiograph, so I could see the mess of scar tissue on his lungs.

As with all clients, I met Leland roughly four weeks ago. A month before the *terminus*. That term feels cold to me, but I wasn't the one who coined it. I suppose you have to give some kind of name to an event that important. In any case, it's not a word I would ever use around Leland Mumm.

Leland wanted to die the first day I met him. He didn't want time to think it over, because he didn't want to lose his nerve. But I insisted on a waiting period to give my clients the chance to get cold feet. It was my own Brady Bill. Two other clients had changed their minds at their moments of truth. During the first meeting clients were eager. They thirsted for relief and could forget that they needed to put their affairs in order. The good-byes. The legal documents. Sometimes a final house cleaning. When we met, Leland didn't want me to leave. He pulled at my dress with a weak hand, imploring me to ease his pain. The best I could do was morphine.

In most cases, I'd meet the family, usually a spouse. Leland didn't have anyone he wanted me to meet. I didn't push him. A typical client would introduce me to his doctor, but because of her qualms, Her Majesty Dr. Thibeault refused to be in the same room as the executioner. So it was just Leland and me.

Leland was young for a client—only fifty-two, according to his records. He had a long build, and I suspected he'd had more meat on him before the disease. IPF had eaten away at the muscle, especially in his arms and legs.

Over the past month, I visited his hillside ranch house in Clayton once a week. I'd gotten to know the ochre peels of the bathroom wallpaper, the bend where the wood veneer had pulled away from the wall. This was the house where Leland grew up, and it looked like it hadn't changed much. Leland didn't open windows either, turning the house into a gardener's hotbed. Stale sweat and urine fermented the air.

While I helped with the good-byes and the legal documents, we chatted. Leland admitted he didn't have many visitors, and he seemed happy to hear another voice in his home. Because his condition ruined his lungs, he wanted me to do most of the talking. He asked a lot of questions. This was natural. People are curious. People are especially curious about the woman who's going to kill them. I shared anecdotes about myself, but never real facts. For my own safety, I didn't use my real name. My work required anonymity. My parents also raised me with an audacious sense of theatricality. If I were honest with myself, I also enjoyed having a stage persona.

Kali. That's the name I used with clients.

Kali is the four-armed Hindu goddess of death. She has been appropriated by hipster flakes as a symbol of feminine power. Maybe that's fair too. But make no mistake, Kali is a destructress. In one of her hands she holds a severed head.

I know, I know, so fucking dramatic. I'll admit to a little cultural appropriation for choosing a name like that. I don't know squat about Hindu culture. I don't even practice yoga. Since I was so gung ho about picking the name of a goddess, I could have found something more fitting. The best match might have been Ixtab, the Mayan goddess of suicide, also known as Rope Woman; but really, who was going to pronounce that? I almost chose Kalma, a Finnish goddess of death and decay, whose name meant, "the stench of corpses." But way too gruesome, right? I wanted to comfort my clients. Kali sounded like a normal name. I needed a fake identity, but I didn't want to be flippant about my work.

Because of his staccato breathing, Leland sometimes needed two breaths to cough out my name. "Ka-li." He pronounced it the way people pronounce "Cali" instead of saying "California." Some clients pronounced it "Kay-lee." It's actually "Kah-lee," but I never corrected anyone. It was a fake name, so what did it matter? I wasn't going to be the snooty five-star waiter who tells patrons it's pronounced *fi-LAY* instead of *fillettes*.

Leland was slow with words, but that didn't mean he was speechless. To imagine the way he talked, you'd have to insert ellipses every two or three words, and not where you'd want to put them. On our last visit, he asked with effort, "What does your dad think of all this?"

This edged against my boundaries, but I indulged the question. "He died." *Dad, not stepdad.*

"Sorry."

"Me too. He was a good dad."

"Did you help him pass?"

"Not unless I talked him to death."

"What was his name?" We both knew this was forbidden territory, but he couldn't help himself.

"Mr. Kali."

He smiled. We were just playing.

Slowly, I found out more about my client. A geologist, Leland spent most of his career working for mining companies. The hardest stint he'd ever pulled was a gold mine up in Canada, within a hundred miles of the Arctic Circle. As a sci-fi geek, he called it Ice Planet Hoth. In the summer he couldn't sleep. In the winter he drank too much and got belligerent. He showed me a scar on his stomach from where a feverish colleague stabbed him after twenty days without sun. It's not unreasonable to guess that he'd gotten lung disease after years of particulate pollution. Then again, he'd been a smoker for decades. After his diagnosis, the company gave him a settlement. Not fat enough to live like a rap mogul, but enough to keep the house and feed himself.

I was getting close to Leland's, curving through the octopus-branched oaks in the Mount Diablo foothills. Parched grass the color of camel fur scrambled up the slow grade where the hiking trails picked up. The neighborhood, if you could call it a neighborhood, was a sparse network of small homes buffered by a half mile of wild land. Leland told me wild boar roamed back here. That might have been horseshit, but I believed it.

Leland lived in a tumbledown single-story home with loose brown shingles. The roof slouched, and the sun and rain had wrung out the sides like driftwood. It had the sort of beat-up charm that might attract attention from budding photographers and painters. I thought scientists made a lot of money, but not him. Perhaps he spent it on something else.

I parked alongside his cream sedan, a Chevrolet Monte Carlo from the eighties, which, like the house, must have been perfect three decades ago. Like one of those old refrigerators that kids locked themselves in. *A classic.* Now the mountain's clay dust streaked the tires and the trunk didn't close all the way.

The neighborhood had banished noisemaking, unless you counted hawk screeches. So Leland probably heard my engine. He would be expecting me, but I stayed in the car a moment longer to collect myself. This was all part of the preparation. After five years and twenty-seven clients, my nerves still rattled before the final meeting. This was more stressful than my paramedic work. When I charged into buildings in my other job, there was at least a chance I might save someone.

My ritual was similar before every terminus. I used my rental car as a dressing room—a green room, if you will. Any driver who's spewed hellfire at another motorist can tell you cars offer the delusion of privacy. So in my car I soothed myself, pretending no one was watching. My particular mode of relaxation began by flexing my body. I mean toes to top—every muscle. It sounds stupid, but it works. Flex and release. Flex and release. Loosens up the whole body. Prior to something this important, it also reminded me I was strong. Everyone has a point of pride, and mine was muscles. Mine weren't so big that they were scary, but notable for a girl.

I adjusted a purple wig so the bangs paralleled my eyebrows and painted lavender liner on my eyelids. My lips darkened to burnt wood. The last patches of makeup came from two dainty ziplock packets in my purse. If it weren't for the gray coloring, the packets might have looked like flour or cocaine. They were tiny ounces of ash, two bags worth. I dipped a pinky in each, and applied a smidge to each side of my neck. Nothing to alter the overall look of my costume—the smears of ash were added for my own benefit and undetectable to my clients.

This particular outfit matched Leland's tastes, but I always dressed loud for this work. An old boyfriend once said I had a kitten face. Another boy said my face was too soft to be on a body like mine. I took this to mean that people thought my features looked infantile, or at the very least juvenile, and I didn't want my clients feeling like some toddler was steering them into the afterlife. The makeup matured me, sharpening my features, so I looked fierce, even lethal. Like a scimitar-wielding death goddess. When I looked in the mirror, the severity of my face now fit the character I adopted for this work. Kali stared sharply back at me.

Rental cars have such sweet air conditioning, and as soon as I stepped outside I started to sweat. Sun scorched the driveway here on the ass-side of the mountain. The wet warmth of the morning foretold a muggy afternoon. I dabbed my forehead with a tissue. I didn't get two steps out of the car when I saw the black spider running across the walkway. Jesus, they moved fast. And this was a big one, the size of a goldfinch. But being Kali charged me with courage, and I thrummed with epinephrine. Without hesitation, I brought my heel down and crunched it like an ice cream cone, scraping my sole off on the pavement.

When I entered, the fetor almost pillowed me. Leland didn't

smell like other clients. Most smelled like they were dying, but this was worse than death. The air rotted like a summer dumpster. I stifled an involuntary gag, nothing Leland could have seen. According to Dr. Thibeault, a nurse cleaned him every few days, but it didn't help with the fumes. This suffering man managed to emit a decay that seemed inhuman.

With a compact layout, the main living area was open with oak floors and a window the expanse of a wall. Because the building squatted on the slope of Mount Diablo, the view faced away from the summit toward the minor rolling hills, without any homes to interrupt the scenery. Architects built-in custom cabinets, originally intended for dishware were now taken up by clothing and medical supplies. Outlined by sunlight, Leland lay in bed where I'd left him. Three weeks ago we'd moved the mattress to the living room because it gave him a better view. Now he swaddled himself in white sheets, his head rolled to the side that offered him sun and hills. He reminded me of Winslow Homer's *The Gulf Stream*, the black sailor on the brink of dehydration among the sharks.

I eased the door shut, but I still woke him.

"Kali." Leland's voice trailed by the end of my name. With effort he lifted his arm to wave.

"I'm here." I went to his bed and kissed him on the forehead. He tasted briny.

Leland was a dark man with a gaunt face and high cheekbones. If I were to guess, I'd say his lineage was Ethiopian or Somali. A descendant of African runway models. I'm tall for a woman, but he had several inches on me. Maybe six two. It was hard to tell since I never saw him standing. Leland Mumm was bedridden by the time I met him. He shuffled to the bathroom and back, but never during my visits. The way he looked now, he seemed like he'd collapse if he tried to stand. His bones stuck out all over. He didn't keep photos of himself around, so I couldn't tell how much body mass he might have lost. At this point, he couldn't have weighed much more than me.

I rumbled a chair across the floor and sat beside the bed,

covering his hand with mine. "You've got spiders outside."

"I know," he rasped. "They're everywhere."

"If it makes you feel any better, you have one less."

He laughed faintly. "Big or small?"

"The size of a volleyball."

"And you survived."

"Barely."

Leland's wide smile reminded me of Steven Tyler. I've heard that teeth are the bellwethers of someone's overall health, but that's a load of crap. Leland Mumm was about to die, and his enamel gleamed. Not a filling in there.

He complimented my clothes. "Nice getup."

Death should feel special, so I always dressed for my final meetings. What, was I going to waltz in with mustard-stained sweats? What I wore completely depended on the person. For Leland I wore a form-fitting white cocktail dress with purple piping to match the wig and the eyeliner. As a self-proclaimed sci-fi geek, Leland wanted me to dress like the kind of expo booth hottie you'd find at Comic-Con. Back when he could walk, he apparently made annual pilgrimages so he could meet Stan Lee. Clients have asked for weirder outfits—one wanted a nun habit, and one wanted me in scrubs so I would seem more like a medical professional.

"That wig. Like the Jetsons." Leland's laugh hacked up something. Weak as he was, he still ogled my legs. He didn't keep photos of his wife out, so I couldn't tell if I was even his type. But I didn't mind. If I were in his boat, I'd want something decent to look at on my last day.

"You requested it."

"You look good. Real good," he wheezed and squeezed my hand. "Gloves to match."

Purple satin opera gloves stretched from my fingers to elbows. "As good as latex. I can still handle the delicate stuff."

"Gloves, like a criminal," Leland mused. "You feel like a criminal?"

A client had never asked me anything like this, and Leland

was usually so playful I would have shrugged it off, but there was something abrasive in his tone. Something in the way he shifted his look from my left eye to my right, possibly trying to detect some guilt in my reaction. I had to catch myself so I didn't rebuke him. There was that combative streak the doctors always complained about. Like a jack-in-the-box, it sprang out so fast, and took so much more effort to push back down. "So long as there are laws, I'll feel like a criminal breaking them. But I don't feel like it's wrong." I stripped off the gloves. "We don't need these." With bare hands I touched his hair as if primping a floral bouquet.

He wore oversize flannel pajamas with trains on them. Such a sweet nerd of a man.

"You hot in these?"

"I get cold." He drew his blankets closer to his body, withdrawing his arm under the covers like an eel back into its crevice. He shut his eyes, and I noted the slight tremor of his lids before he opened them and nodded to the nightstand. "It's all there."

A stack of documents fanned across the small table. He'd also been reading Dr. Jeffrey Holt's *The Peaceful End*, marked toward the back with a green plastic book clip shaped like a tongue. Most of my clients had read it, and all of them had heard of it. A handbook for people who want to take control over their own deaths, it covers everything anyone needs to know about assisted suicide and provides a selection of methods. A popular option described is the bag-and-helium method. Basically, a turkey-sized oven bag hooks up to the same kind of tank used to inflate balloons. Many have tried to convince me how quick and painless it is, but I've never met someone who really wants to die with a bag over his head. But the book is important in many ways, and Leland Mumm followed many of its recommendations, which included preparing the materials that now lay on his nightstand. In addition to the DVDs, these included a living will and durable power of attorney document. Finally, a sheet of paper with thick red letters: DNR. *Do not resuscitate.* I would leave this on Leland's chest when I left, in case anyone came afterward and thought to revive him.

I opened one fat envelope with my name on it. Leland had given me a quarter-inch of cash. As I thumbed through it, he noted my confusion. "That's for you."

I reminded him, "I don't take money."

"It's a donation."

"Someone else can have it."

"Who else?" He spaced out, perhaps remembering his wife.

This wasn't the first time someone tried to pay me. Some people weren't comfortable receiving anything unless they gave something in return. "Thank you." I slid the envelope into my satchel. After this was over, I'd put it back. I wouldn't take the money, but I wouldn't insult him by refusing it either.

"How are you feeling?"

"How do you think?" The playful tone ebbed out of his voice. "God awful."

He seemed afraid, and I pressed my fingers into his palm.

"You're strong," he remarked. Then with several breath breaks, he asked, "Can we please do this? The wait is killing me."

"You're ready?"

He answered without hesitation. "I was ready weeks ago."

I unlatched my leather satchel and assembled my equipment. This part was the hardest for me, and I found it difficult to keep from tearing up. Death is sad. Every time. Not even the process of death so much as the frailty that leads to it, the helplessness. It always got to me. Leland Mumm also felt different than other clients, and I'm not just saying that in hindsight. My fellow paramedics—the ones who were parents—were the ones shell-shocked when they saw kids get hurt. Similarly, I thought that since Leland Mumm was roughly the same age my dad would have been, this hit close to home. But Leland didn't really remind me of my dad. He just didn't have anyone. Without family and friends to surround him during his quietus, the bleakness of his solitude ate at me.

I wish I'd learned to ape the poker faces I saw on other paramedics and docs, but I never mastered detachment. As I prepped the needle, my stomach churned. It always felt like this, and

I always considered it a weakness. No one wanted to see his personal Hindu goddess get all blubbery. To stop my eyes from watering, I practiced a look that made it seem like I was concentrating on my job with laser precision.

"Different kind of needle."

"It's called a butterfly syringe." Also known as a winged infusion set, this was a tool of the trade. Kevorkian himself used these. Most of my clients were on the older side, and the needle was designed to ease into smaller and more brittle veins.

"Walk me through it again," he said. Under the covers, he wrapped his arms tightly around his trunk, embracing himself. Many clients liked to talk through our final meeting so they could diffuse the fear.

"The first dose puts you to sleep. The second will turn off the lights."

"How many people have you helped?" He asked.

His tone shifted again, and now he sounded suspicious. It triggered my fiery impulses, sending a hot swell through my blood, and requiring a deep breath to calm down again. "Enough to know what I'm doing." The answer was twenty-seven.

"You'll find the vein all right? You're not going to play darts with my arm?"

"You shouldn't feel more than a pinch." I was a trained paramedic, and kept up my accuracy by sticking needles into oranges at home.

He breathed louder, faster. "I'm scared."

"I know. You know you're in control."

"I know that." He seemed certain on this point.

"Are you sure you want this?"

He nodded, maybe too eagerly. "Badly."

"I can give you a sedative if you want."

"I don't want more needles."

I shook an orange pill bottle from my satchel. "Diazepam. Valium. It can take the edge off."

His eyes danced around the room while he considered it.

"How long?"

"You'd feel it in under a half hour."

"How long after you stick me?"

"After I give you the first injection, you should fall asleep in under a minute."

"Stick with plan A." I stroked his arm. An invisible layer of semidry sweat had greased his skin. He tried to smile, but his mouth just twitched. He ran his tongue between his lips and teeth to try and moisten his mouth.

I readied the needle at his arm and tried to find a vein. He was dehydrated, so I had to tap a few times. "Do you want to close your eyes for the pinch?"

"Give me one more moment," he implored.

"All the time you want."

"I'd like to pray." Leland had never brought up religion, and this wasn't my area of expertise, but other clients had asked. He held my hand to his chest, and his ribs quaked with a violent heartbeat. "Pray with me."

"Of course."

We closed our eyes.

Lost in a meditative moment, I almost ignored the sensation of something hard brushing against my wrist. Hard, like a bracelet. Cold metal pressed into my skin, first lightly and then sharply. Then I heard the click. Eyes open, I saw a gleam of silver steel clasp around my right wrist. A chrome chain draped from the cuff in a wide arc to a thick teak bedpost topped with a carved pinecone. Leland Mumm had chained my arm to the bed frame.

When he spoke, his voice was clear and resonant. "Kali, I'm with the police."

Trigger temper. I latched onto Leland's neck with one hand. My volatile impulses set loose, I tried to crush his windpipe. I'd never attempted to hurt someone like this, but I dug my knuckles deep into his neck. To protect himself, he hunched his shoulders and stiffened his tendons into wires. His muscles flexed with a shocking power. This man was suddenly vital and dangerous. Leaning over him, I bore my weight down on his body. When my thumb wormed into the ribbed hose of his trachea, he gagged. His hands clawed at my arms, but in my furious blackout I kept my arms stiff as dowels. My palm clamped down over his arteries, and the way his eyelids flickered, I could tell he was losing oxygen fast. A few more seconds, he might have blacked out. I might have killed him.

Something fast flew into my face, like a kamikaze bird smacking a window. His fist hammered my left cheekbone, and my head snapped to the side. The impact shook me loose. My fingers lost their grip. Slackening with the force of the punch, I slid off the mattress. When my skull struck the floor, needles burst through my brain before the pitch darkness enveloped me.

CHAPTER 2

"You went rabid on me," he said, delighting in my ridicule. There were no ellipses between the words now.

Leland only had a few seconds after he knocked me down, but he made use of them. He flopped me onto the bed and kicked my leather satchel across the room. Then he patted me down for weapons, even though the most dangerous thing on me was the syringe. He rolled that across the floor, too.

Our positions reversed: I lay on the death-stink covers, tethered like a sacrificial goat. The mattress was still warm from his body heat. Leland was on his feet, looking down at me. *Miracle recovery.* His locomotive pajamas sagged at the crotch.

With my left arm pulled across my body, I yanked the chrome chain taut with the hope that it might decapitate the carved pinecone atop the bedpost. Leland kept his distance, which was a smart move. As soon as my head cleared, I kicked like crazy. When I couldn't reach him with my boots, I grabbed what I could with my free hand and chucked it at him, including his coffee-stained copy of *The Peaceful End.* The green plastic book clip fell out and into the covers, and the book only flapped a few feet. Envelopes whirled like Frisbees, but few hit him, and nothing hurt him.

Leland gave me the same smirk as when he'd ask, "When are you going to tell me your real name?" But he'd mutated into a different man, fast and formidable.

A residual ache swelled under my left eye, and Leland appeared blurry as he hovered over me. I savagely tore at my handcuffs. As a firefighter, I should have known this wouldn't have gotten me anywhere, but the pain and panic prevented rational thought.

It's not that I'd never been punched. On plenty of calls, an addict half out of her senses could crazy it up and clobber me when I didn't expect it. It wasn't ever pleasant, but the shock of being punched was worse than the pain itself. Years of sparring taught me how to take a shot, and how to hit back. Leland Mumm hit hard, but he wasn't Wladimir Klitschko. Just a tad stronger than my stepdad. He'd caught me off guard and landed a lucky blow. If I'd been ready for it, he wouldn't have pushed me off my feet.

He seemed to marvel at my flushed face and gurgle of obscenities. The past several moments had changed me too. My legs thrashed whip-wild, and my growls and swears sounded feral.

The chain held. After a few minutes, my wrist burned and my lungs heaved. My skin pinked around a thread of crimson where the cuff sliced a faint incision line. I wasn't about to break the bed frame. Not teak. The wood was too dense to crack the bedpost and too heavy for me to upturn the whole thing and whack apart the joints.

I split my attention between my shackles and Leland. I was still finding new pain from the punch, shooting down through my jaw now, and found it impossible to concentrate on any singular thing. I stared at Leland's face above me, trying to focus on the tip of his nose with my foggy eye. Leland seemed taller now, or maybe that illusion was created from him on his feet and me on the mattress. When he sneered, all those healthy teeth reminded me what a goddamned sucker I'd been. I should have known something was up when I saw those pearlies. What I wouldn't have given to chip a few with a boot heel.

"Who are you?" I ran a finger over the handcuff keyhole, as good as spinning a safe dial without the combination.

I kept expecting Leland to climb on top of me, but he hadn't moved since he shackled me. "I told you. Cop," he said with no frailty in his voice.

"No, you're not. No fucking cop would chain me to a bed. Punch me in the face."

"Sorry you think that. Because that's exactly what a cop would do."

Blood warmed the plumping welt under my eye. Where the cheek split, a trickle ran down my face and tickled the skin over where it hurt. "Fucker—I'm bleeding!"

"Believe what you want, but you're good and busted."

"Bullshit. What about Miranda?"

"Keep your mouth shut if you want. Call a lawyer when you can. That about cover it?"

I rattled my handcuffs, but if I fought anymore, I was going to spring a vein. Instead, I looked for weapons. I'd thrown all the loose stuff at Leland, leaving nothing on the nightstand. Pivoting off the mattress and stretching as far as the chain would allow, I stood on the floor and mule-kicked the nightstand at him. The flimsy table was light enough to sail at him, but he sidestepped it like fucking Fred Astaire. When it splintered on the wall behind him, he seemed amused. I went back to fidgeting with the lock, desperate enough to try working my pinky nail into the keyhole.

"It's not going to work," he said.

Handcuffs were easy. All I needed was a paper clip to spring it. But I didn't have a paper clip. As Leland predicted, my pinky nail didn't fit. All my tools were in my cowhide satchel, and that satchel sat by Leland's ankle. Frustrated, I grasped the chain with both hands and tug-o-warred with the bedpost, but only succeeded in tearing the skin on my palms.

"You're not going to pull the chain apart. You're going to hurt yourself."

The friction of steel against flesh dug down to the bone, and that hairline incision in my wrist began leaking rivulets of blood. The pain was enough for me to give it a rest.

The loss of control overwhelmed me. I couldn't control my own body, not with my heart shuddering and my lungs on fire. I couldn't remember breathing this hard, not even during the physical aptitude test for the fire department, and for that I had to sprint up and down six flights of stairs with fifty pounds of gear. Worse yet, I couldn't control the man in the room. Leland was out of my reach and unpredictable. If I expected him to zig, he might zag.

He spoke like a toastmaster. "We're going to have a long talk, but there's something I've really got to do first." He unbuttoned his flannel pajama top, button by yellow button. When I saw his bare stomach, I wrenched the chain again until the pain shooting up my arm made my shoulder spasm.

He bunched the flannel and absently tossed it against the wall. I didn't want to look at him, but I felt like I needed to monitor Leland in case he came at me. I imagined him on top of me, his hot mothball breath steaming up my nostrils. The baggy clothes had hidden his musculature. Leland Mumm was thin but tight, a welterweight. *Sneaky mofo.*

"Kali. You killed nine people." Again, it was twenty-seven. He'd counted wrong. "Did you expect this would have a happy ending?"

I writhed against my clasp. Smears of my blood rouged the sheets.

"Jesus Christ, calm down!" In the same breath, he pulled his pajama bottoms over his hips, and they dropped to his ankles. "You can't imagine how good it feels to take these off." He wore stained white briefs. In a moment he'd be naked. "I'm sorry to be so open about this, but we're on intimate terms by now, aren't we?" I dry heaved. He snapped. "For Christ's sake, get a hold of yourself. It's going to be a long day for you."

I waited for him to charge at me. My mind raced, fishing for defensive options. He was naked, I reminded myself, and I was clothed. I could squat 260 pounds. His nuts were right there at the level of the mattress. If he ran straight at me, I might crack his pelvis. I drew my knee to my chest, readying my left leg, the strong one, for a kick.

But Leland turned and walked through the bathroom door.

A few seconds later, the shower ran.

"I hope you don't mind," he called through the open door. "I have to get clean. You have no idea what it takes to stink like you're dying." His voice sounded like it came through a soup can. "I figured you'd have been around death enough to smell it on people. That means I haven't showered for a week. I'll be honest, that was tough. You ever been that long without a shower?"

Now that he was out of the room, I fished around the sheets, in case I could find a stray object under the covers narrow enough to stand in for a paper clip. *Nothing.* The entire house had been staged, and since no one really lived there, no one would have carelessly discarded items during day-to-day routines. Leland had only packed in enough props to make the place believable. I'd knocked a pill bottle off the nightstand. It was close enough that I could snare it with a boot, but when I twisted off the lid, the bottle spilled out breath mints.

He repeated himself. "Kali, have you ever been that long without a shower?" Presumably, he was checking to make sure I hadn't popped out of my cuffs.

"Yes," I spat. I felt between the mattresses for a trace of something, maybe a safety pin. *Nothing.*

"You know what the secret is to smelling like death?" He paused for effect. "FlyNap! You ever heard of it?"

This time I didn't wait for him to ask again. Maybe if I kept our banter going, we'd keep things congenial. "Fuck no." Maybe not that congenial.

He rinsed out his mouth in the shower cascade and coughed the backwash into the tub. Revolting. When someone is repulsed by the sound of body noises like eating, there's a name for that. *Misophonia.* Mine flared up listening to the swish of his saliva while he hawked up the shower water.

Soon enough the pipes whined and the water stopped. The curtain ripped back. Leland appeared in the doorway, dripping with a terrycloth towel wrapped around his waist. "FlyNap!" He sounded like a kid excited by something he learned in class. "It's an anesthetic they use to put drosophila to sleep—fruit flies."

I positioned myself back on the bed so I could kick easily. "I know what drosophilas are."

"Of course you do," he said dismissively. "I guess geneticists use the stuff to put flies to sleep, so they can count out which ones have red eyes, or some nonsense like that. It has the same compounds you find in rotting meat. So after a week of not showering, the added element you're smelling is a few drops of…"

"FlyNap. I get it."

"You know what you get? A perfect death cologne. I was worried you couldn't be fooled, but I'm very happy you were." He disappeared from the doorway. "You have no idea how bad it was. I mean, you only had to be around that smell for a couple hours tops. I had to live with it for weeks. A few days ago, I had to run a menthol stick under my nose just to get some relief."

The master of the quick change came out in charcoal slacks and a T-shirt. Over the tee he buttoned up a blue Oxford, like he was getting ready for a business meeting. "You ever heard of Richard Angelo?"

"Is that the inventor of FlyNap?"

He scoured my face for signs of sarcasm. "He was a nurse. I'm sorry, let me restate that. He was a murderer. He killed ten patients using pancuronium bromide, a muscle relaxant."

"Never heard of him."

"How about Efren Saldivar? Called him 'The Angel of Death.' Respiratory therapist, probably killed more than a hundred patients. Drug of choice? Pancuronium."

"I don't know who those people are. And I'm not one of them."

"Pancuronium's a funny drug. They use it in executions. You probably know that."

I did. It was one of three drugs. Sodium thiopental to induce coma. Pancuronium bromide to shut down respiratory systems. An optional third would be potassium chloride to stop the heart. But what he didn't say was that they used the same cocktail without the potassium chloride in the Netherlands, where they had done the greatest work around euthanasia to date.

"Nine other people in Northern California dead with 'DNR' cards on them. Pancuronium in the blood." He snatched the syringe from the floor and flicked the barrel. "And I bet you I'd find it in here too." He studied me, maybe waiting for a change in my mood, an "I gotta come clean" moment.

My mood did change. I grew more afraid of him because the danger he represented was turning from a physical threat to something much worse. My diaphragm trembled as I forgot how to breathe.

"That's why this is happening to you."

He grabbed my satchel off the floor. Seated in the chair by the bed—now dragged outside my kicking radius—Leland dumped out its contents. "Let's see what we have."

A different kind of panic crept into me. This guy might really be a policeman. If he was telling the truth, he was going to arrest me. We'd mentioned Miranda—maybe he had already arrested me. I thought about having all my dark secrets exposed for my shame and others' judgment. All the infinite possibilities of my life whittled down to captivity. Beyond butterflies now, I really thought I might puke. This man had tricked me; and above everything else, I felt indignant that all of this had come about because I'd been the rube in an elaborate prank.

I talked so I wouldn't hurl. "You're not even sick, are you?"

Leland picked through my purse litter without looking up. "'Fraid not."

"You look sick."

"Just skinny. Always was."

"You should get yourself checked. I've seen a lot of sick people, and you look sick."

"In the pink. Just had my annual physical. I have a quick metabolism." He found my backup syringe and squinted into the empty barrel.

"You had medical records. X-rays."

"Borrowed from a hospital."

I remembered the phantom phone physician. "Dr. Thibeault. Who's she?"

"My partner." He unscrewed my eyeliner and sniffed the brush. "Where is she now?"

Maybe he would have answered, but he jubilated in something he snatched off the floor. "Yahtzee!" He held up my driver's license, eyeballing the photo and comparing it to the purple-wigged gal on the bed. *Crap.* I felt my wig. In the scuffle it had been pulled off kilter, and some of my own plain caramel-colored hair showed through.

Leland's joy didn't linger. Not when he read the name on the license. "Martha Stewart."

This should go without saying, but the license was phony. I sassed, "I have to explain it a lot, but it's what my parents wanted."

Sunlight glinted off the lamination as he scanned for the golden seal of California. "You actually get by with this?"

"I rented a car with it."

"People are morons." Now he rolled my lipstick between his fingers, uncapped it and twisted the charcoal tip out of the tube. "You're smart, I'll give you that. Fake license. Rental car."

On this point, I felt victorious. Anything with my real name on it was back in my apartment. "Sorry to disappoint."

Examining my ID again, he mused at my photo. "You have a great smile. When you do smile, that is."

I didn't want this man judging my appearance, for better or worse. Plus, he was patronizing me. I looked goofy and toothy in that photo, surprised at my own happiness as if the prom king had just asked me onto the dance floor. I have pale and pinkish skin, but I'd been out in some sun back then. The sun brought out my nose freckles, and my teeth stood out like marshmallows in cocoa.

He found cash in my purse, and not just what he tried to give me as a donation. "You just carry cash? No credit cards? What happens if you run out of gas?"

"I plan ahead." More than he knew. In addition to the purse money, I toted a hundred-dollar fold in my underwear.

"Kali, Kali, Kali." He said my name like it was a dessert he was about to gorge. "Why don't you tell me who you are?"

I tried to confirm for myself that he was a police detective. "Where is your partner?"

"Somewhere busting some other jackass," he said halfheartedly.

"You're not going to give me your name?"

"What do you think?"

"Worth asking, though." He rustled a packet of travel tissues decorated with illustrations of She-Hulk. To himself, he noted, "Cartoon superheroes. Interesting." Then to me: "We're going to be at this a while, huh?"

"Looks like it."

Leland poked through the items on the floor with a pen and found my car keys. He dangled them in front of his nose as if trying to spy a wasp in amber. "Now we're getting somewhere. Don't go anywhere."

He bounded off the chair and walked out the front door, leaving me alone. The door gaped.

As soon as he was out of sight, I was back at my handcuffs like I was buried alive and tunneling my way out. I rolled out of bed as far as the chain would allow and fished under the pillows and sheets to find something that could pick a lock. Nothing bigger than a sandy breadcrumb ran between my fingers.

A moment later, my rental car honked as he tested the locks. Hopefully he'd comb through it a while. Nothing of mine was in there.

I thought about screaming for help, but the first person on the scene would be Leland Mumm. If I made enough noise, maybe a distant neighbor would phone in a disturbance. That just meant more cops would show up. I remembered that Leland never showed me a badge. If he wasn't a detective, then I'd be inviting law enforcement into a situation, putting myself in serious legal jeopardy. Then again, if Leland wasn't with the police, he might do much worse if no one came. I told myself that if he wanted to rape or kill me, he might have gotten started by now—but I wasn't sure.

My fingers poked something sharp and thin by a leg of the bed frame. A toothpick? A paper clip? Whatever it was, it was a *prize*. I snatched it. It was the green plastic book clip he'd used for *The Peaceful End*. I pinched it gently, and then snapped off the delicate loop around the outside. The fragment gave me a piece of curved plastic that fit into the keyhole. I worked the green plastic shard around the hole, but popping the lock was harder than when I'd practiced. My hands quivered. Leland would return any moment. Every few seconds, I snapped my head over my shoulder to check the front door.

While my right hand maneuvered the plastic, my left hand shivered in the manacle, raw and slowly swelling. The lock shivered with it. Time after time, the plastic slipped around the keyway.

"Now we're getting somewhere." Leland spoke two seconds before he came back through the door, allowing me to palm the plastic and pounce back on the mattress, as if I'd lounged the whole time he was raccooning through my car. "I saw the remnants of that tarantula on the walk. You really don't like spiders, do you?" I said nothing. There were plenty of those crawlies around there, and just to fuck with me he might pluck another from his lawn and let it scrabble around under the sheets. "I get it. They're creepy. Good to know, though." He tapped his temple. "I'll file that little factoid away in the safe deposit."

Leland slid a waiter's mini spiral notebook out of his pocket and scribbled. "You removed the plates. Very smart." I rented the most generic car I could; in this case, a silver hatchback. Replaced the plates with a generic dealership placard, so it looked like I'd just bought the thing. "Not as smart as you could be, though. Know what you missed? The VIN." The triumphant bastard sang to me: "The...fucking...VIN."

I didn't own a car. Hence, I didn't know what a *vin* was. *The Vincent?* Leland noticed. "VIN. Vehicle identification number. Right in your glove compartment." The VIN. The fucking VIN. "You know who they tracked down using the VIN?" No guesses from me. "Timothy McVeigh."

The way my left hand stretched over my forehead, I might have been swooning on a fainting sofa. This provided just enough of a blind spot for me to work the lock with my right hand. Clumsy so far, I kept missing the keyhole. My fingers started cramping.

Leland opened a cabinet and produced a laptop. When he

sauntered back to the chair, he ignored me while he unfolded it and clacked at the keyboard. I fidgeted with my lock. We could have been miserably married for all the attention we paid one another.

"Eureka," he said dryly to himself. "Got the rental agency." Detective or not, he had access to some kind of restricted information.

The plastic pin snapped. Leland lifted his head and combed over me with his eyes, trying to identify the source of the sound. Blood flushed my face, and my chest rose and fell. After the scan, Leland looked back down at his screen, and I felt between my fingers. Half my plastic needle had dropped behind my pillow, and I choked up on the remaining splinter and found the keyhole again.

Leland typed a number on his cell phone and raised a polite "one sec" index finger. To someone on the other end, he said, "Got something." He read the name and address of the rental agency. "Used a fake name. Draw a five-mile radius around the rental place and check for gyms. She has muscles." He studied my shoulders and legs from across the room. Coming from my captor, the comments about my body again made me uneasy. "Trains with weights. She looks broke, so start with cheapo gyms and mom-and-pop joints. I'll send you a headshot." He hung up, and then angled his camera phone over me. "Cheese." *Flash*. My scowl shot out into the ether.

As he messaged my photo, I felt something magical at my fingertips.

The point of my plastic pick found its pressure point. The cuff unclasped from around my wrist.

Open a rabbit cage and the bunny won't rocket out. Similarly, I stalled to consider my options. Leland still had my car keys. Sprinting to my car wouldn't get me anywhere. If I ran for it, I'd tumble down the grade in clunky heels. The neighbors, if I reached them, might not be home. If they were, they might believe him over the raggedy tower in the white and purple cocktail dress. They might even call the police, and I'd be back to square one.

Another option would be to physically subdue Leland Mumm and take my keys back. He was strong, but I hadn't gotten the chance to properly fight him.

Right after Christmas last year, the firehouse got a call on Jerrold Avenue in Hunter's Point. Gunshot through the thigh. A massive 300-pounder had just got out of prison and didn't want to go back. Wrestling him down to the stretcher was Herculean, even with a partner. He thrashed around, and between the latex gloves and the blood, our hands were slippery. That guy was like a wet bar of soap, and strong. But when he bashed me in the forehead, I caved in his nose with an elbow and he went limp. If I could immobilize that monster, I could handle the bean pole.

Leland passed on instructions through the phone with his back to me in the bathroom doorway. When I stood, my legs creaked from lying down for so long. I stretched out my fingers to test their strength and rotated my swollen wrist. Stalking toward him, I stayed quiet as a ghost, even in the boots. I snatched a syringe off the floor. Not the winged infusion set I was going to use, but the backup hypodermic, dart-shaped with a two-inch cannula. Extending the plunger with a thumb, I siphoned air into the barrel. I had no idea if an air bubble would actually kill him. The air bubble heart attack was a kind of urban legend, and I'd never tested it. I didn't like the idea of having to stab someone, much less kill him, but I would today. Kali might have come there to dispatch Leland Mumm, but I shouldn't have to explain that this kind of death was a different breed of chinchilla.

I skulked toward the bathroom door, lifting my feet lightly and rolling my soles on the ground. My ribs shook from my heart throbbing. I should have just run for it, but I needed to destroy this man if I wanted to escape. He wasn't ready for me, lollygagging in that doorway on his cell. And as I approached him, I fumed with anger. My face felt hot. I wanted to hurt him.

Leland thanked the person on the other end and disconnected. After a few seconds of heavy silence, he spun, noticing the silence in the room. We stood face-to-face.

"Son of a bitch!"

I lunged with the syringe, but not fast enough. That wiry prick had some fast-twitch muscles, and he dodged me. Maybe I was too hesitant and didn't thrust deep enough to be lethal. Still, I got him the second time. The tip punctured his stomach, but only far enough to break skin, just to the side of the scar he'd told me came from his Arctic knife wound. Someone had taught Leland what to do during a knife attack. Moving with a fluidity that came from trained repetition, he clawed my forearm and twisted me counterclockwise. The hypodermic rattled on the floor. Twist an arm the right way, and the attacker can be on his knees in seconds. A potential game ender. But someone had taught me this move and how to defend against it. I jabbed my free thumb into his neck, and we broke apart, stumbling farther into the bathroom. He tried to say something, but only gargled.

Elbows are a girl's best friend, because the whole body goes into every blow. When Leland covered his throat, his face opened up as a target, and my elbow caught him on the cheek. He reeled back into the shower, cracked the tiles and smeared a little blood on the ceramic. I landed a couple more heavy elbows to his head. When he tried to prop himself up on the tiles, he lost his footing. Backing into the shower stall, his leather sole slipped on the porcelain and Leland collapsed, knees over the tub rim, feet in the air.

I dropped to my knees and used my fists. When Leland threw up his forearms to protect his ears, I got inside and belted his solar plexus. He wheezed, but I didn't debilitate him. An hour ago this guy's body seemed like it could snap like a biscuit, but now his arms rigidly braced over his face. I always knew I was winning in a scrap when my opponent's arms started to get lazy. This guy was a rock. I pounded harder because I could feel how his muscles coiled. Like Ali against the ropes when Foreman was laying into him, he took the punishment and waited for his chance to spring back when I stopped. A disorienting high surged through me, and I stopped thinking about where to place my punches and started whaling on him. Trying to get to his face, most of my punches landed on his arms.

I should have used my legs. Such a dummy, getting down on the floor with him. With legs hanging over the sides of the tub, I could have driven a heel into his shins. Knocked out the knees. It would have been so easy. But I got carried away, fueled by a numbing heat, which made me forget the pain in my right wrist as I brought down both fists with equal abandon. I kept battering, and he just waited until I punched myself out.

The moment I gasped for breath, Leland came alive. One of his hands dropped. He pulled something out of his pocket roughly the size of a small vibrator, not much larger than a lipstick tube. I owned one of these in pink and kept it in my nightstand drawer. In the moment, I thought Leland Mumm might be attacking me with sex toy. He snaked it under my arm, then sprayed me in the face. A moment later, the most intense pain of my life burned my eyes blind.

Pepper spray doesn't necessarily paralyze the victim. On the contrary. With my sockets searing, I went wild. My arms and legs swung like medieval flails. Unsure of where to aim, I flagellated my limbs in all directions. Guttural screams punctuated the movements. Instead of disabling me, the pain only stirred me up. I kicked a dent in the plaster and bashed the sink out of the wall, so it sagged on the pipes. Somewhere in the maelstrom, a distinctive crunch told me I'd crushed the hypodermic under my heel.

Leland had the advantage, and he found a way to evade my punches and kicks. I felt his body maneuver around me, and his arm slithered around my neck from behind. He threw a sleeper hold on me and dragged me back to the bed, my heels sliding on the floor. I thrashed my legs and toppled the bedside chair, but that didn't help me. The handcuff found its way back around my wrist. It hurt more this time when the steel cut against my bones. I scratched some skin with my free hand, but it didn't stop Leland. Seconds later a cuff closed over the other wrist. I lay flat on the mattress again, now with both of my wrists lashed to the bedposts. All I could do was scream in protest.

Sometime between a half hour and an hour later, my eyes registered blurs, the most prominent being a smear shaped like Leland's face. Hovering over the headboard, my legs couldn't get him. Then he started with the water. He poured water over my eyes and dabbed them with a towel. I thought the prick was waterboarding me and bucked as much as the chains would allow.

"Hold still," he said. "This will make the pain go away faster."

One might think that this kind of pain would limit my ability to speak, but despite the panic, I was able to curse just fine. Someone walking through the front door might have thought they stumbled across an exorcism.

Diligently, Leland Mumm poured the water over me, talking me through it as he went. "I know, it's the worst. I've gotten sprayed three times. Once I nailed myself while making an arrest. I was just starting out. I pointed the thing the wrong way and blasted myself in the face. Can you believe that?" Initially, the water made the pain even worse, like vinegar in a wound, and I writhed in response. "Second time, we were in the same kind of situation, trying to hold down a guy hopped up on PCP, back when PCP was still a thing. My own partner missed the guy and got me." He softened. "Open your eyes to let the water in."

I shook my face and moved every part of my body that I could. The bed bounced on its teak frame.

He waited for me to calm down, and then went on. "Third time was plain trickery. I washed out the canister, and the steam carried some of the vapors into my face. It got in deeper, the way the cold can creep in under your clothes."

I fought the towel, but he found a way to dab my face.

"Kali, hold still. Open your eyes to let the water in." More water drizzled over my face. Some snorted up my nose. "Have you ever taken chemistry class?" He asked.

I responded by howling into his face like a crazy person.

Without raising his voice, he said, "I know you can hear me, and I know you can respond. Have you ever taken a chemistry class? Kali." He stressed *Kali*.

I articulated for the first time since he sprayed me, and my voice croaked from all the screaming. "Yes. I've taken a chemistry class."

"Remember the water fountain? The one you use to flush out

your eyes? That's what this is like. I'm flushing out your eyes. You need to open them. It will make the pain go away faster. I promise." Opening my eyes was a challenge, but I did it. The water eventually helped. Eventually, the piercing sting faded to a dull soreness, no more painful than dry eyes after an all-nighter. The skin around them smarted like a mild sunburn.

He picked the chair off the floor and returned to his seat. "You're a dangerous woman, no doubt about it." I squinted, and some of the excess water and tears drained out. Slowly, he came into focus.

"Stops you in your tracks, doesn't it? Nice belly ring, by the way." My dress had torn, and my navel was exposed.

He laughed heartily and patted down his body, especially a few inches left of his navel, where I'd stuck him with the needle. "You almost gave me my own belly button piercing." Now that our tussle was over, he seemed gleeful. "You got me good. I have to hand it to you. *Jesus!*" He prodded around his ribcage where I'd landed some of my deepest punches. "Do you realize how phenomenally *fucked* you are right now? You just assaulted an officer."

"Show me your badge."

"Fair enough." He opened a closet door and found a suit jacket that matched his trousers. From the inside pocket, he pulled out a gold shield and flopped it close to my face. In the time afforded me, I could read the words "Alameda County," and the number "5417." It looked real enough. The moisture drained from my tongue.

"You've never been arrested, have you? Probably never been stopped." I didn't reply, but he guessed the answer. "Lucky duck. Don't worry, I'll guide you through every step of the way."

Having just traded blows, I was less afraid of him. "If this is an arrest, why am I still here?"

"Technically, I haven't arrested you yet. I'm detaining you right now." He retrieved the copy of *The Peaceful End* and thumbed through it in his chair. He breathed deeply as he settled into his seat and cracked the cover. "I'm not sure what to do with you yet."

CHAPTER 3

The sun passed to the western side of the house. The living room dimmed until Leland turned on the overhead so he could continue reading his book. He hadn't said much to me except to occasionally offer me water. I refused, and my tongue had toughened to hide. I thought about asking for a lawyer, but I didn't have a lawyer to call.

"This book is handy. Even has illustrations," he said. "You ever try using the helium tank?" It wasn't a good idea to say anything about my work. But when Leland Mumm was a client, we talked about different methods I could use—different options for him. He remembered. "That's right, you didn't recommend it. I can see why. Look at these photos. Dying with a bag over your head? It's like going out dressed as the Unknown Comic. You know that guy? He was on 'The Gong Show.' A comic that dressed up with a bag over his—you know what? It's not important."

"I've seen 'The Gong Show.'"

"Must have seen it on reruns. Too young to see it on broadcast, that's for sure. Probably watched it with one of your folks. More of a guy show, so probably your dad?" He studied my reaction until he determined he'd guessed correctly. "You must love your dad. Putting up with bad reruns just so you could sit with him."

This felt like it was never going to end. "Why are you holding me captive?"

"Captive? What do you think is happening here? I'm detaining a mass murderer."

"I don't believe you're a cop," I said. I'm not sure what I believed. I'd seen that badge—he might have been law enforcement. I was just being contrary. It took some will for me to say this, not to mention some physical effort since my mouth was dry. I was essentially daring him to book me. A police station would mark the end of my free life. I didn't want that to come any sooner, but if Leland wasn't planning on arresting me, he was planning something worse.

"I guess that's the beauty of me being where I am and you being where you are. I don't need you to trust me. But I am a cop, and you are in deep shit."

His cell phone jangled. Leland picked up and listened. He didn't take his eyes off me this time. He scribbled in the margins of the book. Something ignited his face. The call ended in less than a minute.

"Pamela Wonnacott."

Leland had just spoken my name. If my insides were a room, all the paint would have melted down the walls. I didn't know how to react.

"Pamela Wonnacott," he read off his sheet of paper. "The miracle of mobile, baby. Found your gym and messaged your headshot over. The general manager knew you in a blink. He says you're there every morning. One thing you don't have to worry about in prison will be your access to free weights."

From the notes in the book he then read off my street address in Bernal Heights and my social security number. He was dead on for both of them. "Born in 1984. Five ten. I'd have guessed you were six feet, but it's probably the boots and the broad shoulders. Eyes...*green*." He looked at me intently from across the room. "How about that? I don't see those very often. I thought you were wearing contacts. Now let's seen...hair *brown*. I would amend that—brown... *sometimes*. Right?"

I felt like such a jagoff for wearing that purple wig.

"Everyone can be found out, Kali." I was properly horrified, which was exactly what he wanted. "So let's pull the walls down and get to the studs." He sipped his water. "Pamela. You don't look like a Pamela. Wonnacott. What the hell kind of name is that? Sounds like you're a pilgrim."

I puked. I didn't have much in me, but whatever I had dumped out over the mattress. The acrid smell burned in the back of my nose. Leland rolled his eyes and threw me another towel. With effort, I angled my arms *just so* to wipe my mouth. "You'll be even more dehydrated after that, and you can bet your ass we're going to be here a while."

By his feet he kept a second water glass, the one he kept offering me all afternoon. "You want it?" Reluctantly, I nodded this time. That dull ache behind my right eye throbbed that much more passionately from the dehydration. He walked behind the headboard and slowly fed me the water. I finished the glass, and he wiped my mouth with a clean corner of the towel.

"What do you think your folks will think of this?" he asked. "I'm going to call them, you know. They'll be the first people we talk to." This must have worked on the born-yesterdays.

"Good luck getting a hold of them," I said.

He read my face. "Your dad really is dead, then? Mom too?" My lack of response confirmed it. "Mom too. I'm sorry for your loss."

He refilled the water glass in the kitchen and came back to me. "More?" I didn't refuse, and he poured the water slowly into my mouth.

"What did your father do? Mr. Wonnacott. I'm going to find out anyway."

My will was crumbling. Since he already had my name and my social, it wouldn't take much to find out details about my parents. Still, this eased out of me unexpectedly. "He was a musician."

"Trombone?" He loved messing with me, as a client and then a cop.

"He scored movies."

"Like John Williams. There's good money in that, right?" I nodded hesitantly. "Any movies I would have heard of?" He mopped up the water that ran down my cheeks.

"Depends how much you get out." He would have heard of a lot of the movies my dad worked on.

"So, you're a rich kid."

I started to wonder if this was a kidnapping and he wanted ransom. "Do you want money?"

Leland scoffed, "If you've got money, why did you take mine?"

"So you wouldn't be insulted when I refused." My mouth started to feel moist again. "I'm not a fucking assassin."

"Whatever you call yourself, the outcome is the same, Pamela." He stewed over the name. "I don't like the way that sounds. I'm going to call you Kali." He nosed into the notes he'd jotted in *The Peaceful End*. "You have a falling out with your folks? Trust fund runaway?"

"I loved my parents."

He shrugged. "Kids from good homes usually don't find themselves in situations like this. It's not that it never happens, just not as much. How did they die?"

I'd already said too much. "You're a detective. Detect."

He studied my face. "Someone got to you, though. As a kid, someone got to you. Something bad happened. Was it your mom? She cross a line with you?"

"My mother didn't molest me."

"I never said she did."

"You implied it. And she didn't. I loved my mom."

"Not your dad either. He was a good dad. I can tell by the way you talk about them both. Shame. It would be so much easier to blame them."

I was going to have to pee soon. My bladder had started to swell.

He said, "Listen, I really don't give a shit about your parents. You don't have to tell me about whatever happened to you as a kid. Really, I'm just being polite."

"What do you want from me?"

"Your confession."

When I closed my eyes, a tear rolled down the side of my face.

Leland said, "You're not done yet. You just need to cook a little more." He read his book.

. . .

I fell asleep. I'd fought to stay awake, but somehow several hours escaped, and now it was morning. The sun came through the windows in a cathedral beam and baked me gently. If metal weren't grinding against my bones, this might have been a perfect morning.

Leland was still reading. His shirt now rumpled in places, his sleeves rolled to his elbows. He looked tired as he combed over the last few pages. He blinked slowly and rubbed his eyes. His spare hand propped up a leaden chin. When he saw me budge, Leland regarded me in passing, and then flipped a page.

My bladder was bursting. "I need to use the bathroom." My throat dried again overnight.

Leland hadn't moved. "Too bad."

"You can't keep me here like this. This has to be illegal," I thought aloud.

"But you're not sure, are you?"

"Eighth amendment."

"You have no idea how it all works, do you? I haven't hurt you any more than necessary to detain you."

"I still need to use the bathroom."

"Do you have something you want to say to me other than please?" When I didn't say anything, he laughed with less oomph. "Worth a shot."

My heart beat the way a wing flaps on a wounded bird. I twisted in my cuffs. My left wrist had swollen visibly in the shackles, and now my right wrist chaffed as well from hanging in chains. The cuts and bruises on my knuckles—the ones I'd earned from punching Leland—smarted this morning. I didn't mind them as much. I scanned my body, especially between my legs. I didn't feel different down there, just a little musty. As far as I could tell, Leland hadn't fondled me while I was out.

"I need water."

"That I can do." Leland had a glass at the ready and poured it into my mouth from behind the headboard. On the back of the chair he'd draped both his suit jacket and a shoulder holster with a black semiautomatic. I still wasn't completely assured that he was a lawman, but his props were convincing.

"I need to pee."

"Can't let you off the chain."

"You have a gun."

"You can't be trusted."

My eyes watered. This man wasn't going to arrest me, and I had no idea what he was going to do. I hadn't eaten for a day, and although my stomach squealed, the abundant cortisol shooting through me killed my appetite.

A detective would have driven me somewhere by now. He would have called his partner and at the very least, the two of them would have been watching me together. My interrogation would be hosted in one of those cinder-block rooms with the big mirror. They'd give me a cell with a bed and a toilet. At this moment I craved those things. My eyes ached from the pepper spray and fountained with tears. I coughed up the extra mucus in my nose, and then the coughing avalanched into sobs.

"That's an appropriate reaction." He let me cry a while before he put his book down. "This can go on for a lot longer, you know. But you can end it."

A watery gasp from me: "How?"

"Just talk to me."

Again the confession. He wasn't going to arrest me without it. Maybe he didn't have much hard evidence, and he needed me to fess it all up. If this was all he wanted, then I could talk. It was the smallest morsel of hope.

"You're a good actor," I said. "I thought you were dying."

Leland smirked. He pointed to my purple ball of hair, now bunched in a pile with the rest of my purse chaff. "You're pretty theatrical yourself." His voice relaxed. We were both tired. He noticed something else in the pile he'd missed. Pinching them between his fingers, he picked up one, then both of the ziplock bags.

"Those aren't drugs," I said.

"Of course they're not," he said, examining them against the light. "They're ashes, aren't they?" He held them in his open palm.

"Let me guess. Your mom and your dad?"

"Please don't empty them," I said, realizing that I was pleading.

"Don't worry about that." He placed them inside his jacket pocket. "I'll keep them safe."

I felt like I should keep talking, because the conversation gave me a wobbly sense of calm. "My dad was in opera before he did movies."

"Name like Wonnacott—of course your dad was into opera." Leland's voice was tender now. I knew he was manipulating me, but I didn't care. Fake kindness was better than no kindness.

"I liked the costumes. I got lost in the wardrobes backstage."

"Do you dress up every time?"

I remembered I should be defending myself against prosecution. Deny, deny, deny. "What do you mean, every time?" This came out coy.

"When I told you to talk to me, you know what I meant. No reason to dodge anything now. I caught you red-handed." Leland drifted. His all-nighter must have got to him. "Ever wonder where that came from—red-handed?"

"It means you've got blood on your hands."

"That would make sense." He chewed his pinky in thought. "How long have you been doing this?"

I was ready to talk, but not to confess. "Doing what?"

"How many people have you killed?"

Not a squeak.

"Do you have any idea how long we've been trying to find you?" I did wonder—very much. "Roughly two years." He could've earned a master's degree in that time, and yet he chose me. "The way we've counted it, there have been nine unexplained deaths of senior citizens in the Northern California area. I'll admit, I don't know if this number represents your full portfolio, but I do know that all of those people suffered from terminal illnesses. They all died in their homes. They were unattended, except by whoever killed them. Big note with 'DNR' written on it." He waved the book over his head. "Do Not Resuscitate—just like the good Dr. Holt suggests. In every instance, death came from an intravenous high-dose barbiturate. Thiopental and pancuronium. One-two punch." He leaned toward me. "Did I get the number right? Nine?"

As I mentioned, he didn't have the number right. He'd missed several clients in Southern California, Nevada, Arizona and New Mexico. Twenty-seven clients. He had counted nine, and I didn't even know if his nine matched mine. His lack of data boosted my confidence.

"It's been more, hasn't it? Doesn't matter. We only need to get you on one count."

He was right. What a goon I'd been. I let my guard down a little, and now I was screwed. With every twitch of my face, I was giving myself away. "We can figure out the full count later. Killer's a killer's a killer."

I couldn't imagine saying it out loud. I wouldn't have confessed to myself in a locked closet back in Bernal Heights. I killed twenty-seven people. That phrase would never get its proper volume.

"I'm not a killer." This just came out. He'd riled me. I knew I shouldn't have spoken as soon as I heard myself. A second later, I thought, *So that's how people get caught.*

Maybe I needed a lawyer, but I didn't ask for one. Leland hadn't officially read me my rights, because he hadn't arrested me. But it was becoming inevitable. If I were an active participant in my own ruin, it would only go faster. I imagined how I'd look in my best suit, standing during the sentence reading. Momentarily, I indexed my wardrobe and chose a heather gray suit that hid my shoulders, softening me. Kevorkian got eight years, but he was a doctor and had a lot of good will behind him. The right legal team could paint me as a piranha and toss me in a dungeon.

"Does the name Nancy Donavan mean anything to you?"

Of course it did. Nancy was Kali's first official client. Nancy had tightly wound ringlets. Her thick glasses prevented much direct eye contact. She was eighty-seven years old, suffering from delusions brought on by an inoperable tumor behind her right eye. She didn't remember her family on most days. Nancy's daughter and son-in-law brought her to live with them. I was queasy the whole time, and popped one of my own Valiums so I wouldn't hyperventilate during the video good-byes.

I might not have had the gonads to go through with any of it, but Nancy guided me. She wanted it so badly. The whole family wanted it. Even with a house full of witnesses, it didn't feel wrong. We bunched together, quiet as she drifted off on her side, mouth open in an interrupted yawn. Most of us wept, including me. I didn't know what killing was supposed to feel like. I suppose I guessed it would feel like stealing. But when her fingers gave a final tremble, I felt like I had gifted her mercy.

"Did Nancy Donovan give you a taste?"

Yes, but not in the way he meant.

"What about Merrill Stromberg?"

Leland had done his homework. Merrill was client number twelve; probably number four by his count. She was younger than most. Younger than him. Forty-four years old and suffering from uremia. Accompanying kidney failure, uremia occurs when urea and waste products stay in the blood instead of being excreted through urine. It gave her a lot of bruising and bedsores, and she couldn't hold any food down. She'd withered down to a stick. Uremia lowers the body temperature, and her body felt cold when I touched her. Merrill's husband, Peter, sat with her and read Erica Jong poems until she fell asleep.

"You took money from her."

"I did not."

"You had to."

Merrill came from a very wealthy family, old money New Yorkers who relocated to the West Coast. The Strombergs ran one of the more successful drugstore chains in the region. Leland Mumm assumed that a family of means would have naturally paid me for services. The truth was, she contacted me the same way everyone had. Some people sought me out because they didn't want to be alone. Some because they didn't want to botch the job. Some, like Merrill, wanted discretion.

"Nothing that you say or do will ever make that statement true."

"That rhymed," he said.

"Unintentionally." I couldn't ignore my bladder anymore. "I really have to pee."

"*Tough. Titty.*" Leland meticulously intoned.

"I'm serious. You want me to wet your floor?"

"Go ahead. What makes you think this is my floor?"

"You want to humiliate me on top of everything else?"

"It won't be the first time I've ever seen someone piss their pants."

I tried to shame him. "Does it get you off?"

"A grown woman soaking her own crotch with urine? No, it does not. Nice try, though."

"Have a crumb of humanity."

"I'm not inclined to uncuff you."

"You're going to have to eventually."

"If you're looking for privacy, you're not going to get it. I've lived with women, Kali. A little urine isn't going to bother me. And don't worry about the bed. I was going to throw it out anyway." Leland walked around to the headboard and loomed over me. I tried to kick him, but my boot wouldn't reach. Some of the sheets had bunched in the corner of the mattress. For a moment, I thought he was going to drape the sheets loosely over me for a modicum of privacy. Instead, he snapped them out from under me, swiftly as a magician doing a tablecloth trick.

Son of a bitch. He really wasn't going to let me use the toilet. He wouldn't even turn his back. So I opened up my bladder, locking hateful eyes with him. The mattress became warm and wet, and seconds later the dampness around my crotch made my underwear chafe like sandpaper.

Above me, Leland seemed satisfied. He excused himself and made for the bathroom, where he loudly emptied his own bladder into the toilet, flourishing it with a proud flush.

This was my breaking point, the final humiliation that cracked my will. I sobbed again, but this time without any restraint. I had no defiance left in me when he returned to the room.

Leland gaped wide when he yawned, like a crocodile. "They've got a few nicknames for you. Florence Nightingale is the one that stuck, but some folks call you the Night Nurse, and Belladonna."

When I collected myself, I said weakly, "Why not Kali?"

"Not as fun for them."

I paid more attention to my gritty crotch than to what I was saying. Coy evasion wasn't working for me. Leland read my facial tics, and knew how to coax the truth out of me, even if it was just serving up yes-no questions and detecting when I was lying. Now I'd offered a tacit confession by not refuting the implication that I was Florence Nightingale or whatever the hell they wanted to call me.

Between the shame and the exhaustion, I stopped caring about my own safety. Leland had broken me. So instead of telling him to lick his own balls, I started talking. "So, they think I'm a nurse?"

"We assumed you had some sort of training, but we weren't sure how much. I knew you weren't a nurse from the questions you asked about my medical records."

"The questions I asked Dr. Thibeault."

"She told you how to spot the scar tissue on my lungs. Someone who went to med school would have already known how to spot it."

"Fair enough."

"We knew you were a young woman and tall. Some witnesses pegged you going in and out of homes, and a security camera caught you in a parking lot in Orinda."

He waited for a reaction, and I finally gave him what he wanted. "I can't believe I missed those. I usually check."

Leland seemed pleased I was opening up. "Now we're getting somewhere."

I'd never felt so deflated and yet relieved that I could share the truth instead of concealing it. "What do you want to know?"

"I want to understand. I'm trying to figure out if you're redeemable, or if I should just throw you to the lawyers and be done with you."

"You haven't already made up your mind?"

"This is a tricky crime to suss out. You could be trying to help people in your own misguided way. And you could be a full-tilt psychopath. I'm wondering which one it is."

"What if I'm doing something courageous?"

"You'd like to think that, I'm sure. But tell me, where's the courage in killing someone who's mostly dead? Sounds like hunting at a zoo. It's just target practice."

An instinctive indignation released my combative streak. "The courage comes in defying an immoral law."

"Then you could say there's courage in every criminal, which there is, at some level. But it doesn't make it legal."

"If it's the right transgression, it makes it moral. And that's enough."

He mocked me in a church voice. "If it's wrong, I don't want to be right!" His contempt ruffled me, but I didn't have much strength to retort. If he unlocked the cuffs and I tried to punch him, my arms might swing as weakly as air guitar windmills. "See, this is the kind of logic that I've come to expect from the misguided. You're twenty-six, old enough to know better, but still young. Idealistic and highly malleable. I get it—I was that age. But what you're considering an immoral law has been part of mainstream morality since we've been making laws. It's never been considered moral to kill another human being. You could argue that it's the foundation of why we even made laws. So people like you wouldn't go around on willy-nilly killing sprees."

"It's not a killing spree."

"Quite right," he considered. "A killing spree would imply the heat of passion. A rash, irrational act. That's not you at all, is it? All of these were very methodically planned."

"It's not murder. None of them were." There I went again, seeping out my confession.

"I believe that's what you believe. That's a good sign. That means you're not a psychopath. Probably. These people make you feel something?"

"It's mercy."

"Listen, when you've got laws on the books as old as ours—I'm talking Hammurabi Code here, and even laws that were made before that—people created punishments when one civilian killed another. People don't want to see people kill other people—it is an undeniable part of human morality."

"It's up to individuals to take action so people can identify what laws need to be changed. Remember slavery?"

Leland looked as if a balloon had just popped. Then he laughed with his head between his knees. "Oh, that's good! You're going to talk to me about slavery. All right, let's see how bad you hang yourself."

"Slavery was around for thousands of years, way before anyone from Africa ever got to America."

"That's right. But it was never considered a moral absolute. That's what made it tricky. Slavery was an economic system that necessitated the violation of human rights. Some people knew it was inherently wrong. But as an economic system, it was open to different perspectives. On the other hand, when someone gets killed in civil society, everyone always gets their nuts in a bind."

"It's the same thing to me. Different ways to legitimize human suffering." Not sure how much I believed this, and how much I was trying to push his buttons.

"You're not going to sell me on your argument."

I asked, "Do you feel like people in chronic pain have the right to die?"

"In fact, I do. That's why we're talking. That's why you're not in a jail cell yet." His voice lost some of its amusement.

My adrenal surges ebbed, and I was left quaking and nauseous in their wake. Leland nursed his water. The talking was drying me out. Now that I'd unsuccessfully tried to link my work to the abolition movement, I wasn't sure if I could even ask for more.

"You want more than a confession. Please tell me what it is." My teeth chattered as I said it. Any answer to this would terrify me, and I shivered thinking of all the weird things he might do to me.

He propped his elbows on his knees. "You know what I find

remarkable? That I've had you chained up here overnight and you haven't asked for a lawyer. You haven't even screamed for help."

"I didn't think anyone would come running. Maybe all the homes around here are empty, like that town in Nevada where they dropped the A-bomb."

"No," he shook his head. "You didn't think that. You didn't want anyone to come and save you."

He didn't sound anything like my mother, but it didn't stop me from answering like a petulant daughter. "Think so?"

"Know so."

"Why would I need rescuing? You're a detective, right?"

"Indeed I am. But cop or no cop, I represent a threat to you. And I've done something completely unorthodox for the police. Namely, I've kept you captive. And you haven't squealed for help the way anyone else might have." He shot me another one of his puzzled stares. "That tells me you don't want someone to come and fetch you."

"And why not?"

"Any number of reasons. You might be used to being independent, so you might not be in the habit of asking for help. You might still think you can save yourself. Maybe you think I'm a psycho, and you're worried if someone else comes into the scenario, they might get hurt too. But I think you have what the law calls *mens rea*, 'a guilty mind.' You know this is wrong, and you want to be caught."

Though I surely lacked the strength to grapple with him now, I tossed out, "Why don't you uncuff me and test the theory?"

"Listen to you now. No fight in your voice. You don't even want me to let you go now. You wouldn't know where to go if I did." He was confusing me. In the pauses, his lips gently sucked at his water.

"So what do you want from me?"

He placed the glass by his ankle. His long fingers twiddled. "I want us to trade."

"I don't know what that means."

"You will." He started again. "Kali, do you know why all this is happening?" No, I really did not know, and that was the worst part. "I wanted to give you a taste of captivity. How do you like it so far?"

My thoughts mixed a mob of voices into a babbling welter. Already I'd fantasized about how to hurt or kill Leland Mumm. California was a death penalty state. For the crimes I'd committed, a court would entertain life imprisonment. If I killed a detective, I'd get the needle. How was that for irony?

Leland continued, "This is just a taste. An *amuse-bouche*. A lot of people don't get how bad it is when you lose your freedom. Here, you're still in a warm house. We're in a little chalet compared to where we could be. You don't see any bars on the windows. Not here. Not yet. No guards, except me, and I'm a puppy compared to the folks in lock-down. And I haven't given you roommates. I suspect you're not the type of person who would warm to constant companionship in a locked cell. Granted, women's prison isn't as bad as being thrown in with the boys, but it's no Magic Kingdom. And I'm guessing by the way you act, the way you dress—you've never come across ladies like this, unless you passed them in a bus station."

He was getting to me. My wrist churned against the cuffs again, the steel digging into my open cuts.

"Now, you might be the sort of person who would want to end it, but it's tough to kill yourself in prison. People are watching you all the time. Even if you could get someone to sneak in a razor or a rope, you probably wouldn't have the privacy you wanted. Making a makeshift rope out of torn bed sheets? Tougher than you'd think, and it takes quality alone time to do it. Puncturing yourself with the corner of a bedframe—tough to pull off. Most likely you'd knock yourself out and be stitched up at the clinic. So you'd end up living a long, *long* and miserable, *miserable* life. Isn't that what you're trying to help all these people avoid?"

He was good with words. He might as well have been reading my tarot cards and narrating my future. My body should have dissolved into the mattress. I wanted to be invisible.

"That's my future, then."

"It could be."

I hated myself for asking, "But?"

"If there was a way out, would you take it?"

"What's the trade?"

"Freedom for a favor."

That's what this was all about. Offer a drink to the sweaty chick in the desert, just when the turkey vultures coast down for a sniff. All this time I'd been petrified this was going to end with parts of me packed in suitcases. Turns out I was more afraid of the shame and torture of prison. When it really sunk in, captivity terrified me more than death. Piss-stained, exhausted, and terrified, I would listen to any hypothetical.

Leland dragged his chair closer, near enough that I might lash out with a leg. But there was no chance I would pull something like that now, and he knew it. Dictators have been known to quell rebellions with an infrasonic "brown note," a frequency so low it would loosen the bowels of an angry mob. Leland had neutralized my defiance with another form of self-soiling—my pee-bleached undies. This was what it felt like to be broken. It wasn't the biological wear and tear he inflicted. Compared to what a lot of people endured in interrogations, I'd gotten off light. I still had all my fingernails, and he never went near my pelvis. He didn't have to. Once I lost hope, he held dominion.

My jaw sawed on its hinges before I responded. "What is it?"

"What if I told you all you had to do was see another client?"

Suddenly he was calling them clients instead of victims. "Who?"

"There's a woman. Her name is Helena." His face tightened into a triangle. I couldn't identify the emotion, but it shooed away his jolliness. "She has an advanced stage of pancreatic cancer, and she's also diabetic. Only a few months left. She's toyed with suicide, but she can't work up to it. All the ways you can kill yourself, there's still no real dignified way to go. I think that's what she wants—some dignity."

This I understood. "There's always the helium tank method. You could be with her."

"I can't be with her. I'm a cop."

I found it hard to suspend my skepticism since Leland had fooled me once already. "That's what this is about?"

"You said it yourself. It's mercy."

"You don't think it's mercy."

"But she does." Leland retrieved his laptop from the floor and scooted to the bedside. Sitting right next to me, I could feel warmth from his body. Overnight on Leland smelled horsey, but at least he didn't reek of FlyNap. "I'll show you."

My arms tensed against the cuffs, but I didn't move.

He rested the computer on my stomach, apparently unconcerned that I might buck it off.

A video window popped up and played.

On the screen, an obese black woman with the face of a Shar-Pei sat in a pink hospital gown. The woman wept violently. She rocked rhythmically, trying to face the lens head on but having difficulty. Her bulk creaked the joints of her folding chair. The microphone distorted her weeping into a tinny trumpet. She might have been Leland's age. The camera caught her with a murky frog eye, rendering her slightly grainy but clear enough to see dark dots of pigment around her eyes from various chalazia, consistent with diabetes.

None of my video good-byes had felt like this. Sure, some of my clients cried. But this woman sounded ashamed. Having just bawled shamefully in front of the detective, I knew what this kind of shame sounded like. She couldn't get a hold of herself. If I'd been filming this, I'd have stopped the camera to give her some air.

The woman moaned to the camera, "I want to die," but that's all she could get out. Seconds later the video ended.

"Sometimes she forgets who she is. Who I am. She doesn't remember why she's in pain sometimes, and if I'm there, she thinks I did something to her. Like I'm torturing her."

It was such a weird thing to hear from this man with my hands still in cuffs.

I listened, but all this felt wrong. Kali would never consider a client under duress. I wasn't thinking about the woman's needs.

For a typical client, I needed to speak to them personally. But I considered Leland's trade for the selfish reason that I wanted to get free of him. A manhole opened a passage out of the sewage, and I monkeyed up the ladder. So Kali pretended to be attentive when all I gave a poop about was my freedom.

"I have medical records," he assured me. I nodded, even though I would have accepted his trade without them. His face loomed so close to mine. His eyes boldly earnest, he pleaded with me, even though he had stolen my will to resist. "She's suffering."

This I believed. There was no disguising that woman's genuine suffering on the video. Without a doctor, I couldn't be sure what kind of suffering she was enduring. Whatever the woman had, she seemed to be going through something awful. But what most compelled me was how badly Leland wanted my help.

"Who is she?"

"My sister."

CHAPTER 4

Leland had planned my encounter with his sister before we met. As her health deteriorated, he plotted out how to find me and coerce me into granting his sister a merciful death. She only had a few months left now, maybe a few weeks.

After he uncuffed me, we reviewed a printed agenda on how I should tend to Helena Mumm—prepared lines to say if she got delusional, emergency phone numbers in case it all went kabluey, that kind of thing. We role-played at the ranch house in Clayton, me as Kali and Leland Mumm as his sister, while I gobbled PB&Js and ibuprofen for the dehydration headache. The polymer pistol in his armpit reminded me I couldn't act up.

He led me to my rental car. Both a courtesy and an indignity, Leland placed a towel on the passenger seat so my pee didn't soak into the fabric. He slid back the seat to make room for his long legs. Then we drove back to my apartment for a change of clothes and supplies. I didn't want to bring him home, but he already had my address, and I had no choice.

There wasn't much to my apartment in Bernal. A top-story flat in a two-floor salmon stucco box, my bed lounged by the windows. The one thing the place had going for it was the peekaboo view of Bernal Hill. If I craned my neck, I could see the round green lump rise out of the city thatch work like a blister.

A baby grand piano proudly hogged most of my living room. This had been passed down to me from my dad. My stepfather, Gordon Ostrowski, had wanted to sell it off or junk it, but my mom placated him by sticking it in storage, which is the only reason it was still intact. The instrument was horribly out of tune, but I didn't really play it. I treated it like a valet stand. But I loved it. I kept the shades up, even at night, because I liked seeing sunlight and street lights cascade off the black lacquer. Admiring the piano from the bed, I reconstructed memories of my father playing back when I was dazzled by the gong of felt hammers hitting the wire.

"I thought you had money," Leland remarked.

"Did you expect a champagne pyramid?"

"I expected more than a phone booth."

I really didn't want Leland Mumm near my stuff. Other than the few hours I'd lost in Clayton, I hadn't slept. I didn't feel rested. On my best day I wouldn't have welcomed an armed stranger into my apartment, but today I was edgier than usual, and I felt downright twitchy with him in there.

Leland made himself at home, beelining to the piano. Two urns sat on top of the lacquer, one brass and the other wood. He guessed, "Mom and Dad, right?"

I didn't correct him. When he lifted the lid on the brass urn— my father's—I said something, just to interrupt him as he peeked inside. "I can't trust myself with ceramics." Leland smiled and secured the lid back over my dad's dust.

He found the ziplocked bags of ash from inside his suit jacket and laid them beside one of the urns. "These belong to you." This show of kindness should have comforted me, but I felt more agitated that he was so close to my parents' cremains.

He sat down at the piano and plunked. His fingers on my dad's keys felt like catching a stranger reading my diary. Everything was manipulation with Leland. By invading my home, he must have known that he was spurring me on to help him that much faster, so I could push him back out of my life. He didn't want to give me any time to get cold feet.

Leland fingered the whites while I went to shower. "Keep the door open," he instructed. I tried not to let this creep me out.

"Do you play?" I asked.

"Not a lick."

This didn't stop him from pecking out a few chimes while I rinsed off. The tuning made the piano sound like an antique toy. Leland's playing didn't help. At least his plunks told me how far he was from the shower stall, just like a cat with a bell collar.

When I passed back through the room in a towel, he barely looked. "Don't worry about getting dolled up. Just wear normal stuff. Helena will flip out if you look like you just stepped out of a Broadway musical."

"Your wish is my command." I pulled some clothes from my closet and retreated to the bathroom.

As much as my wrists stung back in Clayton, the soap made it worse. The skin around my left wrist had inflated, soft as a marshmallow. Where the metal had sliced through the skin, I dabbed rubbing alcohol and wrapped gauze from my medical kit. If a cop weren't in my living room, I might have shrieked.

Dry underwear never felt so good. While I slipped them on under my towel, Leland crossed the room and gawked at my bookshelves. Without a divider to duck behind, I was grateful he kept his back to me. "Lots of textbooks."

"I like to study."

"Ever think about medical school?"

This felt like he was taunting me with hopes of a limitless future. In fact, I had considered medical school. But I answered, "I think about a lot of things."

He lost interest in the books and combed over my wall photos. "This your dad?"

Hopping around on bare feet as I slid on corduroy pants, I was concentrating on minimizing the exposure of bare skin. I dropped my towel for a flash and wriggled into a camisole before he could catch a glimpse of nipple. Long sleeves covered the gauze. After the regular clothes, I added a second layer of loose-fitting scrubs while he stared at my father's photograph, close enough to steam the glass.

"He's a good-looking guy. Tall like you, too."

In the photo I was six years old, sitting on my father's lap. An orchestra surrounded us, brass viscera everywhere. It had been taken while he was recording a score for a blockbuster alien movie. My dad dressed like he was clamming at the beach, boat shoes with no socks, and a light cotton sweater. My smile jagged all over because of the baby teeth worming through my gums, and I was too lost in awe of my dad and the musicians to face the camera.

Leland remarked, "You were a cute kid." The way he said it implied, *what happened?* "Who are the boys?" He'd moved on to another photo, a shot of me with a group from the firehouse.

"Firemen."

"Good-looking guys. I guess firemen usually are. Any of these your boyfriend?"

"No." In truth, I'd dated two of them briefly. Mistakes, both times.

"So, none of these guys knows how you spend your off-hours?"

"Absolutely not." I toweled my hair dry and skipped off this subject. "I'm done."

"You're wearing scrubs." Leland seemed surprised.

"You wanted me to look like a nurse."

"I didn't think you'd own scrubs."

"I have a whole closet full of clothing."

"It just doesn't seem like something Kali would wear."

"She wears what she needs to wear. Let's get going."

On the drive to Helena Mumm's house, Leland and I rehearsed the plan some more. Occasionally he made eye contact to make sure I'd digested the details: how long to wait before I administered the first dose of thiopental (so he had enough time to be somewhere else with witnesses), the lot on The Embarcadero where he'd leave the rental car, specifics on where she didn't like to be touched—for Helena, it was anywhere around the collarbone. Despite the peanut butter sandwiches and the hot shower, my blood sugar plunged. *My kingdom for a candy bar.* I squeezed the gauze around my left wrist so the pain would keep me alert.

"You've really charted this out, haven't you?"

"I'm a planner. I get my Christmas shopping done by

Halloween." He added, "It's my sister. I want to make sure it's done right. And she doesn't have much time, so it needs to be done right and right now."

Helena Mumm lived in the Excelsior District, not far from Bernal. Cutting through the southern half of San Francisco didn't take long, even if we stopped every other block.

Leland said, "It'll feel remote, like the house in Clayton. Police don't hang around there. Or if they do, they'll patrol it at night. You can basically come and go as you please. After everyone leaves for the morning commute, it's a ghost town. So no nosey neighbors to worry about."

He was right. When we crossed into the neighborhood, ours was the only moving vehicle on the street.

"Since when are you so concerned about my safety?"

"Since it could be traced back to me."

Even though we'd covered each triviality, I asked out of habit, "You sure you don't want to be with her?" Families went both ways. Some wanted to say their good-byes but didn't want to watch their loved one expire. Out of loyalty, others wanted to stay until the last breath.

"I'm a cop. I can't be part of this. If someone thinks I've helped kill my own sister, that's the end of my career." He omitted the threat of jail time. Maybe he thought a detective would be impervious to imprisonment.

"So, you're going to drop me off and drive. What makes you think I won't just run?" Leland was putting a lot of faith in me by leaving me alone with his sister. I wondered if everything I'd endured back in Clayton was his way of ensuring that he could trust in my compliance.

Leland said, "Anywhere you go, unless it's the Marianas Trench, I can find you. And you won't like what happens when I do." He continued, "You understand that I'd find you again, right?"

"You seem sure of it."

"I'm very good at my job."

I tried to add some levity. "Would you smother yourself in

FlyNap next time?"

Leland eased the car to a standstill. He took his eyes off the road so we could lock pupils. "Next time, I won't detain you. From here on out, you would link me to a crime. If I arrested you, I'd open myself up to legal action, definite disgrace, and possible prison. So if there's a next time, I will kill you." To make sure I took this in, he asked, "Do you understand what I just said?"

I nodded, but this took the wind out of me, so I didn't immediately say anything. I shrank in my seat. To protect myself, I asked, "Won't I be a liability if I tend to your sister?"

"No. Then we'd be equally culpable for the same crime. We'd be bonded together by mutually assured destruction. You couldn't touch me without hurting yourself. We'd have reached a détente." He shifted back into drive, and we rolled on. I caught myself holding my breath.

I hadn't spent much time in the Excelsior, a forgotten neighborhood. When people thought of San Francisco, they didn't think of these hideaway enclaves, where the paint peeled and the wood moldered in the salty fog.

According to the GPS, we were almost there. I started to imagine Helena. This would be the first time I'd complete a terminus with a client I'd never met. I thumbed through her medical records in the car. They seemed legit, but then again so did Leland's X-Rays.

"Your sister knows I'm coming," I confirmed.

"She knows. We've discussed it in the same detail as I have with you. Once the doctors gave her the final prognosis, she planned it out with me. But she won't remember everything. That's the trick. She was lucid when we made that video, but she goes in and out."

"So she may not remember she's expecting me."

"That's correct. She'll expect a nurse though. Even if she forgets the rest of the plan, she'll remember that a nurse pays her a regular visit." He repeated what he told me earlier, "She gets a weekly house call so she won't forget to keep up her regimen. It makes it easy for you, because she'll be expecting an injection anyway."

"And I won't overlap with her real nurse."

"I called her regular nurse and canceled for today."

"You can do that?"

"I should be able to. I'm paying for it."

Helena lived on Urbano Drive, which looped in a giant ellipse. Some of the guys I rode with in the department were amateur history buffs, and one of them told me Urbano Drive used to be the Ingleside Racetrack. When the track turned into residential housing, people raced their cars until the city installed street humps and roundabouts. Now the street was a stretch of road no one really wanted to live on and no one really wanted to develop. The homes were rashly constructed white stucco buildings, what my dad would have called gingerbread houses.

We stopped along the curb and Leland pointed to a building. His sister's house shared a similar anonymity as the ranch house in Clayton, which made me doubt whether any of this was on the level.

"Your sister's in there?"

"She'll be in the living room. She doesn't use the bed much anymore." Leland lost his sense of play. He turned somber, almost fearful.

I wanted to clarify about her condition, so I asked, "How delusional is she?"

"She forgets who I am. She forgets where she is. She might ask about a guy named Walter. I think he was some crush she had as a teenager."

"Was she ever married?"

"She has an ex-husband. It didn't end well, and now she doesn't even remember the guy. They didn't have kids."

I tried to think about what I would say to her. Because Leland didn't allow me to wear a more theatrical costume, I looked more like myself. And that meant I felt more unsure of what role I should play. My job flowed so much easier in disguise.

"Does she have guns?"

Leland snorted, "No. Why?"

"I don't want to be shot as an intruder."

"Pretty white girls don't get shot."

"They do when people with guns are delusional and a stranger comes into their homes."

"She doesn't own a gun." He pointed to the glove compartment. "And you'll be using what's in there."

We hadn't discussed this. Inside the glove compartment, a black leather case snuggled against his electronic toll sensor. Flat and long, the right size for a necklace, it revealed a preloaded hypodermic needle.

"What is this?"' The syringe was much larger than mine. A cook could baste meats with it. "Are we dueling with needles?"

"Do I honestly have to explain it?"

"We covered every inkling, and you never mentioned this."

He said, "It slipped my mind. Sometimes the most obvious things do."

"I have my own tools. And I don't know what's in this."

"First of all, your syringe is broken. We crushed it when we scuffled."

"I remembered. I packed extra supplies." I raised my satchel, restuffed and fully packed with my usual gear.

"You'll use this needle and only this needle. My sister's a big woman. I needed to size the dose appropriately. Did you ever hear about Tookie Williams?"

The name was vaguely familiar, but I didn't want to entertain this strand of conversation. "He was a gang leader. Who gives a crap?"

"He cofounded the Crips. But for the purposes of this story, he was a bodybuilder on death row. Big guy—used to lift down at Venice Beach. When it came time for him to get the needle, they screwed up the dose, because they didn't account for his size. The nurse botched it a few different ways, actually. He woke up in the middle and died in agony. I don't want that happening to my sister."

"You don't think I would have considered that?"

"I've had more time to consider it. That's the right dose."

"What's in here?"

He frowned to tell me it was none of my business. "Saline solution." When I registered that he was being a wise-ass, he said,

"It's sodium thiopental, same as you use. The same thing you gave Maxine Jook. And Burton Ott. And Carlotta Vieira. I could go on." He'd done his research—all three had been clients. "I consulted my own experts to assess the proper dosage."

"You mean the illusory Dr. Jocelyn Thibeault?" I quipped.

"The San Sebastián execution team. They know their thiopental." If he meant the prison, the team had been called incompetent for botching a number of executions in the same way he'd described the last moments of Tookie Williams. "You only need one large dose of this. You don't need two needles. The dose you have here could put a lion to sleep."

"I have a system. Two doses. My doses. That's how you do it right."

"This needle and this needle only. You'll leave your other equipment in the car with me, so I know you won't use it."

Crafty SOB. This was the most important aspect of the process, and we had ample time to talk it through. He'd skirted the issue and led me to his sister's door, because he knew if he got me this far I wouldn't balk. Captive or not, I would have raised a one-woman riot if he'd sprung a syringe swap on me earlier.

He tried to soothe me. "It's not just the dosage I'm worried about. I told you she forgets things. She forgets a lot of things. But she knows she gets a visit from the nurse. She expects it. A nurse comes each week and gives her one single injection, from a needle just like this one. Helena will expect that single injection. I don't want to deviate from that pattern. I want her last moments to be peaceful. She sees a second needle and she'll react. Badly. She might become violent. Don't let her roundness fool you—she's strong, like me. She can be mean if she wants. I don't want that to happen with my sister, nor do you want that happening to you."

"She forgets who you are, but she'll remember what the needle looks like?"

"The mind's a funny thing, isn't it?"

My stomach churned. I couldn't fathom why he would insist on his own needle, but by now Leland had convinced me that I would be leash-led to freedom. I was too tired to argue on a point like this. What needle and the specific drug and dosage used to end his sister's pain were minor decisions compared to my decision to collude.

The engine murmured as we hovered at the curb. Not a head slipped into a surrounding window to inspect us.

"What happens afterward?" We'd covered this, but I needed to hear it again. It was my version of checking the mail drop twice to make sure the envelope slid down the postal chute.

He fumed out his nose before repeating himself. "You walk out of the house and pick up your car—no taxis. You walk all the way to the parking spot and pick up your rental car. Burn the clothes."

"And you and me?"

"We never see each other again."

"You're sure about that?"

"Why would I want to see you? It puts me at risk to be in contact with you. You move on, and I move on, and we both know we were silent partners. You'll have helped give my sister some peace, and I'll be grateful."

"What happens to your case on Kali?"

"Goes cold. I can't say whether someone else will pick up where I left off. I can't control the rest of the police department. But I can promise that I would let the investigation dead-end."

"What about your partner, Dr. Thibeault?"

"I can guarantee that she forgets about this. You have my word on that."

"Do you still think I'm a killer?" I shouldn't have taunted him when I was moments from stepping out of the car, but the thought came to me like a hiccup. Without rest, my brain operated under the governing assumption that it was drunk.

"Kali. Point of fact, you do kill people. I believe that you have deluded yourself into believing you're helping them, but deep down you know it's wrong. I'm willing to overlook that because your clients seem to want the services you provide. Make no mistake, if these people didn't consent to your services, we wouldn't be having this conversation. I'd bring you in or put you down. And my sister's values aren't my own. If I were dying, I wouldn't want you to call on me. But I'm trying to fulfill someone else's wishes. Because of what Helena wants, I'm willing to trade favors and let you go. Doesn't make me innocent, and it doesn't make you innocent. We are complicit in an ill deed to help ease someone's pain. For that, I can forgive myself and forgive you."

I removed my own syringe and wedged it into the glove compartment, and then slipped Leland's jewelry box into my satchel.

CHAPTER 5

Leland motored off in my rental car, leaving me on Helena's driveway in my lime green scrubs. Barely used, the fabric creases poked at me through my camisole. A chill from the Pacific wind crept under both my layers and prickled my shoulders.

The doorbell ding-donged some church hymn on brass pipes. Despite his fake prayer in Clayton, Leland didn't strike me as religious, but maybe his sister was. Helena didn't keep her door unlocked like her brother. The chimes knelled a few more times with no answer. Eventually I stage whispered, "Helena, it's your nurse. I'm here for our appointment."

Leland had given me keys, but I didn't want to use them. I imagined that mammoth of a woman behind a shotgun. Don't ask me why. Something in the video made her seem volatile, and if violence ran in the family, she could be ready to fire that cannon as soon as I entered.

When I rode the rig—sorry, the ambulance—I'd gotten weapons pulled on me. If the police were involved, the paramedics would park the ambulance in a safe area, and we only came in once the suspect was restrained and the cops had made a sweep. Still, stuff happened. Suspects struggled free and found hidden weapons. One guy waved a knife around like a conductor's baton; another aimed a gun at the bridge of my nose. All it took was someone off kilter who felt threatened.

"Helena?" Louder now. "Helena?" I hoped she might actually have died. Suspending my compassion, I imagined a cadaverous lump in repose. I heard the faint jabber of daytime television in there. Possibly she passed on while watching her stories, death grip on the remote. *Deus ex miracle.* I'd never felt so callous toward someone I'd considered a client, but Helena Mumm wasn't a client. She was an appendage of the man who had just treated me to an express Guantanamo sojourn.

Leland had color-coded the keys, and the purple one turned the bolt. I was supposed to drop them in the cactus on the porch when I left.

The house was filthy. A heap of unlaundered clothes stewed up musk in the entryway. The ranch house in Clayton had reeked of decay, but this smelled of human underarms and unwashed feet. To be sure, I checked for traces of staging in the foyer—price tags behind the picture frames, that sort of thing. On the entry table, I found a handwritten Post-it reminder for "knee-highs for right," whatever that meant. Someone had spilled water on it, blurring the ink and drying the paper to the consistency of a thin potato chip. Someone lived here and rarely left.

Piles of yellowed *Time* magazines and *San Francisco Chronicles* towered as I passed down the center hallway. Like the Post-it, their pages warped and dried crinkled. Wine stains from ancient celebrations ghosted the beige wall-to-wall carpeting. If Leland had manufactured this setup, he'd done a more meticulous job than back in Clayton. A stack of mail fanned out on the table with Helena Mumm's name printed on a few shutoff warnings from the utilities.

"Helena!"

"What?" She bleated from down the hallway. I'd probably just woke her up.

Helena Mumm reclined in a leather TV chair in a small room at the back of the house. The way the black lounger bent under her body made me think she might sleep in it. She appeared heavier than in the video. Since paramedics are in the business of hauling bodies, I got pretty good at judging what people weighed. Helena probably weighed around 280 pounds, just north of what I could squat. I'm not sure if I could have carried her out of a burning building by myself. Hard to fathom how this woman and stickman Leland came from the same DNA, but genes can get divided up in strange ways.

Her reading glasses slipped halfway down her nose, so she could alternate between the book in her lap and watching the television above the rims. The TV was set to a soap, and a blonde with ironed hair presently slapped a chesty man across the cheek. Helena wasn't dressed for company. Her hair grew in matted seaweed tangles. A moth-ravaged T-shirt damped at the pits. Matching navy sweatpants unveiled one bare swollen foot, and a black knee-high sock stretched over the other foot and outside the pant leg. She hadn't showered recently, but compensated by spraying floral air fresheners around the room. An invisible cloud of synthetic gardenias only added to the funk.

Her eyes were still dreamy from napping. "I thought you were the pizza delivery guy." An open pizza box monopolized the coffee table. If this were a pie chart, it would have told me that she had 25 percent left to eat.

"Looks like the pizza guy was already here."

"I thought he forgot something." Her voice sounded richer, more buttery than Leland's, and lacked his rasp. "Who the hell are you?"

"I'm your nurse."

"No, you're not." At least she knew that a nurse was supposed to visit her. That was something.

"Well, I'm not the pizza guy."

"If you were the pizza guy I'd know why you were in my living room." She seemed lucid, more so than I'd expected. Remembering how fragile she seemed in Leland's computer video, I'd imagined someone more docile.

I stumbled through my practiced lie. "I'm a substitute. My name is Kali. We talked on the phone." She looked past me at the wallpaper to try and remember. Wallpaper was a rare find, and for good reason. Customarily hideous and a bitch to scrape off, I only found it in homes left to disrepair. Helena Mumm patterned her walls with red rocking horses like a baby's room.

Eventually Helena drifted back to me, and I saw the telltale twinkle that she was too ashamed to admit she'd forgotten. "That's right. Thank you for coming." She'd lost her self-certainty, and it relieved me that she showed the symptoms her brother described. I tried to feel a kinship with her, because we were both sisters of broken will. "Come closer."

I've visited enough sick people that I should have felt right at home, but I was apprehensive as hell. Leland warned me she could be violent. If she was anything like her brother, she might lunge from her seat and slap me, stab me, shoot me. I checked her hands. Other than the remote control, she wasn't holding anything. No weapons. I stepped within striking distance.

Her eyes puffed, and her lids were dotted with the pinprick moles I'd seen in the video. From the grainy footage I'd assumed they were chalazia, but I was wrong. They were milia, bumps built up by dead skin cells. They were linked to some dietary imbalances, so they wouldn't be unusual to find on a diabetic either. Helena smelled sugary, or maybe I imagined it. The nose can smell what it wants sometimes.

She muted the TV and tugged at my scrubs. "You just get out of surgery?" Her usual nurse, if she remembered the man, probably didn't wear these kind of OR scrubs. Helena wasn't testing me now. She was trying to get comfortable with me, and had a gentle laugh that contrasted the brash tone she used when I first came in.

"Brain surgery," I cracked.

"Is that right?"

"You got a drill? I can take care of you right now." Gallows humor. It's my favorite kind.

She remarked at my physique, accusingly. "You're tall."

"I get that a lot."

"What are you, six feet?"

"Not quite. About five ten. But you add heels…"

She peeked at my shoes. "You've got clogs on."

"That's a kind of heel."

"Look at me. When I was skinny, I was a tiny little thing. You could carry me in a change purse. I wanted to be tall like you."

"It's not as nice as you think it would be."

"Says the tall person…" She shared Leland's sharp wit. I liked it more on a person who wasn't holding me captive. "You've got a cute figure."

"Thank you." I looked for a chair to sit and unpack my satchel.

Her attention drifted to the soap opera. "Jill had more curves, but you probably have a foot on her." I didn't know who she was talking about, and she nudged, "My usual nurse. You've met her, right?"

Leland prepared me for this. He had given the name of Helena's regular nurse. "I know Dimitri."

"Who the hell is that?" Either she was testing me or she forgot. I couldn't tell.

"That's your usual nurse."

She laughed, "Says who?"

"The hospital, your medical records, and Dimitri." Helena's smile froze. She was trying to figure out if she'd forgotten. Then it came back to her, unless she was just faking recall for my benefit. "Dimitri—ass like a coconut. That's why I picked him."

"That's him."

Around the room, Helena's belongings overflowed from cardboard boxes. A couple of previous clients had done this—packed up their possessions to make less work for their family. Like Leland's staged home in Clayton, I couldn't find any photographs on the walls either. No smiling Lelands looked on while I got to work. Normally a client's house was full of family pics. Perhaps the Mumms weren't sentimental. For all I knew, Leland and Helena hated each other, and he was tending to her now out of a fraternal obligation. Still, even in the most strained family dynamics I'd see photos of kids, parents, friends. *Someone.* I'd shrugged off the anomaly with Leland, but took note of it now. I told myself she'd just boxed them up with her other things.

The only thing hanging on the walls was a framed black and white poster of a half-naked woman who might have been a darker Josephine Baker, sexualized with long lashes and a fan of feathers obscuring her breasts and pelvis. If I could add a third certainty to death and taxes, I would add that the woman in the poster was not Helena Mumm.

Without a chair handy, I placed the pizza box on the floor and sat on the corner of the coffee table. Her scent cut through the gardenia fumes. Hygiene is as much social ritual as health, and most clients fall out of that ritual. They peed and pooped a little in their clothes, and you could smell it for miles. Hospitals did a better job at masking it by bleaching out the pores in the linoleum, but they never cleaned out the smell entirely. I used to snort a little perfume so I could sit next to a client and not look like I was sniffing the expired milk. Helena smelled a little of excrement, and I found it comforting, because it smelled the way someone who was dying should smell. She didn't smell like FlyNap.

I almost liked her, as much as I could like anyone related to Leland Mumm. The empathy didn't come easily this time, because I didn't want to be there. Helena must have sensed it too. But we both faked it, and as I was faking it, I found her false smile assuring. Her contrived effort was still an attempt to put us both at ease.

On the edge of the coffee table, I unzipped my satchel. Leland's black box waited inside, but I wouldn't take it out yet.

While I stared into my satchel, Helena suddenly latched onto my wrist. She couldn't see the gauze under my sleeve, but her hand clamped right where Leland had cuffed me. Indian sunburn.

My eyes went wide and I jerked my arm away. "That hurts!" I fumed, shaking out my wrist. "Why would you do that?" Kali didn't get angry with clients. Not ever. But my fist balled up, and I pushed the coffee table away from her chair.

Helena withdrew her hand, stunned at my reaction. "Just trying to thank you for coming," she said. "Just trying to show you affection."

Neither of us spoke. We were both confused. For me, it wasn't so much that she had held my arm, or that she had grabbed the tender part of it, but that she had so much power in her grip. For someone with an advanced disease—and let's face it, at least another co-occurring disorder—she was stronger than I'd have guessed. Most clients don't have much physical strength by our final meeting. I'd gotten used to quavering hands. Not Helena. She'd clamped down on my wrist like a lobster claw.

I wondered if she was healthier than I'd been led to believe. I wondered about the different ways Leland Mumm might have lied to me about his sister. People killed their relatives all the time. But he couldn't be killing her for money, not unless she'd buried a pot of gold in the backyard.

"I didn't grab you that hard."

I rolled up a sleeve, "See the gauze? I'm hurt."

She squinted at the bandages. "Did you try and kill yourself?"

"Of course not."

"Because it looks like you slashed your wrists." Abrasive like her brother. Often I wondered how I'd get along with a client if I met her when she was healthy. I don't think I'd have liked Helena.

If this sort of interchange had happened with another client—which it hadn't—Kali might have asked if that client was uncomfortable. Kali might even offer to leave. But there against my will, I couldn't walk out. Bitch or not, I needed to get this over with.

Leaning forward, she snatched at my scrubs again and reached my other wrist. She twisted harder this time, to let me know the first time hadn't been an accident. The pain ripped through my arm as she pulled me into her. "Who sent you?"

I chopped her radius with the meaty part of my hand. She was strong, so I had to whack her arm twice before she let go. If we arm wrestled, she'd give me a run for my money. I rose to my feet and shouted, "Psycho!" This would never have come out of Kali's mouth. I gasped at my outburst.

Helena repeated, "Who sent you?" Furious this time.

Leland had requested that I not mention his name. She had problems remembering her family, and, according to her brother, she got angry when she couldn't remember. In Clayton, I'd been willing to believe anything, but now I wondered how much of Leland's story was bogus. "The hospital sent me."

"Which one?"

I pulled from Leland's script. "UCSF Lakeside."

She sensed I was lying. "Who really sent you?"

I didn't know how to answer. The woman wasn't too addled to understand what was happening. She simply didn't trust me. Had we bonded in the traditional Kali-client relationship, trust would have been forged through several meetings and phone conversations. This wouldn't have been so awkward.

"You're not going to touch me until I know," she said.

I'd minimized how much I spoke. Leland had instructed me to keep as quiet as possible. But this was such a deviation from my traditional process, I wasn't sure how to bullshit my way through it. Helena waited for a response. I didn't see her opening up unless I built some trust. I said the first thing that violated Leland's instructions. "Your brother sent me."

Her mouth stretched into a bullfrog frown. "I haven't spoken to my brother in years." I didn't trust Leland, but she might have forgotten that her brother visited yesterday. Some people are good at faking recognition, and appraising the authenticity of delusions wasn't part of my training. For that matter, I didn't even know with certainty what diseases and disorders currently degraded her, so I didn't know what would be symptoms of her degeneration, or simply personality quirks. As she considered the possibility that I'd been in touch with her brother, she asked, "What did he say about me?"

"He briefed me about your condition—"

"What did my brother say about me?"

"We didn't talk about your relationship." Kali had never been this cold with a client. "It wasn't my business."

"What was my brother's name?"

This one I didn't know how to deflect. "Leland."

I could tell she recognized the name. The way she digested the word "Leland" looked as if she'd just found a bone in her food.

"Sit down," she said. I hesitated until she softened. "Please." Slowly, I lowered myself to the edge of the coffee table, hands at my hips to keep my wrists out of reach. Piecing my story together, she said, "You're my nurse?"

"That's right."

"Your name again?"

"Kali."

"That's right." She nodded to herself, lost in thought as she examined the rocking horses on the walls.

I watched Helena's hands as I unpacked the satchel. I brought out some rubbing alcohol to clean the arm. Kali would have explained every step of the process. For all I knew, Leland already had. I couldn't tell what she thought was happening. Helena might have decided to die in a moment of lucidity, but now she might have been expecting her weekly injection of Byetta, which controls blood sugar for type 2 diabetics.

Helena may not have been comfortable with me, but she resigned herself. The chair creaked as her body sank further into the recliner.

"You're here to stick me."

"That's right."

"Well, start sticking." Checking the time on my cell phone miffed her. "You got some place you need to be?"

"I'm trying to assess the timing of the medication." That statement meant nothing. I needed to wait per Leland's instructions, until he could be clear and in the company of whatever colleagues could vouch for his whereabouts. I had to stall.

"You're nervous," Helena observed.

"I'm fine."

"You new at this?"

"No, I'm not."

"Then why so jumpy?" She focused sharply on my face and deliberately rolled up her sleeve. "Kali, whatever your name is. I know you're not my nurse. Dimitri doesn't have a coconut ass, although I wish he did. He's about my size, but a white Russian." She offered me her arm like a gift. "I know what this is, and I'm fine with it. Everyone's got to go sometime."

I had to remember to breathe.

Inebriated with thought, I swabbed her arm with alcohol and rubbed too hard.

Helena admonished, "You're not going to wipe the black off, sweetie."

I stopped. "I'm sorry."

"If you're going to prick me, prick me. But don't think I'm a vegetable. And don't you believe Leland. He's not what you think he is."

I didn't want to derail us, but I needed more explanation. "He said you had delusions."

"I know what's going on, don't you worry."

"Is Leland your brother?"

"He might as well be family."

"Are you ill?"

This dispirited her, either because it reminded her that she was actually ill, or because she considered how Leland must have conspired to bring about her death in this way. "That I am. I'm sick in all sorts of ways."

"Are you dying?"

"Probably have a few months, so this works. Might as well be now. Might as well be you." She held out her forearm again. "Do what you're here to do."

"You didn't ask for this—"

"No," she confirmed. "But I deserve it."

I hesitated. Helena Mumm hadn't chosen this. This didn't fit Kali's criteria, and it felt nefarious. Now I didn't even know who Leland really was.

"You want this?"

She nodded. "I do. Stick me." Sweetening her tone at last, she urged, "Please."

I fondled Leland's black case in the satchel, still hidden from her. For me to get out of this house, I needed to move this along. "I have sedatives. They can take the edge off."

"Pills? What kind?"

"Valium."

"Would you believe I've never taken those?"

"If you really want to go through with this, they'll ease your nerves."

"They'll relax me. And then you'll stick me."

"If you want me to."

"Give me the pills."

I dug out the orange bottle and rattled it. Calculating her weight, I tapped a few into her hands. I handed her a half-empty, three-liter jug and she washed them down with cola. "You'll feel them in twenty minutes or so."

"What happens while we wait?"

"Is there someone you'd like to call?"

Helena gave it some thought. "No one who can come."

I tried to think of her like any other client. Now that the sedatives were in her body, we just needed to talk. The same way Kali would talk to anyone. "Who are you thinking about?"

Helena's eyes glossed over. She smiled, not Leland's toothy grin, but a wistful widening of closed lips. As if enjoying a pleasure as simple as sunlight. "Walter."

"Your husband?"

"We weren't legally married. But he's my soul mate."

That she used the present tense made me ask, "Where is he now?"

"Near but far."

I didn't ask for explanation. If Leland had been truthful about Helena's lapses, she was thinking about an old boyfriend. Now she thought about him quietly and reached for my hand. I held her callused palm. Her index finger stroked the back of my hand too familiarly, but I didn't pull away. We watched her muted soap opera for a bit.

"What's he like?"

"Walter? A pain in the ass." Somehow, this came off good-naturedly. The drugs hadn't kicked in, but she was loosening up. Helena was getting used to talking to the intruder in her house. "He was a wall climber."

"Is that a euphemism?"

"No. He liked to climb walls. As in, up the sides of buildings. He wanted to be Spider-Man. He wasn't any good at it. He broke both ankles. Pain in my ass."

"He did this as an adult?"

"God no—he grew out of it. He was like that as a kid." She joked to herself, "A grown man trying to be Spider-Man..."

"How long did you know each other?"

"Most of our lives."

"That's romantic," I offered.

"Is it?" She shrugged. "He wasn't pretty to most folks, but he was pretty to me, because I loved him. And he was smart—he had a mind like a boxer. We grew up watching the fights. You watch the fights?"

"Not often."

"With all those muscles, I'd figure you were one of those female boxers. You like girls or boys?" She retracted her question. "Never mind. You don't like boxing then?"

"I've watched some fights. I like Ali."

"Of course you do. Not liking Ali is like not liking Santa Claus. But my point is, if you watch enough of them, you can tell a smart boxer from a stupid one by how quick they are. The body doesn't do anything the mind doesn't tell it to. Quick body, quick mind." In her own appraisal, I wondered what she thought of herself.

I withdrew my hand from hers. Now that we were talking about fighting, I readied myself in case she tried to grab me again. "Even Mike Tyson."

"Not an educated man, but smarter than you think he is. If he grew up in your neighborhood instead of Brownsville, Brooklyn, I bet he would've turned out different." Her eyes fell on her forearm, possibly wondering where the needle would puncture the skin. Her voice slowed down. "That was Walter. Quick like a cheetah. You could tell by how he moved he was going to grow up smart." The croak in her voice told me the sedatives were working their magic.

"I can call him." We still had time.

"No you can't." She was emphatic. "And I wouldn't want you to."

Her chin lolled, and she cat stretched in the recliner. I'd given her a healthy dose of diazepam, and it now streamed through her blood. She asked drowsily, "Can I tell you a secret?"

"Of course."

She looked about the room. We were alone but she still made sure this would be private. "We had a boy, Walter and me."

This did stun me since she didn't display family photos. I wondered if Leland might have been right about the delusions.

She slurred now, loopy as a spring breaker taste testing Long Island Iced Teas. "We never had our own kids. We couldn't, the two of us. But we took some in. We kept a little garden with those kids. A little garden in the woods."

"Kindergarten," I thought aloud.

"Excuse me?"

"Kindergarten. In German it means, 'children's garden.'"

"Funny. You'd think I'd have learned that along the way. But that's what we had together with those kids. A children's garden. It was a beautiful thing. The boy, he was like a son. Like a little Walter. He was the special one."

"Are you still in touch with him?"

"We lost him. And that was the end of us."

"I'm sorry."

I lifted Leland's leather case out of my satchel, cracking it open so she could see the needle. "Are you sure you want this?"

Some clients gagged when they saw the needle, but not her. "Yes, I do."

"You don't want to say good-bye to Walter?"

"We said our good-byes a thousand times." She was choking up now. A tear—something I didn't expect from this woman—rolled down a cheek. "And we were rotten together."

In what I presumed was a regretful wince, Helena froze her face for a long time. She stared into the television. The TV blinked to a black screen. She discarded the remote control onto the carpet. The blur of daytime drama had given the illusion of activity in the room. Without it, we seemed very still.

Her forearm extended to me once more, and I stroked it lightly. "I'll wait until you're asleep. Then you'll keep sleeping."

"You won't do anything wicked to me when I'm out?"

I shook my head. "Promise. You won't feel anything. Just rest."

My hand rested on hers, sensing a slow pulse. She breathed in soggy heaves. Eventually, the air swelled in and out with less effort. Her stomach rhythmically billowed, and Helena's chin nestled into her shoulder. Her eyes fluttered as she lapsed into sleep.

While listening to her snore, I packed up my equipment. I closely examined Leland's syringe before I repacked it into its case. Whatever chemicals he'd put in there, not a drop would be injected into Helena Mumm. On the way out I snatched a few pieces of mail, and left the woman to sleep off her benzodiazepines.

CHAPTER 6

Without packing, I drove straight up to Shallot, Oregon, and got there by the next morning. The town clustered around a short main street dotted with vintage diners and brawl bars. If it weren't for the redwoods, I could fool myself into thinking this was somewhere in the US heartland.

A half hour past the town center, I came to a junkyard hidden from the street by a chain link fence with plastic slats, where a hard sun blasted a sea of crumpled cars. Once proud automobiles tamped down to bricks of wrinkled steel and those bricks stacked up in a formidable wall. A chained Rottweiler barked outside a vinyl-sided office trailer. A pristine white minivan stood out as the lone vehicle that survived the wreckage. Beside it, Dr. Jeffrey Holt spoke with some guy I didn't know.

Jeffrey was a tall, older man with round spectacles and a white beard trimmed like a baseball infield. A hundred and fifty years ago he'd have made a good pioneer. He ran marathons, ate vegan, and, I suspected, had crystalline bowel movements. His breezy linen clothes magically repelled grime, even in a dusty lot like this.

The man who stood with him had a black chin beard and a keg torso. Heavier than Helena Mumm, but also taller. His rolled flannel cuffs revealed a dense thicket of tattoos that spread down to his wrists. Their body language suggested that Jeffrey knew him well, but Jeffrey made friends quickly.

I *skurched* to a stop in the gravel. When I approached them, my mouth twitched more than it smiled.

"Come here." Jeffrey waved me in close and hugged me, more

stiffly than he'd ever hugged me. He was going through the motions, but without any affection. "Kali, this is Henry."

The other man wasn't so happy to see me, but perfunctorily gripped my hand. They'd waited in the sun long enough for his palms to moisten.

"Henry's going to help us out. We can trust him."

Jeffrey had never given me reason not to trust him, but I scanned the lot, checking for human humps in the gaps between compressed steel. I needed to apologize. "I didn't know who else to call." To Henry, a man I'd never met, I said, "I'm very grateful." At least that made him smile.

"We prepared for this kind of emergency. It's not the first time the police have looked in our direction."

"You ready for this?" Henry asked. "Lots of people get attached to their cars."

"It's not my car." I didn't relish destroying a car that I didn't own, but Henry smirked with a sickly elation.

Jeffrey asked, "Did you bring any bags? Any clothes?"

"I didn't have time. I just took cash out of the bank and drove. I don't have anything with me."

"Except your cell phone," said Henry.

"Except that."

"Give it," Henry ordered. Jeffrey gave the man a reproving glance, and he amended his request, "Please."

I handed it over. Henry pulled out the SIM card and stomped on it, then tossed the fragments into the hatchback before squeezing inside and starting the engine. Jeffrey and I watched as my compact rolled over to a giant red steel bin, something that looked like a disjointed car from a mammoth Ferris wheel. Scrapes marred the bin's interior from where steel had resisted being crushed. Henry abandoned my car and locked himself in a glass booth across the yard, where he maneuvered a giant claw that lifted and then dropped the hatchback into the bin with a thunderous toll. The process had a carnival feel to it, without the fun.

"So that's how a car crusher works," I muttered.

"Car baler, technically."

"Car gallows."

"We'll get you another car. That's the beauty of stuff. Somewhere, someone's always making more of it."

We stood far enough so flying debris wouldn't hit us, but the noise still rattled me. The press collapsed the car with the same effort my firehouse boys exerted crunching empty cans between their palms. The hatchback offered weakling resistance. With the shrieking of crumpling metal too loud to talk, Jeffrey and I silently watched as the car and my cell phone compressed to a tight box the size of a footlocker. I wanted him to look at me. Without a real father for most of my life, I wasn't familiar with the feeling of disappointing one. I assumed this closely approximated it. As the hydraulics dwarfed us all with its magnificent show of strength, I shrank to the size of a titmouse waiting for my mentor to speak. Even another hug would have done it. I swayed in the dust waiting.

When it was done, Jeffrey compensated Henry with a fold of money thicker than my own emergency cash.

We got into his minivan, and as he drove off, he finally asked, "Are you hurt?" I hadn't told him all the details of what had happened in Clayton, but he eyed the gauze peeking out from my sleeves. "I can take a look at you back at the house."

I addressed what I suspected Jeffrey was most concerned about. "I don't think anyone followed me."

"Seriously. Were you injured?"

"I'm fine." I clipped my words, less comfortable jabbering away with him so frosty. "I didn't see any cars stick with me on the trip up."

"You have to be tired." He rubbed his beard with a free hand. "You've been through something horrible. I want to make sure you're healthy." He forced empathy, earnestly wanting to care about my well-being, but the tone of his voice and the clench of his jaw told me he was anxious. Still, this was the first compassion I'd received in days. My eyes watered a bit.

"I'm all right."

Before he published *The Peaceful End*, Dr. Jeffrey Holt was a pathologist. His wife developed breast cancer young, and after long treatments that failed, he attended her suicide six years ago. It shouldn't have happened the way it did. Mina Holt was much younger than Jeffrey, and she should have easily outlived him. He was a pathologist, and yet all his medical expertise failed to save her. When recovery became impossible, she asked him to end her suffering. They used the helium-and-bag method, and he was acquitted when it came to trial.

They had two daughters, whom Jeffrey now raised alone. Around when I met him four years ago, at the height of his notoriety, a right-to-life extremist shot him during a university lecture in Baltimore and winged him through the fleshy part of the hip. Jeffrey had a mild limp, indiscernible if you weren't aware of it. He stayed up here in Shallot, Oregon now, in a house tucked in the wooded part of town, more to keep his kids safe. Jeffrey was as outspoken an advocate as they came, but he'd learned to protect himself. As we drove, he scanned the road left to right and scrutinized the faces of the two people we passed: a mustached dog walker and a female jogger in pink. "I don't know her," he said about the jogger. "Probably visiting."

He glanced across at me. "He knows your real name. But you don't know his."

"Leland Mumm is the only name I have." I paused and gnawed on my chapped bottom lip. "I'm sorry, Jeffrey." I was extremely sorry. I was, after all, a trail of breadcrumbs to his door.

"You suspect he isn't related to this woman, Helena Mumm."

"They know each other, but I'd bet there's no relation."

"You're sure that her name is actually Helena Mumm."

"No, but I have mail with her name on it. It's more than I have for Leland."

"You still think he's a detective, even though you know he gave you a fake name? Did the badge look real?"

"The badge looked real enough, and he seemed to know how the law worked."

"He tied you to a bed for a day—you really think he knows how the law works?"

"You had to be there." The trees grew denser the farther we drove; their trunks often as wide as the minivan. The deeper into woodland we went, the safer I felt. "I'm really not sure what's going on, Jeffrey. And I'm sorry I'm putting you in this. I didn't know who else to call. If I could have done this on my own, I would have."

"Speaking of calls." He reached over and opened the glove compartment, finding an outdated flip phone. "Sometime today, call work and tell them why you didn't come in. You're sick, and you will be sick for the next week. Use it sparingly, but no one can trace you on this."

It occurred to me that I'd probably lose my job. Even if the law didn't get me, I could only be absent so long. Open slots in fire departments didn't come up that often either. I'd had to wait two years to take the entry exam.

When I took the phone, he felt my hand tremble. Jeffrey observed, "You're shaking. Did you know you were shaking?" I placed my hands and the phone between my legs. "We'll figure it out. You're a tough cookie." His concern was as close to compassion as I was going to get right now.

The minivan pulled off the road into a shopping center. "Next stop." To a stranger, his voice would sound calm as a yogi's, but Jeffrey never followed a strict agenda like this. He liked to yak, and we'd said almost nothing to each other.

I bought a few days' worth of outfits from a boutique athletic shop: butt-hugging yoga pants and layers warm enough for the woods. I changed in the dressing room, and we bagged my old clothes.

Jeffrey drove on until we reached a landfill, where he announced, "Final stop."

Tractor tires piled atop a heap of paper debris and the occasional stray television. Herons picked at the detritus. Without a soul in sight, he doused my clothes in lighter fluid and tossed a lit match on the mound. He asked regretfully, "Your wallet."

"You sure that's necessary?"

"You were unconscious. You don't know what he planted on you. I know you'd expect a recluse like me to wax conspiracy, but you'd be surprised how crafty law enforcement can be."

I handed over all of my identification. I would have taken the cash too, but Jeffrey cautioned, "Only keep the money you withdrew after you left the detective." The bank had given me an envelope for the few thousand I'd withdrawn, and I'd kept it separate from my billfold. I probably had sixty bucks in the wallet, but I didn't know when I'd be at my next bank, and I couldn't use credit cards.

"They'd mark the cash?"

He said, "You've just destroyed a car, and you're worried about saving sixty dollars?"

I surrendered the wallet. He tossed it on the pyre and we watched my belongings reduce to ash. The only items spared were the syringe Leland gave me, still in the case, and the mail I'd stolen from Helena Mumm; and they were only saved because he wanted to examine them.

"Do you have anything else on you he might have touched?"

"No. I've got nothing."

"Then let's take you home."

Redwoods curtained off Jeffrey Holt's house from the street. The place was so remote he didn't even get his mail delivered. The P.O. Box was back down on Main Street in Shallot. After the shooting, he'd bought an old sheep ranch and rebuilt on the land. Only someone with serious funds could have afforded this. The house was one long floor on the top of a hill with windows everywhere, looking out onto vast contours of pine tops. An aircraft carrier on a sea of conifers.

The house hadn't changed much. In the four years I'd known Jeffrey Holt, I'd visited three times, when he hosted annual dinners for volunteers. I belonged to a group called Friends, a subset of a larger organization known as Gifts of Deliverance. Jeffrey had chosen the name because the acronym spat in the face of religious right-to-lifers like the man who shot him. When a client wanted someone like Kali to visit her, she would contact Gifts of Deliverance and ask for a Friend. About fifty Friends attended the last annual gathering.

When we pulled into the driveway, I ducked down in the backseat of the minivan while Jeffrey went inside. He hurried the nanny out and tapped the glass when I could come out of hiding. The girls were back from school. He didn't keep the kids around while the Friends got drunk at his house, so I'd never met Stacy or Jess Holt. I recognized them from photos. Once we got inside, I watched them bounce on a trampoline in the backyard while Jeffrey examined my cuts and bruises in the bathroom.

We moved to the kitchen, and I started peeling carrots and yams in the sink. While I skinned vegetables, Jeffrey moved through the house and drew vertical blinds across the big windows. With every yank of the pull cord the blinds lurched until the striped sunlight cast prison bar shadows on the floor. Another twist and the room was dark. This was the first time I'd ever seen his windows covered. I'd once asked him if he ever felt exposed in a house this open, and he'd said the forest gave him all the privacy he needed.

The kitchen window gave me another view of his daughters playing. Both girls were under ten, smiley with long limbs and fingers like their dad. The older one, Stacy, had her mom Mina's lopsided dimples. Unlike either of the Mumm's homes, family photos lined the walls, allowing me to compare faces. Once Jeffrey made his rounds to every room and drew the blinds in each, he returned to the kitchen, gave a longing look at his daughters, then reached over my shoulder and pulled the shade.

When he called the kids inside, Jeffrey hugged them tight, almost to show me how much affection could be poured into an embrace when someone deserved it. Or maybe today he felt more protective. He introduced me as an afterthought, but didn't call me over from the sink, and the two girls hesitantly waved to me from across the room. The older one, Stacy, asked why it was so dark inside, and her father said he was getting the house ready for movie night. The kids cheered.

He joined me in the kitchen while the girls changed. "On movie night they dress up like Hollywood celebrities." He sliced the yams I'd peeled and kept his eyes on the knife. "It will keep them busy until we eat." He kept his eyes on the counters while we cooked.

We roasted root vegetables and he stir-fried tofu with garlic and chili paste. With Jeffrey lost in thought, neither of us spoke. Cooking usually zenned him out, but he operated like an automaton as he prepared the food, and I pivoted to keep out of his way.

By the time we gathered the kids for dinner, the sun had gone down. Through the narrow gaps in the blinds, the night was the pure black only found in deep, dark nature.

The kids stampeded to the table in garish costume gowns and tiaras, Halloween costumes modeled after Disney princesses, with vinyl frills that imitated lace. Stacy wore her dress with Crocs, and Jess ambled in a pair of her mother's loose-fitting heels. Jeffrey had held onto a closet of Mina's clothing.

At the table, the girls fiddled with their napkins and kicked their legs. They were chuckling, blond monkeys who hadn't learned to sit still. Both of them eyed me curiously. From what I picked up, the girls seemed to know little about their father's euthanasia work. He told them I was a friend from work, but not much else. While he forked his yams into mash, his restless leg quivered. The soft scrapes of steel against ceramic kept the room from going completely silent.

Stacy tried to piece together our friendship from the factoid her father fed them. "You work with my dad. Are you a doctor too?"

Jess couldn't contain herself. "You're tall. Are you a man?"

Stacy was at the age where she tried to act like an adult. She scolded her sister. "She's not a man. She's pretty."

Jess pointed at my bicep. "Her arms are too strong."

"Want to feel them?" I asked.

"Yes," said Jess without hesitation. I made a muscle, and her eyes bugged when she felt it. "Awesome." Her hand slipped down to my bandaged wrist, and I tried to be subtle about my wince. She saw the gauze. "Are you hurt?"

"Not that hurt."

"What did you do?"

"Stunt girl. I fell out of a building for a movie." Jeffrey had been stewing in thought, but this momentarily jogged him out of it. He smiled with a momentary eye twinkle.

"Really?"

"No, I'm just kidding."

Stacy asked, "Are you a beaver or a duck?" I had no idea what she was talking about.

Jeffrey looked up from his food. "It's an Oregon thing."

"Neither?"

Jess tried to braid her own hair while she assessed, "Not a beaver or a duck, and not a doctor. Not a stunt girl. What do you do?"

Jeffrey didn't offer much help—he was back to staring at his sweet potatoes. "I'm a firefighter—kind of like a stunt girl. I put out fires. Occasionally, I have to look for people and make sure they're safe—it's called search and rescue. And I work as a paramedic." I asked her dad, "Do they know what a paramedic is?" This forced Jeffrey to acknowledge me, and he shrugged, managing a smile. "It's someone who brings people to the doctors when they're hurt."

"You're a fireman?" This wowed the older sister.

"I told you she was a man," Jess said.

This pulled Jeffrey out of his ruminations. "She's not a man." To me, he said, "I'm sorry." Either the delight of his children or the wine had begun to pacify him. He was unknotting into the man I admired, and now joined the conversation.

I took this opening to remind him. "Thank you for having me here. I know what you're doing for me, and I appreciate it."

"Is she staying over?" Jess asked her dad.

"She is," he confirmed.

Stacy finished spelling the word "be" with her carrot segments, and her father judged that the meal had concluded. "You guys want to start the movie?"

Jess bolted from her seat and out of the room.

Stacy told her father. "We get to race with her tomorrow."

"Fair enough," he said to her, then to me, "Good luck. They're fast and they know how to dodge trees."

He left the table and started an animated movie while I cleared the plates. With the kids engrossed, we talked in the kitchen over running water. He washed and I dried.

He continued with the question that had been nagging him. "Why are you convinced he was real police?"

"When I go on calls I run into cops. He reminded me of some of those guys. Not the rookies, but the veterans who've been through it a thousand times over."

"I need to ask. Does he know you know me?"

"It never came up, and I sure didn't bring it up. If he knows, it's not because I told him." I didn't mention that Leland chose to read Jeffrey's book during my detainment. To win his confidence, I added, "I don't keep anything on the organization in my apartment. He won't find anything there."

"Your computer…"

"My computer is registered to Pamela Wonnacott. The only place Kali got e-mail was my cell phone."

"You know there's a lot at stake here, right?"

"I'm not taking this lightly. I don't want to put you in jeopardy."

"Too late for that," he snapped. "I'm sorry, but I can't get over the fact that you didn't consult the doctor face-to-face. You didn't verify the records. We have those rules in place so things like this don't happen." He chewed on a fingernail. He was absolutely right, and hearing my mistakes aired aloud made me shrivel inside. In some ways, disappointing Jeffrey Holt was worse than fending for my own safety.

"Would it be better if I left?"

"No it wouldn't." Covered in a wet yellow canner's glove, his hand covered mine. The way I held clients' hands. "I knew a long time ago I'd be at risk doing this. Even before that little man shot me in Baltimore. The work we do inherently pisses people off. You piss off enough people, someone's going to come after you. I knew that. But I'm not worried for myself. I'm worried about the other people in this house. The people in this house, and the people in our network. You know how many people this organization represents?"

"About fifty Friends," I said.

He stared at the stream of running dishwater, perhaps wondering whether he should say more. "Gifts of Deliverance, as an organization, represents a network of about 2,600 people. And the potential for calamity is the reason you didn't know that until now."

I'm usually easier with words, but I was speechless.

He patted my hand. "We're going to fix this. You'll see tomorrow."

I slept well. My bed smelled like cut wood and mildew, unfamiliar odors that promised refuge from the known, vengeful world.

Voices woke me in the morning.

Two new people sat in the living room with Jeffrey and the girls: a big oafish white guy with a beard orange as a campfire, and a petite Asian woman with honey skin and Malcolm X glasses. Both of them were in their late twenties. They occupied distant points on an L-shaped sofa set. The big guy absentmindedly plucked pentatonic scales on an acoustic guitar while they talked, even though it distracted the girls from watching cartoons on TV. The guitar belonged to Jeffrey—it came out every year during the parties.

Silence fell when I walked in. Jeffrey forced a cordial, "Ga' morning."

Christ, I was the class dunce.

"Where are the girls?"

Jeffrey said, "Dropped them off at school. Wouldn't want them around for this anyway."

He introduced the red-bearded guy as a lab tech named Morton Ross. "He's done impressive work on drug interactions."

The Gifts of Deliverance network conducted research. Hence, it made sense for Jeffrey Holt to retain a bullpen of researchers, people who could test forms of assisted suicide such as the helium-and-bag method. The term "drug interactions" had devolved into pharma jargon, but it referred to how one medication impacted the effects of others. For example, did Valium compound the effects of sodium thiopental and pancuronium bromide? Researchers like

Morton Ross helped Dr. Jeffrey Holt perfect the most painless ways to end lives.

Morton stopped plucking the acoustic. In glass-rattling baritone, he jollied, "Dr. Holt tells me you have a syringe full of a mystery fluid?"

I retrieved it from the bedroom. Morton cracked open the case and turned the hypodermic barrel up and down. Had it been a dirty novelty pen, a girl's hula skirt might have rolled up to reveal her nethers.

Morton looked at Jeffrey. "No sweat. Two days, three tops. If it takes more than that, I'll try drinking it." When the other woman gaped, he assured her, "I'm kidding."

Jeffrey introduced the woman as Lisa Kim. Five feet even and slim. Built like a ballerina, her haunches were slightly more developed than her bony ribcage.

I tried to be friendly. "You look familiar. Have we met here at one of the gatherings?"

Lisa Kim almost snorted. "No, we haven't."

"Sorry, I thought you might be another Friend."

Her witchy cackle suggested that was the best joke Lisa Kim had heard in some time. "I'm Jeffrey's general counsel. If I look familiar, it's probably because you've seen my photo on the website. Definitely not a friend."

Jeffrey said admiringly, "Lisa helped put together several of our ballot initiatives."

In the time I'd known him, the organization had lobbied on four euthanasia and assisted suicide bills in three states.

She said, "I do a lot more than that. I'm the hog that roots out truffles." She sprang from the sofa and asked me, "I hear you got mail. Where is it?" I pointed down the hallway to one of the guest rooms, and she disappeared and reappeared with the junk mail addressed to Helena Mumm. She said to Jeffrey, "I can make this quick."

Morton set up a portable laboratory in a guest bedroom. Jeffrey secluded himself in his private office. That left Lisa Kim and me together at the dining table, which we converted into a workstation. She had ample elbow room, but set up her computer right across the table from mine; I can only assume, to make me uncomfortable. Every few seconds, she peeped up above the horizon of her laptop screen to see what I was doing. She struck me as someone with OCD, because she fidgeted more than Jeffrey's daughters. Every few seconds she made some extraneous movement: checking her cell phone, loudly slurping her coffee, *dinking* the side of her water glass with a fingernail. She even flicked her hollow cheek in a way that sounded like raindrops. As it turned out, she was trying to draw my attention. Finally, she said, "I know who you are, Kali. Pamela Wonnacott." It sounded like an accusation. "Jeffrey talks about you." I hoped for a compliment, but no such luck. "I expected something different."

"What did you expect?"

"I expected Joan of Arc, to be honest. Some freaking superhero. But you're a kid." She spoke in rushed bursts, reminding me of how a tetra darts about in an aquarium.

"You can't be more than two years older than me, " I said.

"I'm thirty-eight, but I look young."

Law school had trained her not to deviate from her own line of argument. "You're prettier than I thought you'd be, I'll give you that. Everyone always talks about your muscles. I thought you'd be one of those women who looks like a man with a wig, but you're normal enough."

"Are you disappointed?"

"Maybe a little. I expected big, snaky tattoos. Do you even have a piercing?"

I stood and lifted my shirt to show her the navel ring, hoping my playfulness would soften her up. "Indeedy."

Kim navel-stared until she was satisfied. "Turquoise?"

"Yes."

"You get it at Bonaroo or something?"

"I've never been."

"I know what happened to your family." With this she blindsided me in a cross-examination. "Lots of press on that story."

When people found out about my family history, about my stepdad Gordon Ostrowski, about the fire, most people offered something apologetic. Even if they stumbled through an awkward sentiment, I appreciated the attempt to communicate empathy. Lisa Kim made no such effort.

"You're a visible woman, Pamela Wonnacott. Is that why you don't use your real name?"

"You'd be hard-pressed to find someone who would recognize my name."

"So, why the alias? I know other people in the Friends network. They don't use fake names."

"Maybe I'm just more careful."

She gesticulated to our laptops, reminding me that we were all here trying to cleanse my colossal error in judgment. "Clearly not."

I gritted my teeth. "Maybe I just like the name."

"You want to be someone else, that it? Pamela Wonnacott was a victim. Kali is someone new, someone who doesn't have to live with that legacy."

I noticed my clenched fists, then remembered that I was there because Jeffrey had been kind enough to grant me sanctuary in his home. For his sake, I pressed my palms flat on the table to keep them from balling up.

"I understand how you got to where you are, you know. I could describe the life cycle of Pamela Wonnacott since you were a tadpole."

"Shouldn't we be researching Leland Mumm?"

"I checked—there is no Leland Mumm. It's a fake name," she said dismissively, momentarily glancing at her monitor at whatever she had looked up to confirm this for herself. Then she continued on the subject of me. "First your dad died, then all this stuff with Gordon Ostrowski happened. You felt weak. You packed on the muscle so no one could push you around. You gravitated to a profession that requires strength—one that even allows you to save people."

I felt an eyelid twitch.

She kept going. "Lots of firefighters end up becoming EMTs because they go on medical calls." Her nails pattered on the table. "Not many become paramedics. You need extra training for that."

"I like to study," I said flatly.

"Not hard enough to become a nurse or a doctor though. Your transcripts could get you into medical school, but you didn't go."

"You've seen my school transcripts, then."

"Remember—I'm the pig who finds the fungus." Her dexterous fingers tap-danced. I willed myself not to reach out and snap them. "No medical school," she confirmed.

"Maybe I couldn't afford it," I fumed.

"Charity case like you? Dead parents, daughter of a Hollywood composer? Admissions would cream." She folded her laptop shut and leaned on her elbows. "You didn't go to medical school because you don't have your act together. Work like this—Jeffrey's work— draws its share of the misguided."

"And yet you tolerate them so well."

"Most of them don't bungle this badly." Lisa flicked a raindrop noise from her cheek. Such a strange woman. "Jeffrey likes you. I used to think it was because you two had a thing going, but now that I'm here, and I can see you two in the same room, I know there's nothing sordid going on. Someone less enlightened might take a look at you and assume you're a lesbian, but you don't like girls. You're neutered. Declawed. You can't find the pleasure in life."

My nostrils flared, and I couldn't help clenching my fists again, so tight this time that my fingernails dug sharply into my palms. "I date."

"Not much. Your most recent fling lasted two months. A boy from another firehouse who you met at a softball game."

I shot daggers at her, and my reaction confirmed everything she said.

She pointed at herself. "Pig." Then at me. "Fungus." She swigged her water and swallowed far too audibly for a woman without dentures. "Jeffrey likes you because he has a soft spot for suffering. But this isn't a place to work out your problems. If you come here for therapy, you're just another client, and the rest of us are forced to be your caregivers."

"I don't want to be taken care of." If I were anywhere else, this table would have been lifted out of the way, and this woman would have been bent into a pretzel.

"And yet that's exactly what's happened. We're all taking care of you. That's why we're here. I flew halfway across the country to be here. I live in Dallas. Now, I hate it in Texas. It's not like I don't jump at the chance to get out of town when I can, but it's still not convenient for me to do it. I came here to do a job. My job is to protect Jeffrey, and in doing so protect the larger movement we represent. So my role here is to minimize the damage you've done. In the short-term, that means figuring out what just happened to you and neutralizing the threat. In the long-term, it means neutralizing you." She opened up her laptop so the screen pointed at me. "Here's your woman."

In a few minutes, Lisa Kim had uncovered a slew of articles from a sensational court case involving Helena Mumm. The trial earned far more coverage than Gordon Ostrowski's ever had. Lisa Kim watched my reaction as I pored over the press.

Almost twenty years ago, Helena Mumm worked for the postal service in Livermore. In a blotchy photograph, Helena's figure was a similar shape two decades ago, but without as much breadth. She'd told me she'd been skinny once, but either she'd lied, or her skinny days were over long before this photo had been shot.

At the time, she lived with a man named Walter Gretsch—according to the photos, in an innocuous-looking single-story stucco dwelling where dirt collected under the siding lips.

The couple wanted children but could not have them. So they created a family. Helena and Walter abducted three children and held them captive for two years. They killed one who tried to escape. They mutilated another to prevent her from escaping. Eventually, they broke the will of those who survived. The two remaining kids—neither of whom were named in the articles—began to refer to themselves as the children of Walter and Helena. They became docile enough that Walter Gretsch even took them on errands. This apparently lasted some time, until one of the children alerted the authorities at, of all places, a post office.

Walter Gretsch did what he could to seem unfit for trial. He spewed Bible verses, even sang Christmas carols to convey how crazy he was. Walter's defense argued the PTSD from his own father's abuse led to crystal meth, making him incapable of controlling his sexual urges. Those urges led him to abduct the children. He had deluded himself and Helena Mumm into believing they were making an honest attempt to build a family.

The law didn't buy any of it. A court-ordered psychiatrist labeled Walter Gretsch a drug user and sexual deviant, but competent—competent enough. He was sentenced to life without parole, narrowly avoiding the death penalty. Currently he resided in San Sebastián, the same prison as my stepfather.

Helena Mumm got a lighter sentence for testifying against Walter, but it didn't save her. She spent thirteen years in prison for abduction and conspiracy to commit murder, but the parole board took mercy on her and let her out last year. She was terminal, and with a few months left to live, she won over the parole board with her "warm spirit and contrition," according to the news. They released her so she could die outside the confines of prison.

Lisa Kim had pulled Helena's sex offender profile. It featured a chinless photo and the address in the Excelsior, an old family house she'd inherited and let decompose on its foundation.

Helena Mumm was also Walter Gretsch's sister.

Lisa reveled in how my face sunk. "You dropped us in a steaming heap, didn't you?"

I couldn't make sense of all of this, not all at once. Jeffrey's general counsel might have been baiting me, but she was right. I didn't understand how this might impact the Gifts of Deliverance organization, but I knew this made our situation very serious. I searched for more articles on my laptop, and the two of us read quietly for some time. I scanned old photos for a face that looked like Leland's, only twenty years younger. I didn't find anything.

When Stacy and Jess got home from school, they invited me to race in the woods. I went without hesitation. I needed something to clear my head from everything I'd been reading and some distance from Lisa Kim. With a little fresh air, maybe I could figure out how it all connected. The lawyer scowled at me when I left the table, but she was ready to judge me no matter what I did.

They picked a trail behind the house. Down and back, down and back, we weaved around the trees on either side of the trail to make it interesting. Between the roots and the incline, it was harder than I thought. The exertion helped—while I was huffing cool air, I momentarily forgot how much trouble I'd gotten us into. Jeffrey hadn't said as much, but he must have been worried about his daughters as much as anyone in our professional network. They only had one parent now, and if he went to prison, they would be orphans like me. Running around back there, I could tell they had no awareness of the danger that threatened them. And because they were so carefree, I let myself relax with them, trying to put out of my mind the fact that I might be the person who would destroy their lives.

The stillness helped slow down my brain. Redwood forests aren't like regular woods. They're tidier, because of how straight the trees grow. The forest floor had its share of needles, but no scrambling brush to scrape your shins. The soil odor was hearty, and a woodpecker jackhammered bark with a cathedral's reverberation.

Stacy was old enough to control her strides, but Jess didn't know what to do with her arms when she ran. Her limbs flopped around, and when she lost a relay, Jess complained that her older sister was cheating. I jogged behind them both so they could win. Sometimes I pretended I was chasing them, and they squealed. We hauled down a few hundred yards, caught our breaths, and scurried back down the decline. So long as we kept moving, they didn't ask me questions.

After a few runs, Lisa Kim appeared between the trees. She'd thrown on a citrus yellow running outfit that probably cost as much as a business suit. Speaking to the children the way crazy cat people talk to their pets, she twittered, "Girls, could you go in the house?"

The kids clammed up immediately. As if magnetically repulsed by their father's attorney, they stepped away from both the adults and walked back to the house with their heads down. Lisa waited until the front door latched, and we were alone in the woods. "The girls like to race up here. When you're confined to a place in the middle of nowhere, you find ways to amuse yourself." She braced a thick trunk and pulled one foot to her butt to stretch out the quad. "You all raced out?"

"You can't be serious."

"It's either that or girl talk." She wasn't going to leave me alone. Weighing my options, I considered that the more effort I poured into physical exertion, the less tempted I might be to punch this woman.

So we ran. I bolted, then Lisa Kim charged after me.

What initially started as a race quickly began to feel like a chase. While we ran, she shouted questions and comments, just to remind me how close she was to my heels. "Jeffrey's cabin is a good place to get some clarity. Not so many distractions out here. It helped me get a handle on your situation."

I didn't talk when I ran. It's not like I was winded, but exercise was one of the few times when I could extinguish all my extraneous thoughts. So I said nothing, and without my responses to dam it up, her prattle flowed like the Yangtze.

"You know how bad it's going to look if they bust us? It's going to be bad. I mean, *national news* bad. They'll call us a death cult. You'll be our Squeaky Fromme."

I sped up. With longer legs it shouldn't have taken much effort to outpace her, but she was fast. She trotted alongside me like a hunting terrier. "How long do you think I've known Jeffrey?"

She gave me an open-ended question. I couldn't just grunt an answer. "A long time."

"Eleven years. A lot of us have been around longer. Much longer. Remind me, how long have you known Jeffrey?"

The faster pace was getting to me. Cold wind ran up my nose, and I had to gulp air to speak. "You know the answer."

"Four years."

Since I couldn't outrun her, I tried to avoid her. I rounded a redwood trunk, but Lisa Kim found me on the other side. "You'd think that was a long time, but in the grand scheme of things, not so much. A ton of us are more vested in this organization."

I was tempted to run off trail but didn't want to get lost. I sped up, but Lisa picked up her pace too. Light on her feet, her legs a blur.

This time, when I turned to round another trunk, my foot caught on a root. I spilled hard, and rolled out in the dirt. The ground was soft, so I didn't scrape up the way I would have on the pavement, but dried needles and blood freckled my palms. Because I braced the fall with my hands, my wrists stung beneath the bandages. My chest heaved harder once I stopped running.

Despite her size, when Lisa Kim towered over me she seemed formidable. Hands on her hips. Unlike me, she showed few signs of exertion. "You need to leave. I'm good at assessing risk, and it's riskier having you here than not."

I puffed. "How do you figure?"

"This guy's going to find you. It'll be better if he doesn't find you here."

She was right. I hated her for saying it without empathy, but my carelessness might have doomed the whole network. Coming here had only heightened the danger.

She turned and walked back toward the house. "I'll give you the night."

Inside, the kids watched TV in the living room. Jess was lost in her cartoons but Stacy waved. The dining table had been cleared for dinner except for the laptop Jeffrey had loaned me. A Post-it stuck to the screen. In bubbly cursive, Lisa Kim had written: *Cindy Coates. Victim.* I peeled it off and tucked it inside the envelope with my emergency money. I'd look this up later.

As I powered down the computer, Morton emerged from his bedroom laboratory, using the singsong voice of a carnival tarot reader. "Come with me and have all your questions answered."

In the bedroom, Morton's microscope, centrifuge, and computers sat across two folding tables. Soft lights cast the equipment in a vintage glow. All the adults clustered around the monitors, and Jeffrey looked disappointed that I was late. He said, "We've been waiting for you." Behind him, Lisa Kim beamed at my expense.

Morton was so excited, his body jiggled. "It's a drug. And I know what you're thinking, but it's not heroin, or any kind of heroin derivative."

Jeffrey squinted at onscreen charts and tables. "Not a poison?"

"You could kill someone if you used enough of it, but it's not a poison. It's largely used recreationally."

"You're going to make us guess?" Lisa asked.

His cheeks flushed—he was too excited to hold it in. "There's a drug used by shamans in the Amazon. It's a very strong hallucinogen, stronger than LSD. They call it ayahuasca. They use it for," he tried to find the right words, "spiritual journeys."

Lisa had heard of it. "Rich white folks also use it to find themselves. You're supposed to shit and puke your guts out. I hear it feels like dying."

Jeffrey peered over his glasses at his attorney. "I've done it."

I was pleased to see Lisa's derision blow up in her face.

"Sorry, Jeffrey."

"I was in the Amazon with a real shaman—and with a lot of other rich white folks. It felt like I died and I was reborn, several times." He turned to Morton. "What I had was cooked. It's organic. What's this in the needle?"

Morton awed at the findings on his monitor. "A synthetic version. They call it pharmahuasca. What cocaine is to coca leaves. The experience is much more intense—so I'm told."

"I can't imagine something more intense than what I went through," Jeffrey thought aloud.

I asked, "Why would Leland want to give this to Helena Mumm?"

Lisa added, "What would this do that poison wouldn't?"

We all looked at Jeffrey.

"Torture." He shrugged. "It would torture the patient. What I went through was administered during a ceremony, with someone who could guide you through the process. And it was still the most terrifying experience I've had in my life. The visions seemed as real as anything I'm touching now." He prodded the centrifuge. "I saw myself crucified nine centuries ago. I saw my life begin and end across several lifetimes. The pain was agonizing. I'm trying to imagine what that would be like without a ceremony, when I wasn't prepared for it. Honestly, I can't imagine anything worse. It would make death seem easy."

I didn't talk much at dinner. The kids asked me questions, but that night I wasn't as responsive. They ended up gravitating toward Morton, who made faces at Jess and joked with them. Lisa glared at me throughout the meal, until I excused myself and brought Jeffrey's laptop into my bedroom. There I searched for more information on Helena Mumm, Walter Gretsch, and pharmahuasca until I finally fell asleep.

The next morning I ambled into the kitchen for water. I bent the blinds to look outside, and a soft beltway of mist lingered on the trees, tinged red from the first hint of sun over the valley.

A laptop glowed on the dining table, even though no one manned it. Maybe Lisa Kim beat me out there, set it up, and went for a jog in her hornet outfit. Another Post-it stuck to the screen, left for my benefit. It read, "Time to go."

The onscreen browser had two open tabs. Lisa Kim had called up nuggets of information for me to look at before she sent me off. The first browser tab showed Cindy Coates's home page. The woman had written a book about her captivity with Walter Gretsch and Helena Mumm, and customers could purchase it directly from the site. The home page footer contained an info@ e-mail address. I jotted down the URL.

The second tab was about me. An old article with crime scene photos. The images felt fresh, because I remembered them daily. Often they flickered in dreams. But I hadn't looked at the photographs themselves in years.

The first showed a house on fire. Flames belched out the windows and rose from the roof like a wild surf of light and smoke. Helmeted men in the foreground fought in a blur to douse it.

The second in the series had been snapped twenty minutes later. Same scene, but the beams had collapsed and now firefighters were just watering down the ruins. One of the men had removed his helmet and was breaking the news to someone over a radio while mopping his head with a rag.

The third and final in the series showed paramedics in yellow lifting the sides of a stretcher like pallbearers. The woman's hair had burned to the roots. Her scalp, and the skin visible around her oxygen mask, was either black or the color of raw salmon.

A toilet flushed, and Lisa Kim emerged in flannel pajamas decorated with pink toads. She froze when she saw me. Lisa had wanted me to find what she'd left on the monitor, but not at that precise moment. Possibly, she thought I'd wake up later or that I would see the computer and let myself out without disturbing anyone. I'd surprised her, and she flinched in a flutter of blinks, like someone coming out of a cave into noonday sun. With the rest of the house asleep, we were alone. I guess I could have resisted for Jeffrey's sake. Instead, I walked slowly toward her so she wouldn't run. When I got close enough, I hit her so hard in the cheek I knocked her off her feet. She bounced against the wall and dented the plaster.

That woke everyone up.

When Jeffrey assessed the situation, he let us both have it. I'd never heard him raise his voice, and now he ranted like a rush hour cabbie. "Jesus Christ, Lisa, show some discretion!" He thrust a finger at me. "And show some goddamned restraint!" To Stacy and Jess, who stood openmouthed at the kitchen door, he lowered his voice and said, "Pretend you didn't hear that."

I can't say I regretted that punch, but it made this very uncomfortable retreat all the more awkward and reminded me that I had violated the generosity of my host. Lisa Kim might have been right on one account. Right now they were taking care of me, and I was being a difficult client. "I'll pay for the wall."

Jeffrey said, "You think?" Stacy and Jess had probably never seen a fight in their home. When I tried to look at them, their gazes danced away. The big muscly woman in their house had gone and socked the ice princess. Morton sat on the couch the whole time, eyes to the ceiling, possibly hoping a UFO tractor beam might come along and vacuum him up.

Lisa pressed a sandwich bag of ice to her face while she paced on the other side of the room. Sitting down would have been a show of weakness.

Jeffrey called to his daughters, "Stacy and Jess, could you leave us for a moment?"

"Why?" Jess asked.

"Because I want to say bad things to our guests, and I don't want you to hear them."

They disappeared.

Without his kids in the room, Jeffrey vented behind a scarlet face. "You know we're trying to save your ass, right?"

I nodded.

He turned to Lisa. "You know why I brought you here, correct?"

She nodded.

"Do either of you realize how close we are to the precipice? I invited you into my home. Both of you. Our goal, and it's sad I have to remind you both of this, is to protect our family. I have two. Those girls in the next room and this organization."

Not one to be deterred by someone's rage, Lisa Kim interjected, "Jeffrey, I am looking out for both. This woman is a liability. She can't be here—she'll ruin us."

"So you antagonize her by throwing photos of her mother in her face? That's how you've decided to help? We've discovered tiny bits of information. Instead of making sense of it, you're both adding to the chaos by picking at each other like caged rats."

"I wanted her to leave on her own, because I know you're loyal to her."

"You say that like it's a bad thing. I'm loyal to you too. Remember that the next time you think about being a sadist. That's not who we are."

Lisa's shoulders rolled forward, an attempt to make herself seem smaller. Her voice lost a little of its confidence. "I apologize."

"Goddamned right." He addressed the only other beard in the room. "Morton, what do you think of all this?"

"I just want to get back to the lab, Dr. Holt."

"Too bad, Morton. Like it or not, you're a part of this too. Please come here. All of you."

Morton looked like he'd had a glass of bad milk, but he rose from the sofa and joined us.

Jeffrey motioned all of us closer, until we made a circle around him. I was close enough to feel Lisa Kim's warmth. Jeffrey leaned into our faces like a coach, never so terrifying as when he spoke so softly, issuing warm breath into our faces. "Would you all say I've done something for you?"

That I said "of course" came as no surprise. But Morton and Lisa Kim sheepishly nodded too, reminded that, at one point, Jeffrey Holt had helped them as well.

"Have I ever asked anything of any of you in return?"

We all agreed that he had not.

"Then figure it the fuck out. You're here to save my ass too."

Jeffrey Holt dropped the f-bomb. My insides curdled.

He composed himself. "Stacy! Jess!" he called.

The girls came out of hiding. "Let's go." Our mentor strode to the front door holding his daughters' hands.

Lisa called after him. "Where are you going?"

"To get some air."

He flung open the door, but didn't walk through it. Jeffrey stood rooted in the threshold, fixed on something none of us could see, something on the doormat. Slowly, he turned back to us, face ashen.

A package sat on the welcome mat. The size of a brick, wrapped in brown butcher paper. We all approached the doorway to look at it. My mouth opened but I didn't breathe.

Jess was the first to speak. "We don't get mail here."

"No we don't, sweetie. No we don't." Jeffrey motioned to his lab technician. "Morton, could you take the girls out the back? Far out the back."

Morton picked up Jess by the waist and escorted Stacy by the hand. The kids must have sensed the urgency in their father's voice, because they went along without protest. In seconds, they hustled out through the rear entrance by the kitchen. Jeffrey's hand ran along his hip where he'd been shot four years ago.

I imagined we all thought the same thing: that this package was a plainly wrapped brick of explosives. The right bomb this size could create an explosion that would raze the house and any number of trees within a wide disc of incineration.

"Please leave," I said. "Everyone should leave. Jeffrey, follow your family."

The three of us checked the trees to see who might be out there watching us, but I only found a red-crested woodpecker clinging to a trunk. In a flash of panic, I considered who might be waiting in the woods behind the house for Morton and the kids, but we hadn't heard any noise, and I hoped they were safe. "Jeffrey, please go." I stepped between him and the doorway and crouched by the package, wishful that my body might shield him from the blast.

"What are you doing?"

"Someone's got to see what this is." I spoke stiffly, and I'm sure others could tell I was petrified. Still, I didn't see another solution. "What are we going to do, call in the bomb squad?"

Lisa Kim had likely played out the same scenarios. She started retreating along the same path that Morton and the children had taken. She implored, "Jeffrey, come with us."

"I'm not going anywhere."

"We can't call in the police. Because when they come, I'll be here."

Lisa said, "She's right. Jeffrey, we've got to get you somewhere safe."

"This is my home," he said.

"The beauty of stuff, right? Someone's always making more of it," I reminded him.

"You're not stuff," he said. "You're not the bomb squad either. What are you thinking, you'll just tear this open and cut the blue wire?" Honestly, I was planning on waiting for them to reach a safe distance, and then pick up the package, expecting that it might discharge the moment I touched it.

"Jeffrey, you need to go," Lisa insisted. Her footsteps scuttled to the rear door. Then the door slid shut and only Jeffrey Holt and I remained.

"Be with your daughters," I insisted.

"So you can be blown up by a bomb that was meant for me?"

"You're assuming it's meant for you."

"If this is for you, then it's still ultimately for me. I brought you into this," he said.

We examined the package for a long time. Long enough to ensure that Stacy, Jess, Morton, and even Lisa Kim had reached what we considered would be a safe distance. I wondered what kind of bomb this might be. I'd heard cell phones could detonate IEDs now, in which case someone could dial their phone any second and a sphere of fire would engulf us.

"We have to open it." I said.

Jeffrey nodded, businesslike. He masked his anxiety well, but his face tightened. I briskly walked to the kitchen, and for a moment Jeffrey might have thought I was hustling for the rear entrance, but I found the knife I had used the night before to chop carrots. Crouching by the package again, I shivered, then stretched my fingers.

"We can't just drop it in the trash," I said to convince both Jeffrey and myself.

Jeffrey nodded, blinking furiously behind his glasses.

I felt like I was reaching out to touch a rabid animal. I pressed the paper lightly. I didn't know what exactly triggered an explosion, how hard you would need to press before it went off. Or if I would feel anything if it burst in my face. My fingers shook a bit from the force of my own pulse.

I wanted it to be heavy. The package was the right size for a brick, and I wanted it to be a brick. Something harmless. But the box was light. Hollow. I didn't know if an airy box was better or worse than heavy. I got onto my knees and cradled it in my palm.

"Last chance."

Jeffrey shook his head. "Let's open it together."

We hunched over it like battlefield surgeons. He squeezed my arm for luck. I thought about my father and sitting in on those recording sessions, the orchestra playing while the films showed behind them on the big screen. Colton Wonnacott didn't have a beard like Jeffrey. He was handsome in an unconventional way, with a crooked nose and a long face. But they both showed a lot of teeth when they smiled. And when they smiled, I didn't want to disappoint them.

I slid the blade under the tape. The box had been wrapped tightly, which was a promising sign, because whoever had dropped this here wasn't shy about pressing down when they sealed it. The flap sprung free. I gently rotated and sliced down the seam.

Peeling off the paper, I uncovered a white pastry box. Not heavy enough to contain pastries though. I couldn't resist giving a gentle shake. Something was in there. Maybe a small muffin. Jeffrey's mouth twitched. He didn't want to open this package any more than I did. But I went ahead and unsealed the side.

It opened. I should have been relieved the whole thing didn't combust in our faces, but I wasn't. Both of us screamed at the same moment. Jeffrey howled the f-bomb again. My voice sounded as shrill as it ever had. I worried it would change the way Jeffrey thought about me—especially because I couldn't stop screaming. Not even when he held me to his chest for support. The box dropped out of my hand. An expired tarantula tumbled out, furry legs curled in on itself.

CHAPTER 7

We bugged out, in the army sense of the phrase. Lisa and Morton drove back to the airport. I would have driven out of Oregon immediately if I still had the rental car, but I was stranded. Jeffrey called someone, presumably another member of the network, and arranged to borrow a used cobalt sedan. It was waiting for me on Shallot's Main Street within a few hours. In the meantime, the Holts hastily packed the minivan, and Jeffrey went into hiding with his kids. He wouldn't tell me where. We didn't exchange many words, and he further deflated my spirits by leaving me without a hug or a handshake.

Inside the trunk of the borrowed sedan I found an envelope with cash, a laptop, and a cell phone. I couldn't use my credit cards or access my bank accounts without giving up a location, so Jeffrey had made sure I could support myself while this blew over, whenever that might be. He'd promised to call me on the burner phone, but I couldn't count on when.

The car fumed petroleum, and its springs creaked under my seat. Its lawnmower engine chugged all the way back down to California. I looked at the car mirrors more than the highway, convinced someone must me following me. Without the temporary sanctuary of Jeffrey's home, I was alone again and everything felt unsafe.

At a highway motel in Santa Rosa, I drew the shades and hunted around the Internet for Helena Mumm, Walter Gretsch, and the man who held me captive in Clayton. With spotty Wi-Fi, the hunt went slowly. Subsisting on chocolate and chips from the vending machine, I did pushups and body-weight squats next to the bed.

Occasionally, I peeked through the shade to try and spot cars in the parking lot with men in them. I didn't find any, but I couldn't help but feel exposed, even as a motel shut-in. *Law & Order* reruns without the volume provided the illusion that someone else was in the room with me. The local news didn't say anything about me, so if the police were searching, they weren't public about it.

Since Leland had assuredly dropped off that spider package on Jeffrey's welcome mat, I assumed that he was conducting his own manhunt. I looked for him first. I didn't find much. Even though Lisa Kim had assured me the man wasn't using his real name, for due diligence, I scoured the web for Leland Mumm. No shocker—I didn't come up with anything. His police badge had looked real enough, so I looked for photographs and interviews with police in Alameda County and any of the towns included within Alameda County. Fruitless.

There was plenty to dig up online about Walter and Helena. Handwritten love poems, some in pentameter, had been scanned and posted, making it clear that Helena worshipped her brother. Walter Gretsch was her romantic grail. He might have loved her back, but I couldn't find similar notes or quotes from him.

The box with the dead tarantula had also stirred up memories of Gordon Ostrowski and cemented connections between my stepfather and Walter Gretsch, despite that Leland was the one who had left me the spider. In the same way Jeffrey Holt shared traits with Colton Wonnacott, Gretsch had much in common with Gordon, not the least of which was that those two psychopaths were both housed in the same prison. Helena Mumm even had similarities to my mother, much as I hated to admit it. My mom's inexplicable crush on my stepdad was easier to explain than Helena falling for her brother, but both women had been drawn to monsters.

Walter and Gordon diverged physically. Gordon had been manufactured with clean, waspy features. He was both handsome and plastic in a Ken doll kind of way.

Walter had been a skeletal teen. With freckles and hazel eyes inherited from a white father, his skin was a few shades lighter than his sister's. His hair frizzed into stubby tentacles, and his cheeks caved in behind fish lips. T-shirts hung off him. The photo garnering the most media attention showed a skinny kid swimming in an XXL Oakland Athletics jersey. His look changed over time. On trial and in prison, Walter added muscle and fat under his orange jumper. In an interview conducted only a few years ago, his cheeks puffed out into the face of an exhausted fugu.

Walter and Helena had different fathers, so I suppose I should clarify, they were half-siblings. This explained the different last names, and made their relationship only slightly less repellent. Walter's dad was a white, unstable German aviation mechanic named Bodo Gretsch. He hanged himself when Walter was seven months old.

Gracie Mumm had been a burlesque performer and pinup model with fleshy thighs popular during the era. I recognized her from the poster Helena kept on her wall. She stood over six feet tall and had devilish cheekbones. Between the money from her career and a modest inheritance from Bodo Gretsch, she purchased a small home in the Excelsior District. Helena Mumm was born soon after from a nameless boyfriend.

Gracie favored corporal punishment, both in and out of her blackouts. Specifically, when she wanted to discipline her children, Gracie stabbed them with kitchen forks. Neglect, abuse, and little contact with anyone other than Mom, and *voila*—you got two kids who loathed humanity.

Polaroids chronicled their time together. Walter wasn't much taller than Helena. There was something frighteningly confident in the way he glared at the camera. Unlike his sister, who simpered in her photos, Walter didn't smile. He defied the camera. For each photographer, from his parents to prison, he tucked his chin the way a wolf might look at a snowshoe hare before the lunge.

I wondered how Helena Mumm could have disregarded one of society's biggest taboos. I suppose they would have clung to each other when the rest of the world shut them out. Maybe his tortured fish face brought out her nurturing urges. Plenty of bullies find spineless mates—Gordon and my mom were examples—but Helena didn't strike me as that kind of dummy when I met her. Remarkably, she'd stayed with him when things escalated—when the children came into the picture. She might have been like the frog in a pot that didn't have the sense to jump out as the water slowly boiled. That would be the kindest way to see her. Regardless, she most definitely loved Walter. I didn't need the press clips to convince me, not after hearing her pine away in the Excelsior.

After a while, the articles on Walter and Helena just retold the same story, and what I knew of them didn't give me any stronger a sense of how they connected to Leland. And Leland was the one who was after me. The only real lead that I had was Cindy Coates, one of the victims of Mumm and Gretsch. I went to the website Lisa Kim had found for me, the one that promoted her book account of Cindy Coates's abduction. The site didn't say much. Out of desperation, I e-mailed her with a fake story about being a recently released abductee. This was nowhere near my proudest moment.

The rest of the day, I stayed inside my crappy motel because I didn't know where to go. None of my research had given me an idea of how to move forward. If I stepped out the door, I was convinced Leland would find me. He'd tracked me to Shallot, Oregon. There was no reason to think he wouldn't find me in the Santa Rosa motel. If I jumped to another hotel, there was no reason to think he wouldn't find me there. In public, I stood out, even without the Kali costumes. As a tall woman with muscles, people noticed me no matter what I wore. Those people would remember me when Leland came around asking questions. My best bet was to stay hidden.

I missed my own apartment and wondered if Leland Mumm, or whatever the hell his name was, had already plundered it. I thought about my dad's baby grand, one of the items I couldn't replace. I wondered how he would vandalize it, raking scratches into the side, bringing an axe down on the keys. Worse yet, he might have emptied my two urns, spreading my mother and father all over my apartment as if spilling a vacuum cleaner bag. I couldn't save them or the piano right now. I couldn't go anywhere near my apartment.

Because Leland had separated me from my possessions, I no longer owned anything. It struck me how much of identity is tethered to ownership. My money sat in a few accounts, but without access to it, I couldn't rightly say I was wealthy, certainly not in my motel. My laptop and car were borrowed. My clothes had been purchased for me by Dr. Jeffrey Holt. If ever there was a good time to convert to Buddhism, now was it.

Jeffrey had planned for this sort of emergency. He'd socked money away and kept a safe house in an undisclosed location, his own Abbottabad compound, someplace even farther off the grid than Shallot, Oregon. I had done no such planning, because I was twenty-six years old and untouchable. Thinking back, I should have buried a tin of cash and kept a treasure map. Without it, I was dependent on my thin stack of dwindling dollars.

By the next morning, I was already sick of candy and fake cheese powder. Left to spiral through hopeless thoughts, I began to understand what true desperation could do. At any moment, a knock on the door could herald another plainly wrapped mystery package on the doorstep. Leland seemed so sure that he could find me again. Having no contact with Jeffrey Holt or the network, and no sure way of protecting myself against the unexpected, I would have entertained anything to save myself.

In the middle of ab crunches to CNN, Cindy Coates e-mailed me back.

* * *

Alameda might as well have been Oregon, since it felt similarly removed from any metropolis. A small flat runway of land just across the water from San Francisco, and cut off from Oakland by canals and the highway, the community was a cut through to shipyards.

Here in a small coffee shop, a long queue waited for their caffeine. I tucked myself behind a table away from the windows with an espresso and an iced mocha, neither of which I'd touched.

To disguise myself, I'd purchased a roomy hoodie and mirrored aviator sunglasses, which probably made me look more suspicious. Coffee soot gave the room a rustic scent, and when the grinder discharged its invisible plume of coffee dust into the air, I sneezed into a napkin.

I was here to meet Cindy Coates. She'd asked to meet me in Alameda, and I'd agreed despite that it brought me to Leland's backyard. I remembered his badge—Alameda County, number 5417. The county region covered Oakland, Berkeley, and busier areas of the East Bay. The town of Alameda was sleepier, but I still had a greater chance of stumbling into the man who was chasing me. On the way here, Alameda felt as quiet as the Excelsior. But with all those commuters in the coffee shop, a café was possibly the worst place for me to avoid strangers. Or police.

A pair of local patrolmen stood in line for java. They looked at me, but not in the way I was used to being looked at. Kali was typically regarded with admiration or fear, if not outright objectification. My droopy sweats and lack of makeup neutered me. I hunched my back and sank lower in the chair. As far as I knew, the police weren't looking for me, so there was no reason to think they would detain me. But I wasn't thinking rationally, and the cops stared too long. For all I knew, anyone in a uniform could have been Leland's ubiquitous eyes and ears, the "Elf on a Shelf" of law enforcement. The police uniforms made me blench. I pulled my hoodie farther down around my face and chewed on the sweatshirt collar so I could cover my cheeks and chin, until I was just a nose in a sea of cotton. They kept staring.

Then a young woman walked into the café and recognized me instantly, even though we'd never met, even though I was covering my face. Proving my point—even in camouflage, I stuck out.

Cindy Coates walked with a deliberate bounce in her step, which was no euphemism. Her right leg was missing below the knee. She walked on a prosthetic called a running blade, designed for runners with below-knee amputations. It was shaped like the "xistera" they use to fling balls at the wall in jai alai. The blade made her bob. On the phone, Cindy had explained, "I'll be the one on stilts."

"Are you Cindy?"

"Of course I am," she said brightly.

Her body reminded me a little of Lisa Kim's, but her athleticism was more obvious. Her shoulders were bulkier, and her biceps were blessed with that sinuous vein earned by the ultrafit. She was dressed in tight black Lycra, and her horse-mane ponytail lashed out side to side in time with her gait. The patrons in line admired her from the waist up, and then gaped at her leg.

Even behind sunglasses, I felt it was apparent I was staring. The two officers were as well. However, now that she was there, their attention was drawn to her instead of me. After studying her running blade, they caught me watching them. Busted for gawking at the amputee, the officers pivoted on their heels and focused on the menu board as they shuffled forward in queue.

Cindy possessed a radiance I wished I had, a deep love of herself that made her skin glow. Perhaps it was simply the sheen of sweat from running. Her pert musk smelled clean as tea steam. "Are you Pamela?"

In many respects, Kali felt more like my real name than Pamela Wonnacott, so giving her my real name felt like I'd provided an alias.

"Thank you for meeting me." I stood, removed my glasses, and unhooded my face.

"There you are," she remarked. She took my hand in both of hers, embracing it as if holding a dying bird. "It took guts for you to reach out. I'm glad you did. That's why I have the website."

Cindy maneuvered herself into the seat with gymnastic balance on the good foot. She wiped her face with a spare napkin on the table. "I hope you don't mind—I usually train in the mornings, and I just finished."

"Not at all." Even with her legs below the table, my mind lingered on the prosthetic. I imagined what her injury would have looked like fresh and how she might appear if I'd tended to her as a paramedic.

"Cool, isn't it?" Cindy was used to stares. Maybe it felt similar to when I fielded comments about my height, but I suspected it would seem more dehumanizing. She joked, "It makes me feel like a cyborg."

"I've only seen them in photos."

"It's a Lightning-Flex. Do you know anything about them?"

"I've seen them on that Australian runner." I added before I could stop myself, "The one who killed his girlfriend."

"He's from South Africa. He uses something a little different, but the principle is the same."

I asked, "Do you wear them when you're not training?"

"I've got others for daily use. But, honestly, I like the way it looks. It's badass."

I slid the lukewarm espresso I'd ordered for her across the table.

"Thanks. I hope you don't mind that we met someplace public. I have to build in safeguards. You'd be surprised at how many people try and find me. Most of them are nuts."

"It makes sense to be careful." At that precise moment, I felt like the world's grandest asshole. To meet Cindy Coates, I'd spouted a sonnet of lies, first by e-mail then by phone. She was so eager to help me. Rapt, she listened to a story of my abduction trauma, all of which was pure fiction. When I was finished, she said I was brave. That's why she wrote her book, she'd said—so others would come out and share their stories. So none of us would be afraid. My Lord, did I feel like a rodent. Leland's detainment in Clayton might have counted as kidnapping, but that wasn't the story I gave her. Over the phone I'd spilled out an elaborate yarn of being thrown in a van and bound to a radiator for three weeks. In my story, the kidnapper made me eat dog food—both the dry kibble kind and the moist horse meat kind. The postman heard me one day when I chewed through the gag, and I'd been released the previous week. That explained the bandages on my wrists—this was where I was handcuffed to the radiator in my fabrication. In my story, my kidnapper was out getting groceries when the postman found me, and when the police caught up to him, he was ripped apart by bullets in a bodega gun battle. All bullshit.

Over the phone she'd said, "You know, the post office rescued me too, in a way."

I did know, and it made my insides squishy.

At the café, Cindy asked, "Are you comfortable talking where people can hear us?"

I hesitated. "I am if you are."

She reached across the table. "Is it okay if I touch you?"

Funny—I asked a version of this question when I picked up people on medical calls. I nodded, and she grasped my fingers. Her hands were smaller than mine, soft and dewy from the run.

"It's nice to meet you, Pamela."

Across the room, the police officers picked up their drinks. One of them shook a few sugar packets and stirred while his partner gave me an over-the-shoulder glance, again stealing a glimpse of Cindy's prosthetic. I boldly smiled at him, and understanding that it was rude to stare at Cindy, he gave me a good-neighbor grin back. They left moments later.

The night before when we spoke, I'd told Cindy I'd read as much as I could about her, but I hadn't had time to purchase the book. This was true. If I'd had the time, I would have gone through it before I reached out. Since Clayton, everything had unraveled so fast, I had little time to prepare. So now that we were speaking in person, Cindy gave me the rest of the details about what had happened to her at the hands of Walter Gretsch and Helena Mumm. The more she talked, the less I had to speak about my own fictional abduction.

Of the three children abducted by Walter Gretsch and Helena Mumm, Cindy was the only one who spoke about it in public. In her book, she chronicled her own experience, but was mindful not to call out the other two kids by name. Both families had apparently requested privacy. Several years after she was found, Cindy made the rounds on talk shows. She reinvented herself as a paraplegic athlete and trained disabled runners when she wasn't competing. At the London Paralympics she'd earned a silver medal in the 100-meter sprint. In her victory photo, she'd reached to the sky with two fists, looking like she was dropping down a roller coaster decline.

"You look like you're still all nerves. That's normal," she said, mistaking the cause of my anxiety.

"That's good to hear."

"It's too soon to really think about this, but have you thought about writing a book? It helped me work some of it out."

"I'm not sure my story is worth a book," I said, fidgeting in my seat.

"Don't diminish your own experience. Sometimes it helps just to get it down on paper. Why do you think I wrote my book? It helped me find peace. I wanted to help other people like yourself who'd lived through the same thing, but to be honest, writing about it helped me as much as anyone else. You don't even have to make it public. It can be a diary, something to help you make sense of what happened and put it in perspective." Her compassion reminded me of how Kali would treat a client. I was such a bird turd for doing this. "Later you can worry about whether you want the publicity. Once you put yourself out there like that, it will draw attention. For me, it helped by giving me community. I've met a lot of friends this way. People like you. But the publicity isn't for everyone."

"I'm not ready for the publicity."

"Have you been approached by the press? 'Cause those vultures are relentless."

I wasn't sure how to answer. Tentatively, I said, "Yes. But I don't talk to any of them."

"Good for you. I have to admit, I dug around the web to find out more about your case and was impressed that you've been able to keep it out of the media. I thought maybe I didn't spell your name right."

It seemed like she was asking, so I spelled it for her now. The Internet didn't have much to say about Pamela Wonnacott, so I didn't see the harm in sharing. She whipped out her phone and typed it into her browser. I didn't think anything interesting would come up, but I suddenly second-guessed whether it had been safe to give her my real name.

Something came up in her search results. "You're a firefighter?"

Huh, so that's out there, I thought. "For the past four years."

"That explains how you're in such good shape. We should go running sometime."

"I'd like that," I said.

"Fireman," she mused. "That's real superhero stuff. Must have been a tough kook to try and pick a fight with you."

I nodded, "Pretty tough."

She reached across and squeezed my hand again. Mine felt cold compared to hers.

Cindy interpreted my nerves as a symptom of recent trauma, and not guilt for being a rotten human being. "Those wrists look pretty raw." I'd unwrapped the gauze from around my arms, and my wrists were purple and scabby from where they'd ground against Leland's handcuffs. The abrasions had authenticated my crap story. She said, "They threw manacles on me too. On all of us. They suck, don't they?"

"They do." Finally, I got to say something honest.

"There's something about losing your freedom. Not being able to walk across a room if you wanted to, because you're shackled to a pipe. That freaked me out, even before any of the really nasty stuff happened." She showed me her own wrists where thin scars crisscrossed along the undersides. "I fought against my handcuffs until I cut myself."

"Same here."

My time with Leland shared similarities with her experience. I wondered if Leland found me again, how he might torture me before fulfilling his promise of killing me.

Her forearms were dotted with a different type of scar. Clusters of four small points in alignment stippled both arms. Cindy saw me looking and explained, "Helena stuck me with a fork if I got out of line." She added with some pride, "I was out of line a lot." She winced at the memory, for a moment shedding her veneer of confidence. Then she remembered herself and beamed like she was invincible.

Now that we were talking details, I had the chance to extract information from her that could help me. I fumbled through it. When I asked for details about her abduction, I explained that they might help me make sense of my own experience. I could tell this made her uncomfortable, but she told me anyway. I asked her how she escaped, and she said, "I didn't escape." Her perennial smile vanished for a moment. "I tried. We only tried once."

Walter and Helena had kept the kids in a cabin on the compound. This much I'd read in the news articles. It was a glorified tool shed. Walter had soundproofed it because he'd tried to be a musician, and he'd built a modest recording studio like the Manson Family. Walter had recorded a handful of songs from that shed. The MP3s I found online played a lone, canned voice and an aggressively strummed acoustic guitar. His lyrics bitched about things—the government, women, white folks—in a blues voice inspired by Howlin' Wolf.

I had found maps of the property. Behind the house, the yard extended in a long, thin rectangle. Halfway to the rear border, they'd grown a hedge that bisected the property, so the yard looked about half the size. Once, police visited them when neighbors reported screaming. Officers came to the house, looked around, and walked around the backyard but never got farther than the shrub.

Cindy talked about her attempted escape with the tone of someone who'd been interviewed by reporters. She had practiced how to dish about her trauma without crumbling. Only an occasional eye squinch hinted at the flood of emotions behind her composure.

A couple of months after they'd taken her, Cindy had tried to run away with one of the other children. She said, "I was just following Julie. Julie tried to escape, and I went with her."

This was the first time I'd heard a name of one of the other children. I coaxed the full name out of her. Perhaps now that she'd seen my scars, she trusted me as a confidant. "Julie Diehl. She was one of us." She paused, and I reached out and gently squeezed her arm to keep her talking, hating myself for doing so. I asked her who else was with her.

She said, "Just three of us. Me and Julie, then Veda. Veda came third."

"The third child."

"Veda Moon."

I tried to lighten the mood. "Hippie name."

"Berkley hippies," she acknowledged. "Bona fide."

"How do you even spell that?"

"V-E-D-A. Apparently, it's Sanskrit for 'knowledge.'"

After a few months, Walter realized that the children were getting sores from the chains. The sores got infected, and he didn't want to bring in doctors. So he let all three off the chains so their arms could heal. They were still locked in the shed, but now that they had some mobility, Julie decided to tunnel out. The shed had a dirt floor, so the kids burrowed under the wall. It didn't take more than a few days. Each of them had been led to the shed with a bag over her head, so they couldn't know how close they were to other houses. On the maps I'd seen, houses on either side looked as close as a run to first base, but the children wouldn't have known that.

Cindy's nostrils flared as she spilled her story. Kali would have told her she didn't need to continue if it was too painful to talk about it. But that day I was Pamela Wonnacott.

Julie was the oldest and the most adventurous of the three children. Cindy was scared. By then Walter had already done things to her. I'd read the reports of sexual abuse that came up during the trial and didn't press her for details. Despite her terror at the time, Cindy had decided to try and escape. She said, "I assumed my expiration date was approaching, and I would have preferred to die doing something than doing nothing."

During their escape, Julie and Cindy made it out, but Veda got cold feet at the last moment and stayed behind. When they ran through the hedge, they jangled some brass wind chimes, and Walter heard them. Cindy recounted the ensuing events distantly, as if describing something that happened to someone else. Some of this was reported in the trial coverage, but not all of it. Walter Gretsch lost control when he tackled Julie, and caved her head in with a rock. Cindy made a point of saying that Helena protested, but there was no stopping Walter at that point. He and Helena buried the girl in the ground under the shed, and the remaining two children could smell her through the soil.

As we hovered over our drinks, Cindy relived all of this for my benefit because she had promised herself she'd help people like me. Her eyes watered. I handed her a napkin, but I was enough of a monster that I didn't interrupt. I wanted to leave. More than that, I wanted to hug her and apologize for putting her through this. But her information might connect to Leland, so I kept egging her on with reassuring strokes on her forearm.

Cindy had been punished but not killed. To keep her from running, Gretsch and Mumm strapped her to a worktable in the basement, where they sawed though the bottom portion of her right leg with a hacksaw. They seared the wound with an electric charcoal starter, a heated coil used for barbecues, so she didn't bleed to death. The amputated portion of her leg was buried with Julie Diehl in the dirt beneath the tool shed.

At the end of Cindy's story, I realized my mouth hung open without my choosing. I needed to fill the silence with something and managed to say, "I'm so sorry."

Cindy took some time to compose herself. She wept and blotted her eyes with the napkin. She asked, "You were captive for how many weeks?"

I had to remember what I'd told her. "Three."

"I'm not sure if you got there, but that Stockholm syndrome thing is true. I never had good feelings about Walter, but Helena grew on me." According to Cindy, Helena gave them extra food after that, and sat outside the shed door at night and read stories to them. Tiny perks didn't make up for the atrocities, but she became the lesser of two evils. "When they finally found me, I even stood up for her. I told the police it wasn't really her fault. She just wanted to have kids."

"That's really what it was about?"

"They wanted a family, and they couldn't have kids. Or at least they thought it would be wrong to try." When she laughed a twinkle came back in her eye. She dabbed it with the napkin. "That's where they drew the line, morally."

"Did you know they were related?"

"Not until the police told me. I mean, they don't look much alike. Helena kept talking about how she wanted to give Walter babies, but she couldn't. I just assumed she was infertile." She drifted into another memory. "I still sleep with the lights on, you know. I think it has to be the shed that did it. It was dark in there. They boarded up the windows, so we only got sunlight through the cracks in the day. They didn't light it at night, because it would have been easy to spot. That's one of my quirks now. That, and I keep a lot of toothbrushes. Thirteen months without regular brushing, I have to brush after every meal now. Do you have anything that sticks with you like that?"

I had to make something up. I could have brought up my spider thing, but it wasn't the same kind of quirk that she was talking about. I thought about Gordon Ostrowksi—specifically, his smell. "He had a cologne. It was something that a woman would wear, but he decided it was for guys too. I smelled it on a woman once and it made me puke." This was actually true.

Her smile disappeared. She raised her glass, and for some reason we toasted. Some of the joy drained out of her voice, and she added somberly, "Veda has a thing about smells too—Walter's smell."

"Was it that bad?"

"It was memorable." This talk of smells brought back something else: the smell of FlyNap cloaking Leland in fruity decay. Maybe my real-life captivity had affected me more than I thought. My head spun talking about how atrocities clung to their survivors. Hearing about Cindy's leg, imagining how it would have felt to be held in place as that hacksaw detached a limb, then the blinding pain of searing steel. My forehead felt clammy, a feeling that usually precedes nausea.

"Can I excuse myself? I could use the bathroom."

"Of course." As soon as I left the table she played with her phone.

Inside, I washed my face and stared at myself in the mirror

for some time, channeling the same self-reflective mood as when I pumped myself up for a terminus. I tried to convince myself that not only was I helping myself, but by reaching out to Cindy Coates, I made her feel valuable by playing the part of a victim whom she could help. Such was my logic. All this talk of psychopaths kept bringing up memories of my stepfather as well. More than Leland, Gordon Ostrowski came to mind when I imagined a captor, so when Cindy talked about Walter and Helena, her story freshened up my old wounds from Gordon. Maybe I wasn't so different from Cindy. I had a different breed of childhood trauma, but Gordon's imprint stayed with me in the same way. Cindy had coped with her trauma through athletics, and I started building muscle so people couldn't push me around. Not so different, the two of us.

I'm not sure how long I was in there, because I lost track of time. I wanted to apologize to Cindy and leave, but I needed to ask her about the police she'd been in touch with. I needed to find out if she had met an officer who matched my description. I ran through various ways I could broach that subject, trying out various lines in the mirror. Someone finally pounded on the door to snap me out of it.

When I returned, Cindy was absorbed by her phone screen. She grimaced at whatever she was looking at. Without looking up, she said, "You were gone so long, I kept reading more about you online." She sounded different, somehow bitter.

As soon as I sat, something whizzed at my head, and I barely had time to see the motion before it collided. Roughly the same spot where Leland had coldcocked me. Right before it hit, my eyes took a quick snapshot of the running blade. Cindy had detached it and swung it like a club. After Leland had gotten the best of me, I should have been on my toes, but her attack was so unexpected, I didn't have time to defend myself. Her prosthetic whacked the side of my head. I saw stars and tumbled off my chair.

"Who the fuck are you?"

I fell on my back. Cindy tipped the table and climbed on top of me, continuing to beat me with the running blade. With a fuzzy head, my best defense was throwing my forearms up. Patrons stopped talking. I didn't see them, but I heard the hush fall over the café, quiet as a wake. They were too stunned to intervene. I guess none of them had ever seen a paraplegic cudgel another woman with her prosthetic. They didn't know whose side to be on, and if I'd been in their shoes, I'd have probably sided with the amputee.

The rubber-coated aluminum could have caused real damage too, if I didn't have my arms up. She gashed the middle of my forearm, close enough to my wrist injuries that I felt it there too.

"Who the fuck are you?" Whatever composure she had learned to disguise the deep, lasting suffering caused by Walter Gretsch and Helena Mumm, all of it was gone. The way Cindy screamed at me, she seemed both terrifying and terrified.

Sparring teaches you to take a punch. For a while, I stayed on the ground and absorbed the punishment. I deserved it. But I also thought her rage would dissipate. Not so. After a minute of hammering, I knew I had to fight back, if only to stop it. Cindy was strong, but not as strong as me. Plus, as we grappled, I remembered the last time I fought with someone, and our struggle reminded me of my fight with Leland in the bathtub. When I fought back, I was fighting Leland as much as Cindy. I caught her prosthetic and bucked her off me. She weighed a little less without the lower leg. With a flailing arm, she ripped down the shelves, and an avalanche of silver coffee bags rained down on us. I scrambled to my feet and fended her off with her prosthetic, holding it out like an épée.

"Who the fuck are you!" She kept wailing.

Two men with café aprons came toward us, and I knew I had to make a quick exit. Her phone was at my feet. I needed to see what she had seen. I dropped the running blade and snatched her phone for a quick look. "I'm so sorry—please believe me," I told her. I held up my hands to the café staff in a *mea culpa* gesture, and stole a glance at the cell.

Search results for Pamela Wonnacott had led her to a registry. Specifically, an online sex offender database, the kind parents would use when they wanted to make sure their neighborhoods were safe.

A profile on that sex offender registry showed my name, as well as my address in Bernal Heights. Some basic stats on me too—they even got my height right, down to the inch. The headshot accompanying this profile was the angry camera-phone pic Leland had snapped back in Clayton, welts and all.

CHAPTER 8

At my new motel in Hayward, I Googled everything I could remember from my conversation with Cindy Coates. After 800 milligrams of ibuprofen, my head eventually stopped throbbing. Cindy got me pretty good with that running blade. Served me right. When Lisa Kim threw my childhood trauma in my face, I reacted with a punch. I couldn't begrudge Cindy Coates for pummeling me after I'd made her relive her thirteen months with Walter Gretsch and Helena Mumm.

First on the list, I looked up my sex offender profile. I'm no hacker, so there was no way I could pull it down. If I tried to contact the site manager, I'd probably only succeed in alerting Leland. Once notified, Lord only knew what he would do. He'd caught up to me in Clayton and could have killed me, but he didn't. The sex offender profile was just another way to wound me. If he wanted me dead, this might turn into a death-by-a-thousand-cuts scenario. Or his shadow might suddenly fall over me, and he might end me quickly with that semiautomatic he carried. I tried to convince myself that all he wanted was for Kali to go back and stick a hypodermic into Helena Mumm, but I honestly didn't believe it was that simple anymore, or that I could save myself that easily.

The next day, my scalp started to heal. Under a curly black wig in a warm afternoon, it itched like poison oak.

I was walking in Berkeley. Cindy had given me the name Veda Moon, and once I had the name, it didn't take much to locate the place. Frankly, there weren't too many Veda Moons out there. Public records pointed me to an address.

The Moon family lived in a midsized craftsman on a quiet street lined with knotty oaks. A wooden swing dangled within the covered porch, and a fresh-ish paint job made the trim glow white. What might have been a small front lawn had been manicured into a flower garden, accessed by a rustic wooden gate. Betty Crocker quaint.

Cindy Coates would probably have called Veda by now. She would have told her that some predator stalked her to a café. She would describe a lanky woman in loose sweats and a hoodie, so I costumed myself to look radically different. Kali dressed in a navy blue A-line dress, purchased at a thrift shop for the cost of a gourmet sandwich. I chose an outfit that would attract minimal attention. Even in something this simple, my legs stuck out like stilts and drew a few looks. But the wig was unruly and gave me the look of someone who didn't believe in unnecessary bathing. Tortoiseshell reading glasses cast me as a bookish Cal postgrad, someone who'd turned off the plumbing downstairs until she finished her degree.

The most important prop was the dog. A six-month-old puppy named Emmanuel trotted beside me on the sidewalk. He was a mutt, but between his black and white coat and amphibious eyes, I guessed he had some Boston terrier in him. Emmanuel chomped at the fresh air. Unsure what direction he was supposed to go, he lurched at the leash and jumped up on my calves. Plush-toy adorable, he was. The local animal shelter let the public take dogs for walks— play with a dog long enough, you might get attached and want to keep him. We promoted this shelter at the firehouse, and it's where we got our mascot. Most of us wanted a Dalmatian, but they didn't have Dalmatians, and the captain ended up bringing back an ancient Chihuahua with a walleye.

Emmanuel was an important distraction. The dog gave me an excuse to patrol Veda Moon's neighborhood. Now, I was just a girl walking her puppy. Passersby stooped to let Emmanuel jump all over them and barely paid attention to me. A police cruiser slowed down, and I stiffened until one of the guys rolled down his window and asked for the dog's name. In a crackly murmur I told him Emmanuel, like in the Bible. He didn't try to chat me up.

With the dog in tow, I made several passes by the Moon house. Whatever qualms I had about reaching out to the victims of Walter Gretsch and Helena Mumm, those vanished when I found myself on the sex offender registry. Survivors learn to scavenge. I'd obviously traumatized Cindy Coates, but I was prepared to do it again with Veda Moon. I'd feel worse this time because I knew more about how they'd suffered.

Apparently, Veda was a runner like Cindy Coates. Her name popped up a few times in Internet race results. She'd completed a few half marathons and clocked the San Francisco marathon at 3:17. Not bad. She was twenty-two years old now and still lived at home. That alone said something.

If I found her, I would need to trick Veda into talking to me. I'd hoped to run into her outside. I'd recognize her by her age. In my scenario, Veda would stoop to play with the puppy. Kali could be charming. If I could get her to play with the dog, we could strike up a conversation. I would be new to the neighborhood, full of questions. "Could you give me some advice on restaurants?" I might ask. "What about dog parks?" If I got her talking, Veda might open up. Clients confided in Kali. If she could confide in me, maybe I'd learn something about the man who was chasing me.

Round and round I went in a long loop, past the Moons' house then up to a bakery on Shattuck and back again. Dinner was a cronut—half doughnut, half croissant.

The shelter closed at six, but I didn't return the dog. They'd be pissed, but I'd drop him off in the morning.

During my laps I made small talk with every woman in her early twenties. Like I said, people liked talking to Kali. All of them gave me their names, and none of them were Veda Moon. By eight, the block darkened and everyone who was coming home had come home. I thought about going home, but in my last lap, the front windows were lit, and a silver Volkswagen was parked in the driveway.

The Moon craftsman was designed in a cluster of rooms, so that a peek through any of the windows gave the peeping tom—me—a good sense of the overall layout. Through the front windows, I spied a woman all the way in the back, standing at a kitchen counter. Her arm jiggled in a way to suggest she was chopping vegetables. She had her back to me, and was dressed in a gray business suit with an updo. She had coiled hair and wide hips, and when she turned to the side, light skin. I was too far away to tell how old she was, but the woman was too old to be Veda.

I could only see more if I ventured closer. The wooden gate swung with a subdued whine, and I tromped through the garden to the window. I tugged Emmanuel to follow. Rose bushes grew along the building perimeter, and when I pushed branches out of my face, the thorns felt like unhitched safety pins. The crown of my head rising above the windowsill, I watched the woman work.

The dog found a patch of dirt to pee, but soon got bored and pulled at his tether. He yowled grumpily—not loud, but loud enough. The woman snapped her head toward my window. Maybe she caught a little motion as I dropped below the windowsill. Maybe the reflection off the glass was too strong, and she didn't see anything. I crouched and waited. But I couldn't be there long. Out in front of the house, I felt exposed. The neighborhood was quiet, but if someone walked by they wouldn't miss me.

I worked my way around the side of the building, following the brambly rose hedge. The house was longer than wide. After I passed the living room windows, I edged past the dining room windows, inching toward the kitchen and the back steps. Emmanuel caught his leash in the bushes, and we cracked a few twigs, but nothing to rouse anyone. The dog thought we were playing the whole time. When I ducked my head to keep it out of sight, he took it as a cue to try and lick my face.

I raised my head cautiously into the kitchen window. Just a broomstick reach away, the woman stood in profile, slicing onions with her sleeves rolled up. Deep frown lines carved into her face, and she wore generous slicks of eye shadow. She seemed consumed with worry.

The dog abruptly snorted through its nostrils, so I ducked. It would have been so easy to blame it on Emmanuel, and I'd like to say that the dog gave us away. But in the end, it was me. The grass grew spotty on this side of the house, and when I slid down under the window, I lost my balance and slipped in the damp sod. I reached out for a branch, and my hand closed around thorns. I squealed.

Ducked below the meridian, I couldn't see her, but she must have heard me. Branches surrounded me, and on the shadowy side of the house, webs laced the thorny shrubs. Silken spider threads caught in my mouth. *Not now.* I rubbed my face frantically and swatted at whatever might be crawling on me. The dog saw me paw at my face and barked at me.

Heavy-heeled shoes clunked toward the window. Coiled into a catcher's crouch, I stroked Emmanuel, aiming to placate him into silence. She approached the window and cast her silhouette, boxed within a long rectangle of light in the garden. The dog smelled something on my fingers tasty enough to lick, and that kept him too busy to make noise. After a few breaths, a descending shade eclipsed the light. Heels clicked away from us, and a long blade drummed on a cutting board. A skillet quietly sizzled.

I realized I wasn't closer to meeting Veda Moon while I was scrunched in a rose bush. I couldn't just knock on the door and talk to this women either, because if she was Veda Moon's mother, chances were that Cindy Coates had already alerted her. I needed to leave and regroup. But Emmanuel became impatient. His licking turned into teething. He was probably hungry—I hadn't fed him since we'd shared part of my cronut. He yapped. Loud. I was astounded by the amount of noise that could come from an animal that size. Inside, a knife clattered on a counter. The sound outside was too loud to be a neighbor or a passerby. Her heavy shoes hammered back toward me.

I rushed to a hiding place, to the garbage pails by the back stairs. Three of them aligned in a row—green for compost, gray for recyclables, and brown for regular old trash. Flat on my ass with Emmanuel cradled in my arms, I shushed him, then let him lick my face—anything so he wouldn't make noise. The faint bouquet of rotting foods attracted his interest, and he sniffed like crazy to take it all in. If only I could have duct-taped his snout. Cruel, yes. But just for a few minutes.

The back door opened.

I couldn't see her, but sensed her. The woman scanned the yard, along the side of the house to the street. I should have just bolted, but I didn't. Dumbass that I was, I pretended to be tiny behind the trash barrels. It was absurd. Too little too late, I dug out a tiny hot dog treat for the Emmanuel, but even when he ate he wasn't quiet, and slurped it down. The door stayed open. From where I was, I couldn't see her shadow cast into the yard. She might have stayed on the stoop, or she might have gone back inside. I didn't hear heels, but maybe she slipped off her shoes so she could tiptoe. Aside from the dog's chewing, I only heard the ambient noise from distant cars, and I hoped those noises might be enough to cover up the sound of a small dog eating a fake wiener.

When I stood up, the woman was two feet away, on the other side of the barrels. She pointed a handgun at my face and assured me, "If you run, I'll shoot you."

• • •

The woman led me back inside and sat me down on a white sofa in the living room. She drew the shades in case other voyeurs were gendering through the front windows. I kept my hands on my knees. Emmanuel squirmed in my lap.

This had to be Mama Moon. Tesmer Moon—her name was on the title of this place. In my myopic search for Veda Moon, I hadn't bothered to find out if the father lived there too, but I only found one name through the public records. My research had been expedient—I learned enough to find the place and had rushed there on impulse.

This woman was in her early fifties, with some muscle but a diving suit's worth of padding that augmented her curves. Her ancestors came from the Fertile Crescent, but I couldn't place her heritage more specifically than that.

So far, I hadn't seen a trace of her daughter. Around the living room they had plenty of photos, but each one featured a clump of people, and I couldn't get a good look to decide who might be related to whom. The Moons knew a lot of people. Modern day hippies too—Cindy was dead on about that. The coffee table displayed a book titled *Tropical Hallucinogens and the Shaman's Way*. I would have leafed through if I weren't scared of getting shot.

Tesmer dialed someone on her cell. In the briefest of conversations, she asked, "Where are you?" A few seconds later, she added, "Get here faster," and hung up.

Visibly nervous, she handled the gun like she knew how to hold it, but not like it was second nature, the way we carry our cell phones. The barrel wandered—toward the floor, the kitchen, me—and after holding it up for a few minutes, her hand wavered from the weight. At the windows, she peeled back the shade to double-check the street. "Did you come here alone?" I hesitated, listening to the spitting oil of the skillet in the kitchen. "You can talk now," she said.

"I was just walking my dog."

"I know who you are." She circled the sofa and yanked off my curly wig, tearing at my real hair and scratching the welt Cindy Coates gave me the day before. I didn't try to defend myself. With her free hand, she found the lump on my scalp and pressed as if it were a doorbell. "Cindy called. Told me she gave you that." My stomach sank. When Tesmer circled back around to face me, I'm sure I wore some pitiful expression. Emmanuel and I were posed as the most pathetic Pietà in history.

An alarm blared, like a toy ambulance racing through the house. We both jumped. The gun barrel bounced about, and I was worried she might squeeze off a round by accident. Smoke hit my nose a moment later.

"Goddamn it!" Tesmer ran to the kitchen. "Don't even itch." Fish burned. Maybe catfish. That stink would get worse once it had time to breathe.

I could have run, but the house wasn't that big. She had a good chance of hitting me if she had a second to aim. With the gun pointed toward the living room, she dropped the pan into the sink and ran steaming water into it. I craned my neck to watch her. Like a compass needle, the barrel always found a way to point in my direction. "Now we have no dinner," she said. On top of everything else, she was trying to make me feel guilty about dinner.

Tesmer spoke with the crisp confidence of an educated professional. Something about her voice was familiar, but I couldn't place it yet. Her range was lower than the typical woman's voice, with buttery tones.

I tried to defuse the tension. "I'm not what you think."

"And what's that? A burglar or a predator?" She'd spoken to Cindy Coates. Had she seen my sex offender profile? I had to assume so.

"Either of those."

"Don't you dare make a joke of this."

"I don't mean any harm. I just want to speak to your daughter."

"Daughter?" For the first time she regarded me without seeming threatened. "I don't have a daughter."

This stumped me. Immediately I thought I might have visited the wrong house. In which case this wasn't Tesmer Moon, and we weren't waiting for Veda Moon. But Cindy Coates had called her, so this had to be the place. I was confused. My eyes tracked where the gun pointed, especially when she pointed it at me, employing the revolver the same way one might raise an accusatory finger to shut someone up.

Opposite the sofa, she sat down on an ochre hog leather reading chair. "Why are you here?"

Now that I wasn't certain about her relation to Veda Moon, I didn't want to mention the girl by name. "Because I'm in trouble. I thought someone lived here who could help me."

"How would they help you?" Her gun hand rested on the armrest, and the barrel angled so its would-be target was two cushions away.

I chose my words carefully. "I hoped they would tell me something that would help me figure out my problem."

"This girl—you were looking for a girl—would say something

and you'd figure it all out." It sounded bad the way she said it.

"That was the plan."

"You expected this of a child?"

"She's not a child now."

"No, he's not." She turned the gun so it angled farther away from me. Now if it discharged it might clear the couch and hit the wall.

I was in the right place. "You're Veda's mother."

"That I am."

"He's your son."

"That he is," she confirmed.

I nodded to myself as I absorbed this. "I assumed it would be a girl."

"People take boys too." Some humanity eked into her voice. "What did you expect him to tell you?"

"I don't know. His story. Walter Gretsch and Helena Mumm."

She waited for me to elaborate.

"Somewhere there's a man who wants me to kill Helena Mumm. I don't know why, although it's becoming clearer. I don't even know who this man is. I just wanted to learn more so I could figure it out." I felt compelled to add, "I'm not trying to exploit your son. I'm not a reporter."

"I know you're not, Kali." My name came out of her so easily, it took a moment to remember that I'd never said it. I brimmed with dread. The gun turned again, now pointing back toward my chest. This woman shouldn't know that name. Cindy Coates had only met Pamela Wonnacott.

"Who are you?" I asked her.

She said flatly, "You know who I am. My name is Tesmer Moon, and you're in my house." She brushed back a tendril that had fallen on her face.

She hadn't phoned the police. We were just waiting, her as much as me, for what would happen next. "Was that Veda on the phone? Is he coming home?"

"He is coming home," she smirked at me. "Soon."

Her voice. It was starting to come to me.

Emmanuel yipped in my lap. I corralled the dog awkwardly, like fumbling with a wet bar of soap.

Tesmer concluded, "That's not even your dog, is it?" For some reason this seemed to disappoint her.

"No."

"Jesus Christ," she rolled her eyes. "That's deplorable." Emmanuel pawed at my arms. "He wants to run around. You should let him."

But I didn't want to let Emmanuel off my lap, because then I wouldn't have a cute baby mammal to dissuade her from firing her pistol at my stomach. "He'll pee," was the best protest I could produce.

"I'd rather he peed on the floor than the couch." She waved the gun. "Let him run wild."

She didn't seem eager to hurt me. I hoped I could talk her out of holding me there. "Honestly, I can just go. This was an honest mistake. I don't need to speak with Veda. I crossed a line, and I don't want to add insult to injury by letting my dog pee on your rug."

"It's not your dog. And you're not going anywhere." She lifted the revolver just to remind me she had it. The weight of the gun was apparent in the effort it took to aim it, and that reminded me of its explosive power and how a bullet would rupture me if the gun discharged. I'd seen my share of gunshot wounds. If they weren't lethal, they were messy and painful.

I lowered the wriggly Emmanuel onto the carpet. He romped over to her, but she ignored him, so he scampered off to explore the house.

It dawned on me. "You were the doctor on the phone." A second later, I remembered the name she'd used. "Dr. Jocelyn Thibeault."

She huffed; a sound intended to pass for a laugh. "You want a gold star for that? It took you long enough." She chided, "You should have insisted on meeting me. I couldn't fathom why you didn't. Don't you have a vetting process for what you do?"

One of the few things I had once everything else had been

taken from me was pride in my work. I resented the criticism. "I made an exception for you."

"What would make you do that?"

"I felt sorry for your patient."

Car brakes whined outside. The way Tesmer's face relaxed, I could tell it was a familiar sound. She eyed the door.

A young man walked through it. "Whoa, fish!" He fanned his hand in front of his nose. An instant later he froze when he saw me, his mother, and the gun.

Tesmer soothed, "It's all right, baby."

Veda Moon was Cindy's age, early twenties. Only a few years younger than me, he seemed younger, and rolled his shoulders forward like a kid. Six feet tall and bony all over. Trim-fit Oxford shirt and skinny jeans. Clean-cut. He was so light on his feet. I could see how he'd make a fast runner. His face was sharply defined, with smooth amber skin and light hazel eyes. He was a beautiful young man. Some African blood had mixed with his mom's, angled his features and turned his eyes into gemstones. I understood why Veda was chosen by Walter Gretsch and Helena Mumm. If seen in public, people might actually think Veda was Walter's blood son. He was the closest approximation of the biological son they could have borne together.

"Mom?"

I don't know why I expected Veda and Cindy to be similar, but he didn't have her huggy energy. I could already tell he tiptoed through life, and he was scared now. I guessed he'd never seen his mother hold a pistol. Maybe he didn't know they owned one. It was that moment when the mafia kingpin's kid stumbles across his dad stuffing a corpse into an oil drum. Veda Moon was trying to reconcile what he knew of his mother with the woman who would hold a stranger hostage.

His voice warbled. "What's going on?"

Walking in on this scenario would have been confusing to most—I got that—but confusion is different from fear. Veda was afraid, for his safety and of his mother. As if the gun itself were an

IED that could blow us all to chum. He looked at me curiously and cautiously, trying to see if he recognized me from somewhere.

Tesmer told him, "Cindy Coates called today. She told us to keep an eye on this one. Said she'd try and find you." She gestured to me. "She's been passing around a fake story about how she just got abducted and released herself." To me she faux-praised, "Balls on you, girl."

Veda hovered within a lunge of the open door. Part of me wanted him to back out through it. His mother might follow him, and I might excuse myself.

I suppose not knowing what else to say, but feeling like he needed to interject something, Veda asked, "Why does it smell like fish?"

"Because I burned it."

"It smells like shit." He pinched his nose. I didn't know if this was the awkward spilling of a random thought, or if he was trying to diffuse tension. Hard to read this kid.

Tesmer seemed irritated—at her son, at me for putting her in this situation, and possibly at the gun for being so heavy. "He's sensitive to smells."

"Can we open a window?" he said.

"No, because then people will hear us."

An unseen voice through the door announced an adult man. "Veda, you don't have to be here for this." That familiar voice.

My tendons tightened like gurney straps as Leland stepped into the house. He wore a gray suit and rooster-red tie, with shoes scuffed around the toe box. The jacket under his arm bulged from where he carried his semiautomatic. He had brought a second gun into the room. Leland looked at me with a victorious smugness, and I felt invisible fingers encircle my heart and squeeze.

CHAPTER 9

My fingernails dug pink crescents into my thighs.

The Moon family conversed with a rote ease that might make one think they didn't in fact have a stranger on their sofa fighting to breathe.

"Where am I going to go, Dad? This is our house." Veda's voice was deep like his dad's.

"Your son has a point," Tesmer said.

Leland, or the man I knew as Leland, waved at his nose. "That is strong."

"It's nasty," Veda said.

Tesmer dismissed it. "You're sensitive to smells. It's not that bad."

Now would have been the time to scream. Bunched all together as a family, perhaps they would be less likely to discharge their side arms. Tesmer and Leland seemed concerned about alerting the neighbors. They should have been. We were close enough that a slingshot could have pinged pebbles off the adjacent roofs. Unlike the ranch house in Clayton, someone might have come running in Berkeley. But I didn't scream. Stiffened in terror, I could not move or make a sound.

The man I knew as Leland Mumm gently shut the front door. Like his wife, he peeled back a flap of the shade to peek outside and make certain no one else was out there spying. Once my exit closed, anything could happen. Tesmer could shoot me as an intruder. Leland could whip out the handcuffs.

He stood behind the ochre reading chair and affectionately

rubbed his wife's neck. He said to me, "I was coming for you anyway. You just beat me to it."

I found my voice. "What's your real name?"

Tesmer and her husband exchanged looks. Veda suddenly understood that his father knew me.

"Leland Moon."

"Are you even a cop?"

"Not exactly." He dug into his suit jacket and flopped a badge, too far away to read anything but the abbreviation, FBI. It looked real, but I couldn't be sure I could trust anything he said or showed me.

"Why don't I believe you?"

Leland sauntered to the front closet and opened the double doors to a rack of coats. He pulled one off the hanger—a deep blue windbreaker. Across the back, in giant yellow block letters: FBI.

Holy shit, I was fucked.

The soft mound of black and white fur scampered back into the living room and sniffed around Leland's feet. "What the hell is this?"

Tesmer said, "It's not even her dog."

"She brought a dog?"

"She said its name is Emmanuel."

Leland asked, "Did you steal this?"

"I borrowed it from a shelter."

"Pathetic."

"Exactly," Tesmer added.

Emmanuel got the hint that Leland Moon wouldn't play with him and romped over to Veda. Their son moved for the first time since he'd come inside. He squatted and stroked the dog. Cuteness aside, playing with the puppy was one way to withdraw from whatever his parents had going on in their home. Emmanuel flopped on his back, and Veda gratefully stroked his stomach.

Tesmer warned, "We're not keeping it."

The dog gave Veda some courage to speak up. He nodded at me. "Who this is?"

"Don't worry about her. It'll be all right," his father said.

"She's here because of me, right?" Apparently, Cindy Coates hadn't spoken to Veda. When the threat arose, she'd called the parents instead.

His mother echoed, "It's all right, Veda."

With no answers from his parents, Veda addressed me. "Why are you here?"

I admired this. First impressions what they were, I didn't think he'd have the fortitude to speak to me directly.

I partially fibbed to win him over. "You're not the reason I'm here—your dad is. Ultimately, I was trying to find him."

"Why? Who are you?"

Leland interrupted, "She's a criminal, Veda. One of the ones who got away. It was my mistake, and we're going to fix that now."

"But this has something to do with me, right?" His parents didn't answer, which told him what he needed to know. "Then I want to talk to her." Veda walked past his mom's armchair and stood by the drawn shades, turning our weird little triangle into a square.

Leland and Tesmer traded eyebrow semaphore. They'd been together long enough that they could communicate without words. When they'd reached a nonverbal agreement, Leland asked me, "Are you carrying a weapon?" Then to Tesmer: "Did you check for a weapon?" Tesmer hadn't.

"I don't have a weapon." This was true.

"Are you going to do anything stupid?" he asked.

I looked around the room and marveled at having landed myself in this pickle. "Stupider than this?"

He wasn't as easy with his grins now that I was in his home. "I'm asking if you'll do anything that will make use shoot you. Do you want to get shot?"

"Of course I don't."

"Then we're going to have dinner."

Because of the burned fish, Tesmer heated up leftover stew with gamey beef. The parents sat at the ends of the table, and I sat across from Veda. A dim overhead hung like a pool table chandelier, casting deep shadows under all of us. Leland removed his suit jacket but wore his shoulder holster—I assumed he would have unstrapped for a regular meal. Tesmer's revolver glistened within reach on a side table.

Veda reached to either side for his parents' hands, and then bowed his head.

"Grace—tonight?" Leland asked.

"Especially tonight," said Veda. He sounded like he might have been pranking all of us, but I went with it. Tesmer and Leland looked like they were humoring their child.

We held hands séance style. I had to hold hands with Tesmer and Leland. The last time I'd touched Leland's hand, I thought he was dying of idiopathic pulmonary fibrosis. His talons sunk into me like he was trying to wrench apart a wishbone. Veda kept his eyes shut; sparing himself the vile looks I traded with his father.

"Lord, we gratefully accept your bounty tonight and welcome an unexpected guest—"

"An uninvited guest," Tesmer aired.

Veda corrected, "An *unexpected* guest, which tests our hospitality. We pray that we can share this meal in kindness, without incident. Amen."

"Amen," Tesmer and I said.

Leland was quiet. We let go of each other as soon as we could. As I prepared to pick up a utensil, another hand grabbed me. Reaching from across the table, Veda had latched onto my wrist had, the way Helena Mumm had grabbed me. He gave me a penetrating stare, and turned my hand over to study the cuts and bruises on my wrist and invited me to inspect his old, self-inflicted scars, running lengthways, streaked across the underside of his forearm. He meant business when he'd cut deeply along the vessels. They'd faded into raised stripes just a shade off from his skin. He looked into my eyes as if we were the only two in the room.

Disquietingly, his voice changed when he spoke, from a deep adult timbre into a boy's pitch and tone. Veda Moon was affecting the voice of a prepubescent child, imbued with false innocence. In this mocking voice, he asked me, "Want to share stories?"

His parents were repulsed in the same way prudes react to the punch line of a dirty joke. Tesmer admonished, "Don't use that voice!" Leland pushed away from the table. "Your father hates that voice."

Leland almost shivered. "The baby voice. I keep telling you not to do that voice, Veda—creeps the Holy Spirit out of me."

Veda released my hand before I knew what was happening. When he spoke again, he used his regular baritone. "Just messing with you." His initial fear had been replaced with the sort of semiserious petulance of a kid who just grew out of his tweens and wanted to put one over on adults every chance he got. I got the impression Veda Moon might have been a pain in the ass.

Turned out Tesmer wasn't much of a cook. We might have been better off with the charred fish filets. The beef didn't taste any better than it smelled. She'd thrown too much orzo into the mix, and it sucked up all the broth. We were left with stringy beef porridge. I spooned up the carrots and celery, spooned because none of us had forks. We used stainless steel sporks, the spoon-fork combination utensil customarily employed by boy scouts. These were high-end sporks, specially selected with a brushed finish. The prongs had no depth, and I'd have had a tough time spearing the beef if I'd tried. I remembered the fork scars Helena Mumm had given Cindy Coates. I didn't see scars on Veda Moon, but suspected forks might be an emotional trigger for him.

Veda's baby voice had freaked out his parents more than me, and no one spoke for a bit. I had no idea what their normal dinner chat was like, but it couldn't have been this icy. Utensils clinked in silence. Emmanuel played under the table, and his tail swatted against my ankles. The dog gobbled his portion of stew from a cereal bowl, and assuredly appreciated it more than me.

I couldn't take the silence. "You registered me as a sex offender?"

Tesmer's spork clanged on her plate, even though she wasn't the one I addressed. Leland didn't stop eating. "We had a trade, and you welched on your end. Welcome to the consequences."

"What were you making her do?" Veda asked.

"Never mind," said Tesmer.

"I know about your trades," he said to his father. "Why were you trading with her?" He was still trying to figure me out. "Who is she?"

"She's a killer, son," Leland said with a *leave it alone* tone.

"Who did she kill?"

"A lot of people."

"Is that true?" Veda asked me.

I didn't answer him.

Without making a show of it, Veda rubbed his fingers on his napkin to wipe off my cooties. "And you made a trade with her?"

Neither of his parents responded. This was my chance to get a word in. "When we met, your father told me his name was Leland Mumm. He claimed he was Helena Mumm's brother."

Veda was a bright kid—he put it together quickly. He would know that Helena Mumm had been released from prison. He probably even knew where she was living.

"You told me you weren't going to go after her."

"Technically, we weren't." A naked lie.

"You were going to kill her." Veda gestured to me with his spork. "You were going to get this woman to kill her."

Tesmer tried to soothe her son. "Nothing happened."

I couldn't stop now. The best chance I had of getting out of there was wooing their son over to my side. "Helena is still alive because I refused to kill her."

Leland said to his son, "Helena is dying as it is. She has a few weeks. We had a small window of opportunity to get to her while she was out of prison and before she was in the ground. We took it."

Veda snuffled at his father with palpable contempt. He seemed more interested in me, and looked up and down my arms, possibly comparing my musculature to his own. "Are you some kind of assassin?"

"No."

"Why didn't you kill her?"

"Because she didn't want to die," I said simply.

Leland finally introduced me. "Veda, this is Pamela Wonnacott." Until that moment, I had been nameless to their son. "She kills the old and sick, because she thinks she's putting them out of their misery."

I didn't defend myself. Either someone was going to understand what I did, or they weren't. I didn't want to risk alienating Veda Moon by trying to rationalize my work.

Leland added, "She goes by Kali when she kills people."

Veda absorbed what his father told him. He remarked, "Your fake name sounds more normal than your real name. Does it mean something?"

"It's a Hindu goddess. My parents were in theater. The apple didn't fall far."

"Were they actors?"

"Musicians. My mom sang for the opera. My dad was a composer."

Maybe the kid was asking me questions just to antagonize his parents. Bonding with me marginalized them.

"Are you a musician?"

"I have my dad's piano—but I can only noodle a little."

"Both of your parents are dead," Veda stated more than asked. Not that it took a genius, but he had picked up on the past tense. Bright kid. "Can I ask how?" Veda's face had the emotional expressiveness of a glacier. He could have been pranking me again. Maybe he'd put on that creepy baby voice to mess with me. But he might have been interested in learning about me.

I didn't talk about my parents to many people. Some of the guys at the firehouse knew some of it, but even they didn't know the full story. The guys I dated sure as hell didn't know any of it— sometimes I even lied on dates and told them my parents were happily married in Chapel Hill, even though I've never been to North Carolina.

There at the Moons' table, I opened up to a judgmental bunch to win their sympathy. Anything to get me out of there. "My dad was creamed by a car while he was walking across the street. Nothing spectacular. Just a traffic accident."

"Drunk driver?"

"Just a moron who wasn't paying attention." As casual as I tried to be, this brought up some bitterness.

"How old were you?"

"Eleven." Not true. I was ten. But Walter Gretsch and Helena Mumm had taken Veda Moon three weeks after his eleventh birthday. I was desperate to curry favor.

"What about your mom?"

My guts knotted, having to tell a story that I never gave volume. Leland studied me academically to see what I'd do. The way Leland looked at me, I could tell he'd already found out on his own. Tesmer looked as if she knew what I was going to say as well. It was like both of them were waiting for a favorite line in a movie seen a hundred times; they wanted to hear me say it. They didn't save me with a, "Let's talk about something else," sort of interruption. I hadn't expected compassion, but they let me squirm.

"My mother died in a fire." I choked on the words.

"Two accidents," Veda noted impassively. "Strange."

I could have let it drop, but with Leland and Tesmer glaring like lighthouse Fresnels, I explained through a tight jaw, "The fire wasn't an accident. My mother remarried a man named Gordon Ostrowski. Gordon was an arsonist. He burned the house down." My masseter muscle felt like it might cramp. I didn't want to cry in front of these people, but my nose dripped. All those emotions that I fought daily to repress were issuing out like volcanic fissures, a twitch here and a cramp there.

Veda said, "But you lived." This could have been intended as a comfort or accusation—impossible to tell from his tone.

My eyes watered. In my mind I literally begged him to stop talking. *Please no more.*

"Were you hurt?"

My hands were shaking. *Why won't you stop?* Now came the part I hadn't told anyone. No one. Not my closest comrades. Not my therapist. Only the police would have known, because they questioned me right after it happened. Leland and Tesmer might not have known this part. My deepest shame. And by that, I mean the deepest shame of my life. And here I was in front of these people I didn't like or know, and I couldn't hold it in. It poured out of me. "I wasn't there. I ran away from home and left my mother alone with that man."

When I was fourteen years old, Gordon scared me enough to walk out. I tried to convince my mother that he was dangerous, that we should leave him. When she wouldn't come with me, I protested, then stuffed a camping duffel and stayed at a hostel for two days. I hoped she'd get the message that it was either me or Gordon at that point. Maybe she even got the message. She wasn't able to tell me.

I never saw the house on fire—not in person. I never saw my mom carried out to the ambulance. Those photos I had to find in the paper and online like everyone else. When I came home, all I found was the house in ruins. The smell of smoke still hung in the air. Saying it aloud there with the Moons meant I had to relive that moment of smelling ash in the air, the moment my body knew that catastrophe had happened before my mind could think it.

It was July and too warm for fireplaces. I only smelled a tinge when I was a few blocks away, then it grew more pungent, downright skunky when I turned onto my street. Our house had been a cozy Tudor; a style I appreciate now but took for granted at fourteen. The space where the house stood was just a space. The absence of the building seemed like a hazy mirage. At some point I dropped my runaway bag and tore down the street until I reached what remained of the foundation. Within the ashen pit, black beams toppled on each other like pickup sticks.

I could no longer compose myself at the Moons' dinner table. I collapsed on my forearms and wept. I needed to be someplace private, but when I rose to leave the table, Tesmer retrieved the gun. "Sit down, please." I despised them all in that moment, but I wasn't strong enough to put up a fight. I squatted back down on my seat and cried into my hands, hiding my face from the family. They all observed me.

Veda was the first to speak. "My name's Sanskrit." He wasn't good at small talk.

I snorted. "I know. It means 'knowledge.'"

Veda shifted attention back to his father. "Why didn't you just go after Helena yourself?"

"Because he'd get caught," I answered softly. To add some sand in the ointment, I said to Leland, "You never talked to him about any of this."

Tesmer pinched her spork stem like a dart. "This isn't your issue."

"It sure as hell is now."

"She's got a point there," said Veda. "Why would you bring someone else into this? What were you thinking?" I wiped my eyes with the napkin. It was fascinating seeing a son claim the moral high ground over his parents. "Why didn't you tell me?"

"Because you don't like talking about it," his mother said. "And I don't blame you. But it's our job as parents to protect you. That's how it works."

"Protect me from who? Helena Mumm? Too late!" He laughed bitterly.

"This was our chance to make good," said Leland.

"By killing her?"

"Would you really care if she died?" Tesmer asked.

"I would care if you were caught. I'd care that my parents had killed someone," Veda said. "I don't want Helena Mumm or Walter Gretsch in my life. I don't want to think about them. God, it makes me sick. It's like you've brought them into our house." Some emotion surfaced—maybe fury. I couldn't identify it. "What was this supposed to do for me *now*? How does this help me *now*?"

Something washed over his face—uncertainty, maybe even embarrassment. He sank in his chair, his expression suddenly vulnerable, like he'd woken up nude in a classroom. At first I didn't know what had happened. The dog reacted to it before the rest of us, trotting from under the table with a clipped whine.

Veda bolted up from his seat, and his chair tumbled onto the floor. His hands played fig leaves, but they couldn't hide it. He'd urinated. The khaki fabric around his crotch had soaked through in a wide patch. Neither parent looked surprised. Their son marched out of the room, and Leland simply tossed his napkin onto his dinner plate, signaling the meal had ended. The ammonia stench finished off an already unpalatable meal.

With his son out of earshot, Leland said, "That's what he does now. He pisses himself. He lives with us because he doesn't know how to make it on his own. He can't hold down a job. He can seem like he's in control, but he's got triggers. And if those triggers are pulled, he'll crumble right in front of you." He pushed his plate away and folded his hands as if he wanted to pray. "You think because he's the one who got taken, he's the only one with a say in this. You're wrong."

Down the hall, Emmanuel's collar jangled into what I assume was Veda's room. It sounded like they were playing together.

Leland got up to walk his plate and spork into the kitchen. Tesmer stayed at the table in case I got the urge to run. From the kitchen he called, "Do you drink beer or wine?"

I looked to Tesmer. "We're drinking now?"

She tossed her napkin on her own plate, covering her food like a morgue shroud. "We are. So what is it?"

"Beer."

Leland brought back two beers and a glass of red wine for his wife. Somewhere in the house, a shower hissed. This reminded me of Leland showering off his FlyNap when I was chained to the ranch house bed, pissing myself while he lorded over me. I tried to put it out of my head.

"We're going to have a drink, and we're going to talk." He gestured to both guns in the room. "Unless you do something stupid, we're not going to shoot you."

"Are you going to arrest me?"

"Maybe. Maybe not. But you're still in our home, and we could shoot you as a robber fair and square."

"You think your son would be okay with that?"

Tesmer warned, "He'd get over it."

I cautiously sipped my beer, sniffing the mist at the bottle's mouth to detect narcotics. As if I could. I tilted the bottle and dipped my tongue in the suds. Bitter. Too hoppy. I asked Tesmer Moon, "Are you FBI too?"

"I'm an attorney."

Even the smallest sip of beer made me brave. Not that the alcohol had hit my blood, but the action of pulling lips off the bottle brought back a cowboy cockiness that served me well at the firehouse. I even forgot that I had just been weeping in front of these people minutes ago. "Not corporate. Not with that hair."

"Prosecutor."

"So you two form a little assembly line of legal justice. Good for you." There went that combative urge that my therapist used to warn me about. I swigged. Might as well get drunk at this point.

"It's worked for us so far," she said.

With half the beer gone, I draped an arm over the back of the chair. I saw clearly now. A lawyer and a federal agent were taking revenge on the woman who took their son. Kidnapping me as their instrument. Not a crime of passion, but punctiliously staged. Frigid even. If this ever saw a courtroom, a jury might even sympathize with them, but the case would forever tarnish them and destroy their careers, even if they avoided prison.

In an abandoned ranch house on the ass-end of Mount Diablo, Leland Moon might have been able to kill me and dispose of me in secret, but not here in Berkeley. Even if they killed me without a gunshot, one of their neighbors, wheeling out the weekly compost, would catch them hauling me out, feet flopping out of one end of a coiled carpet.

"You honestly think both of you have less to lose than me right now?"

Leland sucked on his own beer, and then leaned toward me. It was as close as our faces had come since we'd grappled in Clayton. For the first time, I noticed the micro-wrinkles around his eyes. "It's all out in the open. We have our story, you've got yours. Gordon Ostrowski was a real scumbag." Christ, he was trying to bond with me. This was a good sign—he was on the defensive.

"Did you know about him before you lured me to Clayton?"

He admitted, "I only knew you by Kali. I didn't know your real name until we met, so I didn't know about your family. It wasn't too hard to find out afterward. It was a big case."

Right he was. On morose days I could Google myself and still dig up all sorts of archive articles about the Ostrowski case. Now that Cindy Coates had the correct spelling of my name, I wondered if she'd looked all of it up too. To torture myself, I sometimes found images of Gordon's smug profile at the defense table, contemplating his 257-year sentence as if deciding which appetizer to order.

"I'm sorry you had to go through that. I'm sorry your mother had to go through that." He sounded sincere.

"The spider package was a cheap shot."

"That was my idea," Tesmer admitted. "We were working with a limited window of time. We had to motivate you, and quickly. And we didn't want anyone else involved. We wanted to keep Holt out of it."

Leland added, "We have no present plans to go after Jeffrey Holt. That might change, depending on you, but we have no *present* plans." Now he went back to threatening me by putting the Holt family in jeopardy.

"How did you track me up there? I burned my clothes and wrecked my car. Was there a tracking device on the syringe?"

"When I put you to sleep in Clayton, I put something on your body." I should have known. I had way too much adrenaline pulsing through me to pass out on my own.

"Where?"

"Your navel ring." *Fuck me.* I lifted my shirt and examined my stomach. That tiny turquoise nub I'd worn for so long it seemed as much a part of me as a fingernail. Never thought to check it. Sure enough, when I felt the underside, the tiniest of bumps rose from the surface of the ball bearing.

Leland could boast about outsmarting me, but he didn't seem proud of himself for duping me, nor did he wish to belittle me for having been duped. He brought us back to my stepfather. "Did you ever want something bad to happen to Gordon?"

"Today and every day."

"Then you can understand where we're coming from. I've been acting as that boy's father here, not a federal officer. Justice was not served for Helena Mumm. You saw the softer side of Helena when you met her. She's been worn down by disease. That's what the parole board saw and that's why they let her out. She gets all smiley and people think she's a saint. The reality's much different. She's a psychopath, just like Walter. Just like Gordon. She destroyed children, and the families of those children."

"Their crimes are unimaginably horrible," I said.

Tesmer said, "You meant that."

"I do mean that."

"Then help us." Tesmer said.

"You can't be serious." Empathy was one thing, but they were flip-flopping between bullies and buddies. My head spun.

Morbidly serious, Leland said, "We're trying to be nice here. We could still shoot you. I could arrest you. You're still a registered sex offender. There are any number of ways things could go bad. Then there's Jeffrey Holt—the entire Holt family. What's going to happen to them? And once Holt goes down, there goes the movement with it. All because of you."

He'd made those threats before, and I hadn't numbed to them.

Tesmer cautioned, "Leland, don't." Tesmer was going to be the nice one. I wondered if they'd practiced this yin-yang style of coercion. "Let's just talk for a while."

I wasn't eager to help anyone in that family. Threatening me and the Holt network didn't help their cause. I had stamina, and I hoped the talking would wear them down. "What exactly does my sex offender profile claim I've done?"

Leland explained, "You were a babysitter, and you molested a few of your neighbors' kids. Mostly kissing, but some touching as well."

"You fucking prick."

He assured, "That can all go away."

The sound of running water from the bathroom stopped, which brought back thoughts of Veda. "Your son doesn't want this."

"Our son doesn't know what he wants. You saw him. For God's sake, he just wet himself. You don't have kids—you don't know. Sometimes you have to make decisions without them."

In my esteem as a nonparent, this was a hot fudge sundae of bullshit. I'd rescued my share of injured children, where their negligent moms and dads excused themselves with, "You don't have kids, do you?" Gordon Ostrowski had married into my family and told others he was my father. "In my experience, not every parent makes the right choices. Not everyone deserves to be a parent."

"Let's try this out a different way," urged Tesmer, tapping her skills in argument construction. "Kali, why do you do what you do?"

"She means, why do you kill people?" Leland clarified.

I'd already thought through this plenty. I wouldn't have committed to this work without knowing why I was doing it. "I remove suffering."

"You're obviously not a Buddhist," said Leland. "The Dalai Lama himself would argue that suffering is inevitable. Part of the challenge of life is coping with that suffering."

Christ on a crumpet. They were going to beat me down with logic.

"Then the D.L. and I have a divergence of opinions. I never said I speak for everyone. Just myself and the people who want to end their suffering."

"You're comfortable with the idea that death is inevitable."

"Of course I am. You'd have to be delusional not to be."

Tesmer argued, "If we're going to die anyway, and you're comfortable ending lives, how much of a stretch is it to extend this to someone who deserves to die, thereby easing the suffering of the families involved?" She was trying to corner me. I could see how she'd make a good attorney.

"It's the difference between mercy killing and vigilantism. My clients ask for it."

Leland weighed in. "Do you believe that some people deserve to die?" Like a professional wrestling duo, the Moons played off each other well. In my imagination I outfitted them both with colorful Lucha Libre masks.

"Yes, but I'm not the person to give it to them."

"What about Gordon Ostrowski?"

I puckered. "Even him."

"Why not?"

"Because it would make me as awful as him. It's the difference between compassion and execution. If you can't see that, you really don't understand what I do." I finished my beer and squint-eyed through the bottleneck as if it were a telescope.

Leland stood. "Let me show you something." He walked toward the kitchen.

Tesmer took a hold of the gun, but didn't point it at me. "Come on," she said. This was not a suggestion.

Overly bright lights weren't kind to the kitchen. The fixtures needed updating and the linoleum blistered. Across the room, a door led to a dark descending staircase.

Leland noted, "It's rare to have a basement in Berkeley. Not unicorn rare, but pretty uncommon."

"There's no way I'm going down to that basement with you."

Tesmer switched the lights onto a carpeted floor. Not as foreboding as cracked concrete, but not inviting either. "There's nothing bad down there." She saw I was afraid. "We're not monsters. We're not Helena and Walter."

Leland corrected. "We may decide to destroy you. But if we did, we wouldn't do it like this."

I walked downstairs with the Moons following me. If not aimed at my back, Tesmer's gun was pointed vaguely in my direction from behind. The wood moaned with weight. I involuntarily shivered.

At one point, the Moon's basement had been refinished as a family room. A couch and bookcases abutted shabby oak veneer walls. Its current state looked as if angry robots had gone wild.

Holes ripped through the walls. The paneling had been punched by something toothy, possibly a hammer claw, exposing the studs. Dust settled on the furniture, and scraps of drywall and insulation scattered across the rug. Mildew spores clogged the air.

Up in the kitchen, dog toenails skittered across the linoleum. Apparently bored with Veda, Emmanuel ran to join us. He appeared at the top of the staircase, but he wouldn't come down. Possibly it didn't feel safe to him.

Leland gestured to the debris. "When Veda first went missing, we didn't know what happened. He didn't come home, and we thought he'd been hurt—maybe he'd wandered out with friends and there was an accident. But when enough time went by, we knew someone took him. I thought it was revenge. There had been someone I'd arrested, or someone Tesmer put away, and this was plain old vendetta. But if that were true, someone would have rubbed our faces in it. There was no 'I gotcha' note, no ransom demand. No contact of any kind. And that's when we really started to worry."

Tesmer picked up where her husband left off. "This was still early into the abduction. A couple of months in, our neighbors started looking at us funny. Our minister thought it would be a good idea if we took some time off from services." She touched her husband's arm. "Leland had problems at work."

"Let's not go there," he said.

"No," Tesmer corrected. "Let's tell her everything. He had problems at work. Colleagues wondered about him—about both of us. Same with me. Friends stopped being friends."

Leland said, "The agency eventually found a suspect. Guy in his early twenties who was a dog walker. He was sketchy, but he wasn't the guy. When I got him alone, I was a little hard on him." Knowing Leland, I guessed this was an understatement. At his most docile, I imagined a smashed nose, possibly a few bent fingers. "They didn't let me alone with suspects for a while—any suspects, on any cases. I ended up taking a little time off. Paid time off, but humiliating just the same."

Tesmer drove the message home. "We had a lot of time at home. Time we avoided going out. And we started wondering more seriously if we should be looking for a body. We knew other cases where they'd found the child's body right in the house. So we started down here. Ripped the hell out of it. Take a good look." Now I was compelled to peek into the walls to see how far they'd gotten. "When a child gets taken, the whole family goes down."

I walked around the basement to observe how their shame and frustration had manifested in the destruction of their own home. Veda had been back for a long time. They could have cleaned this up, but they lacked either the desire or the money. They'd even painted the outside to keep up appearances, but vaulted the basement away. They didn't even change all the lights. I counted two burned-out bulbs. They'd sealed off the place tight as the tombs in Luxor.

"I'd like to trade," said Leland.

"I'm not killing Helena Mumm for you." Down there in an intimate cluster with two armed adversaries, I felt threatened. But more than the threat, the pervading energy down there was death. Even if no body had been recovered, the room reeked with mortal corrosion. That repulsion from death made me defiant.

"This is a new trade."

"Does it involve killing anyone?"

Tesmer shook her head, and Leland said, "It does not. If you make this trade, all will be forgiven. You can walk out of our lives with no recourse."

"All will be forgiven," Tesmer agreed. This implied that the Moons would pardon me, but that they had done nothing that might need forgiveness themselves. Kidnapping, torture, stalking, or threatening Jeffrey apparently did not necessitate forgiveness.

"This is a good deal for you," Leland offered. "That sex offender record? Wiped clean."

"I'm not a sex offender," I reminded. "I don't have a record."

"Whatever," he dismissed. "It will all be gone. You'll be free."

By now I'd gotten used to the dim lights down there. My boxing gym had the same shadowy corners. I didn't want to be there, but

I didn't want to seem intimidated. I sauntered to the couch with the ripped cushions and sat down. "Whatever this is, it isn't noble. You're still extorting another human being for your own gain."

Tesmer urged, "Take the trade. You won't have a criminal record. You won't go to jail."

They had no clue how much this dehumanized me. So I decided to inflame them by trying out another argument. "Are you protecting yourselves by trying to use me, or is it that you just can't do the job yourselves?"

This got to both of them. Leland said, "You think I lack the capacity?"

"Maybe the FBI's not all it's cracked up to be if you need to outsource."

With hands on hips, Leland shook his head in irritation. "You think you have what it takes to get into *my* club? Do you know what the bureau requires?"

Tesmer tried to calm down her husband. "She's trying to rile you."

Too late. I kept pushing him. "The bureau requires high moral standards. Bunch of goody two-shoes."

"We're not as good as you think," he said.

"Clearly. But you do have moral standards to live up to. And that means you can't do whatever it is you want me to do to Helena Mumm." For once, Leland had no response. Husband and wife traded frustrated looks. I'd stalemated them. "That also means that you weren't supposed to handcuff me to your bed and torture me for a day." That sounded ugly. Tesmer shot him a dirty glance— he probably hadn't divulged the full details of what took place in Clayton. I would use that to pit them against each other.

"I didn't torture you."

"You pepper sprayed me."

"You attacked me!" he steamed. Upstairs, boards creaked where Veda shifted his weight. Their son was listening to us.

"When you sent me to kill Helena Mumm, you talked about us reaching a détente. I think you said we'd be bonded together by mutually assured destruction, because we'd be equally culpable for the same crime."

"But that crime never happened," he said.

"But other crimes happened." I flashed him my wrists. "I go into the bureau and shoot off my mouth, you'll lose as much as me. Aside from the kidnapping—"

"Detainment—"

"You endangered me by sending me unarmed into the home of a convicted murderer, telling me she was your sister."

For some reason he laughed. "How did you think that woman was my sister, anyway? That's racist as hell! Do you really think we look anything alike? You put us together side by side, and we make the number ten."

I refused to let him steer me off course. "If this goes any further, you'll lose as much as me."

"Not as much," Tesmer said.

"Quite right," Leland said. "Only one of the three of us would ever see the inside of prison. And for you, those are murder charges. Serious business. And if you press us, be sure we'll press back. Because the two of us are as vengeful as the Old Testament."

I thought back to how I felt chained to that bed. They had a point. Maybe my cockiness was unfounded. They weren't going to let me walk out of there. Not without giving them something.

"I'm not killing Helena for you."

"That's not the trade. It wouldn't involve killing anyone." He and Tesmer traded a sidelong glance, appreciating each other. Knowing they had my ear. "Here's the trade. Show me your world, and I'll show you mine."

"I don't get it."

"That's the trade. We understand each other."

"I still don't get it. What do you want me to do?"

"Let's not even call it a trade. Let's call it a gentleman's bet." He threw up his hands like a coach trying to keep me from stealing a base. "You give me a day in your shoes. I'll give you a day in mine."

"A day in each other's shoes."

"I'll *bet* if we do that, we'll understand each other. And if we *understand* each other, you'll want to help us. But if we spend that day and you still don't want to help us, you're off the hook."

"What do you mean by a day in my shoes?"

"I come with you to see one of your patients."

I reacted. "No fucking way. Absolutely not."

"It's a fair trade. Show me your work, and I'll show you mine."

"Why the hell would you want to do that?"

Tesmer looked curious as well. This might have been unscripted. *Ah, the delights of improv.*

He said, "Because we can't do what we need to do without outside help. And the only shot at getting you on our side is for us to understand each other. This is me grasping, as a desperate parent."

"But I told you I'm not going to kill Helena."

"That's not part of the plan. It never was." I waited for him to explain more, but he didn't. If I asked, it would only open us up to more dialogue, and I wanted this to end.

"You're tied into the FBI. You must have a network of friends who could help."

He pleaded with the weakness of a hungry man. "Didn't you hear me? They didn't trust me when Veda was taken."

"But Veda came back."

"And when he came back, they treated me like I was cursed. I may not have killed my boy, but something rotten clung to me, and no one else wanted anything to do with it, or us. This family is tainted." He gritted his teeth. "No one at work is going to help."

A thousand reasons might have prohibited me from bringing Leland to see a client. The most important was that I didn't want him to make someone who was already suffering even more uncomfortable. But what I told him was, "You'd be an accomplice if you came with me."

"I could live with that."

"Honey," Tesmer insisted, "This is a bad idea." She had expected Leland to offer a different kind of trade.

Leland's grandeur had diminished in a just a few minutes.

Now deflated, he fought to keep me interested. Like they'd gone to everyone one else and finally came to me. I was his last chance. Leland might not have idiopathic pulmonary fibrosis, but he lived with his own suffering, and my inclination to help those who suffered kept me from shutting down our conversation, even if I hated him.

"In return, you visit someone with me," he said.

I asked, "Who would I have to visit?"

"I'll tell you later." A few weeks ago, this statement would have been a coy remark. Now he was trying not to scare me off. "But it will just be a visit. I won't expect you to do anything other than accompany me. That I promise you."

Not sure why this occurred to me, but after the spider package, I considered what else they might do to terrify me. "You're not going to make me visit Gordon Ostrowski, are you? Because I'll walk the fuck out right now, and you can decide whether you want to shoot me in the back."

"No," Leland insisted. "You won't have to see Gordon."

Alcohol streamed in my blood. I felt my jaw loosen up, my cheeks blushed the way they always do when I drink. Tesmer's face, shaded under the basement lights, sagged sadly the same way Leland's had. I'd railed against their bullying, and now they'd gotten to me with their hopelessness. All we were talking about was a trade—a visit for a visit. A day in each other's shoes.

"What happens if I agree?" I asked.

"Afterward, if you still don't want to help us, you'll never see us again."

"My sex offender profile?"

"Gone like you woke up from a bad dream. If, and only if, you see it through."

Something moved into the doorway at the top of the stairs. Emmanuel's collar jingled. Veda stood up there. From the couch, I could only see his shadow stretch down the staircase. But because of the way his parents looked up at him, I stood to glimpse whatever struck them.

"The walls are thin. I can hear you talking about me," Veda said.

He wore a towel around his waist and nothing else. I saw more similarities between him and his father. The tight, wiry muscles imitated his father's build, but seemed healthier on the younger Moon. Framed by the doorway, Veda reminded me of when Leland came out of the bathroom in Clayton, towel wrapped and freshly showered. For every compulsion I had to help this family, more things came up that repelled me.

I thought Veda might have been blacking out, standing there in some sort of waking sleep, but his face seemed to say that the show was intentional and meant for me. He ignored his parents and addressed me. "You want to know what you're getting into? Take a look."

He turned to show us his back. I'll admit I shuddered. Not that it was profoundly worse than some of what I'd seen in the ambulance, but it surprised me. From his shoulders down to where the towel cloaked his waist, he was marred with the same punctures I'd seen on Cindy Coates. Sets of four dots in Braille. There had to be more than twenty sets on his trunk. The kitchen lights glossed his back so we could see them in full relief, like little mountain ranges dotting his back. After a few moments, he disappeared from the doorway and left us to continue our talk.

CHAPTER 10

There's an association for anything, if you have an interest. I'm sure if I were obsessed with bending pipe cleaners into miniature grasshopper sculptures, I could find enough like-minded folks out there to form our own club, maybe even an online magazine. For something like euthanasia, the United States has any number of organizations. I found Jeffrey Holt and Gifts of Deliverance largely because he was the most thoughtful. The most fearless. When I had the gumption, I attended a book signing when he came to San Francisco. He could have written me off as a kook, but he invited me to eat with him at an oyster bar.

Jeffrey Holt was a wizard at empathy. Hence, he was easy to talk to. I told him about my paramedic work and why it interested me in his organization. There's an expression, "No one ever dies in an ambulance." That's because it takes a doctor to officially call a time of death, and there's never a doctor riding with you in the rig. So even if your heart gives out in the ambulance, official records will state that you died at the hospital. I'd seen enough people suffering in the vehicle that I often considered the legal gray areas of death, and the morality of ending suffering for those who wanted it. Jeffrey had said, "You can't judge this work based on *my* morality, but whether you think you're doing the right thing by your patient." I tried to keep this in mind as I rode next to a federal agent, remembering that the day's visit wasn't about Leland's approval of my work, but bringing peace to the woman who requested it.

We drove in the junky blue car Jeffrey Holt had loaned me via some generous member of the Gifts of Deliverance network. No power windows on this baby. Leland had to roll his down so the wind could break over his sunglasses. He looked blissful in the breeze. He might as well have flopped his tongue around like Emmanuel, who was still at the Moons' house.

It was a costume day. This time it was a blond Marilyn wig and a leopard-print dress. The faint smears of my parents' ashes were applied just above my left and right breasts, thus undetectable in this outfit. Leland laughed when he saw me, but my costume made sense for Beatrix, a former model. She'd moved to the States from France in the 60s, and in vintage photos she might have been Brigitte Bardot's cousin. My ensemble was an homage to her glory years. Leland, on the other hand, looked like Leland. He dressed in a black suit like an undertaker. Only he didn't wear a tie that day.

We talked to fill time, but the conversation was uneasy. The two of us didn't like each other. My sex offender profile was still out there for the world to see, and he seemed to enjoy lording the threat of incarceration over me. It was hard to like someone in that position. Out of boredom, I steered us into talking about Veda's abduction and he divulged more. "When we first figured out someone had taken Veda, we came across someone we thought was the guy."

My voice didn't carry like his. Because of the wind through the window I had to shout. "The dog walker."

"A guy named Hamilton Berle. You think dog walker, you usually think of some college kid, but that wasn't this guy. He was on parole for a liquor store robbery in Bayview. Things got ugly, and he shot the owner in the neck and nearly killed him. He had sleeve tattoos on both arms. When I questioned him, he spat at me. Hit me here," he dabbed the corner of his mouth. "Anyway, that's why I hit him. I don't normally mistreat suspects."

"You mistreated me."

"I only hurt you when you attacked me."

"You drugged me and you humiliated me."

"I thought you were a bad person." Maybe he felt bad about Clayton. I couldn't say for sure. Like his son, he masked his emotions well.

"And now?"

"I think you might be doing work that I don't fully understand."

"That's an improvement." A teal ambulance passed us on the left. No sirens, but it was close, hugging a bend in the highway inches away from us. This made me think about medical calls, then Kali's client calls, and hence the gravity of what we were doing. "We have to set some ground rules."

He shouted back through the wind, "Fair enough. You want me to be quiet? Like your manservant?"

"I don't want you to be with me at all," I reminded him. "But if you have to be, I want you to be an observer. But don't be a mute. That would creep her out."

"So what do I do?"

"Just be respectful."

"I can do that."

"I haven't seen it yet."

We undulated through the central valley where it gets hot enough to fry bacon on the pavement. More torrid than Mount Diablo. Passing through unambitious brown hills, we cut through the windmills—not the cute Dutch kind, but the industrial turbine kind that looked like Victor Frankenstein had stitched together monsters from airplane parts. The air conditioning was on, but in this junkbox auto it merely generated a hint of chill. Inuit breath. The open window didn't help much. The baked air felt like it was blowing out of a cracked oven door.

Two days had passed since my dinner at the Moons. I'd gone back to my apartment in Bernal, but I didn't feel safe in it. Drawers had been opened, clothing shuffled, and I had the sense that Leland had rummaged through all of my personal items. Leland allowed me to get to the bank, so I could access my own money again. But every other part of my life was still in flux. Jeffrey Holt hadn't been in touch, and I wish he'd phoned. I wanted to tell him that his family and the organization were safe, or they would be once the Moons and I had completed our trade. But mostly I wanted a friendly voice, someone to make me feel less alone in all of this.

I found a radio station that played loud guitars over tribal beats, but Leland kept turning down the music. "It's too hard for me," he complained. "And it's the volume you'd use to extract a dictator out of a church."

"Fuck, you're old."

"Getting up there. Maybe in a year or two you'll make me a client."

He'd noted the ambulance ahead of us now. "Given what happened with your mom, I assumed you'd seen EMTs at the fire and that's what drove you into the work. But it didn't happen like that, because you weren't there for the fire."

I looked at him with a squinty disapproval. "What's your point?"

"Just trying to figure you out. Before the fire, what made you run away?"

It wasn't easy to talk about, but I'd already confessed the most shameful parts of the story days ago. I was so elated by the prospect of completing our trade and getting Leland Moon out of my life, I didn't rankle at talking about my mom now. We had to talk about something, and it would make the ride go by faster. I rattled off details. "Gordon burned most of my clothes. He cleaned out my closet and heaped them all in the fireplace and doused everything with lighter fluid."

I hadn't told the police this fact, but it came up in the trial. I couldn't tell if Leland had researched me well enough to know this. "Crazy evil," he said. "He tell you why he did it?"

"I was fourteen. I wore lipstick for the first time. Gordon told me I looked like a whore—he didn't say *whore*, he said *hooker*. Anyway, I refused to wipe it off. To teach me a lesson, he torched my clothes. Since I was becoming a woman, he said I wouldn't need my baby clothes anymore."

"Remind me, how much time did they give him?"

"He's serving life plus two hundred and fifty-seven years in San Sebastián. But you know that."

"So, after he set your clothes on fire, you took off."

"I packed a duffel. I tried to convince my mom to come with

me. She was afraid to leave him."

"She was afraid *of* him," he suggested.

"Probably," I considered. "Same result either way."

"You think that the house got burned down *because* you left."

"Gordon was unpredictable every day. But he'd never done anything that catastrophic. I'm sure I was the catalyst for it."

"You think it was your fault he killed your mom."

"I go back and forth on how much guilt I'm willing to accept over it. Some days I do. Some days I think he was just some crazy fuck. Like locusts. Like an act of God." The guilt he was talking about was part of a more complex web of fears. Gordon hadn't just given me grief and shame. He gave me the sense that everything could be taken from me at any time, if I only took my eyes off it for a moment.

"I wasn't asking a question. I'm telling you. You think it was your fault he killed your mom. I can hear it in you." He removed his sunglasses and stared at me until I looked back. "You can't take credit for someone else's crime." This was turning into therapy. "Were you ever afraid of fires?"

"Maybe a little more than the next person."

"Joining the fire department. Did that help?"

"It helped me control the fear." I was sick of talking about myself. "Why did you become a federal agent?"

"To prove that I could. To prove that I was good enough, strong enough. Sound familiar?"

I slowed down as we drove through a small town with a burger drive-in and a worn-wood truss tower windmill, the caveman version of the shiny white giants we'd passed on the way here.

"Think of a name you want to use when we get there."

"Are there going to be any other people there? Family or friends?"

"It will just be her," I said.

"Then what does it matter what name I use?"

"Do we really have to cover the benefits of anonymity?"

He assured me, "I'll think of something. You want me to do

anything useful while I'm there?"

I thought aloud, "I've never done this with anyone before. Just try not to distract me."

He was already distracting me. I felt like if I didn't fill the vacant spaces with conversation, Leland would keep prying into my personal history. Whatever would become of our trade, I still didn't trust him. I asked, "Has Veda ever tried to live on his own?"

"A few times. It didn't work out well. He lived with roommates, but he gets night terrors, and the screaming doesn't go over too well with other people. We tried to subsidize him when he looked for his own place, but he couldn't sleep alone. Afraid of home invasions. The tiniest little creak can set him off."

"Does he see someone?"

"A shrink? Of course he does. We have a PTSD expert who specializes in kidnap victims. Why do you think we haven't gotten a new fridge and our basement looks like a wrestling ring? All the money goes to our son." To his credit, I didn't detect any resentment in his voice. "You can't just cure something like this. It stays with you—you know that. You still think about Gordon Ostrowski."

I didn't appreciate him throwing my stepfather back in my face. "I do, but I still have my own apartment."

"Different people heal in different ways." Now Leland squirmed. We were digging too deeply into his family. He redirected back to me. "Are most of your clients women?"

"They skew female. Why?"

"Just wondering." He stared into the wind. "Men die sooner, so it makes sense there would be more women out there on their own. Men are more likely to kill themselves, so they might be less likely to seek out your services." I remembered the scars on Veda's wrists. Suicide was probably top of mind in the Moon family. He wondered, "Why don't your clients just kill themselves?"

"A lot of people decide to go that way," I noted.

"I know. But your clients don't. Why don't they?"

"The person we're meeting today is Catholic. It's against her faith."

"What if you don't have religion?"

"A lot of my clients are afraid. They're going to die, and that fear of death brings up other fears. They're afraid it'll hurt and afraid they might do it wrong on their own."

"You ever try to stop someone from killing themselves?" I thought about the scars on Veda's wrists and wondered for a moment if he was thinking about his son as well.

"I have, yes."

"What do you tell them?"

"I listen to them. I pay attention to what they're telling me. Many of them are lonely and want to make a human connection. They want to be heard. I remind them what they have to live for. Then I refer them to people better equipped than I am to heal that kind of suffering."

He processed this and moved on. "Who are we going to see today?"

"Her name is Beatrix LaCroix. She's seventy-eight, and she has lung cancer." She had reached out to me through the Gifts of Deliverance network. Because of my limited access to e-mail in the past few weeks, I'd initially met with her but then dropped contact. Lucky for me, she was still waiting when I got back on my computer.

"French, right? I thought those people lived forever."

"Not the ones who smoke." That came out meaner than I'd meant it. "That's not even what's killing her. She's only at stage two. She also has Waldenstrom's disease."

"Sounds like you made that up."

"Bone marrow cancer. When it rains it pours. The illness exterminates leukocytes—white blood cells. She's had blood transfusions, but it's past the point where they'd be any help. In a few months she'll die from influenza or another common infection."

"You talk to the doctor this time to make sure this is all on the level?"

I frowned, but had no rebuttal. "I met with the doctor and the family weeks ago. They wanted her to come home to France. They just passed a law that allows physicians to accelerate death for the terminally ill. She'd get what she wants without having to skirt the law."

"Why doesn't she just—"

"She's not strong enough to travel."

Beatrix LaCroix lived in a shoddy apartment complex yellowed by flaking paint. Unattended vines tangled up the side like a squid fighting a sperm whale. When we parked, the wind stream waned, and we humidified. Under my wig, sweat beaded up in moments. Leland's demeanor changed. He adopted a precise, manicured sense of respect, like a mannequin come to life. Maybe this was how he held himself at the FBI field office. "Do you want to go in first?"

"She knows you're coming. You think I wouldn't tell the client I'd have company?"

He'd given me back my brown aviator satchel, and I gathered it under my arm while we paced briskly to the door. Since I was in costume, I wanted to get off the street as soon as we could. Beatrix kept her key above the doorframe, and I let myself in. She waited for us in a dark bedroom.

She was a tiny peanut swaddled in an old pink quilt. She didn't like the sunlight and kept the blinds drawn. A gold-framed portrait of Jesus hung over her bed, anemic with a long horse face. The opposite wall displayed a crucifix made from intertwined driftwood. She rasped, "Kali."

"Hi, Beatrix."

She wore her white hair in a pixie cut. The pillow matted it to the side, making her look Reaganesque. A photo on the dresser showed her in her twenties; back when she looked like Bardot. The oversaturated Kodachrome burst with orange and pink, with Beatrix dressed in a mod skirt that showed off her knees. Back then, before she moved to the States, she had milky skin. After decades of American beaches, she had turned the color of bourbon.

Beatrix never remarried after her husband, Henri, passed away. That was nine years ago. She lost her house, and lived in the apartment because she didn't want to move in with her son or go back to France. On the nightstand, another framed photograph showed her husband holding her tightly around the waist from behind, their cheeks touching. My favorite was a family shot: Beatrix, Henri, and three kids—two daughters and one son all under ten years old. They stacked on top of each other as if they'd just collapsed a human pyramid, everyone was laughing. I met the family three weeks ago when they flew into town, and only the eldest smiled at me to convey gratitude.

"Who's that?" Beatrix cooed. Leland loomed behind me but clammed up, which I imagined was an unusual show of willpower.

"Remember, I mentioned someone would be coming with me?" I had told Beatrix and her family that I'd be bringing an associate. As I've mentioned, the amount of people can vary during a final visit, and since none of my clients or their families had ever been through a terminus before, they believed me when I told them the process worked better with two people.

"What is your name?" she asked the federal agent. When she got agitated, her homeland accent came out. Beatrix turned *is* into *ease*.

"My name's Malcolm, Mrs. LaCroix," he said. I swear I wanted to smack him.

"What do you do that she doesn't?" Beatrix was sharper-toned than when we'd last met. The stranger in her house stirred up something.

Admittedly, it satisfied me to see Leland squirm for a change. Beatrix drew the quilt toward her chin, perhaps questioning whether to go through with it. If she canceled, I'd be fine with it. It would show Leland that he was a fool and prove that I wasn't reckless. If Beatrix really wanted my help, I could come back another day.

"I help with spiritual matters." You wouldn't think a line like that would go over, but Leland was earnest and respectful in a way he'd never acted toward me. He stepped around me and motioned to an empty chair by her bed. "May I?"

"Yes," she said. "Are you a priest?"

Leland sat. "A priest wouldn't be allowed to be here." He picked up the Bible that sat on her nightstand. "I thought we might pray while Kali got ready. Would you like that?"

Fucking stones on this guy. But Beatrix brightened. And Leland was warm, as warm to this frail woman as he was to his son. I was seeing a different man. Beatrix responded well, lowering her quilt. He placed one of his large hands over her petite ones and asked, "Are you cold?"

"Not now," she said.

When my clients prayed, I bowed my head, but I couldn't pray with them. You can't fake faith, and I thought it would have been disrespectful to try.

"Let's get you comfortable. Beatrix, are you ready for this?" he asked.

"I am. I want this." She was physically weak, but vigilant. Leland nodded to acknowledge her wishes.

"Then let's pray." He closed his eyes. Beatrix did the same. He murmured the Lord's Prayer. Even a nonchurchgoer like me knew that chestnut by heart. "Our Father which art in Heaven. Hallowed be thy name…" If you've ever been in a church, odds are you know the rest. Both of them chorused the recitation in earnest. I confess this might have been the first time I'd paid attention to the words. Leland spoke as if he'd written the words himself. She closed her eyes and held tightly onto his hand, maybe hoping she could sleepily ease into the afterworld just by following his voice.

All of this was off script, so I should have been outraged. But it worked. He was helping her. I dug through my satchel while they prayed, slightly mesmerized myself.

When she opened her eyes to his, Leland followed. "I'd like to read something else. Something special for you, for today. Would that be all right?" Beatrix nodded, captivated. I'd never noticed before, but to the right person and under the right lighting, Leland Moon could be handsome. She gazed at him as if he were a matinee idol dipping her for a kiss. From his suit pocket he retrieved a Bible about the size of a cell phone. He'd placed a pink Post-it where he marked the section. "Revelation chapter twenty-one, verse four." He slowed down so they could both savor the words. "And God shall wipe away all tears from their eyes, and there shall be no more death, neither sorrow, nor crying, neither shall there be any more pain. For the former things are passed away." Tears formed in Beatrix's eyes, and Leland plucked a tissue from the nightstand. He dabbed her cheek, familiar as a relative.

Is it wrong to say that I felt left out? Probably. Assuredly selfish. But this was my show, and Leland had nudged me aside. He addressed me as if he was in charge, and I was the associate. "Kali?" He said it in the way a stage manager would precede. "You're on."

What was I to do but go along with it? Any tension between Leland and me would complicate the moment for Beatrix, and she was the most important person there. She had already warmed to him, and I had no selfless reason to make her more uncomfortable.

With a chair placed on the other side of the bed, Leland and I bookended our client. He had cradled her hand for some time. Gently as depositing a stray hatchling back into a nest, Leland lifted her hand and gave it to me.

I'd already explained to Beatrix how the process would work, but like other clients, she wanted me to go through it again. I tried to speak as much like a doctor as my training would allow. I would inject a high-dose barbiturate. She wanted to know details, so I told her—twenty milligrams of sodium thiopental. She would only feel the slightest pinch. Once she was asleep—I avoided using the word *coma*—I would administer a second injection, twenty milligrams of pancuronium bromide.

Leland listened keenly. If he could have taken notes without it seeming too clinical, he might have.

His tone and body language were intended to set Beatrix, and possibly me, at ease, but having him there made me self-conscious. I'd never felt like my work was immoral, but having a federal agent on the other side of the bed made me feel like I was on stage— worse yet, auditioning. Now that he'd bonded with Beatrix through prayer, he'd nullified the caretaker aspect of my role. I was here as a clinician.

When I got through my explanation, she nodded to let me know she understood. She returned her attention to Leland, and he assured her, "We'll get through this together. And he'll be waiting for you." Jesus or Henri—it didn't matter. Maybe both.

Beatrix kept a tight grip on Leland's hand while I prepared the syringe, and they silently prayed together with their eyes shut. I cradled her other arm, and beyond a mild flinch when the needle went in, she remained calm. Leland stayed still with her, respecting the solemnity of the moment. He held her hand firmly. His face grieved for her. With me holding one arm and he the other, I felt strangely connected to him. When her chin rolled to one side, I told him, "She's asleep," while I prepared the second needle. He could have said something, but he only gave the slightest nod. I inserted the second needle and depressed the plunger.

Together we felt the slight tremble when she passed. Only then did Leland open his eyes. He kissed her hand softly.

CHAPTER 11

One day later, I went with Leland on our second visit, the flip side of the trade. This time Leland drove in the family car, a decade-old cream SUV. Tesmer usually sat in the passenger seat, and I pushed back my seat so my knees wouldn't bang against the glove compartment.

I didn't know where we were going, but we ghosted through the Richmond Bridge toll plaza toward Marin County. Like a long, lazy roller coaster, the snaky span rolled over the water. Mild salty air breezed through the window—Leland's open, mine closed. The hills were green most of the year, but without much rain in the summer, by the fall the straw grass colored the slopes beige as a Labrador retriever.

At Leland's request, I dressed in a suit. He told me to look professional. "Office professional," he'd put it. That meant light makeup and no wigs. Leland dressed in a suit himself, even thought it was Sunday, and he even wore a tie. Suits on a weekend made me think about church, and that reminded me of Leland's prayer with Beatrix.

"I didn't know you were religious," I said.

"Most of the country is."

"You didn't strike me as someone with a spiritual bent."

"I guess people can surprise you." He kept his eyes on the road, his voice flat. He'd lost some zest since we visited Beatrix. Leland took no delight in taunting me that day. His manner cold, I suspected he felt he had witnessed something he considered murder and had done nothing to stop it. And he wasn't saying anything about it now because he still wanted my help and didn't want to disrupt the deal by arguing.

I wasn't looking forward to whatever this trip was going to be, but at least we were getting it over with. Wherever we were going, we'd be finished by the end of the day. He'd have seen my world, and I would have seen his, and that would be the end of it. Still, the tension in the car was stifling. I could have just kept quiet, but that unquenchable caretaker impulse got the better of me. Even with Leland. When I saw someone that visibly upset, I couldn't help but try and comfort him.

I asked, "Is something wrong?"

"Something more than usual?"

"Did I do something wrong?"

"You're really asking a federal agent if you've done something wrong?"

"Our last meeting made you uncomfortable."

"You think?"

Kali had attended clients for four years now. The process seemed natural. But to Leland it was new. He had attended his first terminus just the day before. I imagined back when it was new for me, the discomfort I felt, even for someone who was emotionally disposed to this work. I'd puked a few times after some clients' final visits, and sometimes drank myself into tequila bed spins—which meant more puking. I understood why even a seasoned agent like Leland Moon would have been morose. He couldn't have been shocked by death itself, but he hadn't seen death like that. A newcomer might confuse clinical precision with a lack of humanity.

I tried to put him at ease. "You comforted her. That was good. The prayer helped her."

"Glad I could help." He was as tetchy as his son.

"You asked to come."

"I know I did."

"Beatrix was suffering."

"Someone who's starving will take whatever food you give her, even if it's poisoned."

A part of me wanted to ask, "What the hell did you expect? Rainbows and gummy bears?" But there was only so much I could antagonize him. With our trade near completion, there was no need to stir things up now. Fortunately, the way the wind came into the car and made conch shells of our ears, we didn't have as much silence to fill.

To our left Alcatraz stood marooned in the water. I'd toured the prison long ago and seen how small the cells were. Thinking of it now, I wondered about what my life might be like in prison.

"Why aren't you telling me where we're going?"

"You'll find out soon enough."

On the other side of the bridge, we turned through dusty hills until we came to a chain link fence topped with a coil of razor wire. Beyond it stood a compound of uniform white buildings. As the chain link fence wrapped around the compound, it led into a high concrete wall that separated the buildings from the water. We were at a prison. "This is San Sebastián," I said.

The impulse to burst out my door would mean rolling on the pavement. Even if I survived the spill out onto the highway, a car rounding the bend in the opposite direction could plow into me. Poof! I'd be gone like Dad. I couldn't see any guards yet, but I imagined them. Law enforcement types, barrel chests in uniforms straight off of a propaganda poster. I imagined the tight rows of cells in there, and imagined one particular cell, where a familiar figure lay atop a charcoal wool blanket, his blond hair still immaculately coiffed.

He slowed the car down as we approached the entry gate, and I unlatched my seatbelt and lunged for the door handle. Leland seized my wrist, right where the cuffs had gone. "Don't be stupid. I'm not arresting you. This wouldn't even be the place to do it. I've had every opportunity to bust you and I haven't. Look at me." Catching myself after a moment of paralysis, I wrenched my arm free. "This is not why we're here."

I was certainly thinking about captivity, but not mine. "Gordon Ostrowski is here." He would always be here. When he died, they would bury him in the prison graveyard with a numbered marker.

"I told you that wouldn't be part of the deal. I'm not seeing him."

"We're not here for Gordon. He won't know you were ever here."

"I don't believe you." I jostled the door handle.

Leland threw the car into park and pulled his gun out of his holster. I should have grappled. That's what they teach you in self-defense. Charge a gun, run from a knife. But in the moment I froze, considering the potential canon boom of a gun in a tight steel box, the likelihood of shattered windows and ricochets. The bullet might zing around and rip through us both. Before I could properly react, he handed it to me, grip first. "Kill me if I'm lying." I took it from him and held it like a live grenade. Leland waited for a reaction. Daintily, I drew my seatbelt back across my chest and fastened it.

"We're here to see Walter Gretsch." Of course that's why we were there. I'd been too self-involved to remember who else was locked inside the facility. Not that I wanted to be there anymore now, but my fingers released the door handle.

"Don't let the guard see it." We drove around the chain link fence while I dropped the gun in the glove compartment. We arrived at a checkpoint. Through the windshield, I saw an armed guard step out of the booth. He was in his mid-twenties—my age—and his full black beard reminded me of a young Fidel Castro.

When he rolled down his window, the guard joked, "Lost?" Leland flashed his badge. It didn't earn any smiles, but within a few moments the white picket barrier lifted and we entered the compound. A small sense of suffocation squeezed my lungs once the fence was behind us.

The inner compound looked like the worst miniature golf course I'd ever seen. They'd built the sniper tower to resemble a small lighthouse. I couldn't see any guards up there, but bullhorns crowned the top. The main entrance reminded me of a medieval castle, but faced in stucco, complete with peaked cathedral windows and a flat rooftop with crenellations, originally designed for archers. The paint on all of it was the color of bird shit, but occasionally the paint and plaster flaked off to reveal brick. Instead of guards patrolling the rooftops, swiveling cameras perched like crows on every building, watching us from every angle.

"You know why they call it San Sebastián?" Leland asked.

I thought about the guys in the department who regaled me with stories about California history. You go on enough rides with them, you pick up something. "I assume there was a Mission San Sebastián here at some point."

"You're almost correct. There was a Spanish mission here, but it was Mission San Ramon. It was renamed. In the early 1800s, let's say 1830 or so, there was an *alcade*—that's a mayor—up here named…" he had to come up with it, "Fermín Rubio. He was a friar, but he also got saddled with running the politics. He was the local magistrate—that's what guys like that did. Anyway, other than a random assortment of settlers, he was close with the indigenous locals, the Miwok tribe. Got to pick up some of the customs. He was good with a bow and arrow, so good the chief gave him a bow covered in snakeskin. You understand, this was a good gift—he was on good terms with everybody. But then Rubio's own people had to go and screw it all up. Mexico was newly independent, and local Mexican rancheros were kidnapping Miwoks to work on their ranches. Sometimes they'd just slaughter a whole bunch so the rest wouldn't resist. To sort it out, Fermín Rubio found these people, and when he did, he executed them. He'd sworn off guns, but he was handy with a bow, so he would strap the victim to a tree, this tree," he pointed to a gnarled oak by the front gate, with a thick trunk and twisted branches, "and plug him full of arrows."

"Just like Saint Sebastian." We passed the tree and cut through rows of cars in the parking lot as we drove toward the main entrance.

"Till he looked like a sea urchin. So Rubio renamed the mission to send a warning out to the criminals. Given the history of the place, eventually it turned into a prison." He pointed to the crenellations by the roof. "The architect that built the new building in the 1920s designed those as a nod to Rubio, a set of nooks where archers could mete out the traditional sentence for a criminal nasty enough to deserve it."

Two guards waited for us by a parking space that had been kept vacant with orange cones. One of the men waved at Leland as we pulled in. They were huge, bigger than the bearded guard at the gate. Their uniforms were short-sleeve beige tops with forest green pants and gold badges over the left chest, something I'd expect to see on park rangers. Both had smooth faces and shaved heads. In some history class I'd learned that Alexander the Great banned beards in his army so that enemy combatants couldn't tug them in battle. In the chaos of a prison riot, I supposed it would pay to be clean-shaven. More massive and less defined then the boys I worked with at the fire department, they might have been former football players, former semiprofessional wrestlers, or former bouncers. Their overly serious expressions had the bottomless gaze of sharks cruising for fish.

When we stopped, Leland reminded me, "It can't stay in the glove compartment." With no holster and no purse, I had no place to keep his gun on my person, so I opened the glove compartment and gave Leland's pistol back to him. Watching us through the window, the guards looked confused as Leland reholstered his sidearm.

The one by the driver's side shook Leland's hand when he emerged from the car. "Took you long enough." He had the slightest trace of a Southern accent, rare in the Bay Area. Either he'd been here long enough or practiced long enough that I only heard it in the extended vowels.

Leland gestured to me. "This is she." To me, he explained, "Meet Leonard Royce and Milton Kearns." Royce was the one who knew Leland. He stood an inch taller than Kearns with thicker arms. Kearns loitered behind him like a kid brother. Both had shiny scalps, but Royce would have been mostly bald anyway. Kearns might age that way. Both nodded at me, but neither offered to shake my hand, maybe worried if they stuck out an arm I might jab a needle into it.

Royce said to Leland, "You know Helena Mumm was here this morning, paying him a visit."

"That's news, but doesn't surprise me. She probably wants to see him before her time is finally up." Leland said to me, "Maybe someone reignited the old flame. Wrong love is still love." I tried to remember what I had said to Helena.

Royce handed me a laminated identification card with my photo on it. "Put this in your wallet." I barely had time to look it over before he explained, "If anyone asks, you're agent Frances Kali." Indeed, the card spelled it out in bold letters. My headshot was the same fuzzy camera-phone snapshot Leland took of me in the Clayton cabin; the same photograph he'd posted on the sex offender registry. My expression worked equally well in the role of a government employee.

The guards led us through the turreted entrance. Through two checkpoints, they talked to the guards while Leland signed us in. I flashed my fake identification a few times. Each hallway was a combination of cinder blocks, stainless steel, and the kind of glass I'd expect could fortify a shark tank. Through every door my stomach twisted a bit, especially when the sunlight vanished and the sounds from the outside faded.

We were on our way to see Walter Gretsch, but I didn't know what would happen when we saw him. What we could possibly talk about. The uncertainty made me feel as powerless as when Leland had chained me in Clayton. I could have been in a submarine at the bottom of the ocean.

Left, left, right, left, right, right…the prison interior networked into a tight labyrinth of hallways. Turning another corner, I'd gotten foggy on where we were going and simply stared at our escorts' calves. The hallways collected a lonely alkaline smell with a hint of organic compost, perhaps from the unreachable rat turds behind the walls. Leland handed me a tissue and whispered, "Wipe your forehead. You're sweating. And keep your head up. Act like you belong here." Royce gave me a dirty look over his shoulder, warning me that I might blow this, whatever it was.

I hissed at Leland, "This can't be safe."

"You've taken bigger risks. So have I."

"I'm fucking serious," I insisted. Ahead of us, Kearns shot me an anguished look to shush me. He nodded to a camera that clung to the ceiling. I kept my voice down and tried to appear calm enough so that anyone hovering over the security monitors would merely see two federal agents working through a professional disagreement. "Are you leading me through a prison block full of men?"

"I wouldn't do something like that."

Royce spoke loud enough to convey that the security cameras didn't have microphones. "We're not going through a cell block. We're headed to the courtyard." Some of the guys in the fire department had been in the military, and his clipped monotone hinted that he'd had the same training. I admit it did make me feel safer.

We abruptly stopped at the midpoint of a long corridor, dim as a mineshaft. Leland and the two guards huddled by the wall, and Royce pointed to the camera directly overhead. "We can't be seen here."

Royce seemed to loosen up. He was cordial, if not jovial. He shook my hand and avoided giving me a bone crusher. "Ma'am, thank you for coming." *Ma'am.* I'm a sucker for archaic politeness. This made me want to curtsy.

I confirmed, "Can anyone hear us?"

"No."

"No security cameras on us at all?" I wanted to be sure.

"When you get to know the compound, you learn there are a few places the cameras never see. This is one of them."

Leland relaxed a bit too, more comfortable around these guys than he ever was around me. He put on the wry grin I was used to seeing when he goaded me. "I call Leonard the convict whisperer. He has a knack for getting inmates to do what he wants without having to break anything."

So we were chitchatting now. I tried to play along. "Laws or jaws?"

Royce cracked a smile, but his tone was all business. "I listen to the inmates, so they tell me things."

"What does someone like Walter Gretsch tell you?" I asked.

"He doesn't say much. He likes to ask about my kids." I thought that Royce must hate his job some days. "He found out through the

Internet that I have two boys. He called out their names to me and commented on their swim team results. We took away his computer privileges after that."

Royce waved us forward, and we continued until we reached another steel door. Above it, a grated portal let in a grid of sunlight. "The courtyard's through there. He'll be waiting." He asked me, "Your stepfather is here, is that right?" This might have unsettled me, but he looked at me kindly. I nodded. "But you've never visited here."

"No."

"Is this your first time at a prison?"

"It is."

"And your first time with a man like Walter Gretsch."

Leland said, "You're making her nervous."

Royce asked Leland, "You're sure she's up for this?" He looked back at me. "I mean no disrespect when I say that."

"She's has a knack for adapting," Leland said.

Royce gave me an iron gaze that, when needed, probably intimidated inmates. "Remember," he cautioned, "Walter Gretsch is a dangerous man. He might come on quiet, but you'll see how bad he is if you give him a chance." He warned Leland and me. "Don't give him that chance."

When we walked out into the courtyard, everything bleached to sunburst white. In the twenty minutes we'd trolled through the concrete maze, the sun had burned off the residual fog from the morning. Cirrus streaks draped across a blue sky. Anywhere else, it would have been a nice day.

I could smell the crisp brine of the Bay water, but the prison wall, twice as tall as a basketball hoop and coated in that bird shit paint, blocked our view of the ocean. There was no getting over that thing without a rope or a ladder—a ten-finger boost wouldn't get you very far. With cellblocks around us, we found ourselves in a playa of asphalt, cracked in places for ambitious weeds.

As my eyes adjusted to the daylight, I saw chain-link fences that partitioned the open space into livestock pens. Guards in their park ranger outfits stood on the far sides of these fences and on the rooftops.

Leland scoped out the area, his flat hand an eave at his brow. The guards were mildly curious about us, but none waved. None were close enough to talk. They rested matte black weapons on their shoulders, and while two guards looked straight at the only woman there, I didn't get the sense that they took an active interest, not any more than I was interested in the flock of Canadian geese that presently flew over us.

I'd expected catcalls from the inmates, but it was quiet. There was only one inmate out there, wardrobed in a red jumpsuit.

He sat within a chain link enclosure the size of a chicken coop, chained to a steel picnic table with his back to us. A guard we hadn't met let us in with a nod. I didn't know if this guard knew Royce and Kearns, but Leland didn't speak to him. Once inside, we approached the prisoner from behind. Cuffs restricted the man's ankles and wrists. I rubbed my own pink wrists to test how tender the skin was, and they still smarted with pressure.

Walter Gretsch kept his head down. His shaggy clown hair splayed out in all directions, balding around the crown. He'd put on weight since his incarceration. At the trial he was skinny. Now his stomach folded over itself.

Leland stopped to stare at the prisoner, maybe to appreciate the man's captivity. Walter would have sensed our presence, but he didn't stir. Out of Walter's earshot, I asked Leland, "How is he still alive? Pedophiles aren't supposed to do well in prison, right?"

"He's a special case. They keep him away from the other inmates."

"If you want him dead, why don't you just release him into population? Shouldn't that take care of things?"

"It's not as easy as you'd think."

"It worked for Jeffrey Dahmer."

"Well, that's another special case. You can't just go letting people into population every day. People check. People can lose their jobs."

"Like Royce?"

"Leonard Royce is a good person, and that's about as high a

compliment as I can give someone. I don't know Kearns that well, but he seems loyal. I don't want either of them to get into trouble. They've risked their jobs just to arrange this meeting." Leland looked around the yard at the uniformed men. "I count five guards. Maybe more watching us from a window. Leonard only tells me so much about the staffing and positioning of the guards, so there could be many more watching. You see the cameras too, right?" They weren't as obvious as in the front, but several cameras perched on the roofs back here too. Leland tilted his head back to the guard who let us into the enclosure. "You want to keep your voice down for his sake, but the rest of the guards are too far away to hear anything. This is as much an intimate rendezvous as we could get, but keep in mind people are monitoring us."

I still wondered what we were going to talk about, but so much adrenaline charged through me—and not the scary kind, the exhilarating kind—that I mainly wanted to see how this would develop. If anyone was going to misbehave, it wouldn't be me. "Hypothetically, if you were to knife Walter Gretsch right now in this cage, what would happen?" There was the agitator in me acting up again.

I could tell Leland was upset by the question, but he kept smiling, possibly to assure anyone observing us that everything was peachy. "I'd be arrested, lose my job, and go to prison. You'd probably be dragged down with me."

"Would it give you peace?"

Leland looked at me incredulously. "It would not."

When we got to the picnic table, Walter Gretsch lifted his head. He didn't seem surprised to see Leland Moon, but looked at me curiously. Suspiciously. I was too *something* for him—young, white, female. Whatever it was, he withdrew from me. His face had deep frown lines around the jowls, which I remembered from his trial photos. The unhappiness he'd carried with him forever. The creases cut his face the way Hanna-Barbera had outlined five-o' clock shadows in *The Flintstones*. More than anything, he stank. Maybe he refused to wash as a form of protest. When I've smelled body odor like that, it's been from shut-ins and clients who've sworn off hygiene. Not the same kind of smell, but as strong as the FlyNap.

"Walter. How are things?" Leland faked confidence well, but a twitch at the corner of his lips betrayed him. He loathed the man.

Walter rasped like he hadn't drunk water in days. "It's good to get out. I don't see much sunlight. But you know that."

"Don't be so dramatic," chided Leland.

"What's her name?"

Leland answered for me. "Kali."

Walter wouldn't address me directly. I made him uncomfortable. "Cally, like California?"

"That's it." Leland looked about at the various guards. "Walter, can we sit?" He treated the man more respectfully than I would have predicted.

"Of course." Some strength returned to his voice.

Walter's hands tested the chain when we sat down. Even though he hadn't reached toward me, the snap of the chain made me brace myself. Walter saw me flinch and smiled for a tic, then wiped off the smirk in case Leland caught it.

I could tell Gretsch was shorter than me, but he was stocky, and I didn't know if prison had toughened him up or taken the fight out of him. I kept my hands on the table and prepared for a quick hit if he came at me. I'd go for the bridge of the nose. The chain allowed Walter to place his folded hands on the table. He angled himself toward Leland.

Walter spoke plainly. "How's Veda?"

Leland didn't rile easily. Clearly Walter had jousted with him before, and it seemed like Leland had gotten used to questions like this. He even joked back, even though his eyes simmered. "He just got drafted by the 49ers."

"Doesn't surprise me. He was fast, like me."

Leland leaned in my direction. "Kali, you must have questions. Ask away."

Walter didn't look at me. He addressed Leland. "She's a child."

"Not your kind of child," I returned. Walter grimaced when I spoke to him but didn't acknowledge me.

"You'll want to talk to her," Leland urged. Again to me: "Kali?"

Geezum, he could have prepped me better. Until twenty minutes ago I didn't know we would see Walter Gretsch today. I certainly wasn't prepared to speak with him. Leland looked at me insistently. Christ, what did he want from me? The brat in me thought about reciting the same prayer Leland had whipped out for Beatrix LaCroix. That would confuse both of them. But looking at Walter brought me back to my long-ago conversation with his Helena Mumm. A question formed. "Do you love Helena?"

"That's a new one," said Walter Gretsch. I was impressed he responded to me, even if he couldn't look at me. As he considered my question, he brought his hand toward his mouth until the chain jerked, then hunched and chewed his thumbnail. "I have a fondness for her. As a sister."

"But you were intimate."

He snapped, screaming at the table without looking at me. "You think you know me? Don't fucking judge me, cunt!" The raspy voice rose to a growl, and he couldn't make it through the sentence without a spasm that pulled his chin to the right. The transformation was instantaneous. His hands reached as far forward as the chain would allow, and the wrists tensed against the cuffs. But he hadn't lunged for me, just the air in front of his face. At the same moment, my hand darted out to strike him. I would have probably gotten him in the throat, but Leland had anticipated this. He grabbed ahold of my hand and brought it back to the table. Without speaking, his eyes bulged and circled about at the cameras and guards all around us. Any physical contact and they'd come running.

Seeing he wasn't about to snap the chain, Walter relaxed again, congenial as ever. "We don't have to talk about that part," he said.

"I will remind both of you to be civil," Leland said.

"You want her to learn something, buy her a fucking textbook," he snarled.

As Walter Gretsch grew more uncomfortable, delight crept back into Leland's voice. "You got somewhere else to be?"

"You said you'd bring someone to help me," Walter muttered.

"You said we'd trade." My skin crawled to think Leland had forged a trade with someone like Walter Gretsch.

"I'm trying to make that happen," Leland told him. "She's figuring out whether she wants anything to do with you. To be honest, she's figuring out whether she wants anything to do with either of us. So she's asking you questions, and it would be in your best interest to answer them."

So this was an interview. Fine—so be it. The sooner we could end this, the better. If I could agitate Walter Gretsch to the point where he couldn't contain his fury, those guards would come over and send us home. So I cooked up the most inflammatory question from the ingredients I had. "I want to clarify that you had sex with your sister, but you didn't love her." This earned me daggers from Leland.

Walter gave the federal agent a look that said: *she didn't learn her lesson.* "My dick got lonely, and occasionally you have to fuck something. It's good for your health."

"So, you fucked your sister, then." It came out intentionally vicious.

"Everyone always makes a big deal about that. It doesn't feel any different than anyone else, Agent Kali." His eyes darted this way and that.

"She loved you."

"How do you know that?" he asked pointedly. "You ask her?"

There was no sense in lying, especially since I didn't fully understand the point in talking to Walter in the first place. "I did. You can tell by the way she talks about you. She wanted to have a family with you."

He resigned. "That she did."

"That's why she helped you steal the kids."

Leland conjectured, siding with me. "Love does crazy things."

Walter raised his eyebrows at Leland, imploring him to shut me up. He fought to remain calm. "What's her point?"

I asked, "Did you want a family with her?"

He tried to seem self-assured, but his chin spasm betrayed him every few words. "Hell no. What would I want with a family?" He leaned toward Leland and the shackles rattled. I could smell that he hadn't brushed his teeth that week. "You know how it is when you got some crazy bitch that won't let something go? It's everything I could do not to take a hammer to her."

To fake composure, I sounded as mechanical as possible. "But you didn't."

"I did what I could to talk her out of it. Told her we couldn't have kids, because they'd be all fucked up and deformed. But she kept at me." He pointed at the agent to make his point. "Helena hatched that rotten egg herself."

"Are you saying the kidnappings were her idea?"

The way he regarded Leland made me feel like I'd said something egregiously ignorant, like not knowing who the President was. "Taking those kids was her idea. That's a fact. That's what I've always said."

"So, you had no part in the plan?"

"I didn't say I didn't take part," he said. "Only that it wasn't my plan to begin with."

In the articles, I never read that he'd ever owned up to the crime. "Is that an admission?"

"I said as much as I'm going to say on that."

Leland said, "Sounds familiar."

Walter's temple throbbed. I liked that I was getting to him, although basking in his pain made me feel like a sadist. He asked Leland, "When are we going to get to my trade?" They were speaking in shorthand. Leland had promised him something before this meeting.

"Keep answering my questions and we'll get to it soon." I spoke out of my ass. I didn't want to get to the terms of our trade. I wanted to get us thrown out of the prison. "Why are you in such a hurry anyway? You got big plans for tonight?"

He took my question seriously. "I go back to the room and listen through my little window slit for the birds. They got herons and scrub jays up here. I hope one day one might fly in and I'd be able to eat it, but they're too big to fit." Maybe he was crazy after all.

Now Leland spoke, introducing a new topic. "That's because instead of windows, you have loopholes in your cell. You know where the word loophole comes from? It's the arrow slits they carved into castle walls so that bowmen could shoot arrows from their little nooks. They built loopholes into the cellblocks here because of the whole San Sebastián lore. In your cell, that thin sliver of light is coming from a loophole."

Walter mused, "Loophole..." He thought about the word. "A loophole is what gets you out of something. I need a loophole."

"Sounds like you could sure use one," Leland said, guiding the conversation.

Walter finally looked at me. "I need a loophole to get me out of this place." Facing me, breathing toward me, I inhaled the full potency of his stink. "You are my loophole—you know that, right?" He pointed at Leland. "He told you that right? You're going to be my loophole."

"A loophole to get you out of prison," I said for Leland's benefit. This was one hell of a trade he'd made with Walter.

"Walter..." Likely hearing the contempt in my voice, Walter went back to ignoring me. "Walter..." My instinct was to reach toward his arm to get his attention. If I touched him, the guards could end this. Leland should have stopped me—he had been so quick about deflecting my slap. But Leland didn't get in the way of my slow reach toward Walter Gretsch. I expected that if I drew close to him he might attack me, and I would be willing to prompt an attack if it meant calling the guards. But Walter squirmed away from my arm. The prospect of my touch clearly revolted him. "Look at me, Walter. Look at me."

Leland sat back and folded his arms. Now that I was engaged with the convict, he wasn't going to get in the way. Walter eventually swiveled his head toward me.

"You don't think you're getting out of here, do you?"

Walter shook his head.

I asked, "He told you that I would kill you, didn't he?" Leland looked skyward in disbelief, as if I'd just embarrassed him. Walter seemed confused by my tone, but nodded. My guts twisted. If Leland had promised him this, his promises really weren't worth anything.

I decided that we might as well end this, and my best bet was to rile up the convict. "Why would I do that, Walter? You've got a nice home here. Sure, maybe you feel a little trapped, but it's a home. You can lay down roots in a place like this. You know where you're going to be for the next two years…the next twenty…the next fifty. Why would I want to deprive a man of his home?" His limbs trembled as if I'd sent an electric current through him.

I leaned forward, tempting him to lunge at me. His hands might reach my neck before the chain snapped. Walter's hands rose from the table top, quaking, but they retracted from mine. He ground his molars, his right eye blinking faster than the left.

He pleaded with Leland, "You can't let this fucking cunt tease me."

Leland gave me a slight shake of the head, the way a pitcher might shake off a catcher's suggestion. I kept pushing Walter, leaning ever closer so he might get the itch to lash out. The bruise on my throat would be worth it. "By all accounts, someone should have slipped something sharp between your ribs by now. You should be grateful to be alive."

Walter's eyes toggled between Leland and me. His head jerked to the right. "You know I'm not."

Leland saw how far I'd leaned toward Walter. "Keep your distance, Kali." When I didn't move, he placed a gentle hand on my shoulder. I shrugged it off.

Walter's eyes fluttered as if a contact dislodged as he tried his best to stay calm. Leland breathed deeply through his nose. No one was going to lose his temper at the table. Unbelievable. Walter actually inchwormed away from me on his bench, as much as the chains would allow.

I frowned. "What's death worth to you, Walter?"

He looked at Leland. "She doesn't know?" He began breathing hard, on the brink of hyperventilation.

"Kali," Leland protested.

"What would you give me for killing you?"

"Air," he gasped. For a moment I thought he was short of breath and actually asking for oxygen. "There's no air in here." I thought he might be using a metaphor, but he spoke literally. "They suck the air out of my room when I get back in my cell. They do that with all of us. That's how they keep us docile, like fucking cows. They suck the air out so we don't have enough air to think. Like being at the top of a mountain. Like being drunk all the time." He believed this. Walter Gretsch really was crazy. "They're killing me already, just slower."

Viscous drool drizzled over his lower lip. I sensed that captivity might have heightened his delusions. With my own taste of captivity, I sensed how Walter might feel—instead of feeling empathy, I relished the torment he must have endured. I hoped that didn't make me a bad person.

He begged Leland, "You promised."

Since Walter wouldn't answer me, I asked Leland, "What was Walter going to trade for me?"

This was getting nowhere, so I got desperate. I reached across the table and seized Walter's hands. At first, he blenched like I was hurting him. He tried to pull his hands away but I wouldn't let him. His fingers were cold as raw fish, with softer skin than mine. The grime on his fingertips smeared on my hands. Possibly he considered how to hurt me, but if he stood up, I planned to ram my forehead through his nose. I wasn't afraid of this man.

The guards sprung to action when they saw me holding his hands. They shouted for us to stop touching, but I didn't pay attention, so the one outside the pen unlocked the gate. The visit was almost over. Walter Gretsch faced me dead on. He didn't have any more time to waste.

The door to our cage unlocked and rattled on its hinges; then the guard charged inside. I was about to go home. Walter Gretsch summoned the strength to give me an answer, finding the will not to twitch. He said, "If you deliver me, I will tell you *everything*." His eyes found Leland, and then came back to me. "He *promised*."

CHAPTER 12

As we drove back to Berkeley, I was the quiet one. Leland had lied to Walter Gretsch, and that likely meant he had lied to me. If our agreement was worthless, then I might never be rid of Leland Moon. I felt more trapped in that car than I had in the prison.

He assured me, "You'll be all right." I smelled Walter in my clothes. He'd gotten into the fabric.

"Why wouldn't I be?"

"For Walter Gretsch, that wasn't a bad first impression."

"Meaning that it was an accurate impression?"

"Meaning he was well behaved."

"It could have gone worse."

"Much worse. He was put off by you. He can't handle himself around grown women. You made him nervous."

"Likes kids but not adults," I noted.

"Remember why he's in there," he said. "Once they knew that was a trigger for him, they played on that when he was arrested. They showed him porn magazines, and he reacted the same way you'd react to a spider crawling on you. As far as we can tell, the only adult he's ever been with has been Helena, and they only had sex when they were teenagers. She aged out of her allure a long time ago."

My forehead pressed against the glass as I contemplated the man I'd just touched.

"You may think you just met the devil, but you've probably met people just as bad riding the bus. You just didn't *know* what they did."

"You're an interesting man, Agent Moon."

"He wanted something from us."

"He wanted something from *you*. You think I'm upset because I met some pedophile convict? Please. I'm pissed off because you traded with that man, same as me. You promised something you couldn't deliver. You know I won't kill him—you made one of your trades when you knew full well you'd have to welch on your end. Do you think that instills me with confidence, Agent Moon? I believed that if I honored my side of it, you'd finally leave me alone. Now I'm thinking I might never get my life back. And that's what's making me cranky."

"I'm going to honor the trade, don't worry about that," he said. I didn't trust him, but I wasn't about to contradict him.

We'd already gotten back to the east side of the Richmond Bridge. Around us, oil holding tanks turreted the hillsides in muted orange. I hoped he would let me go. I wanted to climb in my car and go home. That night I would celebrate with a wheat beer and a specific flourless chocolate brownie they made at a local bakery in Bernal. I'd kiss a boy, maybe more.

Leland continued, "He's a tough nut to crack. Sometimes I wonder how much is real crazy and how much is pretend crazy. But it all comes down to actions, I suppose. Someone does the kind of things he's done, it doesn't really matter that much if he's aware of what he's doing."

A passing condominium billboard pitched that if I lived there, I'd be home by now. If it meant getting out of the car sooner, I'd have considered it. "So, we're done then?"

"You'll be done with your part of the trade today, I promise. I gave you my word on that, and I'm not going back on it." The highway hummed for a few beats. "But I'd like you to talk to Veda before you go."

"So, we're not done."

"It was his request, not mine."

We got off at Ashby Ave. The parked cars on his street were kissing bumpers. Music grew louder, coming from the Moon house itself. We pulled into the driveway. The front door was open, and people I'd never seen stood chatting on the threshold. A teenager hauled two bags of ice on his shoulders around to the backyard. The beat was vintage funk.

Tesmer stood behind the living room window. She didn't acknowledge us. No one did. The Moons were having a party.

"This isn't a holiday, is it?" I tried to remember.

"No."

"Someone's birthday?"

"No," Leland said. "We just like to be social. You should try it."

In the rearview, two cars sandwiched my cobalt blue jalopy, giving me an inch of clearance on either end. In the one in front, two men sat in the front seat, both young white men with trendy facial hair and sunglasses. They had the look of finance executives trying to be hipsters and seemed to be staring straight at me. The car stood out—a nondescript silver sedan that sparkled in the way that only scratchless rental cars sparkle. Kali drove enough rentals to spot one.

Leland saw them too. He angled himself enough to read the license plate, which he keyed into his cell phone in case he needed it. After Leland waved to the men, the driver started the motor and pulled off. He said, "Just so you know, whatever that was, they weren't here for the party." Too much was happening to think about random men. I'd wonder about it later.

Leland gave the horn two taps to alert Tesmer, and she bounded out to the car. She was dressed in a white suit with high shoulders, and seemed positively electrified to meet us. She tapped his window, joyful in a way that typically comes from a prescription kicking in. Leland rolled down the glass.

She asked her husband, "How did it go?"

"About as well as you think."

"Well, you're here," she said brightly. "Can you come in? Veda wants to say hello."

"You mean good-bye," I said.

"Of course. He wants to talk to you."

I didn't want to go in there. I wasn't feeling social, especially after Walter Gretsch. Especially after Leland made me doubt whether he'd ever leave me alone. Logistically, it made more sense to drive off now that the phantom driver had pulled out from in front of the hatchback.

"Come on—it'll be quick," she assured me.

"You're in the home stretch," he said.

I was so close to finishing this trade. This was the last thing they wanted of me. If I said a quick good-bye, I could go home. "Sure."

As if preparing for a *terminus*, I took an extra moment in the car to pump myself up for the party. I told myself it would be safe in there, because of all the people. I tried to tell myself this would signify healthy closure, making it easier for all of us to part ways.

The Moons walked me inside. Veda sat in the leather armchair, but it didn't appear as though he wanted to talk to me. He wasn't any happier to be there than I was. A crowd of mostly adults milled around him. One woman patted his shoulder in passing, and Veda feigned congeniality, as did I. When he smiled, it was a warm, elastic smile, but I knew he was faking it. Once the woman passed, his face returned to the same impassive, unreadable enigma that had puzzled me over dinner. Most of the guests left him alone. Veda scratched his arms and eyed the hallway, maybe hoping he could dart to his bedroom.

Friends and neighbors—whoever they were—mingled around the floor. Mixed ethnicities. Mixed incomes too, judging from the clothing. I wondered if this was a church group, but other than Tesmer, no one was that formal. Fashion ran the gamut from cocktail dresses to sandals. People watched me keenly as soon as I came in, not curious the way one would look at a stranger, but smiling and nodding like they knew me. One freckly man in plaid shorts strode up to me and tried to shake my hand. Tesmer said, "Not now," and, mildly surprised, he wandered back to his clique.

Tesmer and I sat down on the white sofa. In her suit, she blended into the upholstery. I sat next to her, close to Veda, but as close to the edge of the couch as I could get. Leland pulled an ottoman close to his son, on the other side of me. We formed a little cluster in the middle of their party.

Veda was odd man out in terms of wardrobe. He wore a T-shirt and shorts; the way I'd want to be dressed on a warm Saturday. Palms up, he showed off the two long scars that ran down his wrists. I thought about taking off my suit jacket, but I didn't want to get comfortable there. I wouldn't be staying. With Leland, Tesmer, and me in suits, we looked like a parole hearing.

Veda played with his hands, tapping each finger on his thumb in sequence. Since he didn't say anything, I decided to be the first to speak. "I wanted to say good-bye."

"Yep."

This seemed about as much of a reaction as I was going to get from him. I had a surprising lack of desire to connect with him. When someone's personality flatlines, it's hard for me to give that much of a crap about them. I started to stand, and Tesmer touched my arm. "Please, Kali." Her voice was soothing. Veda seemed suspicious, if in fact I read his expression correctly. She said, "Let's sit for a moment."

We sat in silence, all of us looking at each other. I didn't know what was going on, and I could tell Veda was confused too.

"What is this?" I asked.

"Why are you being weird?" Veda asked his parents. Tesmer and Leland looked at each other, waiting for something to happen. Around us, the conversation softened, and the people seemed to be anticipating something as well.

I almost expected another prayer, but no one said anything. Things couldn't have seemed stranger. But in the spirit of finishing my good-byes and getting back to Bernal Heights, I went along with it. Veda fidgeted, speeding up his finger taps. I didn't know what we were doing. But we sat there, not talking, not praying, and not engaging with other guests.

Then Veda transformed. At first he was just fidgety; he sensed something in the air. His nostrils flared. He smelled me, and he smelled his father. Or rather, he smelled the stink of Walter Gretsch that clung to both of us. His chest curled in on itself, and his lips tightened as if he'd eaten a piece of bad meat and was fighting not to spit it up.

"It's him." He gagged and stumbled to his feet, then elbowed his way through a knot of party guests. Down the hallway, we heard the bathroom door slam. Faintly—so faintly that you wouldn't have heard unless you were listening for it—he vomited into a toilet.

He didn't stop at a few heaves. It got louder, until the phantom chitchat around us died out. All of us mindfully listened to Veda Moon's retching. In that moment I understood that our visit to Walter Gretsch was meant to accomplish nothing, except for us to bring back his scent to Veda Moon.

Leland said, "Now you can go."

Tesmer scooched a few inches away on the sofa.

"What the hell just happened?"

The Moons turned their attention toward their guests. Leland told them, "He'll be okay. It's nothing we haven't seen before."

A young woman in an empire waist top and jeans asked, "Can I take him to the hospital?"

Tesmer kindly replied, "It will pass."

I took a look at the woman who'd just spoken—familiar voice, familiar face. Her blonde hair knotted in what's known as a beachy updo. She walked toward the bathroom, and I noticed an unusual bounce in her step. One of her legs was a prosthetic. Cindy Coates. With an upturned nose and a light complexion, her face was a blank canvas for makeup, and once she dabbed on eyeliner and lipstick, her features looked much different. She didn't acknowledge me. I sank in the cushion once I recognized her, but I was also a wee grateful that she didn't attack me. I rubbed the diminishing welt on my scalp.

I looked to Leland to explain. "Why would you do that to your son?"

"This is what I wanted you to see." When he spoke, he didn't murmur. Clearly, none of this was a secret to any of those in the house.

Tesmer added, "You needed to see him like this."

Everyone around the room watched me. They reminded me of sidewalk looky-loos during medical calls. Not that I feel like the world revolves around me, but in this instance it felt like it. Every guest had stopped their socializing and stared. Their attention pinned me to the sofa. Some looked at me as if they'd just found a silverfish in their clothes. Others saw how little I understood about what was happening and appeared more sympathetic. I suspected all of them knew who I was. Maybe one of the Moons told them about me, maybe they even knew we'd just visited Walter Gretsch in prison. Likely they all knew why Veda Moon was throwing up.

I addressed the room collectively. "Who are you?"

Leland said, "Friends." This earned a few nods from the group, even from the ones who couldn't hide their contempt. One blocky guy in a Darth Vader T-shirt managed a smile when he remembered he was supposed to be friendly.

I asked, "Who's going to help Veda?"

Tesmer said, "He'll be in there for some time. He probably won't eat for two days." Leland looked slightly ashamed of himself. Not so Tesmer Moon.

"At the very least, you are the worst parents in Berkeley, California. Congratulations," I said.

Leland insisted, "He'll be all right. We didn't want to do this, but we needed to show you...we needed to show you how bad it was."

Had I been alone with Tesmer and Leland, I would have gone to check on Veda in the bathroom. Jesus, someone should have. He was turning himself inside out in there. Either that or I would have walked out.

Instead, my shoulders went slack and I leaned my head back on the couch. "What do you want from me?"

Leland said, "Let's start with punch."

• • •

Guests started talking again; and fairly soon the crowd seemed alive, if not outright festive. Tesmer looked after her son in the bathroom, leaving Leland to walk me through the crowd. I suppose part of the reason I stayed was curiosity.

We cut through the kitchen and out into the backyard. Berkeley homes weren't known for having yard space, but their trimmed lawn fit a good forty people. Coolers held beer, but most dunked plastic cups into open vats of sangria. Leland and Tesmer had bought old cooper's barrels from a winery in Napa, lined them, and filled them up with the punch.

I frugally nursed my sangria, gnawing on a pineapple chunk. No way was I getting tipsy around those guys. I might wake up in a bathtub of ice without a kidney.

Now that the talk-talk had started back up, the guests didn't focus as much on me, so I felt slightly less conspicuous drifting through them. Occasionally I got a nod from one of them, but most tuned into their own acquaintances.

Cindy Coates approached us. Seeing her coming, I braced myself to bolt for the front door, but she charged too fast to go anywhere. This prosthetic resembled a regular human leg, and was hence less exotic than the running blade. Managing the subtle terrain of the lawn, I couldn't detect any lopsidedness when she walked. She gave us that sporty smile that welcomed me at the café in Alameda. "Getting drunk—good idea." She clinked Leland's plastic cup then mine.

I fumbled for something nice to say. "You look pretty." *Dumbass.*

"I was pissed at you, but I can understand you doing what you did," she said. "If things were reversed, I might have done the same."

"Really?"

"Naw—it was pretty rotten. I mean, come on." She chuckled. "But I feel bad about socking you with my leg."

"I feel awful about that."

"It's okay. Now I get free coffee whenever I go in. I'd find another café though if I were you—you don't have many friends there."

"I'm not much of a coffee drinker."

"I heard you met Walter today—it's probably a lot to take in. What did you think?"

"Creepy."

"He's a sad little asshole." I liked her brassiness. She said, "The irony is, I would kick both their asses right now—him and Helena. I was just too young to do it at the time."

"You're different than Veda."

Leland shrugged in a way to suggest he didn't disagree.

"Don't get me wrong. I'm not sure I could be in the same room. He's like my kryptonite. But if I didn't know him and he tried that shit today, I'd whoop his ass." Her candor had surprised me when I first met her, but I started to see some of the true hatred that she still had for them. I could tell she both loathed and feared Walter and Helena, and the lightheartedness was another way of coping. Maybe she was convinced she could cream a jail-hardened convict who'd bulked up since his trial, even with the prosthetic. I wouldn't contradict her. Her bitterness would have been a natural consequence of the abuse, and her courage, in my opinion, that much more commendable.

Cindy looked around at the other guests. "I'm not sure anyone here would have been able to sit down with that man. It takes some serious gonads."

"She's right about that," seconded Leland. An older woman in a floral sarong waved to Leland Moon from across the yard. He excused himself, and for the first time, left me unattended in his home.

I conferred to Cindy in a sisterly voice, "Why are all these people here?"

She seemed surprised I didn't know. "It's a periodic get-together that the Moons run. Leland and Tesmer built this community so we could all get to know each other. So we know we all have each other's backs. Like a survivor's group, except we don't have round-table talks in a church basement. We get to have parties and eat ribs."

"A survivor's group?"

"Everyone who's been hurt by Walter Gretsch and Helena Mumm."

I took in the number people there, and it didn't compute.

"There are too many families here." It was hard for me to articulate, because I didn't want to belittle her experience or Veda's. "There were only three children taken."

She kitten pawed my arm. "I get it now. You still need to get the full picture. Walter Gretsch was only *prosecuted* for three children." That fact had been omitted in the articles I'd read.

I thought aloud, "There were more."

Cindy nodded.

I studied the crowd to see who might have been other victims. Not a whole lot of people our age. My eyes lit on a girl in her late teens. She looked like a ballerina and naturally stood in first position. But she was younger than either Veda or Cindy; too young to have been alive when Walter went to prison. A woman in her late twenties was scooping out a cup of punch. She wore thick librarian glasses and caked-on makeup. A lek of tattooed butterflies started behind her ear and floated to her shoulder. "Is she one?"

"No," Cindy said, watching me. "No one else lived." She waited for this to sink in and sipped her sangria.

I stared at her. "How many?"

"We estimate that they abducted eleven. Only two made it out— me and Veda." The conversation must have brought back memories of the events that led her to the party. Despite her resilience, her spirit faded. She forced herself to perk up again. "What you're seeing here are parents, brothers and sisters, and some cousins. A couple of close friends, but mainly blood relatives."

"Is your family here?"

"No. They think it's weird. They don't like being around the other families. My dad says they judge them because I'm alive." For a moment Cindy Coates zoned out, lingering on thoughts of her parents. She lazily looked past me to somewhere on the Moons' clapboard siding.

Leland rejoined us, standing at Cindy's shoulder. "Are you all right?" he asked her.

She nodded. He threw an easy arm around her and kissed the top of her head. She relaxed into the hug.

After giving it a moment, Leland asked me, "Can we talk?"

Upstairs might have been an attic in another home. Here, Leland kept an office. Both of us had to duck our heads when we climbed the stairs, and depending on where we stood, either of us might have knocked our skulls on the pitched ceiling. "It's quiet up here," he explained. The ramble of conversation was muted but I could still hear it.

He kept it dark up there. I'd been at the house long enough that the sun was setting, and the streetlights flickered on outside the window. They were the brightest lights up there. The window faced the Berkeley Campanile. Underneath it sat an ebony mission desk covered with heaps of papers. The room stretched the full length of the house. At the far end, a small bed hid in the shadows. Leland said, "That's where I sleep when Tesmer and I fight."

"That bed sees a lot of action, then."

He sighed, "I'm joking. That's a guest bed. You don't laugh much."

"Depends who I'm with."

By the top of the stairs hung a vintage gilt frame that corralled a handwritten note on lined notebook paper. Scrawled in loopy ballpoint was "Veda Moon." I thought this might be the first time his son had written his name. To make friendly banter, I asked, "How old was he when he did this?"

"Twelve. That piece of paper is how they found him."

Leland sat on a swivel task chair at his desk. "You read the case. You know how Veda was found." Socratic method.

"They picked him up at a post office."

"That they did. He'd found a scrap of paper," he pointed to the frame, "*that* scrap of paper—and written his name on it. When Walter Gretsch was right there trying to pay the cashier. Do you know the serious testicles it took to do that? Gretsch had already said he'd kill him, and he'd kill his family. Veda had seen what they did to Cindy. And he still wrote this and slipped it underneath the safety glass to the clerk so that Walter couldn't get it back. That was an act of bravery."

"It was."

Next to the desk sat a Kermit-green beanbag. This was as close as I was going to get to a chair. Leland gestured to it, and I obliged by collapsing into the polystyrene beads. When I was in the chair, Leland loomed over me—a similar vantage as when he'd handcuffed me. He leaned forward in the chair and made a chapel spire out of his hands. He tried to convey warmth, but I was immune to his warmth. Try as he might, he couldn't abuse and manipulate me and expect to come out buddies.

"Everyone needs help. Someone that's been through what he's been through needs more help than most."

Something jangled up the stairs. Emmanuel. I hadn't thought about the dog in days. Last I checked, Leland was going to drop him back at the shelter for me.

"Veda likes him," said Leland. The dog hopped in my lap and settled in cozily as I ran my fingers through his coarse fur.

Bulletin boards paneled the wall. Papers leafed off them like ivy. Some showed portrait photographs of kids. Others featured skinnier versions of Helena and Walter. A large topographical map of Northern California was mounted at the center. Colored thumbtacks dotted its landscape. Leland saw my interest. "The yellow tacks represent places where Walter Gretsch lived or worked. The blue ones where Helena lived or worked. You can see there are a number of places where yellow and blue are paired, when they lived together. This map only tracks their activity in the region, although we don't suspect they did much out of state."

"They moved around a lot."

"They did." He got up from his chair and pointed out different areas of the map. "Largely kept to the general region, but here's them in Stockton, Pleasanton, then over here in Sebastapol, down in San Rafael, then El Cerrito and a few places in Richmond." On the map, he'd written dates by each location with a marker. "The green tacks are where children went missing." Each green tack was a knuckle's distance away from a pair of yellow and blue. "Here's an example. Over here in Sebastapol, Walter and Helena rented a studio apartment from 1976 to 1978. In 1978, right before they moved, Gayle Nelson was abducted on the way from school to her house. Seven years old. The path from her home to school was about a quarter mile, and she walked it every day." His finger landed on a crimson pushpin.

"Where did they find her?"

"They didn't."

I counted the green tacks. Eleven, just like Cindy Coates told me. "They didn't find any of them?"

"The only remains that ever turned up belonged to Julie Diehl. She was captive with Cindy and Veda. They buried her in the dirt under the shed where they kept Cindy and Veda, to discourage them from running." I remembered what Cindy had told me, and as my next thought formed, he amended himself. "Plus, the portion of Cindy's leg they cut off and buried there as well." He tapped one of the children's portraits. "This was Julie."

Julie Diehl had been a freckle-faced brunette who wouldn't smile for the camera.

"You think eight other children were abducted by Walter and Helena?"

"They drove a ratty olive green station wagon, pretty distinctive. Tinted windows in the back. They hollowed out the backseat and installed a box long enough to lock up the kids after they took them. That's how they transported them without being seen. It was a family-friendly vehicle, so people weren't as likely to suspect it. Witnesses saw their vehicle around these locations. We have security footage of the car popping up at local gas stations and convenience stores." He pointed to a few printouts tacked to the board, photographs of the car. They seemed staged, probably taken once they'd impounded the vehicle. The station wagon sat on soft tires and was painted an army green; a color no one wanted, so Walter and Helena might have bought it cheap. The tinted windows back then made the glass purple. It looked dingy, but not so bad I'd immediately call the cops. Leland was right—I'd have remembered that car.

A printout of security camera footage, marked with a time

stamp in the lower left, showed a grainier version of the car, but it was definitely the car. You could read the plates on one of the video stills. Higher quality photographs had been taken once the car was in custody. The windshield had a hairline crack. For some reason, the cargo space held a red plastic sled, even though it never snowed in the Bay Area. Two photographs showed the backseat—on the surface, it looked like a padded vinyl bench, but when the bench slid to the side, like the top of a coffin, it revealed a hollowed plywood cabinet that could hold a child.

"That's all you've got?"

"That's all you need in some cases. In addition to the car, witnesses saw both of them wandering around town. Walter and Helena stuck out."

"This never came up in the trials."

"For a lot of reasons. They lined the lockbox in the backseat with plastic and bleached it, so we couldn't pull DNA. We searched, but didn't have any evidence on the rest of the kids, so we kept a tight case around Veda, Cindy, and Julie."

"Are you sure that they're all dead?"

"That's our educated guess. Walter's in prison. Helena was in prison for a long time and was just released. If they kept anyone else captive, those kids would have died by now. If the children ran away, they would have been found by now."

I pointed to the map, dreading his answer to my next question. "You think you've accounted for everyone?"

"I hope so, but you never know. What we came up with here is a conservative estimate of all the abductions that are probably tied to Walter Gretsch and Helena Mumm. When we started pulling this together, other families came to us thinking that they'd stolen their kids too. We looked at every case. But these are the ones where the patterns matched up."

"What do you think happened?"

"We think Walter and Helena killed eight children and transported them, in that olive station wagon, to some central burial ground. Someplace tucked away." He pointed to the middle of the map, a region what would have been easy to drive to from any of the pins. "That's what we're trying to find. We're trying to find them."

When I visited Helena Mumm, she talked fondly about a garden that she and Walter tended. A garden she tended with their kids. I imagined what that might mean now. Then, I remembered Leland's son emptying his guts in the bathroom. "Why are you doing this? It can't be healthy for Veda."

"You think I don't know my own son? I know it's hard for him to see this."

I accused. "Then why the hell do you do it?"

He rubbed his eyes. "Because I get to give those people hope."

"You're hunting for dead bodies. How is that hope?"

"It's the hope that they might have closure. It's a form of hope. And there's always the tiniest chance that I'm wrong, and that their kids are alive. And if that happens it will bring me a joy that I can't describe."

"Why does it have to be you?"

"Because I never had hope." He clarified. "Tesmer always held out that Veda was still alive. She always believed it. And I knew I had to fake it, so I'd go along with her and tell her he'd be coming back to us any day. But I knew—I *knew*. I'd worked on enough of these cases to know my son was dead. And it was the loneliest feeling in the world." He let me sit with that for a moment. "Look—most of those people down there are in the same boat. They've lost blood. The last time they saw their child, he or she was a child. If they'd have grown up, they'd be your age or older. But those kids probably died *as* kids, and they're still children in the minds of their families. When a child gets taken…it's the worst thing someone can go through. Believe it. Sometimes the parents stick together, but not always. Some friends will stay loyal—but not all of them. You don't have the community behind you the way you think you would, because the mere fact that your child went missing casts you in a suspicion that you never shake. Your neighbors—even your church—might think you killed them. And even if you didn't kill them yourself, somehow you screwed up and let them be killed." He set up a straw man so he could give me a taste of how his network of friends and colleagues had turned against him. "I mean, what kind of parent would let this happen to his own kid? A child's a responsibility, right? So anyone who is negligent enough to let this happen to his child *deserves* it." He rocked back on his chair. "If you'd lived through it, you'd know. You can't *untaint* the taint."

"So nothing changed when you found Veda?"

"I didn't find Veda," he said bitterly. I caught his frustration, understandable from an FBI agent who couldn't find his own child. His shame ran so deep he didn't want to articulate it, only adding, "It was luck. That and the colossal balls of my son to write that note hanging on the wall."

"Your church really asked you to leave?"

"The reverend asked us to take some time off."

"Have you gone back?"

"We switched churches," he said.

"What happened to you as a family…you're sure that's what happens to all those families down there?"

"More or less from what they tell me. Hopefully, what we do makes it less bumpy than it was for Tesmer and me."

"But this hurts Veda."

"I'm doing it for Veda as much as anyone else. This isn't putting him through hell—my son is *in* hell. I'm trying to get him out. I expect him to be uncomfortable, but I'm doing this because I love him."

I scanned the layers of paper on the walls. "Does Veda ever come up here?"

"Hell no." He slid out the bottom desk drawer. "That's why we keep these up here." I nosed over and saw a bundle of forks. Dinner and salad forks, probably sixteen, enough for eight servings. Leland picked up a salad fork. Twinkling off the prongs, the streetlights gave it the illusion of sharpness. "My boy has a phobia of these. Forks of all things."

"Why didn't you just get rid of them?" I asked.

"Because I want him to get over this, eventually. But my son is a fragile young man, Kali. At this point, you've seen enough to know that." I nodded to acknowledge this. "You know, I went to Cal. Got both degrees there—bachelor's and my JD. In a perfect world, I would let all this go and spend my Saturdays having a few beers with my son at the Cal game. But you know what? Every time there's a touchdown and that cannon goes off at the stadium, my son almost craps his pants." He dropped the fork back in the drawer, and it rattled like coinage when it hit the other utensils.

"What's the FBI's role in this?"

His tone sharpened. "The FBI doesn't know I'm doing this. I wouldn't host a barbecue for victims' families as part of an FBI investigation—come on. These are cold cases. What we're doing here is a volunteer effort."

"So no one in the bureau is working with you?"

"No one would want to touch this."

I didn't want to steer the conversation, but this was my first chance to test whether I could be free. "Was the FBI ever investigating me?"

"Of course it was."

"How did you find me?"

"I'm what they call a squad leader—drug squad. We found the guy who was selling you the thiopental and pancuronium. Haven't heard from him in a while, have you?"

His name was Dylan, and someone from the network initially found him for me. "I'm not in touch with him that often. I guess it's been a few months. He gave you my name?"

"Not exactly. He kept a journal—you were the only person he sold those drugs to. No one else made anything of it, but I know those aren't recreational. I was curious to see who would bulk order chemicals that they use in lethal injections."

"Is anyone else curious?"

Leland assured me, "The bureau can live with another cold case."

I brought the conversation back around. "Walter never confessed to any of this."

"He played the crazy card. He never outright confessed to anything. All that babbling about demons giving him urges—it wasn't a confession. He never gave us anything useful. Helena played the victim all along. It didn't work for her at first—she got sent up. But in the end it paid off. The parole board thought of her as a disease-addled woman who wasn't in her right mind. Because they felt like if a woman was head over heels for her own brother, by definition she couldn't possibly be in her right mind. I believe they were wrong about her."

"You think killing Helena Mumm would help you bring Veda to a Cal game?"

He leaned back and fingered his chin. "You keep thinking I wanted you to kill Helena Mumm, but all I asked for was an injection."

"What are you trying to say? I know what was in that needle." Some chemical hallucinogen called pharmahuasca. I didn't know much about it other than what I found through Jeffrey's lab tech.

"The beauty of working on drug squad, you find out about all kinds of things."

Leland unlocked his top desk drawer, which might normally store highlighters and binder clamps. "If you know what it was, you know it wasn't a poison." He pulled out a ziplock plastic bag full of what looked like vitamin capsules. "Aya," he said. "Aya, for short. Although this isn't ayahuasca so much as—"

"Pharmahuasca. A synthetic version."

"What do you know about it?"

"It's peyote with an edge."

He admired what was in his bag. I kept thinking about the moral code that the FBI is reputed to have among its agents. Possibly it was a myth, or Leland Moon may have just strayed from that code to keep illegal narcotics in his desk drawer. "To cook up the organic version, you'd usually need a shaman. He'd mix it up and you'd smoke it during a ritual. You're right about the synthetic version—this version—being more potent. Sort of like the difference between mushrooms and LSD. You extract the DMT—that's dimethytryptamine—and refine the drug to a purer form. It's soluble in water. Mix it with a saline solution and it's even injectable. It lasts for up to twelve hours or so, and you go through extreme visions. Twelve hours of nightmares so vivid you can touch them."

"You've tried it."

"Of course I did. I had to find out what it would be like." So this was something that Leland Moon had in common with Jeffrey Holt. "It was the single most terrifying event of my life, and that includes my own son being taken from me. Because at least Veda's kidnapping was grounded in the known world. This stuff," he said as he held it against the window light, "is like being sent to hell."

"Aren't FBI agents supposed to be drug free?"

"Don't tell anyone," he winked at me, so casual about breaking a bureau commandment.

"How did you get that?"

"We're in Berkley, California. Throw a rock and you'll hit someone who's studied with a shaman." He tugged his clear plastic tote like a puppeteer. "These goodies came off a bust in Richmond."

"Why would you give this to Helena Mumm?"

"Because while I experienced this drug, I would have told anyone anything. I would have been too terrified to keep anything secret. This drug can show you your past lifetimes from the dawn of history. I followed myself back to Africa. Given that perspective, any secrets you've got bottled up seem trivial." He tossed the bag on his desktop papers. "The plan was to have you go, administer the injection as if it were her diabetes medication." He rubbed exercise calluses on his palm. "I planned to go visit her thirty minutes later after the chemicals kicked in."

"You were going to interrogate her?"

Leland nodded. "I need to find those kids." He gestured to the map, at all the green pushpins. "I want a location."

"Why did you need me?"

"We can't just go and ask her. We tried asking her for over a decade. We needed someone Helena didn't know, and, frankly, we needed someone who didn't know Helena. Someone who could be in the same room with her without losing their cool. I wouldn't have been able to get anywhere near her."

"You couldn't overpower her and give her an injection?"

"You know what happened when I went back to the house? She'd woken up by then. She heard me prowling around the door and threatened to shoot me."

"She could barely get out of her chair."

"Don't be fooled. Helena Mumm is extremely dangerous. When we took her into custody, she stabbed one of the agents in the thigh. But even if I could overpower her, I wouldn't trust that it would work. We can't go back to Helena, because she already knows we tried to pull something. If she gets that we're doing something to her, she could clam up just to spite us."

"Even with this drug in her?"

"Helena Mumm would kill herself rather than talk to me about anything. She's extremely defiant. The closest we ever came to a confession was when she was sedated. This was when we first had her in custody. There was a moment when she caught a whiff of the enormity of what she'd done and might have felt some remorse. You saw the video."

I remembered the video Leland had shown me back when Helena Mumm was supposed to be his sister. Rocking in her folding chair, she'd wept into the camera, claiming, "I want to die."

"If we got her in that state again, I thought we had a better shot of drawing out the truth. Now, we've missed that element of surprise with Helena. That makes Walter our best option."

I recalled that afternoon's visit to San Sebastián. "Haven't you already hatched some kind of trade with him? Why can't you just get the information that way?"

"I once traded Walter Internet privileges, more time in the yard, and even a boat ride in the San Francisco Bay. He gave us information in return that had us digging up by Point Reyes for three days. I can't trust he'll give us good information, even in a trade. You understand, I've thought about this quite a bit." He jostled his bag of synthetic shaman dope. "I wouldn't have come up with a complicated solution without exhausting the simple ones first."

I hated that I was coming to this understanding so late, and furious at Leland for not having explained this to me earlier. "Helena was never going to die."

"That was never part of the plan. So long as she's alive, she could have things to tell us. Even if she never does, there's always the possibility."

"You couldn't have explained this to me when we first met?"

"If I'd told you anything, Helena would have seen you trying to act out the lie. It was easier if you were just Kali." After a break, he followed with, "Keep in mind that whatever I did to coerce you, I didn't do anything monstrous."

"Think so?"

"Sure, you peed your pants in front of me, but look at my son. I see that every few weeks. When we met, all I knew about you was that you'd probably killed several people. I didn't want to confide in you. I didn't trust you. All this," he gestured to the walls, "is unofficial. I didn't want you to know about this. I didn't want you to know about my family. Believe it or not, it's been as hard for me to trust you as it has been for you to trust me. Consider that."

Leland saw how uncomfortable I was. I crossed and uncrossed my legs, shifting in that beanbag. He said, "Listen, you could go home right now and that would be the end of it. I've already deleted your profile off the registry."

"The sex offender registry? So, I'm no longer a sex offender? Happy day."

"You've kept your end of the trade, and you can go if you want. I won't come after you. But if you help us, you'd be helping more than me. You'd be doing something for all these families." He paused, unsure whether to articulate his next thought. "And you wouldn't have to kill anyone."

He'd offered a desperate plea, his voice weighed down by fatiguing years of struggle. Maybe the sangria had opened me up to suggestion.

"For the sake of argument, if I helped, how would it work? We go into San Sebastián prison and I narc up Walter Gretsch for you?" I laughed at the thought of breaking into a prison. I tipped to the side on my beanbag chair and laughed in a quake I couldn't rein.

Leland stayed serious. "I think you know that's a bad idea. Why's that?"

"It belittles us both for me to explain why that's a bad idea." I mean, where would I begin?

He said, "There are two issues at play. First, whether this is feasible. Second, whether you have the will to do it. Now, pretend for a moment we could. Would you be willing?" He sensed my churning thoughts. "This isn't a snap decision, but it should be. Will you think about it?"

I wasn't sure how much there was to think about. Aside from busting into a state prison, I didn't know what the plan was or what my role in it would be, other than to stick a needle into Walter Gretsch. The last of my cheesy grin disappeared. I thought about the families downstairs, and the original premise that led me to my work—to ease suffering. Out of respect for all the suffering they'd endured, I forced myself not to dismiss this as absurd. "I need more information."

CHAPTER 13

Leland left me alone after changing the sheets, and I got comfortable. Emmanuel stayed up here, and the puppy sniffed at my bare toes.

The low-watt clip lamp hung under the eaves. Right above me, an ambitious nest of cobwebs stretched across that corner, its builder long vacant. I propped myself up on pillows and gnawed on a pen as I leafed through a few folders Leland had put together for me. Occasionally I looked out the window at the lit houses tiered on the hills. I wondered if I made a mistake staying there.

Many of the reports were formatted like tax forms, so hard to glean information. Some of the documents were copies of handwritten notes and Xerox copies of photographs. Leland had gathered an image catalog of the missing children. Some of them were school portraits. Some were cropped with a cutoff shoulder, hinting that a full family had been in the original frame. The girls were at the age where they were losing baby teeth and some had gap-toothed smiles, proud of their dental voids because they hadn't matured to the age where they would be aware of their looks. Cindy Coates was in there. Her inert delight infectious even at that age, she seemed like a pinball of energy, photographed during the one moment she managed to sit still. I found Veda too. He'd been a gerbil-cheeked kid who grinned like he was trying to get away with something. He'd leaned out like his father after this photo was taken.

Veda and the girls stayed in a shed during the day, with no lights and a dirt floor. They were let out to have dinner at the house. Walter threatened that he would kill their families if any of them tried to run away. Helena preceded each meal by saying grace, always a prayer of gratitude for their new family.

Weeks passed. Instead of threatening to kill their families, Walter now told them all that their families had given up looking for them. Over the next several months, Walter and Helena used a number of methods to ensure compliance. The neighbors had loud dogs, and Walter told the children that the dogs were trained to tear them apart in case they ran. The shed got hot during the day, and the dehydration kept them tired and meek. During meals, Walter and Helena sometimes slipped alcohol into their drinks to makes them woozy. Even with all that wearing down their resistance, they sometimes behaved in a way that displeased the adults. When that happened, Helena bent them over their chairs and jabbed them with a dinner fork. Veda acted out more than the other two.

Eventually, Julie tried to escape and Cindy went with her. Veda was too scared to go. Hours later, Walter dragged Julie's body into the shed, along with something else wrapped in a bloody pillowcase. Walter forced Veda to help dig a hole in the dirt floor. Horrified and numb, Veda dug and covered Julie and the pillowcase with dirt. Cindy was returned to the shed days later, bandaged with part of her leg missing. She remained catatonic for days, and she didn't say much after she did talk.

Veda didn't act out after that, although it didn't stop the bad things from happening. He stayed monastically silent and obedient to a fault. As a reward, they brought Veda into the house and gave him a bedroom. Cindy remained in the shed, coming out for meals, or plucked out at Walter's whim. Veda began calling them "Mom" and "Dad." More rewards were gifted, usually more food or an extra shower. Walter experimented with a few trips to the grocery store, holding his hand tightly so he wouldn't run. Those went well, and then Veda accompanied Walter without needing his hand held.

They visited a post office as part of their normal errands. For the first time in public, Walter took his attention off him while arguing with the postal clerk over the price of postage. Veda took advantage of that moment and wrote his name on a piece of copy paper, and then slipped it under the glass before Walter could stop him. He erupted, screaming at the boy and hitting him with a closed fist. Postal employees and fellow customers tackled and restrained Walter Gretsch until the police arrived.

• • •

I drove back to Bernal Heights past midnight and parked a half block from home. Learning more about Veda's case deadened me, and I staggered across the street before I heard the car.

A silver rental sedan slowly cruised by me. I didn't recognize it as the one from that afternoon until I saw the two men, the same nondescript guys with facial hair, just without sunglasses. I froze on my doorstep and held my breath. I didn't want to fight or run—I was too tired for both—but I didn't know what else I could do. Scream I suppose, and hope the neighbors would come to their windows.

They passed me and only slowed down when they reached my cobalt hatchback. With the silver sedan idling, the man in the passenger seat got out of the vehicle, dressed in a black tracksuit. He glanced at me over his shoulder with a look that told me not to move, and then unlocked the hatchback with his own keys. The two cars drove off seconds later. My loaner vehicle had been repossessed.

When I got to my door, a small plainly wrapped brown package sat on my doorstep.

It was the same size as Leland's spider package, wrapped in the same butcher paper. The small brick waited to be unwrapped.

I sat down in the hallway against the wall opposite my door. I stared at the package for some time. I had to assume the two men who'd just taken back the loaner car had left it there. If so, they would be working with Jeffrey Holt. If Jeffrey had left this for me, it couldn't be a bomb. Outside of euthanasia, Jeffrey was the least violent person I knew. On the off chance he wanted to kill me, he wouldn't drop off an IED that could take out my neighbors too. Still, I didn't like it.

I had to take it inside. I gently lifted it off the doormat. The box was light, like the last one. I rattled it. Something loosely rolled around in there.

In my kitchen, I used a boning knife to slice the tape at the folded seams. Stripping back the paper, I found a pastry box. In fact, it was the same pastry box we'd opened in Shallot, Oregon.

I braced myself as I unfolded the side flap and tilted the box so that whatever was inside would spill out on my cutting board.

A cell phone slid out.

A text on the phone instructed me to call a number. Someone picked up on the second ring.

"What are you doing?" Jeffrey Holt was speaking. I was struck dumb by the sound of my mentor's voice. "Kali?"

"I'm here."

He was stirred up. "The man you're working with is FBI. Do you know that?"

"Were you following me?"

"We put a tracer on the car." That meant he'd known where I was the whole time and just reached out now.

I asked, "Why didn't you call me on my cell?"

"Because I don't know who's listening."

I tried to answer his initial question. "It's not what you think."

"He's the same person who sent a bomb to my home."

"It wasn't a bomb."

"It could have been."

"Where are you?"

"You think I'm going to tell you?" I could only imagine the narrative he'd whipped up in the past few weeks with the nuggets of information he'd found.

"I've solved the problem—it's fixed. I stuck my neck out, and it's paid off. Everyone is safe." And since I knew he would ask, I added, "I'm sure about this." Although I wasn't completely sure.

"Are you safe?"

I couldn't answer that.

"Are you operating of your own free will?"

I had to think about that. "I believe I am."

"Understand—so long as you're associating with someone

from federal law enforcement, I can't see you. Or be seen with you. Ever. And I can't imagine it will end well for you." For the first time since I'd met him, I couldn't tell whether Jeffrey was more concerned for me or for himself. "You need to really think about what you're going to do next."

"It's all I've thought about," I said, disconnecting before he could upbraid me.

CHAPTER 14

The sun was out at San Sebastián, but the wind was strong, and the few clouds in the air swam overhead like white whales. I'd driven there alone in a new rental, a black compact.

Midmorning, the scrub jays didn't have any competition as they picked through the trash in the parking lot. I shuffled through the lot in clogs and green scrubs, a packed canvas duffel under my arm. My lanyard felt too crisp between my thumb and forefinger, too fresh from the laminator. According to the ID, my name was Kali Helms, and I was a registered nurse.

Leland had rigged all of this, but he couldn't walk into the prison with me, not with all those cameras swiveling around on the rooftops. We'd gotten away with coming there together once, but he couldn't be seen with me again. Not when I was in costume.

We'd planned out my visit over several nights. Tesmer joined the sessions, but Veda stayed in his bedroom. I hoped he'd appreciate all of this once it was over.

Whoever was watching the feeds from all those swiveling cameras could see my plain, natural hair. The chestnut bob. No wigs for me that morning. Prison guidelines prohibited hair extensions—anything the inmates could tear off and use. I hid my face as much as I could with geriatric reading glasses. Fake tattoos covered most of my forearms—detailed steampunk clock gears, what were referred to as "biomechanical" tattoos, a fantasy of cybernetic works underneath human skin. Without being able to dress in full costume, I hoped those details would distract guards in case someone wanted to track me down later.

Leland assured me that Leonard Royce knew how to fry the security footage, but with so many people to size me up when they checked me in, I worried whether they'd remember me. They'd remember how tall I was. Prison guards made their living by being able to size up an opponent, but my XXL scrubs fit me like a tent and hopefully hid the muscle. Still, I'd never felt so exposed. If something went wrong today, I would be supremely buggered.

I proceeded toward the two turrets that dominated the entrance. As I walked toward the front door, a heavyset woman toddled out of it. She was dressed in a bright dress, something you'd wear to church. Prison guidelines requested that visitors not wear anything red, because it matched inmate jumpsuits. This woman hadn't paid attention. Amid the tropical muddle, she snuck in a little crimson with a flurry of tangerine. Her lipstick stuck out like a plastic pout on a Mr. Potato Head. *Leland*, I cursed to myself. I was staring at Helena Mumm.

She hadn't factored into the plan. Leland might have arranged for Helena's visit without telling me, or Walter might have reached out to her, desperate for some human connection before I came for him. Regardless, she walked right out the front door and down the walkway, just as I approached the building.

She looked at me. I couldn't dive behind a car, not without attracting attention from her and the cameras. I would need to walk past Helena Mumm. I wore the same set of scrubs as when I'd visited Helena, the shade of faded AstroTurf, but had enough props that I hoped she wouldn't recognize me.

For the first time, I noticed how she moved, back and forth like a metronome at *adagissimo*. She'd mismatched her shoes—one high heel and one flat sole. One leg might have been shorter than the other.

I kept my face down. Although the concrete promenade cut through a wide, trimmed lawn, the path itself was as narrow as a corridor. As we came closer, I saw her face change. She eyed me with pointed curiosity. I'd hoped my goggles and the tattoos would throw her, but no luck. Her face pinched as we drew near. She knew me. My best bet was to walk fast enough that she wouldn't stop me.

When we passed close enough to breathe on each other, it struck her. "Nursie."

I should have kept my eyes forward, but I couldn't help myself. I looked over as she spoke to me. My eyes jogged up to meet hers. I couldn't hide my revulsion. She read the contempt in my face as our eyes locked, and there was that moment of familiarity where we understood the connection between us.

We stopped.

"You're here for him." Her voice sounded uncertain, even fearful. I wondered how much Walter would have told her, or if she just remembered me and pieced it together. She'd expected me to kill her during that visit, so it wouldn't be a stretch to figure out why I was there.

Helena wanted a response, and when I didn't give one to her, she insisted, "Answer me." I needed to get the hell away from this woman, but I couldn't run, and I couldn't fight her in front of the cameras.

It felt strange being so close to her again. Back in her lounge chair, she'd seemed harmless as a beached seal. But now she was ambulatory. She stood a head shorter than me, but her girth made her intimidating.

"I'm late."

Helena, quicker than someone her size should have been, tried to slap me with a gigantic arm. Daunted by the cameras and wired tightly from the tension, I surreptitiously knocked her hand away. It didn't stop Helena. She swung a balled-up fist. I leaned back and the blow landed on my shoulder. Now we were fighting, with cameras recording us.

She closed in on me fast and pounded me in the ribs and breasts. Helena was strong. It hurt. I could see how she would terrify someone much smaller than her. She grabbed my shoulder to steady herself while she hit me, and I kept thinking about what that arm, now touching me, had done—plunged forks into children, sawed off legs. My blood was hot. Images from Leland's files flickered in my head. I remembered a "missing" poster with Veda's photo, posed with a naïve, openmouthed smile.

Cameras be damned.

I swung from the hip and smashed my knuckles into the bridge of her nose. Helena yelped and tumbled back onto her ass. Both hands muzzled her nose to stop the bleeding. Blood ran through her fingers. I cocked my arm for another, elbow at my ear, but didn't throw it. Once she hit the ground I remembered how exposed I was.

In the lighthouse tower, the first guard I'd seen on the catwalk coughed into a two-way radio.

Helena wailed like a child. Like someone who'd never been hit and didn't know what pain was. The fall had knocked off the high-heeled shoe. Her bare foot was bruised and swollen, with gout at the big toe. Still anchored in its shoe, the other foot was out of alignment with the leg. And I realized the foot was plastic.

I hadn't noticed in her home, because she'd worn baggy sweatpants and thick stockings. In daylight it was plain. If I'd paid more attention to her feet when she walked, it would have made sense. I'd chalked up her gait to the obesity.

Behind me shoe soles slapped pavement like applause. Over my shoulder I glimpsed the shadows of two men charging me. Amped up from the fight, I pivoted with my hands in the air.

Royce and Kearns. Their two shaved heads gleamed like ample breasts in want of nipples. I dropped my fists.

Royce drew close, his eyes darting around to the tower guard and the swivel cameras. He muttered, "Are you fucking serious?" I'd expected him to be all throbbing temples, but Royce was calm as a surgeon as he admonished me. "Fighting outside a prison? Do you know what people have gambled for this?" He swept a wave to the tower guard to signal the all clear. The guard didn't stop studying us but seemed less hawkish. "Don't ruin it."

Kearns had been silent, but piped up to his partner. "Let's get her in or get her out."

Royce placed an arm over my shoulder and leaned into me. From a distance, it might look as if he were comforting me. He said,

"You're a nurse who got into a smackdown with a crazy. For the sake of everyone watching, act like you're shook up."

I rolled my shoulders forward and pretended I was in shock from the violence.

Kearns inclined his head toward Helena, and Royce stooped to put her shoe back on and help her up.

"Arrest her," she demanded.

Kearns spoke with the same exasperated composure as his partner. "Go home, ma'am."

"I'm bleeding," she moaned, clinging to his arm.

"Go home and we won't arrest you."

She took her hand away. The blood below her nose looked like she'd won a pie-eating contest. "Arrest me? I'm the one hit! I need a doctor." She sneered. "You're taking the pretty white girl's side? She's on her feet and I'm down here. Who do you think needs arresting?"

Royce leaned in and dropped his voice. "Ma'am, we know who you are."

She pointed to me. "And I know who she is." The tower guard took an interest in us again. The cameras had stopped rotating. At least two lenses aimed at us and only us.

Kearns stood and loomed behind her. Both guards specifically chose their positions to intimidate her by bookending her front and back sides. Just as softly, Kearns said, "And who's that?"

"She's some kind of assassin."

"You realize how that sounds?" Royce might have made a good therapist.

"I don't give a goddamn how it sounds, if it's the truth."

Royce crouched down so his head was at her level, leaning forward on his fingertips. "All right, get this. Say you're right, and she is some kind of *assassin*. Why would you pick a fight with this person?"

Helena explained, "She's after my Walter."

"And if she is?"

That stunned her. "Then arrest her."

"It's like this. We have one holding cell in there for this kind of thing. We honestly don't pay much attention to what happens in there—we've got the rest of these inmates to worry about. If I put her in cuffs, I have to put you in cuffs too, because you hit first. Then we'll throw you in the same room together. Do you really want to be alone with this person?"

Helena's eyes widened. Kearns amplified her fear by resting a heavy hand on her shoulder. Helena babbled in protest as she ran out of options.

"Go home, ma'am," said Kearns, releasing his hand.

Kearns helped her stand and escorted her to her car. On her way, she coughed up a little blood from the punch.

Royce and I walked toward the entrance. Up on the roof, the guard lost interest in us. The cameras began rotating again.

I talked to myself about what I'd just seen. "She's missing a leg."

"Focus now." Royce steered me away from the front door. He led me around the turrets, around the corner of the building where a rusted steel door was plugged into the middle of a massive wall. Around it, paint flecked off in patches as big as dinner plates. "Service entrance," he said.

I didn't ask questions. When he pounded on the door it sounded like he was clanging an empty oil drum. Hinges shrieked when the door opened.

Another guard squinted in the sunlight, as if we'd freed him from a cave. He wore the same park ranger uniform as the others. A bushy white moustache swept over his wind-burned cheeks, and his stomach distended over his belt line. He didn't look at me. "This her?"

"Who else would it be?"

Moustache escorted us through a checkpoint full of steel mesh and concrete. Two guards at a console looked at me with interest but no suspicion. To be friendly, a handsome beefy boy asked, "First time?"

Royce replied for me. "Visiting staff. She's just here for the day."

Our escort signed a registry for me, and then several doors opened in succession. We tunneled through a labyrinth of long hallways and right angles. Fluorescents reflected in recently mopped linoleum. Cameras dotted the corners, more obvious than outside the building.

It struck me that I didn't know where we were headed. "Am I going to his cell?"

Royce kept his eyes forward. "No."

"Prison clinic?"

"Somewhere else. Try not to talk until we get there."

Our escort abruptly stopped at a door. It had been painted to blend in with the hallway, and I might have walked by without noticing. He fluidly unlocked it. The corridor behind it was black as a mineshaft without fluorescent tubes to cast a dim glow.

Royce nudged me. "Walk through it like you belong here." My heart quickened. Along the flame-seared slabs we trod into Gehenna.

Moustache gave us both flashlights, and three narrow beams bounded across the floor and walls as we pushed on. In the absence of light, the sound seemed to resonate more. Breathing seemed louder in the dark. Our footsteps clomped like horse hooves. I tried to guess where we were—maybe a service walkway for janitors and off duty guards. We kept at the same deliberate pace set by the man in front, following the light beams. Soon we approached a riveted door. Royce said, "We're here."

Our escort told Royce, "Don't make a mess." He turned and walked off.

"Gretsch is in there?" I asked.

Royce nodded.

I pointed the flashlight down the hallway and back to the door. "How many other people know about this?"

"Enough."

I had to ask, "Why are you doing this?"

Royce pulled out his wallet, and then a small photo onto which he shined his flashlight. I recognized the image of the young girl from the boards up in Leland's office. I didn't ask how he was related, because it didn't matter.

Royce cranked the handle and we entered. He flicked on the

lights, casting an astringent sheen. The walls were the green hue of ill mucus. In the corner, a table had already been set up for me, covered with a stack of loose maps. A broad window looked into an adjacent room next to ours; it was a viewing gallery tiered with folding chairs.

He said, "This was built for sparky." In the middle of the room, I found a square of singed linoleum and drill marks where the electric chair had been bolted to the floor.

In the corner, a smaller chamber had been constructed within the room. The floor-to-ceiling cylinder was shaped like a space capsule with riveting around the glass portals. To open and close the entry hatch, one would spin a wheel usually found on a submarine.

"When they outlawed the chair, they built the gas chamber," he explained.

Through the hatch, a sickly green table stood at the center of the chamber. It had a medical feel to it, like a dentist's chair stretched flat so the patient could lie horizontally. Two armrests jutted out like angel wings, straps lacing across the padding.

Royce said, "When they outlawed gas, they built this. The warden built a new execution chamber two years ago. Looks like a hospital room. They left this one alone, like a time capsule."

"Hard for me not to feel like an executioner."

"That's what he thinks he's getting."

I closed my eyes for a few deep inhales, smelling hints of vinyl. Back outside the chamber, I stared at myself in the reflection of the viewing gallery's safety glass. I looked homely in my soda pop glasses. I removed them and unzipped my duffel, pulling out a makeup kit and a mirror. I thought about applying lipstick, something to pretty me up. But grown women intimidated Walter, and I wanted to look nonthreatening—at least at the start.

While we waited, I asked, "What if something goes wrong?"

"We're in a prison. Things go wrong all the time."

A short wait later, Kearns escorted Walter Gretsch into the room. In the red jumpsuit and leg cuffs, Gretsch stumbled. His hands folded over his groin. The man had shaved that day, so he looked cleaner than when I last saw him. Walter seemed lost in thought, and he only pulled his eyes off the floor with some effort. When he saw the old gas chamber with the empty green chair, his legs buckled. Royce and Kearns both pulled him to his feet.

Walter Gretsch heaved a few times. His chin spasms were more violent, as if he wanted to unscrew his head from his shoulders. He had requested this—had agreed to Leland's trade, just so I'd come for him—but he wasn't ready for it. As the reality of his own demise set in, the natural biological impulses were taking over and he started to panic, breathing hard and fast.

I shouldn't have pitied this man. He didn't know it, but he wouldn't even die that day. But his abject desperation made me feel sorry for him, even though I found him revolting. I stepped in front of the open chamber hatch so Walter couldn't see the chair. "I'll help you through this," I said.

He brightened a bit when he recognized me. His mouth opened to say something, but he couldn't talk. Walter had trouble walking, and Royce and Kearns carried him the rest of the way to the table. Kearns even offered some consolation. "It'll go fine, Walter."

They laid him flat and strapped down his arms and legs.

I'd never attended a client who had to be restrained.

Now tightly bound, Walter breathed in shallow puffs. No one who ever got my needle was ever this terrified. Because of all the misery he'd inflicted, I wanted to enjoy his terror, but I couldn't. To ease the tension, I tried to get him talking. "I saw," I was going to say *your sister*, when I considered the complexity of their relationship, "Helena. Outside."

He looked at the ceiling as I sat beside him. "She's a good girl," he said to no one in particular. It was hard to say whether he had reappraised his sister since we last spoke, whether he was lying then or just bullshitting now. I doubted he had any feelings that might approximate love, but he seemed fond of her.

I said whatever came to mind as I prepped the needle. "She has a prosthetic foot. How'd she get that?"

Royce gave me a sidelong glance, likely wondering why I would bring that up.

Walter nervously chattered the way a first-time drunk would spill stories. "My momma. Our momma."

I gaped at him. Maybe because I'd just seen Helena, I'd pulled the dose I might have given to her, a woman profoundly more substantial than Walter, even with the weight he'd put on in prison.

"She tried to beat the bad out of her. Didn't work. Too much bad in both of us." He laughed to himself. "One night Helena said she was going to run away. Momma took a hammer to her foot. Busted it open like a water balloon." I didn't want to hear any of this, but I needed him talking when the drugs kicked in, so I didn't stop him. "Got infected. Nasty. So she cut it off." Possibly reevaluating his family at large, he said, "My momma saved her by cutting it off."

"Walter, do you know how this is going to work?" I asked. He shrugged. "I'm going to give you a shot that's going to relax you and put you to sleep. It will take a little while. When you're asleep, I'll give you a second injection. Then it will be over. You won't feel it." Now was my turn to spin some bullshit. The dose of pharmahuasca would kick in somewhere between five and twenty minutes after the injection. He would most assuredly feel it.

His body clenched and his voice cracked, though he tried to sound carefree. "Hunky-dory."

I rubbed the antiseptic swab over his forearm while he kept his eyes on the ceiling. "Least it isn't gas. That would be rough," he said. Walter Gretsch had no idea what he was in for.

I didn't use the butterfly needle this time. I set up a regular IV drip. This was what Walter Gretsch was expecting, because this is how a traditional lethal injection would work—with the exception that the execution team would be in the adjacent room, so they wouldn't have to face the convicted. Now that we started the process, a dreamy serenity cast over Walter.

I withheld the syringe. "Tell us where they are, and we'll get started."

"I already told Agent Moon," he said. Immediately lapsing into a practiced patter, he was more at ease because he was doing what he was comfortable doing. Lying.

"I don't think that's true."

"Honest, I told Agent Moon. He knows." Walter nodded at me, almost believing his lie. He hadn't told Leland anything. We all knew this was how it would go. Walter couldn't resist trying to put something past us.

"These will be your final minutes," I said, spooking myself with the severity of this declaration. "Is there anything you want to tell me that might give you some peace?"

"You a priest too?" He smirked at the men, as if they'd be in on the joke, seemingly at ease now that the end was inevitable.

I remained patient. "Would you want to say anything to the families you've affected?"

He closed his eyes. "You ever watch nature shows?"

"I've watched a few."

"Then you seen it. Every time a crocodile snatches a baby wildebeest. Every time a lion tackles a zebra cub or whatever the hell they call zebra babies. Children are always targets for a good hunter. The weakest always get sorted out. If parents can't protect their own, that's just nature being nature." I supposed this was the closest he'd ever come to a confession.

We didn't honestly think Walter would honor his trade. Nor did I press too much for him to answer. If he did start confessing anything, he might lose his nerve, and I might not get the opportunity to surge his blood with these truth-loosening hallucinogens.

Right before the needle went in, I thought about messing up the injection, stabbing the wrong part of the arm or twisting it just slightly so that Walter Gretsch would feel it more. But I ended up just wanting to get it over with.

"God, I barely felt that," he complimented. He got off lucky, relatively speaking.

I left some in the syringe, the difference between a Walter and a Helena dose, and set the needle on a worktable.

"It will take a few minutes for the drugs to settle in," I said. "We'll wait." I reached for his hand and he flinched. Even as he thought he was dying, he was nervous around a grown woman. "Relax."

After five minutes, the first indications were a fluttering of the eyelids. I excused myself from the room. Walter was too occupied with the sensations overcoming him to remark on my leaving.

Outside the gas chamber, I dug more items out of my duffel. Staring into the small mirror, I prepared. Most of my costume came out of a grease paint can.

Despite the dim lighting and small mirror, I worked fast. As I pulled my scrubs over my head, I caught Kearns stealing a glimpse in the reflection of the viewing room window, but he quickly averted his eyes, pushing the hatch nearly shut to give me a little more privacy.

As Walter moaned in the steel chamber, I smeared my face and arms with blue paint. I'd painted most of my body before I arrived. Tesmer got my back and hard-to-reach spots. In the mirror, the paint up and down my spine held up without major smudging. A low necklace of white skulls had been applied along my stomach and chest. Down went the pants, and I painted my ankles and feet, with touch-ups on the places where my skin was showing through.

Leland had instructed, "I want you to be terrifying." The thing that seemed to terrify him the most was a woman, so I went braless and stripped off my underwear bottoms. In for a penny, in for a pound. I'd be as much of a woman as possible, and watch him squirm when he saw postpubescent lady parts.

When I was finished, most of my skin was a uniform cobalt blue, from pectorals to pudenda. Except for the skulls and the accents and black lipstick. I painted Kali's red tongue down my chin. Crimson accents around my eyes made it look like I'd been crying blood. A midnight black mane cascaded down to my waist. In the mirror, what stuck out more than my unmentionables was the muscle definition. The sharp contours of my shoulders and the veins in my biceps were more severe when defined by the blue pigment. I was tribal, what ancient Anglos would consider a *savage*. Without a severed head or a scimitar, this was as close to Kali as anyone was going to get.

For my final touch, I took out the two tiny bags of ash. With a pinky, I dabbed a bit of my father on my right shoulder and a bit of my mother on my left shoulder.

Walter's moans bounced around the steel metal tub. He kept asking Royce and Kearns what was happening, and he called to me. "Kali…"

The door to the room opened again, and I jumped. Our escort with the moustache was back, and he let in Leland Moon. In the old gas chamber, Royce shut the hatch so Walter wouldn't see him.

I hadn't expected him, but I wasn't shocked to see him. He said, "I had to come." For a tic I remembered I was naked, but when Leland looked over my costume, he seemed impressed instead of aroused. "You look good. Real good." He grabbed an armful of maps from the table and walked into the viewing room. "Don't tell him I'm here." On the other side of the safety glass, he sat down in a folding chair and spread various maps on the seats around him.

When I reentered the chamber, Royce nodded to Leland in the next room. I closed the hatch all but a crack.

The guards hovered over their patient. As instructed, Royce was feeding Walter sips of water through a straw bottle to keep him hydrated through the process. The pharmahuasca had polluted his blood. Walter was squirming like mad against the restraints. One of his legs tore loose, and they had to fasten it down.

Kearns seemed horrified by my getup. He looked to Royce and back to me, hoping someone might clarify that he was indeed staring at painted nipples and privates. Royce gave him a look that told him to roll with it, whatever it was.

Walter's pupils had swollen to minimoons. When I lurched over him, he found my face and fixated on me in petrified awe. His hallucinations had started, and I was adding to them. A urine patch blossomed through the red jumpsuit. Normally the condemned wore adult diapers to prevent this final humiliation. Not on that day. The darkening stain made me think of Veda Moon at the dinner table, and that memory made me think about what he and his sister had done to Veda. It was easy for Kali to be furious.

Walter half recognized me, but didn't understand what he was seeing. Maybe he thought someone had drugged him, but he couldn't be sure. When he spoke, he might not have known who he was talking to or if he was talking to anyone. "What did you do to me?" His limbs thrashed about, and Kearns fastened the straps as if cranking a jib. Walter shouted to all of us, "You said I wasn't going to feel nothing!" He started to hyperventilate.

Walter Gretsch had no idea what was happening to him. The physical restraints must have also compounded the fear. He shouldn't have been in real physical pain, but the disorientation would have been its own kind of torment. Fear isn't pain, but it is the expectation of it.

I let him stare at me. There wasn't anything I could say that would ignite his terror the way a whirly imagination could. The less I spoke, the more inhuman I seemed. The silence made him more vocal. He spewed curses and accusations, favoring the word *cunt*. Finding the guards in his periphery, he gave them hell too. My heart raced as well, and I did my best to retain my serenity, especially nude in a room with three men. I breathed deeply into my belly to ground myself, to remember that this man couldn't hurt me. Walter spat at me, and I didn't react beyond placidly wiping his spittle off my breast.

Walter must have also realized that he couldn't hurt any of us, and so he was completely vulnerable. He shivered under my kind, reassuring smile. As the drugs worked their magic, he began hallucinating visions beyond me, somewhere behind me, possibly a mural of living characters stirring in a melting ceiling. He shrieked like a bird. I fought not to jump when he did.

I masked my own revulsion, not only of Walter, but of myself and of us all. This was what being a torturer felt like, and it felt so much worse than anything I had ever done, even though the victim was as deserving as anyone could be. Walter Gretsch twisted and shook in his restraints as waves of visions came to him. He had expected to be dead by now, and as the full flood of psychedelics coursed through him, he doubtlessly wished he was.

When Walter's convulsions settled down to predictable tremors, Royce went to the hatch and opened it slightly wider, nodding a signal to Leland to let him know we were starting to question him. Walter couldn't see him from the table.

Royce walked out to the viewing gallery and came back with a map and a note, which he unfolded beside Walter's face. I took the note from Royce but didn't open it yet—I didn't want to break eye contact with him, not when he was so mesmerized.

I spoke in the lowest portion of my natural range, with the forced calm of someone who might snap at any moment. "Where are they?"

I had to ask several times before it sunk in. I let the silence do the convincing for me. In the quiet spaces he ruminated about his situation, trying to make sense of me and what was happening to him. By now he might have even put it together that we'd tricked him, doped him up. But eventually the drugs won out. The fear was too much. When he looked at me now, he lost his breath and tried with everything he had to squirm away. I lowered a hand over his frozen, shivering face, and when I touched his cheek, he screamed bloody murder, as if my hand were a branding iron.

"Helena said you had a garden. Do you remember that garden, Walter?"

He barely squeezed out the word, "*Yes.*"

"You brought the children to that garden?"

"*Yes.*" He stared at the map, "*Never used one of those.*"

I unfolded the handwritten note from Leland, which read, "Ask him to lead you there."

"Fine. Take me there, Walter." I needed a specific name, and I pulled one from Leland's files. "How did you take Gayle Nelson there?"

"*Gayle...*"

"That's right. Gayle. Gayle's dead, Walter. You've bundled her up. How did you bundle her? Plastic?"

He hissed, "*We had a blanket. A quilt. Helena made a quilt for them kids.*"

"You wrapped Gayle in the quilt?"

"*Yes. Tight like a burrito.*"

"Then what?"

"*We carried her to the car. Late, real late. Put her in the back seat, in the bench. We put the sled in the back.*"

"Did you say sled?"

"*Sled because of Helena's foot.*" This didn't make sense to me. Royce and Kearns seemed just as confused. The way sound echoed, Leland probably heard us out there. I wondered if it made more sense to him.

"Where did you go?"

"*We drove and drove and drove. Late, real late.*" He was babbling, but not to riddle with us. His mind was probably racing too fast to put together cogent thoughts.

"Where, Walter?" He clenched and bucked on the bench, fighting his own will to keep his secrets. His gaze was lost in a spot on the ceiling, at something that had come alive for him. He gulped at it. "What are you seeing right now?"

"*Them,*" he whispered icily.

"I can make them go away. Stay with me, Walter. Where did you drive?"

"*Down the Thirteen.*"

"Route Thirteen?" I asked.

"*Yes.*" Walter drooled on the *s*.

Kearns said, "He's in California."

"*Then to Pinehurst and into the park.*"

"Is that a town?" I asked.

Royce said, "Pinehurst Road. He's in Oakland. Shit, he's right over in Oakland."

I asked, "Are you in Oakland, Walter? Is that where you're driving?"

He started crying to whatever children haunted the space over the table, "*Yes.*"

I asked, "What park, Walter?"

"*Redwoods.*"

"Redwood Regional Park," said Kearns.

"Is that right, Walter?"

"*Yes. Yes.*"

I felt our momentum build, and I wanted to keep him talking. "Where in the park?"

"*We stopped on Pinehurst at a closed trail. Dark and safe. The police don't go there, not when it's that late.*"

"How did you know where to stop? Was it marked?"

"*One thirty-seven,*" he gasped.

I had problems following him. "What is that? Is that another route?"

"*A tiny sign. One-three-seven on it.*"

Royce said, "Could be a mileage marker." He exited through the hatch to tell Leland. Out in the gallery, I saw Leland starting to check maps.

"Is that what it is, Walter? A mileage marker?"

"*Probably,*" he said.

"Then what?"

"*We carried her down the path. Only the beginning, where it was flat. Helena couldn't take hills with the fake leg. We walked off the trail, just ninety-seven paces in. Then we went downhill. I put the girl on the sled, and she went down first. I dragged the sled back up and sent Helena down the slope on the sled because it was too steep for her. Then I went down the rope.*" His eyes pinged right and left, and he whimpered at something hovering past my shoulder. He talked faster, as if he might be running out of time. "*There was a dry riverbed at the bottom. Muddy with big rocks. We pulled the sled across. From there we carved the big trees to mark the trail. Simple scratches, knee-high. Then a special symbol when we reached the garden. Bigger than the rest.*"

"What did the symbol look like?"

Walter fought for words. Initially my face had melted into something that horrified him, but whatever visions he was conjuring around me spooked him even worse. When he spoke, an innocence ushered into his voice. "*Am I dead?*"

We were so close, and I had to prod him. "You're not dead, and you're not alive."

"*Kill me*," he pleaded.

"The way you're feeling now? It can go on forever. Never living. Never dead. Always like this."

"*Kill me*."

"What did the symbol look like, Walter?"

His right arm tried to rise off the table. The straps wouldn't let him. When the arm wouldn't budge, his finger rose like a dowsing rod and pointed toward the map. He insisted, "*I'll show you. I'll show you. I'll show you.*" He repeated this phrase over and over, occasionally diverting into a screech when some hallucinated shadow leapt at him.

"Free his arm," I instructed.

"No way," said Kearns.

"He'll show us."

Royce seconded, "No fucking way."

"This is why we're here. Free his arm." Neither of them responded. I had to break character, and shout at them in my best firehouse yelp, as Pamela Wonnacott. "It's two of you versus a free arm. What the fuck are you afraid of?" Of all the things that happened in this room so far, this seemed to surprise the two guards the most. To get someone on my side, I looked through the hatch at Leland, and the guards followed my stare into the viewing gallery. Leland had heard all of this. He nodded to us, and they complied.

Kearns unleashed Walter's right arm. It flailed wildly at first, but they easily controlled it. "Easy, Walter," Royce warned. Eventually the flailing subsided.

They brought the map to Walter's stomach, and Kearns handed him a pen. Walter scratched his symbol on the paper. It was a crudely rendered outline of a house, a simple box with a pitched roof. It only took him a few seconds to scrawl it, and he dropped his pen to the floor when he was done. "*That's where the garden is.*"

Walter clammed up. His hallucinations seemed to intensify. His fear paralyzed him, and he breathed as if he were freezing to death. He fixed at a point somewhere below the ceiling at something in the air. His mouth quavered for the words that would express his purest fear. I suspect he was waiting to die.

Kearns asked, "What if everything he tells us is bullshit?"

Royce answered, "Then we do this again."

"*Kali*," Walter whispered. I ignored it the first few times, but he was persistent. "*Kali.*"

I leaned over him. "Yes, Walter."

"*You promised...*"

I felt a pinch on the outside of my thigh. It didn't register right away. Leland sprang out of his chair in the viewing gallery, but I didn't understand why for a moment. The two guards wrestled Walter's free arm, and strapped it down with effort. Leland came into the room and looked afraid.

My syringe dangled from my thigh. When I plucked it out, I could see Walter had depressed the plunger and injected the remainder of the pharmahuasca. It was probably red as a fresh mosquito bite under the blue paint. No curses could properly punctuate the moment. My hands flew to my mouth and I forgot to breathe.

It burned beneath the skin, but the drugs didn't hit me right away. That meant I got to see everything that happened next.

Walter was breathing too fast. At first I thought he was exhilarated from the burst of violence, but his body began to vibrate. Unaware of what to do, Kearns and Royce secured all the bindings. Leland stood over Walter's head and slapped his face to bring him back. The whole table shook and rattled the floor bolts. Unsure of how to help him, the two guards tried to hold him down. Kearns pressed on the man's shoulders, Royce his legs. Leland held his face between his hands and called Walter's name several times.

"You...promised," Walter grunted. He said this again several times until he began to gag.

I'd gone on a fair amount of medical calls that involved overdoses, but never for this drug. I felt for a pulse, smudging paint on his wrist and neck. His heartbeat raced. Sweat beaded up everywhere from the neck up. "Give him some water," I said. This was a guess.

Royce obliged, but Walter wouldn't take the straw into his mouth. His eyes rolled into his skull, and he couldn't even see the straw. Royce tried to pour water into his mouth, but most of it ran over his lips and cheeks. The trickle that got to his throat rolled down his windpipe until he coughed it up. His body had forgotten how to swallow.

"This is going wrong," I warned.

"We can't get him to a clinic," Royce said. "We can't take him out right now." Walter's face was tumid with blood. "What do you have in your bag?"

I'd packed light today. "Nothing that can help him." Walter's shoulders hunched up toward his ears. "We need to move him," I insisted.

Royce shook his head. Leland spoke to the prisoner. "Stay with us, Walter." Walter was not with us. He had drifted into his hallucinations, trembling.

"We need to move him," I repeated.

"A doctor will perform tests. They'll know what we did," Royce said, addressing Leland more than me.

"Let them," I said.

I looked to Leland, who remained impassive. He agreed with Royce. "We can't move him."

I panicked, as much for myself as for Walter Gretsch. Minutes from now I'd feel the same drug in my blood. If my body couldn't handle it, these three might hold me down the same way, praying my seizure would pass. With their refusal to help Walter, I understood they wouldn't help me either.

After the tight coiling of his muscles, Walter's body went slack. His jaw unclenched. Walter seemed to have a moment of clarity, and whispered to the air, "*Girls.*" The next moment his body stiffened as if an electrical current ran through it. His back bowed as much as the straps would allow. I could have run my arm under his shoulder blades. "*Girls,*" he gasped. He shook fiercely, and I could feel the floor tremor.

I'd seen this before. "This man's going into arrest." Moments later, he did just that. "No, no, no," I stammered. Walter's body seized then went limp. I felt his neck and found no heartbeat. I began CPR, and his rubber barrel of ribs gave only slightly. Royce knew CPR and breathed into Walter's mouth at intervals. Kearns undid the restraints. I pumped the man's chest for about ten minutes, until my arms were hot. Until I felt some of the first swells in my brain that told me the drug was taking hold.

When I stopped, Walter Gretsch didn't twitch a pinky.

CHAPTER 15

I knew that chemicals were behind the illusion in my head. But I couldn't deny that Gordon Ostrowski was sitting right there across the kitchen table, real as anything.

I was mute at first. I didn't have the brass I had in the real world. Dream or not, seeing Gordon Ostrowski made me regress to the level of confidence I had as a teen.

Gordon wore his red jumpsuit; the same one Walter Gretsch wore. He was handsome, pink-cheeked, and healthy. I never visited him in prison, so he might have looked like a scarecrow now. The drugs were showing me the Gordon I knew, top of the world again, teeth white as crushed seashells. His preppy hair was slicked back and clear lacquer coated his fingernails.

My palms felt the wood grain on the tabletop, even the familiar scratches I made from playing "surgeon" with potatoes and a paring knife. Our kitchen was spacious, white cabinets and granite countertops. There was a rack over the kitchen island where all the pots hung. The windows looked out onto a long, rolling lawn that ended at a wall of trees. My dad had bought and planted maples out there, so in the fall we'd get a hint of New England foliage. On that day, the leaves had turned orange and red. I could smell a hint of smoke from someone's fireplace.

"Made you breakfast." He slid a bowl of dry Cheerios across the table, which he had done many times. Gordon's generosity was always an opportunity for petty torment. Cereal without milk was his way of getting me to eat dog kibble.

"You never eat anymore," said my mother. Mom must have

been next to him all along, but I only noticed her now. She didn't look like my mom. She was naked, burned head to toe. With her hair singed off, her head was a charcoal orb laced with a network of cracks, and the cracks glowed like embers. Like a human volcano in mideruption. This wasn't how I remember her after the arson, but my imagination haunted me with the worst possible vision of my mother, assembled from stray memories of people I'd pulled out of houses and into the back of the ambulance. Part of me understood that this was my brain short-circuiting, but it didn't matter. My mother smelled like smoked meat. Faulty brain or not, it smelled real, sounded and felt real.

"That's right, Skinny. Eat up," Gordon said. Suddenly, I wondered if I was naked like my mom. It was some relief that I wasn't. I had on jeans and a Radiohead T-shirt, things I would have worn when I was sixteen. Specifically, the clothing I had worn the day I fled my home. The body inhabiting those clothes was bigger, bulkier from the muscle—my adult body. But my mother and Gordon saw me as a sixteen-year-old.

"I don't have a spoon."

"Use this." Gordon produced a fork instead of a spoon. One of the forks Leland Moon kept in his desk drawer. Too fast for me to react, he plunged it into the back of my hand, pinning it to the table. The prongs sank into the table as a knife would into a butcher block's sugar maple. The pain was excruciating, and I screamed soundlessly. Gordon's mouth lifted into his sinister smile as he watched me pluck the fork out of my own hand.

My mother wrapped her black arm around him and leaned her head on his shoulder. "It's just a pinch, sweetie. You'll shake it off." Gordon kissed her on the forehead. Slowly, I wrenched the prongs from between my metatarsals. The fork clattered on the table.

My ankle hit something under the table, and I saw the stuffed gym bag I packed when I ran away. My eyes teared at the evidence of my disloyalty. I was ashamed of myself, and also grateful to see my mother, even this horrible vision of her. "I wasn't gone long."

Gordon flashed his eyebrows and answered, "Long

enough though."

I implored her, "Why didn't you leave with me?"

"Because he's my husband." She'd given me that excuse the night before I left.

I said, "You never saw it, did you?" My mom didn't answer. She smiled at me, and Gordon protectively clung to her burnt arm.

The smell of smoke in the air grew strong, and the room warmed. Around us, flames suddenly crawled up the kitchen walls. The orange foliage through the windows was now obscured by a vibrant curtain of fire. My heart pounded. The fire covered the cabinets, even the hanging pots and pans. My skin roasted, but the fire didn't touch us. A circle around the kitchen table protected us from the flames, if not the heat. I touched my forehead to wipe off sweat and only succeeded in smearing blood on my face.

I waited for my mother to give me an answer, but she kept her head nestled against her husband's arm. She finally said, "He didn't leave me."

"That much is true, Skinny," said Gordon. "I didn't go anywhere, did I?"

"Where did you go?" my mother asked.

"To a friend's." This is what I told other people.

"Don't lie. You know I can tell," said Gordon.

"To the Y," I corrected.

"When did you make it back?"

"The place had already burned."

"You knew I was alive."

My eyes watered more, and I nodded. "I knew you were at the hospital."

"But you didn't come."

"I was waiting for you to get better." This was partly true. I didn't think she would actually die on me. Gordon's crime was still fresh, and I was mad and confused. But the real truth, and I choked on every word of it, was, "I was ashamed."

"I was alone."

I had never spoken this thought, or heard it spoken from my

mother. She passed in her hospital bed by herself, without a visit from me. She'd been drifting in and out for a few days. She might have been awake when she died, but the doctors didn't know for sure. The police hadn't arrested Gordon yet, and wouldn't for another week. I was afraid of him. I'd been too afraid of him to stay and protect my mother, and then I was too afraid of him to risk running into him at my mother's bedside.

What a crushing feeling it must be to die alone. I was terrified of it then and now. I hope my mother wasn't awake, but I always imagined her waiting for me in a blanched room, suffering until her heart finally gave out.

I wept. "I'm sorry."

"Must feel good to admit that," Gordon said. He picked a Cheerio and popped it in his mouth.

"I wanted to kill you so badly," I told him.

"Then do it." He pushed something across the table. I expected another utensil, specifically a knife. Instead, it was a hypodermic. "You know what's in there, don't you?" I knew, because my brain conjured it. This needle had a steep dose of thiopental. Put enough of that in someone and they don't need the pancuronium bromide. They would go straight and deep into a coma.

Gordon rolled up a sleeve and gave me a bare forearm to work with. His arm was miraculously hairless, except for some blond wisps along the back.

"It'll make you feel good."

"No it won't."

My mother said, "It will make you feel like you're taking back some control over your life."

"No it won't." I protested. "I thought it would, but it won't." The fire around us remained outside a perimeter about the diameter of a sumo's dohyō, but my skin cooked. All the times I'd been surrounded by fire, none of it felt this dangerous. The flames crackled even louder, and leapt off the walls, almost licking us. Smoke thickened and coughed and pulled my shoulders tight to my body. Gordon and my mother remained unconcerned, but rhythmic swells of blood surged through my fingers against the cool barrel of the syringe.

Gordon's arm was a phantom, but I believed it was real. His skin was warm. Once I touched him, he unlaced his arm from my mother's so I could focus on him alone. My mother tried to coach me through it. "Go ahead," she said. She stroked my hand with hers, and it was the first time I'd felt my mother in years. Her charred skin flaked like phyllo dough, but the structure of her fingers was still so familiar. I took her hand, careful not to crush it. The needle hovered over Gordon's arm. He was ready for it and pumped his fist to give me a good vein.

I took a breath and moved quickly.

I pushed away Gordon's arm, and, holding my mother's hand, inserted the needle into her forearm instead.

As the chemicals fed into my mother, the flames around us died down to hibachi height, and then extinguished. Within seconds, Gordon's skin browned and blackened deeper than my mom's. His body withered, as if the contents under his skin were siphoned out, and he wilted off the chair, the husk of his skin dark and shapeless as a rotten banana peel.

My mother and I remained at our quiet kitchen table, alone but together. The room was cool, although I sweated from the heat. The fire had blackened the room, but the windows still offered an unmarred view of the yard and the trees. She gazed out and admired the nature, patting my hand while her eyes drowsily fluttered. After my dad and before Gordon, we had plenty of mornings like this, quiet breakfasts with the two of us, where she closed her eyes and basked in the sunlight. Smiling blissfully, she'd savored those moments with a few deep inhales through her nostrils. As the sun gently toasted our skin, she would reach out and hold my hand the way she was now, and say, "I could take a moment like this forever."

Both of her hands wrapped around mine now, and as the serum took hold, she gradually lowered her head to the table. My mother nestled her face against my hands, breathed deeply into her nose, and fluttered her eyes as she rested.

CHAPTER 16

I didn't wake up so much as I came to an awareness that I was lucid again. I stretched out on the bed in Leland's office, back in Berkeley. Cobwebs clustered above me in the eaves.

The room was dark, and the house quiet. With the streetlamps glowing outside, it wasn't even close to dawn. Several bottles of water had been left for me at the bedside with a note reading: "Drink." I drained them. My throat was so dry it felt sore.

A stack of clean clothes, taken from my apartment in Bernal, had been left on a chair next to the bed. On a pile of folded towels, another note read: "You'll need these. We'll throw them away."

If the previous night were New Year's Eve, the vision of my mother would have been the celebratory midnight toast. The rest of my night felt more like the remainder of a debauched holiday evening, especially the bathroom sickness. I remembered hugging a commode, maybe the one downstairs. My ass ached from the runs, and my stomach felt tender from incessant purging. After I drank the water, I drifted off again from exhaustion.

Some chittery bird outside the window woke me up in the morning. My joints hurt. My thigh was knotty and tender where the needle had stuck me. I shambled downstairs to pee and stumbled into the hallway bathroom. The Moons weren't up yet, and the toilet rim was smeared with my stomach dross. I polished it clean with one of the towels.

My hair frizzed in the mirror, as much as my capellini locks could. Someone had washed the paint off my face, although blue crusts shadowed under my ears. I was wearing a loose FBI T-shirt and track pants that I had to cinch so they wouldn't fall. When I stripped down, I found that most of my body was still covered in blue paint. No one had scrubbed my body while I was out. I was happy about that.

The paint came off fairly easily in the shower, but it still took a while before I felt I'd cleaned all the blue off my body. When I was finished, I put on the T-shirt and jeans they had brought from Bernal.

Leland waited in the kitchen for me. He sat on a stool where a counter divided the kitchen and dining room, blowing steam off coffee in faded FBI sweats. I sat on the other side of the counter.

"Made you breakfast." He slid a bowl full of dry cereal across the counter. My heart forgot to beat. "It's not much, but it's all we've got this morning. Skim milk all right?" *Milk in my cereal.* I breathed again. I nodded, and he poured from the carton and slid a spoon and napkin in place. "You a coffee person?"

"Today I am." He poured a cup for me in a Cal mug, and I stirred it with milk and sugar. "How long was I out?"

"Most of a day."

"So only a day."

I could have wolfed down the cereal, but restrained myself. I began to recall everything that happened the day before. "We killed a man, didn't we?"

"It was ruled that Walter Gretsch had a coronary arrest in his cell. The prison officially found him in the morning."

"Is that the end of it?"

"The death of a sexual predator in prison doesn't earn much speculation. San Sebastián will cremate him tomorrow. Helena will claim the remains, I'm sure." While this didn't completely ease my conscience, it assured me I was safe from criminal investigation.

I ate while Leland talked. "You sad he's dead?"

I shook my head and wiped milk off my chin. "I'm sad I was the one who did it."

"It shouldn't have happened like that," he said. At first I thought he might have been blaming me for Walter's death, and then

I realized that this was as close to an apology as I'd get from him.

"We frightened that man to death."

"If he was scared going out, that's some kind of justice."

I said, "If his information doesn't lead to anything, there won't be another chance."

"Then we've done as much as we can. That'll have to be good enough. All this has to stop sometime." This was a new sentiment from Leland. Something felt different in his tone. Walter Gretsch's death might have been his call-it-quits moment. Even if we didn't find the rest of the children, maybe the death itself would serve as some sort of closure.

Around when I saw the bottom of the coffee mug, cars cranked their parking brakes outside the house. From the counter we could see across the house and out the living room windows. People piled out of cars, and I recognized their faces from the party.

He said, "You don't need to be here for this. You can go home if you want, or sleep it off upstairs. But we're going to find the garden today."

I wasn't necessarily feeling up for seeing anyone, but I didn't feel like sleeping, and it was a bad time for me to bail on those people. Casually, they breezed in through the front door. Some of them even brought their dogs, which sniffed the wood flooring entrance to exit. Roused by the noise, Tesmer shuffled out in sweats. She patted me on the back as she drifted past us to greet them. Emmanuel sprinted to the front door to sniff the dogs.

Within the next quarter hour, the house was filled with thirty people. Excited people. They beamed when they saw me and introduced themselves. I recalled some of their last names from Leland's files. Then Cindy Coates gaited into the house and threw her arms around me. She said, "You did something we couldn't."

Veda emerged, looking exhausted. Cindy waved at him, so he shuffled toward us. The guests gave him booming "Good mornings" as he cut through the crowd, and he rolled his eyes at most of them. I hoped the shower had washed off all of Walter's smell. I smelled myself, and I smelled strongly of bottled botanicals. When Veda got close, he said without emotion, "So Walter's dead. Did he go down peaceful like your other patients?"

"The opposite of that."

This seemed to give him a glimmer of satisfaction, but it didn't improve his overall sourness. "Bet you think you're a hero."

"Anything but," I said.

"So, you think you're part of the family now?" he asked.

"Don't get like this, not today," Cindy said. She reached for his hand and urged him, "Come with us today." I didn't know if it was a good idea for Veda to join the search, nor did I know if I wanted to spend any more time with him.

"To find dead girls? How the hell could I miss it?" Some people scowled when they overheard him. Instead of contrition for his insensitivity, he puffed up like someone starting a bar fight. "What?"

Cindy reached around his back and placed her hand on top of all the four-prong scars. Then she tilted his head and kissed him softly on the lips. I hadn't realized they were a couple until that moment. Veda didn't kiss back so much as let himself be kissed. He let her lean on him like a koala wrapped around a eucalyptus. When she held him long enough, her touch had a tranquilizing effect.

* * *

We packed into several cars, and our caravan drove though the Oakland Hills until we reached Redwood Regional Park. I rode with Leland and Tesmer in the lead car. Veda drove with Cindy. It was still early enough that the trails wouldn't be crammed with hikers and mountain bikes, and we weren't even headed to the main park entrances. Early in the morning, fog blanketed the Oakland Hills, and where the highway let out, the air was a milky vapor between the spectral silhouettes of trees. Pinehurst Road snaked around the perimeter of the park, and we crawled around the turns until we leveled out at the top of the hills. "There it is," Leland said. He spotted a small white sign, which marked our distance at 1.37 miles from the start of Pinehurst. The three black letters were stacked vertically, and the decimal point was barely visible. "One thirty-seven."

We parked at a turnoff just past it. As we piled out, I noticed we were above the fog line. The vast park sprawled down through a steep descent into a gully carpeted by trees. From where we stood, the woodland stretched as far as we could see, with the fog nestled in the ravine. I couldn't hear other cars, and it was hard for me to fathom that downtown Oakland's modest bouquet of high-rises stood less than fifteen minutes away.

Despite what the name might indicate, the park wasn't just a redwood forest. The woods grew wild with a variety of trees and brush. The brambly branches hid the landscape from our gang of thirty, who marched up and down the road along the 1.37 mile marker for some time until a woman in a flannel top shouted, "Found it!"

A screen of leafy brush had hidden the trailhead. The woods grew thick and tangled just a few feet in. Moss and lichens coated the trunks, and ferns and garroting vines filled in the spaces between the trees. A post marking the trail had possibly stood where there was now a hole as wide as my boot sole. Any signposts had been uprooted. We surrounded Leland as he looked over a map of the area. "It's not even on here," he said.

We walked single-file behind Leland, all of us lugging stuffed backpacks. I didn't even know what was in mine. He counted his paces aloud and shortened his strides so they might match Walter's. None of us spoke, and I listened to birdcalls and twig snaps as I performed the same count in my head.

"Ninety-seven," Leland announced. "Ninety-seven paces in." The trail had been flat so far, and aside from the two downed trees we needed to throw our legs over, it had been an easy walk. From that point, the path hooked to the right and began a steep climb, so it felt like were at a proper stopping point. Because of Helena's leg, Walter wouldn't have taken her up the grade.

Leland walked down the column of people and examined the plants along the edge of the dust and rock path. He struck to the side where the path sharply descended into the gully. This wasn't a cliff, but the grade didn't seem walkable either.

"Here," Leland said. He crouched by a pine trunk, and I was close enough to see what caught his attention. The bark of the trunk had worn away in a ring by the base, leaving a few horizontal abrasions as if sawed and abandoned by the laziest of lumberjacks. "See here? Someone could have tied something around this." He pantomimed holding a rope that would have knotted around this trunk, and then drew a line in the air across the trail. "It would have run across the path here, and then down the slope...here." He crouched on the other side of the path and pointed at a few faint tread marks in the earth from where a rope had dug into the soil. "Walter would have tied his sled to this tree, run the rope over here, and lowered a body once it was tied to the sled. Then he would have pulled the sled up and lowered Helena down. Then he could have gone down himself, holding onto the rope to steady himself on the descent. Let's unpack."

He walked behind me and unzipped my backpack, pulling out a bundle of rope. Light, red, and banded like a kingsnake. The pack had been heavy, but not heavy enough to contain some sea-soaked coil of wharf hawser. The two men wrapped and knotted the red rope around the same tree Walter Gretsch had chosen and threw the cord over the hillside. Leland descended first. Royce followed, then me, and then Tesmer.

"Take it slow," Leland cautioned us. "And watch for critters."

"Critters?"

"Snakes. Bugs." He meant spiders too, I was sure of it. Strangely enough, the idea of running into a spider didn't bother me then. As I scaled down the slope, I kept my eyes on my boot tips and anything immediately surrounding it.

The angle wasn't so steep that I felt like I was repelling off a cliff face, but the rope definitely steadied me. On the way down, I brushed away stray branches, and the vines scratched my arms. I kept a steady pace so Tesmer wouldn't slide on top of me. Because I was so close to Leland, I could hear him call out observations to Royce and the rest of us. "Look here. Someone dug in with a foot."

When I passed, the indentation was obvious. I put my own toe in it. I wondered how many years it had been since people had made this descent.

Like an ant procession, we clambered down the slope through the trees and brush until the terrain leveled out. The land challenged inexperienced hikers in the group. An older man with wobbly legs stepped sideways, fiddler crab-style, to traverse the brush and still managed to fall on his butt. The dogs scrambled the way they would paw down a flight of stairs. The descent was probably sixty feet, and it took a while for all of us to get down. I marveled at how Cindy made it down with in a sneaker and a prosthetic, something more like a metal tibia and not the running blade. Veda followed her, morose. When Cindy reached for his hand, he wouldn't hold it.

"There," said Leland, pointing to an aisle of ground where the weeds flattened out compared to the rest of the brush. Kneeling to examine the brush, he pointed to areas where some of the branches had been snapped. "He cut it back a little so Helena could walk it."

Forming a line on either side of what might have been an unkempt trail, each of us stood within arm's reach of the next person, walking through the forest in an approximation of a grid search. Rounding crooked trees and stepping through the growth on the forest floor, we looked for anything that stood out among the leaves and dried needles. Several of us stooped to examine inconsistencies, such as a stick that looked like a bone, but none of us found anything. Eventually, the shrubs stopped, and the ground was matted with crisp orange leaves atop a stratum of decomposed sludge.

I didn't know what to look for. The last child would have been buried twelve years ago, so we were looking for inconsistencies in the soil after twelve seasons had layered the gorge with moss and pine needles. Leland seemed to doggedly follow the path where feet might have trod. Those with dogs let the canines lead on their leashes, sniffing at everything.

At the back of the line, Veda complained to Cindy, not for our benefit, but loud enough for the rest of us to hear. No one else was talking, and voices carried in the woods. He said, "You think we're going to find something? You think it's going to fix anything if we do?" Cindy didn't reply. She knew people were listening.

I was next to Tesmer, and whispered to her, "Do you think he's right?"

"I think he's earned the right to a dissenting opinion," she said.

I tried to imagine coming across the body of someone I loved. In particular, I imagined what it would have been like to discover my mother in the cinders. The girls we were looking for would have been skeletonized by now. If we found someone, we wouldn't even know who she was without testing. I wondered whether unidentifiable remains would lessen the shock for the families. I suspected this kind of discovery wasn't something you could ever prepare for. Speaking as someone who had to cope with a murder in the family, you never get over something like that. You're just graced with the ability to push it out of your mind from time to time.

Veda said, "Seriously, what do you think this will give them?" A few people looked over their shoulders and gave Veda hateful looks.

Cindy murmured, "Then they'll know."

"Knowledge is power," Veda snarked. His irreverence was getting on my nerves. In a different place I might have slapped the shit out of him. He was the only child who came away from Walter and Helena with his life and his legs.

"Here," said Royce. He rushed to a tree trunk and pointed out something to Leland. I saw it shortly after. Four small lines had been carved into the tree, as if someone had raked a sharp fork through the bark.

This discovery sent a ripple of emotion through the group. Many let out deep sighs, some out of worry and others out of relief that we were on the right trail. A few of the couples among us held each other, and eyes watered as we realized we were getting closer.

Leland scanned the forest until he found the next one. "There." An identical carving etched into a trunk twenty feet ahead of us.

Like a slalom course, Walter had carved out markers on the outsides of the path, first to the left, then to the right. Once we knew what we were looking for, we plodded forward more deliberately.

We came to the portion of the forest where the redwoods started. They grew tall and straight, just like at Jeffrey Holt's cottage. We came to a creek bed that had dried to mud. My boots barely sank into it. "I think we're headed in the right direction," Leland shouted at the head of the pack, energized. On the other side, he shouted, "Here's another one," pointing to another four scratches carved into one of the thinner redwoods.

Now that we were under the tall trees, the daylight dimmed even more. The forest canopy diffused the sunlight and made noon seem like dusk. It felt cloistered there.

At long last I came across something notable in the path. A small cluster of rocks. One stone the size of a bread loaf rested on top of two others in the world's chintziest pyramid. I had to remind myself this wasn't a treasure hunt, and I felt ghoulish for my momentary elation.

With some effort I rolled off the top rock.

Out of the crack sprinted a spider big as a kumquat.

I gulped. It was a nasty one, hairless but red with a lobster-like shell and fangs that might have been its ninth and tenth legs. I stepped back, but my heart didn't race. I didn't stomp on it either. After a deep breath, I simply watched it run. It scrambled past me, disoriented from having its roof ripped off, and I let it go. The woman next to me yelped when she saw it.

We kept on. Leland, Tesmer, and Royce spotted the next set of carvings, until we reached a huddled grouping of trees surrounded by a field of ferns. They circled like a crown and rose until the white sunlight blotted out their tops. We passed through narrow crawl spaces between the trunks into a clearing maybe fifteen feet across. Those who couldn't fit into the clearing peered in from between the trees. Dried needles had mounded up over time, and my boots bounced on the soft heap of needles as if it were a mattress.

"There." Leland pointed to a trunk coated in moss. I didn't see it at first, but Leland had spotted hard angles—almost a Z—carved into the bark. Tesmer tore down the moss that obscured the rest of the incision, wiping off the sod with her sleeves, and then ferreting her finger into the groove to scoop out the residue. The carving was a house, the height of my forearm. Like Walter's drawing, it was a crude box at the base, then a simple pitched roof and a chimney the size of a cigar butt. This was home.

One of the dogs barked, and then others barked. Their owners let them off leash, and they sniffed around the grounds, pinning themselves to several spots within this ring of trees. Two of them yelped at a patch of ground close to the house carving. Leland unzipped Tesmer's bag for more tools. He pulled out a shovelhead, then from Royce's bag he retrieved several lengths of dowel that he screwed together until the various segments formed a full-size, five-foot shovel. By then his sweat turned the back of his shirt see-through. He started digging while the dogs howled around him, and most of the crowd looked on in horror and fascination, some of them clinging to the trunks around the perimeter. I caught a fleeting glimpse of Veda Moon back there with Cindy. He looked terrified, his chin receding into his neck, possibly on the verge of crying. If I thought I had any chance of comforting him, I would have gone to him. Cindy held him from behind, weeping into the back of his shirt.

Leland and Royce cleared away the top layer with clumped bundles of needles in their arms. I dropped to my knees and helped them push aside the topsoil. Leland snagged his finger on something sharp and nursed it in his mouth, but it didn't stop him from digging. He dug gloves out of his backpack and gave a pair to each of us. They were nitrile, thicker than latex, thinner than mittens.

Leland feverishly tore up the earth with his hands. I felt his eagerness—he had waited so long for this—and I tried to keep up with him. The moist soil diffused into the air like ground coffee beans. Tesmer stood with the shovel, waiting for the surface layers to be cleaned off before she sunk the spade into the dirt. Our circle of spectators watched, quite literally forming a funeral gathering. At least one woman mopped her eyes with a shirt-sleeve. I wondered whose mother she was.

Once the loose debris was cleared, a subtly humped mound of solid earth remained. The dogs barked at the air as we stirred up trace scents of aged compost. Tesmer started in with the shovel, and I scooped what I could with a trowel from Royce's backpack. I'm sure there was a more methodical way to excavate this plot, but no one much cared. None of us cared about procedure, not even the federal agent. No reason to, really. The criminals had already been caught.

Slowly, we amassed termite hills of clumped clay as we burrowed two feet down.

Tesmer alerted, "Look, look…" She'd found something, and then we all saw it: a sharp nub in the soil. Not a root, not a rock. Leland cast a look back at the rest of the search team. He seemed unsure of whether everyone should be watching this, but it was too late now. Some of the crowd stepped closer. Some averted their eyes and looked up at the branches above the clearing. Crouched by the pit, I could no longer see Veda or Cindy.

Leland's glove stroked away the dirt. The nub became a tine. Its color faded from deep chocolate to birch bark. Daintily it protruded. When enough soil had been cleared away the nub became a knuckle. The knuckle became a hand. Onlookers moaned behind us. Leland's head dropped between his shoulders. At first I assumed it was sadness, but his lips rippled in a silent prayer. When the prayer was over, Leland cleared away more of the soil, fiercely vigilant. Breathing through a clenched jaw, he siphoned loud inhales through his nostrils. Royce, Tesmer, and I worked at the same pace. Our first knuckle was a distal phalanx—the tip of a middle finger. It sat closer to the surface because the body had been buried face down, and the fingers curled. Based on the angle of the hand, we shifted where we dug and cleared away sections that revealed a torso and legs. I felt on the verge of a catastrophic sob, and yet I didn't feel sadness.

As we unearthed a pelvis, a new feeling came: *gloom*, the dread of something unexpected, and the feeling that nothing good would relieve the hopelessness. Those bones were from a girl. Every cubic inch of dirt we cleared away made that more of a glaring reality. The dress, the hair, and the hips—even on a girl not fully developed, there were differences.

Her remains issued the tang of rotten strawberries. Royce's arm covered his nostrils. Given what I've smelled on the job, I'd expected something stronger, but she'd been there for at least twelve years. Anything that would have given off those strong meaty odors had already nourished the ground.

The families around us reacted with wet, sickly sobs. Someone called to God. One man, maybe convinced this was his daughter, buckled to his knees and bit his fingers as he cried. His wife rubbed his shoulders. I couldn't see Cindy or Veda.

Carefully we revealed the full figure. Three feet down in the hole, we uncovered a small skeleton with bird bones. Rags clung to the bone, and most of the fabric had been eaten. The remaining patches faded to an overcast version of baby blue. A pink plastic watch loosely coiled around one wrist. No shoes.

Leland motioned to her legs. He meant to speak to Tesmer, but we all heard. "The right leg's been severed below the knee." I thought this might be Julie Diehl, but then remembered Julie had been buried below the shed. A new dread struck me as I realized that what happened to Cindy Coates might have happened to others.

Leland gently rolled the skull to one side. His gloved finger glided along the teeth and stopped at one that was slightly off kilter. "She's the right age. Most of her baby teeth are out, but there are still a few left. Some of the permanent teeth are still pushing their way in."

I needed air. I stepped back from our fresh grave and withdrew past the rest of our search team, out through the circle of trees. The families were so consumed in their own grief that they didn't acknowledge me as I passed.

As I walked through the ferns, I saw Cindy and Veda against the thickest redwood trunk in the cathedral. No one paid attention to them, and in turn, Cindy and Veda ignored the rest of us. Cindy stroked her boyfriend's forehead. Veda Moon lay stiff with his legs splayed on the ground. He looked somewhere between when he's wet his pants and what I imagined would be a seizure. His body quivered as if freezing to death.

I climbed back inside the circle of trees and whispered in Leland's ear, passing a message along about his son. He discreetly stood back from the bones and circled the crowd to reach Veda, motioning to Tesmer to join us. Once the agent stepped away, the rest of the crowd stepped cautiously forward, taking a better look at the skeleton, wondering if she was theirs.

Tesmer and Leland helped his son to his feet. Veda looked confused, like he wasn't sure how he got here. His father whispered in his ear. I stayed far enough away so I couldn't hear. Veda seemed too consumed with his own emotions to listen, but he nodded when his father finished, faking understanding of whatever consolation Leland gave him. I retreated back to the crowd to give them privacy, but couldn't help watching them. They gave each other a quick, violent hug, only lasting a moment before Veda pushed his father away. The two Moon men stared at each other. Leland tried to touch him again, but his son shrank from his father's hand. Tesmer did the same, with the same result. Veda turned from them and walked back from where we came, toward the slope and the red rope. Cindy followed him, simpering apologetically to the Moons. She caught up to Veda and tried to touch him, but he shrugged off her hand as well. He seemed unreachable. I couldn't articulate why I was so worried, but I sensed that however our discovery made me feel, it hit Veda Moon in a place no one could reach.

When Leland passed by again, I said, "You don't have to be here. You can go with him."

"Who else is going to do this?" He sounded so taxed. "Veda will get over it. Maybe not today, but eventually." When I tried to touch him for comfort, he warned, "My son—my business."

We waited for the local police. At that point Leland had to call it in. Leland also called the FBI, who would arrive later. The forensic team stretched yellow tape around tree trunks. Photographers with long lenses snapped every angle, and the pit was marked with a small yellow sandwich board with the number 1. I wish I'd been able to leave with Veda and Cindy, but the rest of us stayed behind so officers could interview and then dismiss us.

They asked everyone, "How did you know to look here?"

"Leland," we all said. "He talked to Walter Gretsch." The police would only speculate about what must have come up in those conversations.

The crowd petered out after they were dismissed. It was a quiet exodus. No one came back to Berkeley. I wished I'd been able to drive myself home. The same way that attending to every client reminded me of my own mortality, I felt closer to death now. I wanted to be alone. But my new rental car was parked at the Moon house, so I rode with Tesmer and Leland, knees cramped in the backseat.

Veda had left hours before we were able to drive back. Once the police came, we were overwhelmed by the flurry of activity and interviews. Now that we were headed back to Berkeley, I thought about the youngest Moon again. When he left, he seemed changed. The gravity of that girl's remains seemed to eat at him worse than the phantom stench of Walter Gretsch. Without a hint of his usual defiance, I thought I'd detected a resignation in his face.

In the rearview, Leland locked on the oncoming road with a distressed squint. He said, "You made this happen." For a second I thought this was an accusation, but then I realized he was thanking me. Even Tesmer looked over her shoulder and smiled.

I smiled halfheartedly. "I hope it was worth it."

"You seem distant. What are you thinking about?"

I answered honestly. "Veda."

Tesmer had been messing with her phone the whole ride, and she checked it again. She said to her husband, "He hadn't texted."

"Does he usually?" I asked.

She seemed annoyed. "He does when I ask him to." She tried to call her son, but the phone rang all the way to voicemail. She placed a hand over her heart and breathed deeply. It seemed all of us tensed at once.

Leland bit a knuckle. "Call Cindy."

Cindy picked up when Tesmer called and confirmed that she'd

dropped off Veda in Berkeley.

"Where are you?"

"My home," she said through the speaker.

Leland accelerated.

When we reached Berkeley, he rolled fast into their driveway and skidded into park. Both doors flung open as the Moons spilled out of the car. Leland and Tesmer ran to their door. I was afraid to get out of the car.

Through the walls of the house, and through the glass of the car, the unmistakable scream of Leland Moon jolted me.

CHAPTER 17

I burst through their front door to find the living room vacant and the house still. I listened for a moment, but nothing made a sound. I lightly stepped through the hallway toward the bedrooms. A frayed black Persian runner softened my footsteps. All the doors were closed, which kept the sun out of the corridor.

The first door opened to the salmon bathroom I'd used that morning. The toilet bowl still showed streaks from a hasty towel wipe. Stray drops of water fell from the showerhead.

Emmanuel barked somewhere in the backyard, but I couldn't hear people inside or outside.

I continued down the hall and tried the next doorknob, which sat loose in the bore hole with some of the gloss rubbed from the brass finish. I twisted slowly but the spring still whined. Inside I found a shallow closet with towels.

The next rattling knob revealed the master bedroom, where Leland and Tesmer slept. Not a trace of them. The windows looked out onto the backyard, and I saw Emmanuel trot in wide circles on the lawn, occasionally barking up at squirrels in the trees. Amid a predominantly white room, purple bed sheets stretched tight as a hotel mattress. A shallow trough indented the right side of the bed from where someone would have lain. The room connected to a private bathroom, which wafted a warm, damp musk. The mirror through the open door reflected an empty bathtub and deep blue tiles.

One more door remained at the darkest end of the hallway. This would have to Veda's bedroom. My brain flickered with memories of medical calls, entering homes to find broken bodies on the floor and unique blood splashes. For just a moment, I flexed and released my muscles as if preparing for a terminus, anything to steel myself before I turned the knob and found whatever scene I would never be able to forget.

I pushed open the door. Veda's room contained no humans. His running shoes had been kicked off on the gray carpet, one tipped on its side. A sweaty long-sleeve jersey had been dropped in a wad like a used tissue. The room was painted olive green, the same shade as the station wagon once owned by Walter Gretsch and Helena Mumm. Unlike his parents, Veda drew his shades to block out the sun. The room stank with alkaline fumes from a young man who was sexually active with himself. Dresser drawers spilled out clothing. The posters on the walls featured graffiti art, one of which had been stylized to look like a vintage war propaganda poster featuring a monkey in a Mao hat. This wasn't the bedroom of a young man, but a boy's bedroom.

Above me, the ceiling groaned.

From upstairs, Leland let out a stifled scream, sounding as if he'd been holding it back for some time. A second voice barked something too muffled for me to understand. I ran back down the hall and scrambled up the steps.

The staircase to the office was coated in loose papers, and when I ascended to the landing, those papers littered the carpeting like crispy forest leaves. Maps had been torn off the corkboards so fast, pushpins still tacked up shreds. The files formerly stacked on Leland's desk had been torn into confetti and cast across the floor.

I suspected that Veda had come up there and destroyed his father's work when he came home, punishment for having kept his trauma so fresh for so long. At the top step I found a smashed photo frame. The frame had contained the paper from the post office, where years ago Veda had written his name and freed himself. Now it was lost among the rest of the debris.

The family gathered at the opposite end of the office, where the spare bed sat by the far window. Leland lay on the carpet, bleeding.

Flat on his back, the same way I first met him in Clayton. His hand pressed against a large red wound in his abdomen. Tesmer kneeled by his head, and Veda stood over them both, a dark silhouette against the late afternoon sun.

In the corner, where the old spider webs clung under the eaves, stood Helena Mumm. Her nose crooked from when I'd broken it, and bruises hung under both eyes. Helena hadn't seen a doctor to have it bandaged, or felt the need to cover up the injury.

She swayed from side to side, switching her weight from the prosthetic to the real foot. The floor moaned with each movement. Her left foot, the real foot, stepped on Leland's semiautomatic pistol. She wore the same tropical dress she'd had on outside San Sebastián when she had visited her brother. I wondered if she wore it to keep her brother's smell on her. Veda would be able to smell it too, but sallow as he appeared, I neither saw nor smelled evidence that he had vomited.

Helena Mumm held a revolver in her left hand and a chef's knife in her right. The knife was slicked with Leland's blood. Her chest heaved as she wiped the blade clean on her dress. She kept her chin tucked, and her eyes burned under her brows. She was both feral and mountainous.

Helena's pliable expression cast loving looks at Veda and boiling rage at the rest of us. When she saw me, she said, "Scum," and spat on the carpet. In her next breath she sweetened for Veda. "Is she related?"

Veda forced a reply. "Does she look related?"

"You can never tell these days. Distant cousin, in-law—"

"She's not family," he said.

"Family," Helena said to herself. From her inflection, I guessed she had considered this word's assorted meanings. Perhaps she and Veda had even discussed it before we arrived. She might have spoken to him in that wistful tone she used when I first met her.

Veda seemed too terrified to move. The whites of his eyes were as wide as the night he peed himself at the dinner table.

She pointed the knife at us. "I went to pick up Walter's body.

You know they went ahead and burned him without my say-so? Now all I got is ashes." The knife point waggled loosely like a twiddling pencil, so light in her hands. "What, do you think I'm stupid? I wouldn't know what happened? Trash, all of you. Thought you were better than us. Thought I wouldn't find you."

I eased my cell phone out of my pocket, but for a diabetic in a dark room, she had keen eyes. "Doesn't matter if you call the police. It'll be over by the time they get here." She was drawn back to Leland when he gasped from the pain. "He was our son, you know. We raised him. That was my *man*..." She gestured to Veda Moon. "This boy's real daddy."

Tesmer's eyes darted everywhere, searching for a weapon or a shield. I caught her eyeing the gun under Helena's foot. Helena scolded us, "You couldn't just let him be. You had put him down like an animal." In her rage, Helena intentionally let slip her poised manner of speech, and spoke in a tough accent so she could throw her primal disgust in our faces. "Well, I come for you now. I'm *a-finish* it. You want to have it all out in in private? I'm *a-finish* it in private."

She barreled toward Tesmer and Leland. Her hulking mass shook with each step, but she moved faster than I'd have predicted a woman her size could move. She didn't choose to shoot them. She intended to use the knife, and she held it blade up at her waist.

I was too far away to rush her. If I tried to charge her, she'd probably shoot me as if shooing away a bug. I didn't mean enough for her to want to cut me.

Veda stepped in front of his parents and straddled his father's knees, and this intervention brought Helena Mumm to a shuddering standstill.

His face was calm and his voice easy as he said, "Come on, Mama." *That voice.* That sickening, nightmarish baby voice he'd used at the dinner table. Tesmer grimaced when she heard it; the surreality of that voice coming out confused and horrified her. Leland's agony consumed him too much for a strong reaction, but he winced too. But this was the tone that Helena wanted to hear, the sound of a young boy cooing to his mother.

Helena lowered the knife.

Tesmer gasped, fighting not to debase herself with sniveling.

The big woman was captivated by the entrancing stare of Veda Moon, and by his soothing, infantile tone. "Come on, Mama."

I inched closer, until I'd entered the room too far to dive down the stairs if Helena decided to fire at me. The closer I got, the easier it would be for her to shoot me. She only needed marginally decent aim, and she likely had six shots to work with.

I couldn't take my eyes off Veda myself, as he lifted his arm and touched the woman's face. "It's all right, Mama," he soothed.

Helena gaped, her arms atremble at being so touched. She couldn't stop from leaning her cheek into his fingers. Her face brightened. "I missed you," she croaked.

"I missed you too," Veda said in his baby voice. He drew her bulk into his arms. He was such a thin young man, but he managed to wrap his long arms around her easily and kissed the top of her head. She snuggled into his shoulder, whimpering with gratitude. Tears dripped onto his jersey.

"We don't need this, Mama," he said. He stroked the hand that held the gun.

I stalked two steps closer.

Helena had taken her foot off the second gun, which now lay unattended on the floor behind her. I saw Tesmer looking at the gun, and then looking at me, hoping one of us would seize the opportunity. If only it were that simple.

Helena lifted her head off Veda's shoulder, and he smiled at her. I hadn't seen him smile much, and never like that. She looked down at the revolver in her hand, shrugged and simpered, "Baby, we need to do this." She looked down at Veda's mother and father. "You want to come with me, don't you?"

"Of course I do." Another few steps and I was as close to Helena as Tesmer.

"Then we need to do this. It'll be quick, I promise." A tear rolled down her frown line. "Lickety-split and we'll be gone. We'll go wherever you want."

Veda's fingers curled around her gun hand. The same fingers that had lovingly stroked her cheek now tightened on the revolver. "I need this," he insisted. His voice dropped into a man's tone, and his placating smile flattened into a sneer.

Helena was confused. "What are you doing?" My small steps couldn't go unnoticed anymore. I was too close. Suddenly, she looked in my direction. "What the hell is this?"

The gun rose, but Veda steered it away from me as it went off. Glass tinkled. In the enclosed space, the shot shattered our ears, leaving a piercing whine in its wake. The bullet hit a glass pane next to them.

Veda struggled with Helena until he snatched the gun. For a moment, he held the revolver, scorching himself on the barrel before he controlled it by its grip. He only maintained control of the weapon for a moment.

A prehistoric squall came out of Helena. She came at him with arms flying and clawed at him until she'd batted the gun out of his hands. We all watched it fly out the shattered window.

Veda punched her, but he'd never been taught how to throw a punch. He landed a soft blow and yelped when he crunched his knuckles. If he'd caught her in the nose again, it might have been enough to stun her, but he just caught her on the fleshiest part of her jowl.

Helena did know how to fight, and she didn't hesitate. She threw an elbow, catching Veda under his chin. He collapsed to the carpet.

Leland tried to kick her from the floor. His wound took a lot of the fight out of him, and he moaned when he tried to move his leg. Helena stayed out of reach.

Perhaps spurred from Helena knocking her son down, Tesmer lunged across the carpet for the second gun, but Helena kicked the Glock under the bed, swooped down, and slashed Tesmer across the back of the leg. She rolled aside to dodge the second stroke of the knife, and then cried out a few seconds later when the pain set in.

Helena blocked my path to the bed and the gun, so I stormed her. She lashed out, and I barely avoided getting my stomach sliced open. Her movements were powerful and deliberate. If she cut me, there wouldn't be any surface wounds—she'd dig in with the steel. But so long as I was a primary target, she wouldn't descend on Leland or Tesmer and finish them off.

I kept some distance from her, but after a few misses, she was impatient to hurt me and lunged, giving me an opening. I sent a haymaker into her ear. I wanted to knock her out, but her bulk absorbed the hit. Instead of concussing her, I whipped up her fury.

She stumbled after me, tottering like a penguin on the plastic leg. The shiny metal knife tip darted here and there. I couldn't predict how she would move, and it was happening too fast for me to consider fight strategy. I could only retreat.

The next time she stabbed at me, I pulled my hips back, and fell on my ass. I scrambled backward, crab-style, as she hurtled toward me.

I needed something to defend myself with, some kind of weapon. *Why couldn't Veda have held onto the gun?* I thought. It could have all been over by now. But Helena had incapacitated the Moons. Veda had resumed his paralysis. Tesmer rolled in pain from her leg wound. And despite all of his FBI training, Leland lay bleeding out on the carpet.

My back pressed against the desk, so I couldn't retreat any farther. With only a moment of decision afforded to me before Helena pounced, I remembered the bottom drawer. I tore it open. Loose metal jangled. I scooped out a handful of steel.

Helena raised the knife high above her head so she could plunge it deep into me.

I jabbed into her body. Helena yelped. The knife faltered, and she staggered back two steps. A fork dangled from her rib cage.

Instead of plucking out the fork, Helena marveled at it. Pumped full of adrenaline, she might not have felt it. If you plugged four prongs the size of nails into a tender spot below my left nipple, I'd probably drop. Not so Helena Mumm.

As soon as I climbed to my feet, she ran at me. I barely had time to toreador out of reach. As she passed, I sunk another fork into her upper shoulder. The prongs stopped short at the scapula. This time she screamed, and swiped at me, the blade narrowly missing my arm.

She cornered me by the desk, the equivalent of being against the ropes in a boxing ring. She swung her knife in the motion of an upper cut, intending to slice my neck; and by some miracle I dodged it and stabbed a fork into her deltoid. Her momentary disorientation allowed me to skirt around her to the open side of the room.

By the third fork, the pain didn't surprise her. She just became incensed. Helena scowled at me and zigzagged the knife. I thrust my next fork low, and it landed in her thigh.

She groaned. The collective agony of the wounds was wearing her down. Helena was too charged up to remove any of the forks, so the flatware flopped off her like migration tags on a wild animal.

Veda moved behind her, although I'd been too preoccupied to watch him approach. Stepping behind her back, he scooped the remainder of the forks. With Veda behind her and me in front of her, Helena didn't know where to focus. She looked over her shoulder at her would-be son, dumbfounded. "Baby?"

I still had a few forks, and now Veda had his own quiver. The three of us formed a triangle. Helena looked at me and then back to Veda, questioning why he had weapons in his hands. "Baby?"

Veda didn't respond.

She kept us at bay with the knife, but the dynamic had changed. She no longer had the momentum. Instead of lashing out at us, she held the knife to protect herself from us.

Veda struck next, swift as a scorpion. While she aimed the knife at me, he plunged two forks so that they rooted in her middle back and right ass cheek. He howled at her, his voice not as untamed as Helena's, nor as afflicted as Leland's. He sounded lustful for violence.

Helena slashed through the air behind her and nicked his forearm, right atop his self-inflicted scars. He plunged another fork between her shoulders. Another fork found her kidney. She squawked as if something had caught in her windpipe, and then her arms spasmed. I plunged two forks into her chest. I operated without thinking, but looking back, I suppose that was the moment when it started to feel wrong.

Helena's arm dropped, and her fingers uncoiled. The knife fell silently on the carpet. I kicked it toward the staircase. I wanted to stop then. Since Leland first cuffed me, all I wanted to do was walk away. The more I involved myself, the more my actions and their consequences tied to those of the Moon family. I wanted all of this to finish. With Helena Mumm disarmed, I might finally leave them.

I dropped my forks on the carpet.

Veda kept his. He wasn't finished.

He planted his remaining forks into the woman. Now unarmed, her entire body was a target; he drove the prongs until they hit bone. The spilled blood inebriated him in a sadistic frenzy, until his last fork entered her stomach, where she had stabbed his father. When he stepped back, he panted and stared at the blood on his hands.

Helena's legs quavered. She dropped to her knees, her weight quaking the floor. She stretched her arms toward the ceiling, possibly longing for whatever god would have her. A dozen steel rods protruded from her, glinting in the cascade of sunlight from the front window. Helena Mumm had turned into an effigy of Saint Sebastian.

I attended to the Moons. Tesmer held her bloody calf, but the gash in her leg didn't seem major. I was worried for Leland. He could have passed for dead but for a fluttering gasp, as a rivulet of blood drooled from his lips. His eyes couldn't focus, and he was possibly delirious from blood loss. While I dialed 911, I saw Veda from across the room.

Veda had retrieved the chef's knife from the floor. My cell phone was ringing at my ear. He walked back over to Helena, who was sobbing from both the pain and the understanding that she had lost. The emergency operator picked up, but I was too transfixed by the youngest Moon to speak.

With both hands, Veda thrust the knife into Helena's neck until the blade disappeared. Blood sprayed on his arms and stomach. Veda cherished the moment. I saw the relief in his face. His hands stayed on the handle so he could savor the woman's every tremor, and he rotated the blade so she would feel it more. She convulsed as she expired, her eyes frozen on him.

Sometime later, I would realize that I hadn't issued a word of protest.

CHAPTER 18

Mortality may be universal, but people experience death in any number of ways. I can't pretend to understand what that experience is, since I have never gone through it (*yet*, I suppose). When it happens to me, I don't know whether it will come as a relief, even deliverance, or whether it will seem like nagging regret over a life unfulfilled, or even the bleak misery of knowing I'll be orphaned again once I sever my connection to the world of the living. Some clients have expressed a mournful resignation of leaving life incomplete, while others have seemed petulantly exuberant that they were exiting the world on their own terms. Walter Gretsch ended his life in confusion, haunted by his victims, and as I like to imagine, possibly tortured by the thought that he might pass into an eternal torment for the things he'd done. When Helena Mumm died, I sensed that she felt cheated by her life, denied a child and a family, and in denial about the pain she had inflicted on others.

Those who witness the transformation of the living into the dead respond to the phenomenon with vastly different reactions as well. Families of my clients have wept from the possible selfish desolation that comes from understanding that you will never see that person again. After unearthing the offspring buried within that redwood cathedral, the wreckage of those families reminded me how mortality might harrow the best of us. Conversely, Veda Moon took gluttonous satisfaction in watching Helena pass on, and possibly drew the strength he needed to move on from his own trauma.

Since death can be experienced in infinite variations, I cannot place a universal value on it. This also means that I cannot place a universal value on what it means to bring death to another person. Let's just say I can't approach my work with the same certainty as before. So I'm taking a break and considering other ways I might help ease suffering.

Shortly after Helena Mumm died, I visited Gordon Ostrowski at San Sebastián. I didn't say anything to him. Not that I was afraid to talk to him. I simply sat on the other side of the glass and observed him. At first Gordon leered at me, as though no time had passed, and I was the same teen who cowered under his pregnant volcano. But eventually he recognized my contempt, the way I studied him as nothing more than a curiosity, an iguana in a terrarium. He called the guard to take him away, and that's the last I've seen him. I don't believe Gordon possesses the capacity to grieve, but I hope he will buckle under the frustration that he was lost any control he once held over other people.

Almost a year has passed. It is August in Boston, and I'm starting medical school in two days. The MCATs were a bitch, but I have a good head for numbers, and I perform well under pressure. The summer in this city is hotter than what I was used to in California. Muggy too, and the mosquitoes love my pale skin. Everything's brick out here; and the squirrels on campus are smaller and gray. At last, I feel disconnected from where I grew up.

Out here I'm Ella. Pamela to school administrators who don't know better. Pam to some. Never Kali. I feel younger than a year ago. My hair grew longer, and maybe it makes me look more feminine. The university sweatshirt definitely makes me feel girlish. I've started to meet my classmates at some wine mixers. Turns out, med school students can be just as buffoonish as firemen when it comes to drinking. I hope this makes it easier for me to adjust.

Jeffrey Holt visited me when he was speaking in town. The Holt family is back living up at the cottage in Shallot. He's gotten over being angry with me, and we had drinks and watched a Sox game at a bar. He pitched me on coming back to the network. I told him I wouldn't take on clients now, not while I'm in school. He teased out the idea of me helping with some of his policy work, and

I said I'd think about it.

At the site, they found eighteen girls; more than they thought were taken. The FBI let Leland reopen the case. His stomach is mostly healed. He can't run much, but it was a close call when he got to the hospital, and he seems grateful that he survived at all. Leland and I trade e-mails, and that's how I found out that Veda moved in with Cindy Coates. They're coming out to Boston next spring to run the marathon, and I'll give them a couch to sleep on. Leland tells me that for all of Veda's crankiness, Cindy softens him up a bit.

Today I'm shopping for books and wandering the stores in Cambridge. Emmanuel skips on a slack leash by my ankles. In one of the bookstores I find Jeffrey Holt's book.

One of the few things here that reminds me of home is the abundance of vintage clothing stores. Second-hand clothes, whatever you want to call them. Strolling down the lumpy brick sidewalk, I'm drawn to one particular shop because of the wigs displayed in the windows.

Inside, I try on a bright pink bob with bangs. Maybe I linger longer than I should. Looking in the mirror, you can barely tell it's me.

I'D LIKE TO THANK everyone at Diversion Books, including Sarah Masterson Hally, Hannah Black, Brielle Benton, and especially my editor Randall Klein, for taking a chance on a new author and championing the project. I owe a huge debt to Jill Marr at the Sandra Dijkstra Literary Agency for taking me on as a client and bringing a vibrant, positive energy to our work together. You always make me believe everything's going to turn out fine. I couldn't have turned out a draft worthy of publication without the help of Jennifer Skutelsky, who contributed a thorough and thoughtful edit of a formative version of this book. Jennifer, your insights and eye for detail astound me. Thanks to everyone who has helped mentor me over the past few years, including Renée Swindle, Edith Updike, Jessica Trupin, and Elise Proulx. All of you have helped whip me into shape. I'm grateful to Caroline Teagle for designing such a compelling—and let's face it, creepy—cover. Finally, thanks to my family and friends, and especially Sabrina, for loving and supporting me. You make all of this fun.

ALEX DOLAN was raised in Boston, lived in New York City, and currently resides in the San Francisco Bay Area. In addition to writing for several publications, he has recorded four music albums, and has a master's degree in strategic communications from Columbia University. *The Euthanist* is his first novel.

CPSIA information can be obtained at www.ICGtesting.com
Printed in the USA
LVOW07s2035150715

446355LV00008B/974/P